MRS. DALLOWAY

broadview editions
series editor: L.W. Conolly

Virginia Woolf (photograher unknown), originally published in *The Bookman*, January 1928. By permission of Lebrecht Photo Library.

MRS. DALLOWAY

Virginia Woolf

edited by Jo-Ann Wallace

broadview editions

Library and Archives Canada Cataloguing in Publication

Woolf, Virginia, 1882-1941
Mrs. Dalloway / Virginia Woolf ; edited by Jo-Ann Wallace.

(Broadview editions)
Includes bibliographical references.
ISBN 978-1-55111-723-2

I. Wallace, Jo-Ann, 1953- II. Title. III. Series: Broadview editions

PR6045.O72M5 2012 823'.912 C2012-905811-4

Broadview Editions
The Broadview Editions series represents the ever-changing canon of literature in English by bringing together texts long regarded as classics with valuable lesser-known works.

Advisory editor for this volume: Denis Johnston

Broadview Press is an independent, international publishing house, incorporated in 1985.

We welcome comments and suggestions regarding any aspect of our publications—please feel free to contact us at the addresses below or at broadview@broadviewpress.com.

North America
Post Office Box 1243, Peterborough, Ontario, Canada K9J 7H5
2215 Kenmore Avenue, Buffalo, NY, USA 14207
Tel: (705) 743-8990; Fax: (705) 743-8353
email: customerservice@broadviewpress.com

UK, Europe, Central Asia, Middle East, Africa, India, and Southeast Asia
Eurospan Group, 3 Henrietta St., London WC2E 8LU, United Kingdom
Tel: 44 (0) 1767 604972; Fax: 44 (0) 1767 601640
email: eurospan@turpin-distribution.com

Australia and New Zealand
NewSouth Books
c/o TL Distribution, 15-23 Helles Ave., Moorebank, NSW, Australia 2170
Tel: (02) 8778 9999; Fax: (02) 8778 9944
email: orders@tldistribution.com.au

www.broadviewpress.com

Broadview Press acknowledges the financial support of the Government of Canada through the Canada Book Fund for our publishing activities.

This book is printed on paper containing 100% post-consumer fibre.

Typesetting and assembly: True to Type Inc., Claremont, Canada.

PRINTED IN CANADA

Contents

Acknowledgements

I would like to thank Melissa Jaques for imaginative and thorough research assistance, and Amanda Allen for a fine proofreading eye. I would also like to thank Stephen Slemon, always my most challenging interlocutor and a generous editor. Students in my two fourth-year Women's Studies seminars at the University of Alberta on "Virginia Woolf and Feminism" (2009 and 2010) are a continuing inspiration and a reminder of literature's capacity to trouble and inspire. Finally, I would like to dedicate this edition to my stepdaughter, Allie Slemon, who, in spite of her overriding admiration for James Joyce, had the wit and good sense to invent a dessert called Mousses Dalloway.

Virginia Stephen in 1902 (photographed by George Charles Beresford).

Introduction

It is difficult to come to a novel by Virginia Woolf innocently. Her reputation—or, more accurately, any one of her many reputations—always precedes her. There are few readers today who are not familiar with the 1902 photograph of the ethereal and beautiful twenty-year-old Miss Virginia Stephen. But this is not the only iconic image of Woolf to impress itself on the popular imagination. When she published *The Years* in 1937 and it became a bestseller in the United States, her portrait, by avant-garde photographer Man Ray, made the cover of *Time* magazine, an unusual acknowledgement of an experimental and modernist novelist.[1] When Edward Albee's now classic play, *Who's Afraid of Virginia Woolf?*, opened on Broadway in 1962, Woolf's very name became a synonym for both escapist intellectualism and its opposite, the capacity to face reality without illusions. When the film version of Albee's play, starring Richard Burton and Elizabeth Taylor, was released in 1966, Virginia Woolf became—as literary critic Brenda R. Silver notes—"a household name" (Silver 102). Later, Michael Cunningham's 1998 Pulitzer Prize-winning novel, *The Hours*, a retelling of *Mrs. Dalloway*, and the 2002 film version of the novel, starring Meryl Streep, Julianne Moore, and Nicole Kidman, consolidated a very particular version of "Virginia Woolf" for a new generation of readers and viewers.

Cunningham's reimagining of *Mrs. Dalloway* reflects the concerns and preoccupations of the new millennium. *The Hours* (Cunningham borrows Woolf's working title for *Mrs. Dalloway*) traces one day in the life of three very different "characters": Virginia Woolf herself as she writes *Mrs. Dalloway*; Mrs. Brown, the American wife of a World War II veteran, as she prepares a birthday party for her husband; and Clarissa Vaughan, a contemporary lesbian living in Manhattan, as she prepares a celebration for her poet friend Richard, who is dying of AIDS. The novel, like the film version, begins with Virginia Woolf's 1941 suicide by drowning with the clear implication that this was the defining event of her life. This is the Virginia Woolf—depressed and vulnerable—

---

1 *Time: The Weekly Magazine*, 12 April 1937. Web. 8 April 2012. http://www.time.com/time/covers/0,16641,19370412,00.html.

who dominates the popular imagination today, but there was much more to her than that.

The Many Lives of Virginia Woolf

Since 1955, when Aileen Pippett published *The Moth and the Star*, the first full biography of Virginia Woolf, Woolf's life has attracted literally dozens of biographical treatments. While many of them—like those by her nephew Quentin Bell (1972), or by James King (1994) or Hermione Lee (1996)—are exhaustive treatments of her entire life, others focus on one aspect. Phyllis Rose's *Woman of Letters: A Life of Virginia Woolf* (1978) is an early revaluation of Woolf's life and work in light of second-wave feminist criticism. Stephen Trombley's *'All That Summer She Was Mad': Virginia Woolf and Her Doctors* (1981) focuses on Woolf's mental illness and the treatment she received from her physicians. The title of Louise DeSalvo's *Virginia Woolf: The Impact of Childhood Sexual Abuse on Her Life and Work* (1989) is self-explanatory. Natania Rosenfeld's *Outsiders Together: Virginia and Leonard Woolf* (2000) is essentially a literary, textual biography of a marriage. And Alison Light's *Mrs. Woolf and the Servants* (2007) uses Woolf's domestic life as a way of exploring class relations and household service in the early years of the twentieth century. As even this abbreviated list will suggest, for more than fifty years Virginia Woolf's life has served as a kind of cultural ink-blot test, reflecting back to us the concerns of our own times and places. And yet, because all of her novels are so deeply saturated with their historical contexts—and so thoroughly shaped by her responses to her own place and time—it is helpful to know something about her.

Adeline Virginia Stephen was born on 25 January 1882, the third of four children of Leslie and Julia (née Jackson) Stephen. Her two older siblings were Vanessa (b. 1879), who grew up to become the well-known artist Vanessa Bell, and Thoby (b. 1880), whose friends from Cambridge University would later form the nucleus of the Bloomsbury Group. Her younger sibling was Adrian (b. 1883), who, like his wife Karin Costelloe, became a psychoanalyst. It was a second marriage for Virginia Woolf's parents, both of whom were widowed. Leslie Stephen's first marriage, to Minny (Harriet Marian Thackeray), the daughter of novelist William Makepeace Thackeray, produced one child, Laura, who had developmental and other problems and was eventually institutionalized. Julia Jackson's first marriage, to lawyer Herbert Duckworth, produced three children: George,

Stella, and Gerald. As Woolf noted in an autobiographical sketch, their family home at 22 Hyde Park Gate was a typically upper-middle class Victorian household—dark, over-decorated, and crowded with both family members and servants: "Here then seventeen or eighteen people lived in small bedrooms with one bathroom and three water-closets between them.... When I look back on that house it seems to me so crowded with scenes of family life ... that I feel suffocated by the recollection" ("Old Bloomsbury," *Moments of Being* 183).[1]

Virginia Woolf's father—a renowned philosopher, essayist, editor, and mountaineer—was one of the leading intellectuals of his day, and the first editor of the monumental *Dictionary of National Biography*. Her mother was a famed beauty whose family belonged to "the Anglo-Indian governing classes" and was well-connected in "literary, artistic, and political" circles (Lee 87, 89). As Virginia Woolf recognized, her mother was in many ways an ideal type of self-sacrificing Victorian womanhood, serving in this role as a model for her aunt, the well-known Victorian photographer Julia Margaret Cameron, and for Pre-Raphaelite painter Edward Burne-Jones, who depicted her as the Virgin in his 1879 painting, *Annunciation*. In fact, Julia Stephen's selfless commitment to others—to nursing the sick, to supporting her difficult and taciturn husband—probably contributed to her early death from rheumatic fever in 1895 when Virginia was only thirteen. This was the first in a series of devastating personal losses and led to her first nervous breakdown. Only two years later Virginia's newly married half-sister Stella (who had taken over the management of the Stephen household) died unexpectedly. This death dealt a double blow. Stella's engagement and marriage had brought moments of real happiness into a household that was still mourning Julia Stephen's death. In "A Sketch of the Past" Woolf describes her own feelings of "light" and "ecstasy" when she was in the presence of the two lovers (105). All this ended suddenly. Stella's death also left Virginia even more vulnerable to the sexual abuse of her half-brothers, an abuse that started when Virginia was only a child. She describes this issue candidly in "A Sketch of the Past" and "22 Hyde Park Gate" (see *Moments of Being*).

---

1 While Woolf had a longstanding interest in all forms of life-writing, her own autobiographical essays were published only posthumously, in *Moments of Being* (1985). Three of the five essays in that collection were written for presentation to the Memoir Club, formed in 1920 and consisting primarily of original members of the Bloomsbury Group.

Leslie Stephen's death in 1904 precipitated Virginia's second serious breakdown. Her relationship to her father had always been complicated. While she was in many ways his intellectual heir, she disliked what she characterized as his sentimentality and his egotism, qualities he felt especially free to indulge in his relationships with his wife and daughters. His thoughtless self-absorption was, for her, a defining characteristic of Victorian patriarchy. Throughout her 1938 anti-war polemic, *Three Guineas*, Virginia Woolf refers to herself as the "daughter of an educated man." The phrasing is deliberate. Unlike their brothers, who followed their father to Cambridge University, neither Vanessa nor Virginia was formally educated.[1] Although Woolf felt this as a lack throughout her life—consequently becoming one of the century's most passionate and articulate advocates of advanced education for women—she had the complete run of her father's extensive library, and later received private lessons in Greek and Latin (Lee 142-44). Woolf's ambitious self-education, in which she especially immersed herself in biography and history, was a key factor in her ability to completely reshape the modern novel.

Following Leslie Stephen's death, the four Stephen children left the family home at 22 Hyde Park Gate in Kensington and moved to 46 Gordon Square in Bloomsbury, a less reputable and more bohemian neighbourhood. There they threw off the shackles of Victorianism, literally letting in the light of a new century by decorating their home in a plainer, more informal and modern way. Thoby invited his Cambridge friends for regular "Thursday evenings" of conversation and debate, events that included the two sisters. In "Old Bloomsbury," Virginia recalls these evenings as "full of smoke; buns, coffee and whisky were strewn about" (189) and full also of endless talk about "philosophy, art, religion" (190) and, eventually, sex (*Moments of Being* 195-97). This was the beginning of the now famous Bloomsbury Group of influential intellectuals and artists. In addition to Virginia and Vanessa, its core members included biographer Lytton Strachey, literary critic Desmond MacCarthy, colonial administrator and then publisher and political theorist Leonard Woolf, economist John Maynard Keynes, artist Duncan Grant, art theorist and artist Roger Fry, and novelist E.M. Forster. Collectively, its members had an enormous impact on the political and cultural life of Britain.

---

1 As a young woman, Vanessa did attend art school; see Lee 142.

Sadly, the handsome and charismatic Thoby, who was so key to the Group's formation, died of typhoid fever in 1906 following a trip to Greece. Thoby's death precipitated a number of changes for the Stephen siblings. In 1907, Vanessa married art critic Clive Bell, whose proposal of marriage she accepted only two days after Thoby's death, very likely in emotional response to it. Virginia and Adrian moved to 29 Fitzroy Square, also in Bloomsbury. These were the years when Virginia began her professional life as a writer, publishing reviews for the *Times Literary Supplement* and, in 1907, beginning work on her first novel, *The Voyage Out*. They were also years in which, as her biographer Hermione Lee points out, "Virginia Stephen was sexually confused and uncertain" (245), carrying on a dangerous flirtation with her brother-in-law Clive Bell while also clearly experiencing "erotic feelings about women" (245). Finally, in 1912, she accepted Leonard Woolf's proposal of marriage. A former colonial administrator in Ceylon (now Sri Lanka), Leonard began to undertake other professional activities, including writing (his first novel was published in 1913), journalism, editing, and policy analysis for the Labour Party and the Fabian Society. Together, he and Virginia bought a printing press in 1917, ostensibly as a form of manual therapy for Virginia. The small handpress, which they taught themselves to operate by consulting "a teach-yourself-to-print booklet" (Lee 363), evolved to become the Hogarth Press, one of the most influential publishers in twentieth-century Britain. The Hogarth Press published all but the first two of Virginia Woolf's novels (with dust jackets designed by her sister, Vanessa Bell), giving her invaluable control over her work. As she noted in her diary, "I am the only woman in England free to write what I like" (*Diary* 3, 43).

The decision to marry was not an easy one for Virginia Woolf, and it was both preceded and followed by nervous breakdowns. The Woolfs' marriage has been the focus of biographical and critical speculation, much of it focusing on the question of whether Leonard was too controlling, or simply caring. In consultation with her physicians, for example, he determined that her mental health was too fragile to permit her to have children, a decision she always found painful. Moreover, Virginia continued to be emotionally and erotically drawn to women.[1] Her best known relationship was with aristocrat and writer Vita Sackville-West, for whom, in 1928, she wrote the fantasy novel *Orlando: A Biography*. On the other hand, Leonard "provided conditions

1 For a discussion of Woolf's sexuality, see Cramer.

favourable for writing" (Lee 337), and it is almost certain that she could not have accomplished what she did without the stability of their marriage.

And what she accomplished was enormous. She redefined the novel in English; she was a brilliant essayist and diarist; she was a passionate advocate of higher education for women, and a groundbreaking feminist theorist. Woolf's feminism was arrived at through a combination of personal experience (especially of the family home), the influence of older women friends (such as classicist Janet Case, her Greek tutor), and intellectual conviction. As Anna Davin points out, although Woolf was occasionally, and briefly, involved in organizations such as the Women's Co-operative Guild or the National Union of Women's Suffrage Societies, for the most part "she had little active interest (or faith) in organized politics" (viii). The nature of Woolf's feminism—which can best be described as radical and materialist—is most clearly outlined in her two great polemical works, *A Room of One's Own* (1929) and *Three Guineas* (1938). Woolf's feminism is radical because she understands women's oppression to be foundational, to be the model and the motor for other forms of oppression. *Three Guineas*, for example, examines women's oppression, or the system of patriarchy, as the root cause of war. And her feminism is materialist because she believes that material conditions produce social and psychic relations. Woolf spells this out with admirable clarity in *A Room of One's Own*, which attempts, in part, to answer the question of why, historically, there have been so few great women poets. Woolf's answer is as follows:

> Intellectual freedom depends upon material things. Poetry depends upon intellectual freedom. And women have always been poor, not for two hundred years merely, but from the beginning of time. Women have had less intellectual freedom than the sons of Athenian slaves. Women, then, have not had a dog's chance of writing poetry. That is why I have laid so much stress on money and a room of one's own. (162-63)

In addition to arguing that women need access to the material conditions necessary to create great works of literature—education, experience, time, privacy—she also argued, in *A Room of One's Own* and in numerous reviews and essays, that the genres in which women already excelled as writers, such as letters and diaries, were themselves significant literary texts. While Woolf's feminist analysis was frequently limited by her own class biases, its influence on literary studies has been unquestionable and profound.

It is important to recognize that while Virginia Woolf suffered from an illness, she was not defined by it.[1] Rather, and as Hermione Lee notes, she "was a person of exceptional courage, intelligence and stoicism" (175) who, nonetheless, in the midst of World War II, with bombs literally exploding around her, decided she could not go on. On 28 March 1941 she drowned herself in the River Ouse near her country home in Rodmell.

"The design is so queer & so masterful": *Mrs. Dalloway* as Experimental Fiction

Mrs. Dalloway—published on 14 May 1925—was Virginia Woolf's fourth novel and, in many ways, the first to fully realize the experimental, modernist, lyrical style with which she is now so firmly identified. While *Mrs. Dalloway* is today regarded as a major novel of the early twentieth century, it created unease among some of its first readers. Early reviews of the novel recognized the "peculiarly experimental"[2] nature of *Mrs. Dalloway*, but reviewers were divided in their assessment of whether or not its style was a success.

Woolf's friend and fellow novelist E.M. Forster described it as "perhaps her masterpiece, but difficult." Poet Edwin Muir noted that while Woolf's earlier novels "analyzed," *Mrs. Dalloway* "evoke[s]." "The result," he said, is like "certain kinds of poetry" that record "a moment of serene illumination, a state of soul." Poet and novelist Richard Hughes compared *Mrs. Dalloway*'s formal composition to the paintings of the great post-impressionist Paul Cézanne. Writing for the *Saturday Review*, novelist and essayist Gerald Bullett agreed with other reviewers that Woolf's "highly impressionistic" rendering of the "stream of life" was new and original, but he concluded that the overall effect was to leave her readers feeling "detached." Similarly, while recognizing Woolf's "natural and unvitiated talent," J.F. Holms nonetheless described the novel as sentimental and argued that "her writing conveys an effect of automatism that is curious, and

---

1 For a full and reliable discussion of Virginia Woolf's mental illness and the treatments she received, see Chapter 10 ("'Madness'") of Lee's biography.

2 McDowall, reprinted in Appendix A3 below. Selections from all the reviews cited in the next paragraph are also reprinted in Appendix A.

aesthetically corrupt." The anonymous reviewer for *The New Statesman* was almost wholly critical. While recognizing that "Mrs. Woolf has extraordinary gifts," he argued that they are not the gifts of a novelist. "In all this brilliant novel," he said, "there are no people."

Virginia Woolf was always highly sensitive to criticism, a characteristic she sometimes described as a "disease."[1] Even so, the claim by *The New Statesman* reviewer that she had not "created a single character" must have been especially painful. Only eighteen months earlier Woolf had been involved in a very public debate with the prolific—and more traditional—novelist Arnold Bennett about the capacity of a newer generation of writers to create believable characters. Bennett's was the first volley in this particular skirmish.[2] His March 1923 *Cassell's Magazine* article, "Is the Novel Decaying?," singled out Woolf's third novel, *Jacob's Room*, for particular attention. Bennett wrote: "I have seldom read a cleverer book than *Jacob's Room*, a novel that has made a great stir in a small world. It is packed and bursting with originality, and it is exquisitely written. But the characters do not vitally survive in the mind because the author has been obsessed by details of originality and cleverness" (quoted in Monk 12).

Bennett's criticism of Woolf's capacity to create vital characters who live on in the reader's mind provoked from her a characteristic response. In December 1923 she published "Mr. Bennett and Mrs. Brown" as a strong rebuttal to Bennett's criticism. In that essay Woolf affirmed the centrality of "character" to novel writing but also famously claimed that "on or about December

---

1 Her diary entries in the first half of April 1921 chart her reactions to reviews of *Monday and Tuesday*, her first volume of short stories. "I must note the symptoms of the disease," she says, "so as to know it next time" (*Diary* 2, 108).

2 Four years earlier, Woolf had launched a volley of her own in "Modern Novels," an essay published in the *Times Literary Supplement* (10 April 1919, 189). In it she took to task a slightly earlier generation of English writers—represented in her essay by H.G. Wells, Arnold Bennett, and John Galsworthy—for their commitment to a form of social realism (she called it "materialism") that, she argued, ignored the inner life and the workings of consciousness. She reserved particular criticism for "Mr. Bennett [as] perhaps the worst culprit of the three, inasmuch as he is by far the best workman." "Modern Novels" was reprinted as "Modern Fiction" in *The Common Reader* (London: Hogarth Press, 1925) and in *Collected Essays, Volume II* (London: Hogarth Press, 1966); see below, Appendix B4.

1910 human character changed."[1] A great deal of criticism has been devoted to untangling the meaning of this claim, much of the discussion focussing on the influence of *Manet and Post-Impressionism*, the November 1910 exhibit organized by Roger Fry (Woolf's friend and a central member of the Bloomsbury Group) for the Grafton Galleries in London. Fry coined the term "post-impressionism" to describe the work of modern European artists such as Manet, Seurat, Van Gogh, Gaugin, and Cézanne whose work was largely unknown in Britain. Had the exhibit, which was greeted in some quarters by outrage, somehow captured or even effected a change in modern perceptions of time, character, and human relations (see Froula, Banfield)? Regardless of the origin of Woolf's claim that "human character" had changed, it is clear from her essay that, at the least, she intended the claim to mark a strong generational divide between *her* kind of novel writing and the kind of novel writing represented by slightly older writers such as Arnold Bennett. The implication here, and in her earlier essay "Modern Novels" (later republished as "Modern Fiction"), is that a *modern* understanding of character shifts the focus from explanatory, external markers of character (such as lengthy descriptions of an individual's social and material environment) to a more post-impressionistic emphasis on consciousness, the inner life, and the experience of temporal discontinuity.

As Woolf argues, in order to capture the reality of a character, the novelist must create a sense of *felt* existence and experience. "Life," she says, "is not a series of gig lamps symmetrically arranged; life is a luminous halo, a semi-transparent envelope surrounding us from the beginning of consciousness to the end" (Appendix B4, p. 232). In other words, we do not experience our lives as a straight well-lit road, a smooth progression from moment to moment, or as a coherent narrative in which every action has a single motivation or explanation. Nor do we have an unmediated relationship to "life." Instead, everything is filtered through our consciousness, our past experiences, our memories. The foundational motivation of the novelist, according to Woolf, is the attempt to create—or *capture*—a sense of the particular

1 See Appendix B3, p. 227. "Mr. Bennett and Mrs. Brown" was originally published in *Nation and Athenaeum* on 1 December 1923; revised for a talk to the Cambridge Heretics on 18 May 1924; reprinted as "Character in Fiction" in the *Criterion* in July 1924; and published as *Mr. Bennett and Mrs. Brown* in the Hogarth Press Essays series.

"semi-transparent envelope" in which a character lives and moves. The language of seduction, pursuit, and attempted capture runs throughout her response to Bennett's criticism. "Some Brown, Smith, or Jones comes before [the novelist] and says in the most seductive and charming way in the world, 'Come and catch me if you can'" (Appendix A3, p. 226). Woolf knows that the novelist's chances of success in fully capturing a character are limited—"most have to be content with a scrap of her dress or a wisp of her hair" (p. 226). Nevertheless, she argues, character, and especially character as a way of being in the world, is the primary impetus behind the writing of fiction.

It is significant that Bennett's article appeared at the same time that Woolf was working on the novel that would become *Mrs. Dalloway*. Her diary entry of 19 June 1923 records her preoccupation with his criticism along with her excitement about how the new novel, which she was then calling "The Hours," was shaping up:

> People, like Arnold Bennett, say I cant create, or didn't in J's R [*Jacob's Room*], characters that survive.... Have I the power of conveying the true reality? Or do I write essays about myself? Answer these questions as I may, in the uncomplimentary sense, & still there remains this excitement.... I foresee, to return to The Hours, that this is going to be the devil of a struggle. The design is so queer & so masterful. I'm always having to wrench my substance to fit it. The design is certainly original, & interests me hugely. I should like to write away at it, very quick and fierce. (*Diary* 2, 248-49)

It is certainly the case that Clarissa Dalloway, the title character of *Mrs. Dalloway*, haunted Woolf's imagination—or seduced it—over a period of years. Woolf pursued her through numerous incarnations. In fact, Clarissa appears in no fewer than two novels and half a dozen short stories. Together with her husband Richard, she makes her initial appearance as a minor character in Woolf's first novel, *The Voyage Out* (1915). It is the story of a young woman, Rachel Vinrace, who travels to South America on her father's ship. Richard and Clarissa are among the monied and influential passengers, though their personalities in *The Voyage Out* are quite different from those they would acquire in *Mrs. Dalloway*. In the first novel, Clarissa is less introspective, a little more brittle, more of the society lady, but she is nonetheless charismatic and charming. Richard—who forces a kiss on the young and inexperienced heroine, a kiss Rachel experiences in part as sexual awakening and in part as sexual assault—is a little less the failed MP "who had lost his chance of the Cabinet" (*Mrs. Dalloway*, p. 189 below) and is much more closely associated with the centre of political and imperial power: "He seemed to come from the humming oily centre of the machine where the polished rods are sliding, and the pistons thumping ..." (*The Voyage Out*, p. 217 below). In this passage it is difficult to miss the degree to which threatening and violent forms of sexual and political power are intermingled. In *Mrs. Dalloway* Woolf would go on to offer, through her creation of the terrifying allegorical figures of Proportion and Conversion, a more sustained and fully realized analysis of the overlapping nature of political, imperial, and sexual power. The subtler and more mature analysis of the later novel further considers the ways in which the apparently private spheres of medicine and religion are also deeply implicated in the exercise of power.

Clarissa Dalloway made her second appearance in print in 1923 when Woolf published "Mrs. Dalloway on Bond Street" in *The Dial*.[1] She reworked this short story as the opening sequence of what would become the novel, and with each iteration she painted Clarissa with greater depth, sympathy, and poignancy. While Woolf remained interested in Clarissa as a type of the "society lady," she also gave her, in *Mrs. Dalloway*, a pronounced capacity for self-reflection, a keen love of life, and a correspondingly sharp sense of mortality. It is likely that these adjustments to Clarissa's character owe something to the October 1922 death of Kitty Maxse, an old family friend about whom Woolf had mixed feelings. While she appreciated Maxse's capacity for kindness, she also mocked her fashionable and somewhat shallow opinions (see Lee 163-64). One can see much of Clarissa in the October 8 diary entry in which Woolf records her feelings upon reading of Maxse's death:

1 During the period in which she wrote this story, Woolf also wrote "The Prime Minister," an unfinished short story that also would eventually be absorbed into the novel. For a discussion of the chronology of these stories, and of the first draft of *Mrs. Dalloway*, see Helen M. Wussow's introduction to *"The Hours."* "Mrs. Dalloway in Bond Street" is reprinted in *Mrs. Dalloway's Party* (1978) and in *The Complete Shorter Fiction of Virginia Woolf* (1989), which also includes "The Prime Minister."

> My mind has gone back all day to her ... visualising her—her white hair—pink cheeks how she sat upright—her voice—with its characteristic tones—her green blue floor—which she painted with her own hands; her earrings, her gaiety, yet melancholy; her smartness; her tears, which stayed on her cheek. Not that I ever felt at my ease with her. (*Diary* 2, 206)

Just as Woolf turned repeatedly to the character of Clarissa Dalloway, as if holding her up to the light to reveal new facets of her personality, so she returned also to what she called in her diary "the party consciousness, the frock consciousness" (*Diary* 3, 12). This was a theme she would carry through from *Mrs. Dalloway* to her next novel, *To the Lighthouse* (1927), in which the novel's first part builds toward and culminates in a dinner party featuring a memorable *boeuf en daube*. Even after she had completed *Mrs. Dalloway*, Woolf continued to return to the theme of Clarissa's party, exploring it in six additional short stories, and from the point of view of several different guests. These stories are collected, together with "Mrs. Dalloway in Bond Street," in the posthumously published *Mrs. Dalloway's Party*.[1]

Exploring the character of Clarissa Dalloway—capturing the complexities of the very particular "semi-transparent envelope" in which she had her being—was clearly a major impulse behind *Mrs. Dalloway*. But it was not the only impulse. In spite of Woolf's emphasis, at the beginning of "Mr. Bennett and Mrs. Brown," on character as the motivation and foundation of novel writing, the essay soon turns to the even bigger issue of "reality"—"... what is reality? And who are the judges of reality?" (p. 228)—and asks whether, after December 1910 (that is, in an age newly marked by modern art but also by Freud's psychoanalytic theories,[2] Einstein's theory of relativity, the women's suffrage movement, rapid

1 Further undermining any sense of *Mrs. Dalloway* as a stable, self-contained text is the 1996 publication of *"The Hours,"* the first draft of the novel, and the 1965 publication of "The ..." (republished in 1966 as *Nurse Lugton's Golden Thimble*), a fairy tale "found in the manuscript of *Mrs. Dalloway*" (Kirkpatrick 178). The availability of this complicated interweaving of texts—the stories that gave birth to the novel and those that it birthed, its draft and its final version, the coexistence of two "first" editions—makes *Mrs. Dalloway* a particularly rich archive for the study of Woolf's creative process.

2 In 1924 Virginia and Leonard Woolf's Hogarth Press became the authorized publisher for Sigmund Freud in England, making his work available in translation to an English-speaking readership.

changes in technology), the writer requires news ways of creating a reality effect in fiction. Can traditional forms of realist fiction capture the complexities of a world in which toffee is advertised by sky-writing aeroplanes (as happens in an early scene in *Mrs. Dalloway*)? Or of a world scarred by modern forms of warfare? Woolf found some of the new techniques she was looking for in the work of other modernist writers such as James Joyce and T.S. Eliot. In fact, she began writing the first iteration of what would become *Mrs. Dalloway* in August 1922 at the same time that she was reading James Joyce's *Ulysses*, a novel by which she was alternately "stimulated, charmed ... puzzled, bored, [and] irritated." In her diary she famously likened the experience of reading it to watching "a queasy undergraduate scratch his pimples" (*Diary* 2, 188-89). However, in spite of her reservations about *Ulysses* she clearly borrowed from it the idea of setting the complete action of her own novel in one day (see Richter), eventually settling on a day in the middle of June 1923.

From August to October 1922 Woolf struggled with the form of her new work—"laboriously dredging my mind for Mrs. Dalloway & bringing up light buckets"—finally recording on 14 October that "Mrs. Dalloway has branched into a book; & I adumbrate here a study of insanity & suicide; the world seen by the sane & the insane side by side" (*Diary* 2, 189, 207). Eight months later she wondered whether "In this book I have almost too many ideas. I want to give life & death, sanity & insanity; I want to criticize the social system, & to show it at work, at its most intense" (*Diary* 2, 248). It is certainly the case that the plot of *Mrs. Dalloway*, a relatively short novel, is, on the surface, simple: a middle-aged, upper-class woman, hoping that the Prime Minister will attend her party that evening, is reacquainted with an old beau, while, in another part of the city, a veteran of the Great War suffers a breakdown and commits suicide. However, this apparently simple narrative opens up—like a set of Chinese nesting boxes or a Russian matryoshka doll—to an examination of the play of memory, the effects of war, the compromises of marriage, the classed and gendered nature of the education system, and the imbrication of medicine, politics, religion, and sexuality. Far from containing "too many ideas," as Woolf feared, *Mrs. Dalloway* is a powerful and convincing argument for the interconnectedness of the personal and the political, and for the ways in which the small tyrannies of private life spring from the same source as the large tyrannies of military aggression and imperial expansion. She would return to this theme in her 1938 anti-war polemic, *Three Guineas*.

By the fall of 1923 Woolf had worked out the technique by which the mostly mundane events of a single day would disclose the fuller reality of her characters' lives and the worlds in which they moved. Diary entries in August and October 1923 record "my discovery; how I dig out beautiful caves behind my characters," "what I call my tunnelling process, by which I tell the past by instalments, as I have need of it" (*Diary* 2, 263, 272). At this point Woolf was still referring to her novel as "The Hours," a provisional title she would retain almost to the point of publication. As this title suggests, *Mrs. Dalloway* is saturated with varieties of time consciousness, from the numerous London clocks chiming the hours throughout the day ("The sound of St. Margaret's glides into the recesses of the heart and buries itself in ring after ring of sound" [below, p. 84]; "It was precisely twelve o'clock; twelve by Big Ben" [p. 121]) to the ways in which memories permeate and inform the present moments of almost every one of the characters.

These memories are one example of the "beautiful caves" or tunnels by which her characters achieve fullness or, to use Woolf's word, "reality." Memories also constitute one aspect of the "luminous halo" or "semi-transparent envelope" in which her characters move. This is evident from the opening scene of the novel which begins in an abrupt, mid-action present—"Mrs. Dalloway said she would buy the flowers herself"—before moving almost immediately to Clarissa's memory of similar mornings at her family's country home at Bourton when she was eighteen. Like all of us, Clarissa occupies more than one temporal moment at the same time. Life as she experiences it is not a series of temporally disconnected moments, but a continuous interleaving of past and present. Most of the major characters in *Mrs. Dalloway*, with the possible exception of Clarissa's daughter Elizabeth, move not only through that day in mid-June 1923 but also through numerous significant moments or events from their various pasts. Clarissa returns again and again to what, in retrospect, was her momentous summer when, at eighteen, she chose Richard over the more impetuous and jealous Peter Walsh, and traditional heterosexual marriage, to an emotionally reserved but decent man, over her passion for Sally Seton. Peter Walsh—coming from "a respectable Anglo-Indian family which for at least three generations had administered the affairs of a continent" (p. 89)—has spent most of the intervening years in India, yet his thoughts also return to the summer when he realized "Dalloway would marry Clarissa" (p. 95), recalling again and again "one scene after another at Bourton" (p. 168).

Proportion and Conversion: *Mrs. Dalloway* as a War Novel

In one important respect, however, Peter's experience of time is more fractured than Clarissa's. Returning to London for the first time since 1918 has made him sensitive to the changes that have taken place in the years following the war. "Those five years—1918 to 1923—had been, he suspected, somehow very important. People looked different. Newspapers seemed different" (p. 102). In particular, Peter notes an apparent loosening of strict moral codes, respectable young women wearing make-up, an ascendency of youth. Coupled with this, however, are signs of residual militarism: "Boys in uniform, carrying guns, marched with their eyes ahead of them ... and on their faces an expression like the letters of a legend written round the base of a statue praising duty, gratitude, fidelity, love of England" (p. 85). Peter's observations point to the ways in which historical time and political events intervene in and shape the personal, forming yet another layer of the time-consciousness of the novel. Historical and political events are, in the end, inseparable from the personal. This is most obvious in the cases of Septimus Warren Smith and Doris Kilman, the characters whose lives most clearly have been devastated by the events of the Great War.

While early reviews of the novel briefly mention the presence of "a 'shell-shocked' soldier" (Appendix A5) or "poor Septimus, the war victim" (Appendix A3), it is only in the last fifteen years that Virginia Woolf has been taken up as a significant, and significantly new kind of, war novelist (for example, see Froula 2002, 2005b; Levenback; Tate; Vincent). Her war writing covers many genres, including essays and longer polemical works as well as novels, and it is thoroughly informed by her feminism and by the pacifism that was typical of members of the Bloomsbury Group and of her wider circle of friends. What distinguishes Woolf as a war novelist is her refusal to depict either the battleground or the home front. Instead her focus is resolutely on the causes and effects of war, both of which she traces to their most intimate sources and expressions.

It is important to remember that most of Woolf's adult life was framed by war. She was 32 when the Great War started in 1914 and she was 59 when she committed suicide in 1941, in the midst of World War II. At the time of her death she and Leonard Woolf were living full-time at their country home in Sussex, their current home in London, 37 Mecklenburgh Square, having been damaged by a bomb in September 1940 and their former and long-time home, 52 Tavistock Square, completely destroyed by a bomb the following month. Virginia and Leonard travelled to London several times to survey the damage, Virginia recording the following description of the devastation at 52 Tavistock Square: "Basement all rubble.... Otherwise bricks & wood splinters.... I cd just see a piece of my studio wall standing: otherwise rubble where I wrote so many books. Open air where we sat so many nights, gave so many parties" (*Diary* 5, 331). Even in Sussex, however, the war was omnipresent, with enemy planes flying overhead and occasionally firing on the countryside below (Lee 739-40). Invasion seemed imminent. Keenly aware of Hitler's policy toward Jews (Leonard was Jewish) and of the likelihood that they were on the Gestapo's "Black List" for Britain,[1] the Woolfs made plans for suicide in the event of invasion: "This morning we discussed suicide if Hitler lands. Jews beaten up. What point in waiting? ... This is a sensible, rather matter of fact talk" (*Diary* 5, 284-85). Woolf's final novel, *Between the Acts* (1941), published posthumously, evokes the final months before World War II erupts. Through its depiction of a village pageant enacting English history from the beginning to the present, and through its examination of modern marriage, *Between the Acts* offers Woolf's final fictional analysis of the ways in which the fundamental causes of war are always close to home.

Mrs. Dalloway is the second in a trilogy of Woolf's novels, all published within five years of each other, that address the issue of war through an examination of both its causes and its effects, while at the same time resolutely refusing to represent war. *Jacob's Room* (1922), her third novel and the one that immediately preceded *Mrs. Dalloway*, circles around the curiously absent and opaque, upper-middle-class Jacob Flanders, a character we know primarily through the impressions he makes on others.[2] The novel follows him through his schooling in class and gender—a schooling that, Woolf suggests, prepares him for unques-

1 "... it was known that with the invasion plan for July 1940 the Gestapo had drawn up an 'Arrest List' or 'Black List' for Great Britain, the 'Sonderfahndungsliste G.B.' which ran to 350 pages.... On this list, alongside many of their friends and acquaintances, were 'Leonhard Woolf, Schriftsteller, RSHA VIG 1, and Virginia Woolf, Schriftstellerin, RSHA VIG" (Lee 730).

2 The character of Jacob Flanders is modelled on Virginia Woolf's brother Thoby Stephen, who died of typhoid fever in 1906 following a trip to Greece.

tioning acquiescence to war—and reveals only belatedly and obliquely his death on the battlefield of the Great War. In the last scene of the novel, his mother holds out his old shoes: "what am I to do with these ...?" she asks (173). In its final focus on the pathetic remnants of a life cut short, *Jacob's Room* meditates upon the irrevocable nature of death and the inconsolable effect of loss. As critic Tammy Clewell notes, "Woolf believe[d] that writing about the war needed to foster a new consciousness of death, one that stressed its absolute finality" (Clewell 200; see also Walsh).

Like *Jacob's Room*, *To the Lighthouse* (1927), the novel that follows *Mrs. Dalloway*, refuses to heroize death on the battlefield. As in *Jacob's Room*, the war takes place off stage, well outside the main narrative, making an appearance only in one brief and literally parenthetical statement. *To the Lighthouse* is structured in three parts. The first and longest part, "The Window," takes place, like *Mrs. Dalloway*, on a single summer day. The Ramsay family (headed by the egotistical idealist philosopher Mr. Ramsay), together with several of their friends, are summering at their country home in the Hebrides.[1] The children hope to row to the nearby lighthouse, though the weather is unpromising, and Mrs. Ramsay hopes that her evening dinner party will be a success. The middle part, "Time Passes," is an impressionistic evocation of several years, those of the Great War, when the country house is abandoned, the years collapsed into one long night. Three deaths are registered briefly and parenthetically: Mrs. Ramsay's, that of her daughter Prue in childbirth, and, finally, that of her son: "[A shell exploded. Twenty or thirty young men were blown up in France, among them Andrew Ramsay, whose death, mercifully, was instantaneous.]" (127). In the third part, "The Lighthouse," which takes place some years after the first, clearly in post-war Britain, Mr. Ramsay and some of his former guests—including the painter Lily Briscoe—reunite at the country house, and the two youngest children, now young adults, finally row with their father to the lighthouse.

In spite of the fact that the war features only in two buried, parenthetical sentences, *To the Lighthouse*, through its representation of the effects of unthinking patriarchy (on Mrs. Ramsay, on the children, on the aspiring painter Lily Briscoe), is a marked

---

1 The Ramsay family's summer home in the Hebrides is a thinly disguised representation of the Stephen family summer home in St. Ives, Cornwall. The characters of Mr. and Mrs. Ramsay are based on Woolf's parents.

contribution to Woolf's analysis of the causes of war. As she indicates in *Three Guineas* (1937), her lengthy polemical meditation on how women can help to prevent war, the tyrannies of the private house—in a word, patriarchy—share a common root with the tyrannies of the public world.[1] Observing the spread of fascism in Europe in the 1930s, and addressing her comments here to the male reader, she writes that the figures of the "Tyrant," the "Dictator," and the "Führer" (258) are all a type of the patriarch:

> [He] has widened his scope. He is interfering now with your liberty; he is dictating how you shall live; he is making distinctions not merely between the sexes, but between the races. You are feeling in your own persons what your mothers felt when they were shut out, when they were shut up, because they were women. Now you are being shut out, you are being shut up, because you are Jews, because you are democrats, because of race, because of religion.[2] (186-87)

Of these three novels, *Mrs. Dalloway* offers the most sustained and overt analysis of the social and psychic causes of war, and indeed of all forms of oppression. As Woolf noted in her 1923 diary, one of her intentions in writing *Mrs. Dalloway* was "to criticise the social system, & to show it at work, at its most intense" (*Diary* 2, 248). While the novel does this most obviously through the characters of Septimus Warren Smith and Doris Kilman, Woolf also employs other devices to suggest the complex relationship between various components of "the social system": education, medicine, religion, class, politics, imperialism, and the military. For example, as the novel's various characters move through London, they are, time and again, brought face to face with representations of Britain's military and imperial history. Peter Walsh, newly returned from service as a colonial administrator in India, observes the Trafalgar Square monuments to the

---

1 "Behind us lies the patriarchal system; the private house, with its nullity, its immorality, its hypocrisy, its servility" (*Three Guineas* 135).

2 See also Woolf's argument, in *Three Guineas*, that "The daughters of educated men who were called, to their resentment, 'feminists' were in fact the advance guard of your own movement. They were fighting the same enemy that you are fighting and for the same reasons. They were fighting the tyranny of the patriarchal state as you are fighting the tyranny of the Fascist state" (185-86).

great military heroes of empire: Horatio Nelson, Henry Havelock, Charles George Gordon (see p. 86). At the same time he watches the progress of a group of "weedy," working-class boys undergoing military training. While the Trafalgar Square heroes, each the product of a privileged background, are highly individualized and literally monumentalized in their commemorations, the reader, unlike Peter Walsh, recognizes that their heroic actions are underwritten by the masses of rank-and-file soldiers, like the sixteen-year-olds marching toward the Cenotaph in Whitehall, their own individuality trained out of them: "as if one will worked legs and arms uniformly, and life, with its varieties, its irreticences, had been laid under a pavement of monuments and wreaths and drugged into a stiff yet staring corpse by discipline" (p. 86).

The process by which these "boys in uniform" (p. 85) become a de-individualized fighting unit is suggested in one of the great set pieces of the novel, the description of the two allegorical goddesses, Proportion and Conversion. The representations of Proportion and Conversion appear almost exactly at the novel's midpoint, and provide a kind of axis against which events and characters in the novel are measured and interpreted. Proportion, we are told, is "Sir William [Bradshaw]'s goddess" (p. 125). Bradshaw—the Harley Street specialist who is called in to assess and care for Septimus Warren Smith when his breakdown worsens—prescribes a rest cure in one of his own nursing homes. While Septimus's general practitioner, Dr. Holmes, insists that there is "nothing whatever the matter" (p. 118) with him, and recommends merely that Septimus get hold of himself and take up a hobby, Dr. Bradshaw's rest cure is intended to return "a sense of proportion" (p. 123) to the "shell-shocked" and traumatized Septimus. Septimus's emotional, delusional, and *dis*proportionate response to his war experience, which included witnessing the death of his friend and commanding officer Evans, must be contained by enforced rest. Bradshaw "invoke[s] proportion" and "order[s] rest in bed; rest in solitude; silence and rest; rest without friends, without books, without messages; six months' rest ..." (p. 125).

Woolf's depiction of Septimus Warren Smith's breakdown, and of how his physicians approached his condition, drew on many sources—most immediately, her own experiences. Many of the symptoms that Septimus manifests, including his hallucination of hearing the birds "sing freshly and piercingly in Greek words" (p. 64), are based on symptoms that Woolf herself experienced during her numerous breakdowns.[1] The degree to which Bradshaw and Holmes are composites of Woolf's own physicians—particularly Sir George Henry Savage, Sir Maurice Craig, Dr. T.B. Hyslop, and Sir Henry Head—is well documented (see Trombley and Lee), as are the rest cures to which she was herself subjected and which she hated (see Lee 182-83). As her biographer Hermione Lee notes, "Woolf's clinical history keeps pace with the developing history of English medicine and attitudes to mental illness" (182). These attitudes included those expressed by Holmes and Bradshaw in the novel and by one of their real-life progenitors, Sir George Henry Savage, whose essay on "Moral Insanity" attributes the loss of "equilibrium" and "control"—in other words, a sense of proportion—as causal factors in his patients' conditions (see Appendix D1). However, by the time of *Mrs. Dalloway*, the medical establishment's understanding of mental illness in general, and so-called "shell-shock" in particular, was slowly beginning to change with the emergence of modern psychiatry (see Appendices D2 and D3; see also Thomas, Winter). Sadly, Septimus Warren Smith's physicians seem unaware of more progressive treatments for what today we would call post-traumatic stress disorder.

While elements in Woolf's portrayal of Septimus Warren Smith's breakdown and suicide are obviously based on her own experiences, it would be a mistake to reduce the novel's depiction of them to the merely autobiographical. Instead, Woolf was determined, as she noted in her diary, "to criticise the social system, & to show it at work" in all its interrelated complexity (*Diary* 2, 248). While the evidence she adduces in her criticism of the "social system" is autobiographical, it is also at times overtly political. As critic Sue Thomas has argued, it is highly likely that Woolf's analysis of Septimus's treatment owed as much to her "angry response" to the regressive *Report of the War Office Committee of Enquiry into 'Shell-Shock,'* which was presented to the British Parliament in August 1922 and received much attention in *The Times* that fall (while Woolf was working on *Mrs. Dalloway*). As Thomas points out, the *Report* emphasized "the strategic importance of the dominating personality of the doctor in the

1 As she notes in a diary entry of 15 October 1923: "I am now in the thick of the mad scene in Regents Park. I find I write it by clinging as tight to fact as I can, & write perhaps 50 words a morning" (*Diary* 2, 272).

therapeutic encounter" with the shell-shocked soldier, stating that "'The physician must have sufficient force to dominate the situation' ..." (53).

Bradshaw is obviously a dominating physician, but he is also a dominating husband. His wife, we are told, has "gone under," her will over the years slowly sapped by his (p. 126). While Proportion is Bradshaw's public goddess, another and more powerful goddess, Conversion, is "concealed" in his heart: "... conversion, fastidious Goddess, loves blood better than brick, and feasts most subtly on the human will" (p. 126). Conversion is Woolf's term for the drive to dominate and, as Bradshaw's relationship with his wife indicates, it is a drive that finds expression in the "private house" (to use the term she develops in *Three Guineas*) as well as in the public world. The drive to dominate is what underlies not only patriarchal marriage, but also imperial and religious expansion and class domination. As the narrator in *Mrs. Dalloway* states, the goddess Conversion is "even now engaged—in the heat and sands of India, the mud and swamp of Africa, the purlieus of London ... in dashing down shrines, smashing idols, and setting up in their place her own stern countenance" (p. 125).

Along with Sir William Bradshaw, Doris Kilman is the character most closely associated with the drive to convert and dominate. Clarissa Dalloway is immediately attuned to this element in the personality of Miss Kilman, her daughter Elizabeth's privately employed history tutor. Fearful that Miss Kilman will convert Elizabeth to her own "religious ecstasy," Clarissa admits to herself that she hates even "the idea of" Miss Kilman, who has become for Clarissa "one of those spectres who stand astride us and suck up half our life-blood, dominators and tyrants" (p. 54). Miss Kilman's clumsy courtship of Elizabeth is described in vampiric, quasi-sexual terms, and even Richard Dalloway mildly wonders whether Elizabeth's relationship with her tutor "might be [seen as] falling in love" (p. 53). Clarissa appears to regard this possibility as beside the point. Her own relationship with Sally Seton when she was eighteen years old, and the kiss they exchanged ("an illumination; a match burning in a crocus" [p. 70]), is one of her warmest and most precious memories. But the highly possessive and jealous love that both Miss Kilman and the young Peter Walsh display are associated in Clarissa's mind with the drive to dominate and convert. "Love and religion! thought Clarissa, going back into the drawing room, tingling all over. How detestable, how detestable they are! ... The cruellest things in the world, she thought, seeing them clumsy, hot, domineering, hypocritical, eavesdropping, jealous, infinitely cruel ..." (p. 146). The ethos that Clarissa counterposes to a domineering love and religion is that of "the privacy of the soul" (p. 147), a privacy that Miss Kilman and Sir William Bradshaw would violate. When she learns of Septimus's suicide, Clarissa imagines that he died to protect that privacy, that intimate core of self.

However, while Miss Kilman, like Bradshaw, is driven by a desire to dominate, she is also clearly a victim of recent events and of the "social system." A gifted historian, a woman with a university degree, during the war she was driven from her teaching position at "Miss Dolby's school" because of her German ancestry and her refusal to "pretend that the Germans were all villains" (p. 144).[1] Here again Woolf is drawing from well-established issues and events of the day (see Appendix C2). Unattractive, poor, underemployed, from a shop-keeping class background, Miss Kilman possesses an unending sense of grievance, one that leads to her own religious conversion (which occurred, as she frequently recalls, precisely two years and three months earlier) and also feeds her desire to convert others. On the other hand, Clarissa, in spite of her class privilege and the shallowness of her political grasp on the larger world, is somewhat rescued for the reader by her ability to recognize and resist the nascent tyrant within herself: "It rasped her ... to have stirring about in her this brutal monster!" (p. 54).

As the character of Miss Kilman makes clear, the drive to dominate that produces the Tyrant, the Dictator, the Führer and that leads to war is not limited to men, though historically it is men who have had the means to act on it. The question that Woolf addresses in *Three Guineas* is: how can women help to prevent war, especially when all of their training encourages them to accept the world views of their fathers, brothers, and husbands?[2]

---

1 One possible model for the character of Doris Kilman is Louise Ernestine Matthaei, Fellow and Director of Studies at the women's college, Newnham, Cambridge, from 1909. As Christine Froula notes, Matthaei "was forced out in 1916 'under a cloud'; she explained to Leonard, 'my father was a German ...'" (see Froula 2002, 161 n. 40).

2 Even worse, women's lack of access to meaningful education and work meant that war and empire-building offered opportunities women did not otherwise have (for driving trucks, working in munitions factories, etc.). "So profound was her unconscious loathing for the education of the private house with its cruelty, its poverty, its hypocrisy, its immorality, its inanity that she would undertake any task however menial, exercise any fascination however fatal that enabled her to escape. Thus con-

Characteristically, her answer focuses on women's access to formal and higher education and their participation in the professions. Only education can free women from economic and psychological dependence, and from the tyrannies of the private house. However, women must use their education and their newly won access to the professions to "experiment" (206) with different social values and different ways of organizing professional life.[1] In particular, women must refuse to comply with the competitive system by earning only as much as they need, by refusing honorifics such as "medals, symbols, orders" (207), by criticizing the ways in which religion silences women, and by resisting hierarchies. In short, women must seek "a different tradition, a different education, and the different values which result from those" (206). Only in this way can "freedom, equality, peace" (206) become primary and explicit social ends.

In *Mrs. Dalloway* the social system of education is addressed most explicitly through the characters of Septimus Warren Smith and, albeit to a lesser degree, Clarissa Dalloway's daughter Elizabeth. Shortly before Septimus's meeting with Sir William Bradshaw, the narrator offers an almost clinical sketch of his class background, his education, his aspirations, and his position at "Sibleys and Arrowsmiths, auctioneers, valuers, land and estate agents" (p. 114). Septimus, we are told, is "a clerk, but of the better sort" (p. 112). The narrator's representation of him as a type, a kind of case study, is almost casually cruel: "one of those half-educated, self-educated men whose education is all learnt from public libraries, read in the evening after the day's work, on the advice of well-known authors consulted by letter" (p. 112). Readers in the 1920s would have recognized from the narrator's passing reference to "Miss Isabel Pole, lecturing in the Waterloo Road upon Shakespeare" (p. 113) that prior to the war Septimus had attended Morley College, a working-men's college situated in the Old Vic Theatre on the Waterloo Road (see Appendix E1 and E2). Woolf herself lectured on English literature and history to

sciously she desired 'our splendid Empire'; unconsciously she desired our splendid war" (*Three Guineas* 72).

1 The Sex Disqualification (Removal) Act of 1919 (see Appendix E3) gave women in Britain the right to practise the professions, though it reserved the right of universities to determine whether or not to admit women. In *Three Guineas* Woolf refers to 1919 as "the sacred year": "Since that year put it into the power of educated men's daughters to earn their living they have at last some real influence upon education. They have money. They have money to subscribe to causes" (41).

working men and women at Morley College from 1905 to 1907 (see Lee 222-24). Her July 1905 "Report on Teaching at Morley College" describes her experience teaching history to four working women.[1] The judgements and ambivalences Woolf expresses in the report share something of the narrator's tone when assessing Septimus and would alienate most readers today. References to her students' "wholly uncultivated" (203) intelligence certainly reveal the biases and assumptions of Woolf's own class background and her self-description as the "daughter of an educated man" (a phrase that reverberates throughout *Three Guineas*). Nonetheless, in *Mrs. Dalloway* Woolf draws some implicit and subtle comparisons between the effects of Septimus's education at Morley College and that of the men of her class and generation. Just as the classical education that Jacob Flanders receives at Cambridge University—where he is solidly groomed as the natural "inheritor," "satisfied; indeed masterly" (*Jacob's Room* 39)—prepares him for unquestioning acquiescence to war, so does Septimus's education in English literature and the largely cultural values of Englishness. Like so many men of his generation, and across classes, Septimus enlists not because he understands the political implications of the war, but "to save an England which consisted almost entirely of Shakespeare's plays and Miss Isabel Pole in a green dress walking in a square" (p. 114). His experience in the trenches teaches him instead that "The secret signal which one generation passes, under disguise, to the next is loathing, hatred, despair" (p. 116-17).

It is Elizabeth Dalloway who represents the unknowable future and the possibility of change. As Miss Kilman repeatedly reminds her, "Law, medicine, politics, all professions are open to women of your generation" (p. 150). Still very young, still a cipher even to herself, and a little passive, Elizabeth thinks she "would become a doctor [or] a farmer [or] possibly go into Parliament" (p. 155).

Beyond the Ending

While it is impossible to know what becomes of Elizabeth, readers of *Mrs. Dalloway* at the time of its publication in 1925 would know a little bit about the political changes that were just around the corner for Clarissa, for other members of her class, and for

---

1 The report is published as Appendix B in Quentin Bell's *Virginia Woolf: A Biography*, vol. 1.

the unnamed Prime Minister whose possible attendance at Clarissa's party is a question that hovers over most of the novel. When he finally does make an appearance, the effect is decidedly anticlimactic: "He looked so ordinary. You might have stood him behind a counter and bought biscuits ..." (p. 182). The Prime Minister in June 1923 was the Conservative Stanley Baldwin. Only one month earlier he had replaced Conservative Prime Minister Andrew Bonar Law, when Law was forced to resign due to throat cancer. Baldwin inherited a majority Conservative government that could have continued to govern for another handful of years before calling an election. However, Britain at the time was plagued by economic depression and massive post-war unemployment. While these issues have no discernible effect on the Dalloways and their social circles, occasional scenes of privation bubble to the surface of the novel, scenes like the "battered old woman with one hand exposed for coppers" (p. 110) singing outside Regent's Park tube station. Baldwin believed strongly that tariff reform, including the introduction of high tariffs against foreign manufacturers, was the only way to bolster British industry and create jobs. He called a General Election on the issue in December 1923 (see Appendix C4). The result was a hung Parliament, with no party holding a clear majority, and in January 1924 Baldwin lost a confidence vote. J. Ramsay MacDonald, who had been in a decided minority of Parliamentarians (including members of his own party) in opposing the war (see Appendix C1), became Britain's first Labour Prime Minister. His own Government lasted only ten months before it was defeated in another general election and Stanley Baldwin's Conservatives returned to power.

In *Mrs. Dalloway* it is only Lady Bruton—who "has the reputation of being more interested in politics than people; of talking like a man" (p. 130)—who appears to grasp fully the political instability of the times. In addition to predicting the ascendency of Labour ("whenever the time came; the Labour Government she meant" [p. 134]), she exclaims over "the news from India!" (p. 134). While it would be another quarter of a century before India gained independence, it is clear that the India Peter Walsh has left behind, and which his family had administered for at least three generations, is undergoing cataclysmic changes (see Appendix C3).

Mrs. Dalloway takes place on one day in the middle of June 1923. Its plot is thin: a middle-aged society hostess is having a party; she hopes the Prime Minister will attend; she reconnects with old friends from her youth. From these slimmest of premises a whole world unfolds. To some reviewers at the time of its publication, the novel's achievement in the making of that fictional world did not seem to have been a lasting one. And yet—as the success of Michael Cunningham's *The Hours* would seem to suggest—of all of Virginia Woolf's novels, it is *Mrs. Dalloway* that appears to speak most intimately to our own time.

Virginia Woolf: A Brief Chronology

[Virginia Woolf's life has attracted many biographical treatments. What follows is a very brief chronology, outlining major events and listing major publications. For more detailed information about Virginia Woolf's life and context, interested readers are encouraged to consult Hermione Lee's exhaustive biography, *Virginia Woolf* (1996, 1997) and the Virginia Woolf entry in *Orlando: Women's Writing in the British Isles from the Beginning to the Present*.]

1882 25 January. Adeline Virginia Stephen is born at 22 Hyde Park Gate, Kensington, London. She is the third of four children (Vanessa, b. 1879; Thoby, b. 1880; Adrian, b. 1883) of Leslie Stephen (philosopher, critic, and first editor of *The Dictionary of National Biography*) and Julia Prinsep Stephen. Both parents had been previously married and widowed. Leslie Stephen had one daughter (Laura, b. 1870) from his first marriage, while Julia had two sons (George, b. 1868; Gerald, b. 1870) and one daughter (Stella, b. 1869) from her first marriage.

1895 5 May. Virginia Woolf's mother, Julia Stephen, dies at age 49 from rheumatic fever. Virginia suffers the first of a series of nervous breakdowns.

1897 19 July. Virginia Woolf's half-sister, Stella, recently married, dies at age 28. The cause of her death may have been peritonitis, or appendicitis, or complications from pregnancy.

1904 22 February. Virginia Woolf's father, Leslie Stephen, dies of cancer. His death precipitates a second serious nervous breakdown.

1904 October. Following Leslie Stephen's death, Virginia Woolf's siblings—Vanessa, Thoby, and Adrian—move to 46 Gordon Square, Bloomsbury. Virginia, who was recovering with friends and relatives, joins them in January 1905.

1905 January. Virginia Woolf begins teaching English composition, literature and history once a week to working men and women at Morley College, a commitment she maintains until the end of 1907.

1905 February. Virginia Woolf's older brother, Thoby Stephen, begins to host Thursday evening gatherings of his friends from Cambridge University, including Clive Bell, Lytton Strachey, and Leonard Woolf. These gatherings form the nucleus of what would come to be known as the Bloomsbury Group.

1906 20 November. Virginia Woolf's brother, Thoby Stephen, aged 26, dies of typhoid fever following a trip to Greece.

1907 7 February. Virginia Woolf's sister, Vanessa, marries art critic Clive Bell.

1910 February. Virginia participates in the Dreadnought Hoax, initiated by Adrian Stephen and his friend Horace de Vere Cole. Half a dozen friends dress up as the Emperor of Abyssinia and his entourage, and tour HMS Dreadnought, one of the newest and largest warships in the Royal Navy. The Dreadnought Hoax is reported in the British press and is the subject of questions in Parliament.

1910 6 May. King Edward VII dies and King George V assumes the throne.

1910 6 November. Roger Fry, artist and art critic, and member of the Bloomsbury Group, organizes the "Manet and the Post-Impressionists" exhibition at the Grafton Galleries in London.

1912 10 August. Virginia marries Leonard Woolf, a former colonial administrator in Ceylon. Abandoning the civil service in order to marry Virginia, Leonard turns his energies to writing and political work.

1913 The emotional stress of the marriage, together with the pressure of finishing her first novel, precipitates a nervous breakdown in 1913. On 9 September Virginia Woolf attempts suicide.

1914 4 August. Great Britain declares war on Germany.

1915 26 March. Virginia Woolf's first novel, *The Voyage Out*, is published by Duckworth & Co., the publishing house founded by her half-brother Gerald Duckworth.

1917 24 April. Leonard and Virginia Woolf take possession of a printing press. Initially intended as a form of occupational therapy for Virginia, it becomes the catalyst for the establishment of the Hogarth Press.

1917 July. The first publication of the Hogarth Press—*Two Stories, Written and Published by Virginia Woolf and L.S. Woolf.*

1918 11 November. The Armistice goes into effect and fighting ceases at 11 a.m., formally ending the Great War.

1919 20 October. Virginia Woolf's second novel, *Night and Day*, is published by Duckworth & Co.

1921 7 April. *Monday or Tuesday*, Virginia Woolf's first collection of short stories, is published by the Hogarth Press.

1922 27 October. Virginia Woolf's third novel, *Jacob's Room*, is published by the Hogarth Press.

1923 12 September. The Hogarth Press publishes the first British edition of T.S. Eliot's *The Waste Land.*

1923 6 December. A General Election is held, in which the major issue is Prime Minister Stanley Baldwin's proposals for tariff reform. The ruling Conservative Party wins the most seats but fails to gain a majority. The first Labour Party government, under the leadership of J. Ramsay MacDonald, is formed but is short-lived.

1924 29 October. The second General Election within a year produces a landslide victory for Stanley Baldwin's Conservatives. Although the Labour Party increases its percentage of the popular vote, it loses 40 seats.

1925 23 April. The Hogarth Press publishes *The Common Reader*, Virginia Woolf's first volume of collected essays.

1925 14 May. Virginia Woolf's fourth novel, *Mrs. Dalloway*, is published by the Hogarth Press.

1927 5 May. Virginia Woolf's fifth novel, *To the Lighthouse*, is published by the Hogarth Press.

1928 11 October. Virginia Woolf's sixth novel, *Orlando*, is published by the Hogarth Press.

1929 30 May. The first General Election with full women's suffrage, often referred to as "The Flapper Election," is held. The Labour Party, under J. Ramsay MacDonald, wins the most seats but fails to gain a majority.

1929 24 October. Virginia Woolf publishes *A Room of One's Own* with the Hogarth Press.

1931 8 October. Virginia Woolf's seventh and most experimental novel, *The Waves*, is published by the Hogarth Press.

1932 21 January. Lytton Strachey, a central member of the Bloomsbury Group, dies of stomach cancer at age 51.

1932 October. Winifred Holtby publishes *Virginia Woolf: A Critical Memoir*, the first major critical and biographical study of Woolf to be published in Britain.

1932 13 October. Virginia Woolf's second volume of collected essays, *The Second Common Reader*, is published by the Hogarth Press.

1933 5 October. Virginia Woolf's fictional autobiography of Elizabeth Barrett Browning's spaniel, *Flush*, is published by the Hogarth Press.

1934 9 September. Roger Fry, art critic and central member of the Bloomsbury Group, dies unexpectedly due to a fall.

1935 18 January. *Freshwater*, Virginia Woolf's comedy about her great-aunt, the eminent Victorian photographer, Julia Cameron, is performed in her sister Vanessa Bell's London studio. The play was first written in 1923, revised in 1935, and published posthumously in 1976, in an edition by Lucio Ruotolo titled *Freshwater: A Comedy*.

1937 11 March. Virginia Woolf publishes her longest novel, *The Years*, with the Hogarth Press.

1937 18 July. Julian Bell, Virginia Woolf's nephew and Vanessa Bell's son, is killed by a shell fragment while driving an ambulance in the Spanish Civil War. Virginia Woolf learns of his death two days later.

1938 2 June. Virginia Woolf publishes *Three Guineas*, her polemical work about how women can help prevent war, with the Hogarth Press.

1939 3 September. Great Britain declares war on Germany.

1940 15 May. Virginia and Leonard Woolf discuss suicide in the event of a German invasion of Britain.

1940 25 July. Virginia Woolf publishes her biography *Roger Fry* with the Hogarth Press.

1940 14 September. A bomb damages the Woolfs' home at 37 Mecklenburgh Square, breaking all the windows and ceilings. Virginia and Leonard Woolf are at their country home in Rodmell, Sussex, but a week later travel to London to witness the damage.

1940 16 October. The Woolfs' former and longtime London home at 52 Tavistock Square is destroyed by a bomb.

1941 28 March. Fearing the effects of another breakdown, and leaving the second of two suicide notes for Leonard, Virginia Woolf drowns herself in the River Ouse near their home in Rodmell, Sussex. Her body is not recovered until 18 April.

1941 17 July. Virginia Woolf's final novel, *Between the Acts*, is published by the Hogarth Press.

A Note on the Text

Virginia Woolf's *Mrs. Dalloway* is an unusually fluid text. One of the challenges it presents to scholars is the difficulty of establishing a truly authoritative first edition. *Mrs. Dalloway* was the first of Woolf's novels to be published simultaneously in the United States and in Britain. Because of this, "it was not possible to set the American editions from published English texts" (Shields 157), which in turn meant that Woolf was required to correct two sets of proofs at the same time: one for Harcourt, Brace (her American publisher) and one for the Hogarth Press. As it happens, she corrected three sets of proofs, one of which served as an advance copy of the novel for her old friend, the painter Jacques Raverat, who was near death in Paris (Wright 242). Two of these three sets of corrected proofs survive—the Raverat proofs and the Harcourt proofs—and it is clear from them that Woolf, who disliked revision and proofing, was inconsistent in her changes. This has led to some debate among scholars about which of the two editions published simultaneously on 14 May 1925 reflects more accurately Woolf's final intentions about the novel (see Shields; Wright). Although E.F. Shields concludes in her 1986 article that both "can legitimately claim to be the authoritative first editions" (175), she also notes that "One tends to prefer the Hogarth edition partly because Virginia Woolf was able to exercise much closer control over its publication" (173).

Not all editors agree. David Bradshaw, for example, chose the 1942 Hogarth Press edition as the copy-text for the Oxford World's Classics edition. And, for the 1990 Hogarth Press Definitive Collected Edition, G. Patton Wright took a completely different approach, producing an edition of *Mrs. Dalloway* based on a collation of all the American and British editions published by 1990, together with the two extant sets of corrected proofs. Wright's edition also corrects unintended errors in the text, such as an inconsistency in Peter Walsh's age, and the colour of the dress Elizabeth wears to the party (see Wright in Woolf 1990, 179-80).[1]

A definitive textual edition attempts to answer the question, "What were the author's intentions?" This Broadview Edition poses a different question: "What were the individual, social, and historical contexts in which this novel was produced?" Therefore,

1 These errors appeared in both the Harcourt and Hogarth editions.

for this edition, I have chosen to take the first Hogarth Press edition as my copy-text, retaining even the errors. (With the exception of minor variations in punctuation, these are identified in footnotes.) *Mrs. Dalloway* was a text that was laboured over, written, rewritten and proofed, and, in spite of this, it was also a text in which small errors—"accidentals" (Greg 22)—found their way into publication. These errors are the traces of a very human hand and an individual mind, a mind that was not "what we might call ... 'factual'" (Shields 175). Together with parts of *The Voyage Out*, the British Library manuscript edition of "The Hours" (Woolf 1996), and the various short stories that comprise what we might call the Dalloway cycle (see Introduction, p. 19, n. 1), the first Hogarth Press edition permits a glimpse into Woolf's mind and creative process.

The first Hogarth Press edition also serves as a reminder of the unusual control Woolf was able to exert over her work, all the way through to its publication. While her first two novels were published by Duckworth & Co., the publishing house founded in 1898 by her half-brother Gerald (whom she later accused of sexual abuse), Woolf's joint ownership of the Hogarth Press (with Leonard) meant that for the rest of her career she served as her own publisher. This gave Woolf unusual freedom to experiment. Owning a press, setting type, and working as a publisher also influenced Woolf's writing in interesting ways. As biographer Hermione Lee points out, "in the two sides of her thinking about writing—how it comes into being, and who the audience is—the Press was an inspiration" (Lee 374).

MRS. DALLOWAY

VIRGINIA WOOLF

PUBLISHED BY LEONARD & VIRGINIA WOOLF AT THE
HOGARTH PRESS, 52 TAVISTOCK SQUARE, LONDON, W.C.
1925

Image courtesy of the Bruce Peel Special Collections Library, University of Alberta.

Mrs. Dalloway said she would buy the flowers herself.

For Lucy had her work cut out for her. The doors would be taken off their hinges; Rumpelmayer's[1] men were coming. And then, thought Clarissa Dalloway, what a morning—fresh as if issued to children on a beach.

What a lark! What a plunge! For so it had always seemed to her when, with a little squeak of the hinges, which she could hear now, she had burst open the French windows and plunged at Bourton into the open air. How fresh, how calm, stiller than this of course, the air was in the early morning; like the flap of a wave; the kiss of a wave; chill and sharp and yet (for a girl of eighteen as she then was) solemn, feeling as she did, standing there at the open window, that something awful was about to happen; looking at the flowers, at the trees with the smoke winding off them and the rooks rising, falling; standing and looking until Peter Walsh said, "Musing among the vegetables?"—was that it?—"I prefer men to cauliflowers"—was that it? He must have said it at breakfast one morning when she had gone out on to the terrace—Peter Walsh. He would be back from India one of these days, June or July, she forgot which, for his letters were awfully dull; it was his sayings one remembered; his eyes, his pocket-knife, his smile, his grumpiness and, when millions of things had utterly vanished—how strange it was!—a few sayings like this about cabbages.

She stiffened a little on the kerb, waiting for Durtnall's[2] van to pass. A charming woman, Scrope Purvis thought her (knowing her as one does know people who live next door to one in Westminster[3]); a touch of the bird about her, of the jay, blue-green, light, vivacious, though she was over fifty, and grown very white since her illness. There she perched, never seeing him, waiting to cross, very upright.

For having lived in Westminster—how many years now? over twenty,—one feels even in the midst of the traffic, or waking at night, Clarissa was positive, a particular hush, or solemnity; an indescribable pause; a suspense (but that might be her heart,

---

1 "[A] firm of 'refreshment contractors'" (Bradshaw 541) or caterers.

2 Durtnall & Co., "a city firm of 'removal & road contractors & furniture warehousemen, railway carriers & general cartage agents'" (Bradshaw 541).

3 An area of central London that includes such significant historical landmarks as Buckingham Palace, Westminster Cathedral, Westminster Abbey, and the Houses of Parliament (also known as the Palace of Westminster).

affected, they said, by influenza) before Big Ben[1] strikes. There! Out it boomed. First a warning, musical; then the hour, irrevocable. The leaden circles dissolved in the air. Such fools we are, she thought, crossing Victoria Street. For Heaven only knows why one loves it so, how one sees it so, making it up, building it round one, tumbling it, creating it every moment afresh; but the veriest frumps, the most dejected of miseries sitting on doorsteps (drink their downfall) do the same; can't be dealt with, she felt positive, by Acts of Parliament for that very reason: they love life. In people's eyes, in the swing, tramp, and trudge; in the bellow and the uproar; the carriages, motor cars, omnibuses, vans, sandwich men shuffling and swinging; brass bands; barrel organs; in the triumph and the jingle and the strange high singing of some aeroplane overhead was what she loved; life; London; this moment of June.

For it was the middle of June. The War was over,[2] except for some one like Mrs. Foxcroft at the Embassy last night eating her heart out because that nice boy was killed and now the old Manor House must go to a cousin;[3] or Lady Bexborough who opened a bazaar, they said, with the telegram in her hand, John, her favourite, killed; but it was over; thank Heaven—over. It was June. The King and Queen[4] were at the Palace. And everywhere, though it was still so early, there was a beating, a stirring of galloping ponies, tapping of cricket bats; Lords, Ascot,

---

1 Nickname for the clock or clock tower at the north end of the Palace of Westminster. The clock's movement was completed in 1854, its bell cast in 1858, and it struck its first chimes in 1859. Big Ben strikes the hour and quarter hours using the famous melody of the Westminster Quarters or Westminster Chimes.

2 World War I or, as it was known at this time, the Great War or the World War. Britain declared war on Germany on 4 August 1914 and fighting ceased on 11 November 1918.

3 A reference to the practice of entailment, whereby property must be inherited by male primogeniture, or by the nearest male-line descendent of the original or previous owner. The death of an only son could mean that the family property would be inherited by another, even a distant, male relative. Virginia Woolf was particularly attuned to the injustice of entailment because her friend and one-time lover, Vita Sackville-West, had lost her beloved ancestral home, Knole, on her father's death because it could not be bequeathed to a woman.

4 King George V and his wife Queen Mary. George V inherited the throne from his father, Edward VII, in 1910 and reigned until his own death in 1936.

Ranelagh[1] and all the rest of it; wrapped in the soft mesh of the grey-blue morning air, which, as the day wore on, would unwind them, and set down on their lawns and pitches the bouncing ponies, whose forefeet just struck the ground and up they sprung, the whirling young men, and laughing girls in their transparent muslins who, even now, after dancing all night, were taking their absurd woolly dogs for a run; and even now, at this hour, discreet old dowagers were shooting out in their motor cars on errands of mystery; and the shopkeepers were fidgeting in their windows with their paste[2] and diamonds, their lovely old sea-green brooches in eighteenth-century settings to tempt Americans (but one must economise, not buy things rashly for Elizabeth), and she, too, loving it as she did with an absurd and faithful passion, being part of it, since her people were courtiers once in the time of the Georges,[3] she, too, was going that very night to kindle and illuminate; to give her party. But how strange, on entering the Park,[4] the silence; the mist; the hum; the slow-swimming happy ducks; the pouched birds waddling; and who should be coming along with his back against the Government buildings, most appropriately, carrying a despatch box stamped with the Royal Arms, who but Hugh Whitbread; her old friend Hugh—the admirable Hugh!

---

1 Lord's cricket ground, home of the Marylebone Cricket Club (in St. John's Wood, London); the Ascot Racecourse (in Ascot, Berkshire) where the Royal Ascot races are held annually in June; and the Hurlingham Club in Ranelagh Gardens, where polo was played. (Woolf omits the apostrophe in Lord's in this and subsequent editions of *Mrs. Dalloway*.)

2 A hard vitreous or glasslike substance used in making artificial jewels.

3 Reference to the first four British monarchs from the German House of Hanover: George I (reigned 1714-27); George II (reigned 1727-60); George III (reigned 1760-1820); and George IV (reigned 1820-30). George III was the first of these to be born in Britain and to have English as his mother tongue. The House of Hanover remained the reigning family of Britain until the death of Queen Victoria when the succession passed to her son, Edward VII, who belonged to the House of Saxe-Cobourg and Gotha, his father's family. See also p. 58, n. 2.

4 The oldest of London's eight Royal Parks. Comprising 90 acres, it is bounded by the Mall on the north, Birdcage Walk on the south, the Queen Victoria Memorial on the west, and Horse Guards Road on the east (see Weinrib et al., eds., *The London Encyclopaedia*, 3rd ed.; hereinafter cited as *LE*).

"Good-morning to you, Clarissa!" said Hugh, rather extravagantly, for they had known each other as children. "Where are you off to?"

"I love walking in London," said Mrs. Dalloway. "Really, it's better than walking in the country."

They had just come up—unfortunately—to see doctors. Other people came to see pictures; go to the opera; take their daughters out; the Whitbreads came "to see doctors." Times without number Clarissa had visited Evelyn Whitbread in a nursing home. Was Evelyn ill again? Evelyn was a good deal out of sorts, said Hugh, intimating by a kind of pout or swell of his very well-covered, manly, extremely handsome, perfectly upholstered body (he was almost too well dressed always, but presumably had to be, with his little job at Court) that his wife had some internal ailment, nothing serious, which, as an old friend, Clarissa Dalloway would quite understand without requiring him to specify. Ah yes, she did of course; what a nuisance; and felt very sisterly and oddly conscious at the same time of her hat. Not the right hat for the early morning, was that it? For Hugh always made her feel, as he bustled on, raising his hat rather extravagantly and assuring her that she might be a girl of eighteen, and of course he was coming to her party tonight, Evelyn absolutely insisted, only a little late he might be after the party at the Palace to which he had to take one of Jim's boys,—she always felt a little skimpy beside Hugh; schoolgirlish; but attached to him, partly from having known him always, but she did think him a good sort in his own way, though Richard was nearly driven mad by him, and as for Peter Walsh, he had never to this day forgiven her for liking him.

She could remember scene after scene at Bourton—Peter furious; Hugh not, of course, his match in any way, but still not a positive imbecile as Peter made out; not a mere barber's block. When his old mother wanted him to give up shooting or to take her to Bath he did it, without a word; he was really unselfish, and as for saying, as Peter did, that he had no heart, no brain, nothing but the manners and breeding of an English gentleman, that was only her dear Peter at his worst; and he could be intolerable; he could be impossible; but adorable to walk with on a morning like this.

(June had drawn out every leaf on the trees. The mothers of Pimlico[1] gave suck to their young. Messages were passing from

1 A London neighbourhood bordering Westminster. In 1923, it would have been a more socially mixed neighbourhood than Clarissa Dalloway's.

the Fleet to the Admiralty.[1] Arlington Street and Piccadilly seemed to chafe the very air in the Park and lift its leaves hotly, brilliantly, on waves of that divine vitality which Clarissa loved. To dance, to ride, she had adored all that.)

For they might be parted for hundreds of years, she and Peter; she never wrote a letter and his were dry sticks; but suddenly it would come over her, If he were with me now what would he say?—some days, some sights bringing him back to her calmly, without the old bitterness; which perhaps was the reward of having cared for people; they came back in the middle of St. James's Park on a fine morning—indeed they did. But Peter—however beautiful the day might be, and the trees and the grass, and the little girl in pink—Peter never saw a thing of all that. He would put on his spectacles, if she told him to; he would look. It was the state of the world that interested him; Wagner, Pope's poetry,[2] people's characters eternally, and the defects of her own soul. How he scolded her! How they argued! She would marry a Prime Minister and stand at the top of a staircase; the perfect hostess he called her (she had cried over it in her bedroom), she had the makings of the perfect hostess, he said.

So she would still find herself arguing in St. James's Park, still making out that she had been right—and she had too—not to marry him. For in marriage a little licence, a little independence there must be between people living together day in day out in the same house; which Richard gave her, and she him. (Where was he this morning, for instance? Some committee, she never asked what.) But with Peter everything had to be shared; everything gone into. And it was intolerable, and when it came to that scene in the little garden by the fountain, she had to break with him or they would have been destroyed, both of them ruined, she was convinced; though she had borne about with her for years like an arrow sticking in her heart the grief, the anguish; and then the horror of the moment when some one told her at a concert that he had married a woman met on the boat going to India! Never should she forget all that! Cold, heartless, a prude, he called her. Never could she understand how he cared. But those Indian

---

1 "The Fleet" refers to the Royal Navy while "the Admiralty" refers both to the command of the Royal Navy and to one of the complex of buildings—located in Whitehall—housing the work of the Lords of the Admiralty.

2 Richard Wagner (1813-83), German composer; Alexander Pope (1688-1744), English satirical poet.

women did presumably—silly, pretty, flimsy nincompoops. And she wasted her pity. For he was quite happy, he assured her—perfectly happy, though he had never done a thing that they talked of; his whole life had been a failure. It made her angry still.

She had reached the Park gates. She stood for a moment, looking at the omnibuses in Piccadilly.

She would not say of any one in the world now that they were this or were that. She felt very young; at the same time unspeakably aged. She sliced like a knife through everything; at the same time was outside, looking on. She had a perpetual sense, as she watched the taxi cabs, of being out, out, far out to sea and alone; she always had the feeling that it was very, very dangerous to live even one day. Not that she thought herself clever, or much out of the ordinary. How she had got through life on the few twigs of knowledge Fräulein Daniels gave them she could not think.[1] She knew nothing; no language, no history; she scarcely read a book now, except memoirs in bed; and yet to her it was absolutely absorbing; all this; the cabs passing; and she would not say of Peter, she would not say of herself, I am this, I am that.

Her only gift was knowing people almost by instinct, she thought, walking on. If you put her in a room with some one, up went her back like a cat's; or she purred. Devonshire House, Bath House,[2] the house with the china cockatoo,[3] she had seen them all lit up once; and remembered Sylvia, Fred, Sally Seton—such hosts of people; and dancing all night; and the waggons plodding past to market; and driving home across the Park. She remembered once throwing a shilling into the Serpentine.[4] But every one remembered; what she loved was this, here, now, in front of her; the fat lady in the cab. Did it matter then, she asked herself, walking towards Bond Street,[5] did it matter that she must inevitably cease completely; all this must go on without her; did she resent it; or did it not become consoling to believe that death ended absolutely? but that somehow in the streets of London, on the ebb and flow of things, here, there, she survived, Peter sur-

---

1 Like most women of her class and time (including Virginia Woolf), Clarissa received no formal education. She was taught instead by governesses and perhaps occasionally by private tutors.

2 Two of the grand detached houses of aristocrats in London's west end.

3 The home of Angela Georgina Burdett-Coutts, 1st Baroness Burdett-Coutts (1814-1906), an heiress and philanthropist, reputedly the wealthiest woman in England.

4 A recreational lake in Hyde Park.

5 A fashionable shopping street.

vived, lived in each other, she being part, she was positive, of the trees at home; of the house there, ugly, rambling all to bits and pieces as it was; part of people she had never met; being laid out like a mist between the people she knew best, who lifted her on their branches as she had seen the trees lift the mist, but it spread ever so far, her life, herself. But what was she dreaming as she looked into Hatchards'[1] shop window? What was she trying to recover? What image of white dawn in the country, as she read in the book spread open:

> Fear no more the heat o' the sun
>   Nor the furious winter's rages.[2]

This late age of the world's experience had bred in them all, all men and women, a well of tears. Tears and sorrows; courage and endurance; a perfectly upright and stoical bearing. Think, for example, of the woman she admired most, Lady Bexborough, opening the bazaar.

There were Jorrocks' *Jaunts and Jollities*;[3] there were *Soapy Sponge* and Mrs. Asquith's *Memoirs* and *Big Game Shooting in Nigeria*, all spread open.[4] Ever so many books there were; but none that seemed exactly right to take to Evelyn Whitbread in her

---

1 A London bookseller located on Piccadilly Street, in business since 1797.

2 This couplet, from a funeral song in William Shakespeare's *Cymbeline*, runs like a refrain through *Mrs. Dalloway*, appearing, as Jean M. Wyatt notes, "at five key points" (Wyatt 440). The first verse is:

> Fear no more the heat o' the sun,
> Nor the furious winter's rages;
> Thou thy worldly task hast done,
> Home art gone, and ta'en thy wages:
> Golden lads and girls all must,
> As chimney-sweepers, come to dust. (IV.ii.258-63)

3 A comic novel (1838) by sports journalist R.S. Surtees (1805-64), who also wrote *Mr. Sponge's Sporting Tour* (1853) featuring the character Soapy Sponge.

4 Margot (Emma Alice Margaret) Asquith (1864-1945) was the wife of Herbert Henry Asquith, Liberal Prime Minister 1908-16. She published several volumes of memoirs; the one on exhibit in Hatchards' shop window is *The Autobiography of Margot Asquith*, published in two volumes in 1920 and 1922. There is no record of any book called *Big Game Shooting in Nigeria* though there were many books published with similar titles (e.g., *Big Game Shooting in East Africa*, 1905; *Big Game Shooting on the Equator*, 1908; *Big Game Shooting in Upper Burma*, 1911).

nursing home. Nothing that would serve to amuse her and make that indescribably dried-up little woman look, as Clarissa came in, just for a moment cordial; before they settled down for the usual interminable talk of women's ailments. How much she wanted it—that people should look pleased as she came in, Clarissa thought and turned and walked back towards Bond Street, annoyed, because it was silly to have other reasons for doing things. Much rather would she have been one of those people like Richard who did things for themselves, whereas, she thought, waiting to cross, half the time she did things not simply, not for themselves; but to make people think this or that; perfect idiocy she knew (and now the policeman held up his hand) for no one was ever for a second taken in. Oh if she could have had her life over again! she thought, stepping on to the pavement, could have looked even differently!

She would have been, in the first place, dark like Lady Bexborough, with a skin of crumpled leather and beautiful eyes. She would have been, like Lady Bexborough, slow and stately; rather large; interested in politics like a man; with a country house; very dignified, very sincere. Instead of which she had a narrow pea-stick figure; a ridiculous little face, beaked like a bird's. That she held herself well was true; and had nice hands and feet; and dressed well, considering that she spent little. But often now this body she wore (she stopped to look at a Dutch picture), this body, with all its capacities, seemed nothing—nothing at all. She had the oddest sense of being herself invisible; unseen; unknown; there being no more marrying, no more having of children now, but only this astonishing and rather solemn progress with the rest of them, up Bond Street, this being Mrs. Dalloway; not even Clarissa any more; this being Mrs. Richard Dalloway.

Bond Street fascinated her; Bond Street early in the morning in the season;[1] its flags flying; its shops; no splash; no glitter; one roll of tweed in the shop where her father had bought his suits for fifty years; a few pearls; salmon on an iceblock.

"That is all," she said, looking at the fishmonger's. "That is

---

1 The time of year that fashionable people spent in London attending social, sporting, and cultural events. It normally began after Easter and ended with the beginning of the shooting (or hunting) season. As Lady Kitty Vincent noted, by the mid-1920s, "the days of magnificent functions are over ... though, in some ways, the season is livelier than it used to be," with the races at Ascot being "undoubtedly" the "most important function during the season" (Vincent 430).

all," she repeated, pausing for a moment at the window of a glove shop where, before the War, you could buy almost perfect gloves. And her old Uncle William used to say a lady is known by her shoes and her gloves. He had turned on his bed one morning in the middle of the War. He had said, "I have had enough." Gloves and shoes; she had a passion for gloves; but her own daughter, her Elizabeth, cared not a straw for either of them.

Not a straw, she thought, going on up Bond Street to a shop where they kept flowers for her when she gave a party. Elizabeth really cared for her dog most of all. The whole house this morning smelt of tar.[1] Still, better poor Grizzle than Miss Kilman; better distemper and tar and all the rest of it than sitting mewed in a stuffy bedroom with a prayer book! Better anything, she was inclined to say. But it might be only a phase, as Richard said, such as all girls go through. It might be falling in love. But why with Miss Kilman? who had been badly treated of course; one must make allowances for that, and Richard said she was very able, had a really historical mind. Anyhow they were inseparable, and Elizabeth, her own daughter, went to Communion; and how she dressed, how she treated people who came to lunch she did not care a bit, it being her experience that the religious ecstasy made people callous (so did causes); dulled their feelings, for Miss Kilman would do anything for the Russians, starved herself for the Austrians,[2] but in private inflicted positive torture, so insensitive was she, dressed in a green mackintosh coat. Year in year out she wore that coat; she perspired; she was never in the room five minutes without making you feel her superiority, your inferiority; how poor she was; how rich you were; how she lived in a slum without a cushion or a bed or a rug or whatever it might be, all her soul rusted with that grievance sticking in it, her dismissal from school during the War[3]—poor embittered unfortunate creature! For it was not her one hated but the idea of her, which undoubtedly had gathered in to itself a great deal that was not Miss Kilman; had become one of those spectres with which one

1 Coal tar shampoo, used as a treatment for itching in dogs.

2 Miss Kilman is evidently eager to help alleviate the ongoing post-war suffering of citizens of "Russia" (which by 1920, following the 1917 Russian or Bolshevik Revolution, was known as the Soviet Union) and Austria.

3 Numerous German nationals as well as British citizens of German origin were discriminated against during the war (see Appendix C2). See also Introduction, p. 30, n. 1.

battles in the night; one of those spectres who stand astride us and suck up half our life-blood, dominators and tyrants; for no doubt with another throw of the dice, had the black been uppermost and not the white, she would have loved Miss Kilman! But not in this world. No.

It rasped her, though, to have stirring about in her this brutal monster! to hear twigs cracking and feel hooves planted down in the depths of that leaf-encumbered forest, the soul; never to be content quite, or quite secure, for at any moment the brute would be stirring, this hatred, which, especially since her illness, had power to make her feel scraped, hurt in her spine; gave her physical pain, and made all pleasure in beauty, in friendship, in being well, in being loved and making her home delightful rock, quiver, and bend as if indeed there were a monster grubbing at the roots, as if the whole panoply of content were nothing but self love! this hatred!

Nonsense, nonsense! she cried to herself, pushing through the swing doors of Mulberry's the florists.

She advanced, light, tall, very upright, to be greeted at once by button-faced Miss Pym, whose hands were always bright red, as if they had been stood in cold water with the flowers.

There were flowers: delphiniums, sweet peas, bunches of lilac; and carnations, masses of carnations. There were roses; there were irises. Ah yes—so she breathed in the earthy garden sweet smell as she stood talking to Miss Pym who owed her help, and thought her kind, for kind she had been years ago; very kind, but she looked older, this year, turning her head from side to side among the irises and roses and nodding tufts of lilac with her eyes half closed, snuffing in, after the street uproar, the delicious scent, the exquisite coolness. And then, opening her eyes, how fresh, like frilled linen clean from a laundry laid in wicker trays, the roses looked; and dark and prim the red carnations, holding their heads up; and all the sweet peas spreading in their bowls, tinged violet, snow white, pale—as if it were the evening and girls in muslin frocks came out to pick sweet peas and roses after the superb summer's day, with its almost blue-black sky, its delphiniums, its carnations, its arum lilies was over; and it was the moment between six and seven when every flower—roses, carnations, irises, lilac—glows; white, violet, red, deep orange; every flower seems to burn by itself, softly, purely in the misty beds; and how she loved the grey white moths spinning in and out, over the cherry pie, over the evening primroses!

And as she began to go with Miss Pym from jar to jar, choosing, nonsense, nonsense, she said to herself, more and more gently, as if this beauty, this scent, this colour, and Miss Pym liking her, trusting her, were a wave which she let flow over her and surmount that hatred, that monster, surmount it all; and it lifted her up and up when—oh! a pistol shot in the street outside!

"Dear, those motor cars," said Miss Pym, going to the window to look, and coming back and smiling apologetically with her hands full of sweet peas, as if those motor cars, those tyres of motor cars, were all *her* fault.

The violent explosion which made Mrs. Dalloway jump and Miss Pym go to the window and apologise came from a motor car which had drawn to the side of the pavement precisely opposite Mulberry's shop window. Passers-by who, of course, stopped and stared, had just time to see a face of the very greatest importance against the dove-grey upholstery, before a male hand drew the blind and there was nothing to be seen except a square of dove grey.

Yet rumours were at once in circulation from the middle of Bond Street to Oxford Street on one side, to Atkinson's scent shop on the other, passing invisibly, inaudibly, like a cloud, swift, veil-like upon hills, falling indeed with something of a cloud's sudden sobriety and stillness upon faces which a second before had been utterly disorderly. But now mystery had brushed them with her wing; they had heard the voice of authority; the spirit of religion was abroad with her eyes bandaged tight and her lips gaping wide. But nobody knew whose face had been seen. Was it the Prince of Wales's, the Queen's, the Prime Minister's?[1] Whose face was it? Nobody knew.

Edgar J. Watkiss, with his roll of lead piping round his arm, said audibly, humorously of course: "The Proime Minister's kyar."

Septimus Warren Smith, who found himself unable to pass, heard him.

Septimus Warren Smith, aged about thirty, pale-faced, beak-nosed, wearing brown shoes and a shabby overcoat, with hazel eyes which had that look of apprehension in them which makes

---

1 The Prince of Wales in 1923 was Edward, son of George V, who would assume the throne as Edward VIII in January 1936 but abdicate later that year. In June 1923, the Prime Minister was the Conservative Stanley Baldwin, succeeding Andrew Bonar Law who had stepped down due to ill health only a month earlier. In the 1923 General Election, Baldwin would fail to retain a majority and J. Ramsay MacDonald would form Britain's first, though short-lived, Labour Government. See above, p. 46, n. 4; and Appendices C1, C4, and C5.

complete strangers apprehensive too. The world has raised its whip; where will it descend?

Everything had come to a standstill. The throb of the motor engines sounded like a pulse irregularly drumming through an entire body. The sun became extraordinarily hot because the motor car had stopped outside Mulberry's shop window; old ladies on the tops of omnibuses spread their black parasols; here a green, here a red parasol opened with a little pop. Mrs. Dalloway, coming to the window with her arms full of sweet peas, looked out with her little pink face pursed in enquiry. Every one looked at the motor car. Septimus looked. Boys on bicycles sprang off. Traffic accumulated. And there the motor car stood, with drawn blinds, and upon them a curious pattern like a tree, Septimus thought, and this gradual drawing together of everything to one centre before his eyes, as if some horror had come almost to the surface and was about to burst into flames, terrified him. The world wavered and quivered and threatened to burst into flames. It is I who am blocking the way, he thought. Was he not being looked at and pointed at; was he not weighted there, rooted to the pavement, for a purpose? But for what purpose?

"Let us go on, Septimus," said his wife, a little woman, with large eyes in a sallow pointed face; an Italian girl.

But Lucrezia herself could not help looking at the motor car and the tree pattern on the blinds. Was it the Queen in there—the Queen going shopping?

The chauffeur, who had been opening something, turning something, shutting something, got on to the box.

"Come on," said Lucrezia.

But her husband, for they had been married, four, five years now, jumped, started, and said, "All right!" angrily, as if she had interrupted him.

People must notice; people must see. People, she thought, looking at the crowd staring at the motor car; the English people, with their children and their horses and their clothes, which she admired in a way; but they were "people" now, because Septimus had said, "I will kill myself"; an awful thing to say. Suppose they had heard him? She looked at the crowd. Help, help! she wanted to cry out to butchers' boys and women. Help! Only last autumn she and Septimus had stood on the Embankment[1] wrapped in the same cloak and, Septimus reading a paper instead of talking,

---

1 The Victoria Embankment, a riverside road running from Westminster to Blackfriars (see *LE*).

she had snatched it from him and laughed in the old man's face who saw them! But failure one conceals. She must take him away into some park.

"Now we will cross," she said.

She had a right to his arm, though it was without feeling. He would give her, who was so simple, so impulsive, only twenty-four, without friends in England, who had left Italy for his sake, a piece of bone.

The motor car with its blinds drawn and an air of inscrutable reserve proceeded towards Piccadilly, still gazed at, still ruffling the faces on both sides of the street with the same dark breath of veneration for Queen, Prince, or Prime Minister nobody knew. The face itself had been seen only once by three people for a few seconds. Even the sex was now in dispute. But there could be no doubt that greatness was seated within; greatness was passing, hidden, down Bond Street, removed only by a hand's-breadth from ordinary people who might now, for the first and last time, be within speaking distance of the majesty of England, of the enduring symbol of the state which will be known to curious antiquaries, sifting the ruins of time, when London is a grass-grown path and all those hurrying along the pavement this Wednesday morning are but bones with a few wedding rings mixed up in their dust and the gold stoppings of innumerable decayed teeth. The face in the motor car will then be known.

It is probably the Queen, thought Mrs. Dalloway, coming out of Mulberry's with her flowers; the Queen. And for a second she wore a look of extreme dignity standing by the flower shop in the sunlight while the car passed at a foot's pace, with its blinds drawn. The Queen going to some hospital; the Queen opening some bazaar, thought Clarissa.

The crush was terrific for the time of day. Lords, Ascot, Hurlingham,[1] what was it? she wondered, for the street was blocked. The British middle classes sitting sideways on the tops of omnibuses with parcels and umbrellas, yes, even furs on a day like this, were, she thought, more ridiculous, more unlike anything there has ever been than one could conceive: and the Queen herself held up; the Queen herself unable to pass. Clarissa was suspended on one side of Brook Street; Sir John Buckhurst, the old Judge on the other, with the car between them (Sir John had laid down the law for years and liked a well-dressed woman) when the chauffeur, leaning ever so slightly, said or showed some-

---

1 See p. 47, n. 1.

thing to the policeman, who saluted and raised his arm and jerked his head and moved the omnibus to the side and the car passed through. Slowly and very silently it took its way.

Clarissa guessed; Clarissa knew of course; she had seen something white, magical, circular, in the footman's hand, a disc inscribed with a name—the Queen's, the Prince of Wales's, the Prime Minister's?—which, by force of its own lustre, burnt its way through (Clarissa saw the car diminishing, disappearing), to blaze among candelabras, glittering stars, breasts stiff with oak leaves,[1] Hugh Whitbread and all his colleagues, the gentlemen of England, that night in Buckingham Palace. And Clarissa, too, gave a party. She stiffened a little; so she would stand at the top of her stairs.

The car had gone, but it had left a slight ripple which flowed through glove shops and hat shops and tailors' shops on both sides of Bond Street. For thirty seconds all heads were inclined the same way—to the window. Choosing a pair of gloves—should they be to the elbow or above it, lemon or pale grey?—ladies stopped; when the sentence was finished something had happened. Something so trifling in single instances that no mathematical instrument, though capable of transmitting shocks in China, could register the vibration; yet in its fullness rather formidable and in its common appeal emotional; for in all the hat shops and tailors' shops strangers looked at each other and thought of the dead; of the flag; of Empire. In a public house in a back street a Colonial insulted the House of Windsor[2] which led to words, broken beer glasses, and a general shindy, which echoed strangely across the way in the ears of girls buying white underlinen threaded with pure white ribbon for their weddings. For the surface agitation of the passing car as it sunk grazed something very profound.

Gliding across Piccadilly, the car turned down St. James's Street. Tall men, men of robust physique, well-dressed men with their tail-coats and their white slips and their hair raked back

---

1 Bronze oak leaves were issued to individuals serving in World War I who were "Mentioned in Despatches" for acts of gallantry or other forms of noteworthy service.

2 Royal dynasty founded by King George V—the reigning monarch in 1923—who, by royal proclamation on 17 July 1917, changed the family name from the German Saxe-Coburg and Gotha to Windsor. This was due to anti-German sentiment in Britain during World War I. The word "House" refers to a family lineage.

who, for reasons difficult to discriminate, were standing in the bow window of Brooks's[1] with their hands behind the tails of their coats, looking out, perceived instinctively that greatness was passing, and the pale light of the immortal presence fell upon them as it had fallen upon Clarissa Dalloway. At once they stood even straighter, and removed their hands, and seemed ready to attend their Sovereign, if need be, to the cannon's mouth, as their ancestors had done before them. The white busts and the little tables in the background covered with copies of the *Tatler*[2] and syphons of soda water seemed to approve; seemed to indicate the flowing corn and the manor houses of England; and to return the frail hum of the motor wheels as the walls of a whispering gallery return a single voice expanded and made sonorous by the might of a whole cathedral. Shawled Moll Pratt with her flowers on the pavement wished the dear boy well (it was the Prince of Wales for certain) and would have tossed the price of a pot of beer—a bunch of roses—into St. James's Street out of sheer light-heartedness and contempt of poverty had she not seen the constable's eye upon her, discouraging an old Irishwoman's loyalty. The sentries of St. James's[3] saluted; Queen Alexandra's policeman approved.

A small crowd meanwhile had gathered at the gates of Buckingham Palace.[4] Listlessly, yet confidently, poor people all of them, they waited; looked at the Palace itself with the flag flying; at Victoria, billowing on her mound,[5] admired her shelves of running water, her geraniums; singled out from the motor cars in the Mall[6] first this one, then that; bestowed emotion, vainly, upon commoners out for a drive; recalled their tribute to keep it

---

1 An exclusive gentlemen's club in London, founded in 1764.

2 A glossy magazine founded in 1901 and focussing on the lives of the upper class.

3 St. James's Palace, in Pall Mall just north of St. James's Park; it remains the official home of the sovereign, though no king or queen has lived there since George III. "Queen Alexandra's policeman" may be a reference to Marlborough House, in Pall Mall just east of St. James's Palace; in 1923 it served as the home of Queen Alexandra (1844-1925), the widow of Edward VII and mother of the current king, George V.

4 The official residence of the British monarch.

5 The Queen Victoria Memorial, unveiled in 1911, in the Memorial Gardens in front of Buckingham Palace.

6 A 34-metre-wide processional route linking Admiralty Arch and the Queen Victoria Memorial (*LE*).

unspent while this car passed and that; and all the time let rumour accumulate in their veins and thrill the nerves in their thighs at the thought of Royalty looking at them; the Queen bowing; the Prince saluting; at the thought of the heavenly life divinely bestowed upon Kings; of the equerries and deep curtsies; of the Queen's old doll's house;[1] of Princess Mary married to an Englishman,[2] and the Prince—ah! the Prince! who took wonderfully, they said, after old King Edward, but was ever so much slimmer. The Prince lived at St. James's; but he might come along in the morning to visit his mother.

So Sarah Bletchley said with her baby in her arms, tipping her foot up and down as though she were by her own fender in Pimlico, but keeping her eyes on the Mall, while Emily Coates ranged over the Palace windows and thought of the housemaids, the innumerable housemaids, the bedrooms, the innumerable bedrooms. Joined by an elderly gentleman with an Aberdeen terrier, by men without occupation, the crowd increased. Little Mr. Bowley, who had rooms in the Albany and was sealed with wax over the deeper sources of life but could be unsealed suddenly, inappropriately, sentimentally, by this sort of thing—poor women waiting to see the Queen go past—poor women, nice little children, orphans, widows, the War—tut-tut—actually had tears in his eyes. A breeze flaunting ever so warmly down the Mall through the thin trees, past the bronze heroes, lifted some flag flying in the British breast of Mr. Bowley and he raised his hat as the car turned into the Mall and held it high as the car approached; and let the poor mothers of Pimlico press close to him, and stood very upright. The car came on.

Suddenly Mrs. Coates looked up into the sky. The sound of an aeroplane bored ominously into the ears of the crowd. There it was coming over the trees, letting out white smoke from behind, which curled and twisted, actually writing something! making letters in the sky! Every one looked up.

Dropping dead down the aeroplane soared straight up, curved in a loop, raced, sank, rose, and whatever it did, wherever it went,

---

1 Usually understood to be a reference to an elaborate doll's house designed for Queen Mary by the architect Sir Edwin Luytens. Over 1500 artists and craftsmen contributed to its design and construction; however, the doll's house was not completed until 1924 when it was displayed at the British Empire Exhibition.

2 Princess Mary, only daughter of George V and Queen Mary, married Henry Charles George, Viscount Lascelles in 1922.

out fluttered behind it a thick ruffled bar of white smoke which curled and wreathed upon the sky in letters. But what letters? A C was it? an E, then an L? Only for a moment did they lie still; then they moved and melted and were rubbed out up in the sky, and the aeroplane shot further away and again, in a fresh space of sky, began writing a K, an E, a Y perhaps?

"Glaxo," said Mrs. Coates in a strained, awe-stricken voice, gazing straight up, and her baby, lying stiff and white in her arms, gazed straight up.

"Kreemo," murmured Mrs. Bletchley, like a sleep-walker. With his hat held out perfectly still in his hand, Mr. Bowley gazed straight up. All down the Mall people were standing and looking up into the sky. As they looked the whole world became perfectly silent, and a flight of gulls crossed the sky, first one gull leading, then another, and in this extraordinary silence and peace, in this pallor, in this purity, bells struck eleven times, the sound fading up there among the gulls.

The aeroplane turned and raced and swooped exactly where it liked, swiftly, freely, like a skater—

"That's an E," said Mrs. Bletchley—or a dancer—

"It's toffee," murmured Mr. Bowley—(and the car went in at the gates and nobody looked at it), and shutting off the smoke, away and away it rushed, and the smoke faded and assembled itself round the broad white shapes of the clouds.

It had gone; it was behind the clouds. There was no sound. The clouds to which the letters E, G, or L had attached themselves moved freely, as if destined to cross from West to East on a mission of the greatest importance which would never be revealed, and yet certainly so it was—a mission of the greatest importance. Then suddenly, as a train comes out of a tunnel, the aeroplane rushed out of the clouds again, the sound boring into the ears of all people in the Mall, in the Green Park, in Piccadilly, in Regent Street, in Regent's Park,[1] and the bar of smoke curved behind and it dropped down, and it soared up and wrote one letter after another—but what word was it writing?

---

1 Green Park and Regent's Park are two of the eight Royal Parks in London. Fifty-three acre Green Park is bounded by Piccadilly to the north, Constitution Hill to the south, Duke of Wellington Place to the west, and Queen's Walk to the east. Regent's Park, which houses the London Zoo, is 410 acres of mostly open park and grassland in northwest Central London.

Lucrezia Warren Smith, sitting by her husband's side on a seat in Regent's Park in the Broad Walk, looked up.

"Look, look, Septimus!" she cried. For Dr. Holmes had told her to make her husband (who had nothing whatever seriously the matter with him but was a little out of sorts) take an interest in things outside himself.

So, thought Septimus, looking up, they are signalling to me. Not indeed in actual words; that is, he could not read the language yet; but it was plain enough, this beauty, this exquisite beauty, and tears filled his eyes as he looked at the smoke words languishing and melting in the sky and bestowing upon him in their inexhaustible charity and laughing goodness one shape after another of unimaginable beauty and signalling their intention to provide him, for nothing, for ever, for looking merely, with beauty, more beauty! Tears ran down his cheeks.

It was toffee; they were advertising toffee, a nursemaid told Rezia. Together they began to spell t ... o ... f ...

"K ... R ..." said the nursemaid, and Septimus heard her say "Kay Arr" close to his ear, deeply, softly, like a mellow organ, but with a roughness in her voice like a grasshopper's, which rasped his spine deliciously and sent running up into his brain waves of sound which, concussing, broke. A marvellous discovery indeed—that the human voice in certain atmospheric conditions (for one must be scientific, above all scientific) can quicken trees into life! Happily Rezia put her hand with a tremendous weight on his knee so that he was weighted down, transfixed, or the excitement of the elm trees rising and falling, rising and falling with all their leaves alight and the colour thinning and thickening from blue to the green of a hollow wave, like plumes on horses' heads, feathers on ladies', so proudly they rose and fell, so superbly, would have sent him mad. But he would not go mad. He would shut his eyes; he would see no more.

But they beckoned; leaves were alive; trees were alive. And the leaves being connected by millions of fibres with his own body, there on the seat, fanned it up and down; when the branch stretched he, too, made that statement. The sparrows fluttering, rising, and falling in jagged fountains were part of the pattern; the white and blue, barred with black branches. Sounds made harmonies with premeditation; the spaces between them were as significant as the sounds. A child cried. Rightly far away a horn sounded. All taken together meant the birth of a new religion—

"Septimus!" said Rezia. He started violently. People must notice.

"I am going to walk to the fountain and back," she said.

For she could stand it no longer. Dr. Holmes might say there was nothing the matter. Far rather would she that he were dead! She could not sit beside him when he stared so and did not see her and made everything terrible; sky and tree, children playing; dragging carts, blowing whistles, falling down; all were terrible. And he would not kill himself; and she could tell no one. "Septimus has been working too hard"—that was all she could say, to her own mother. To love makes one solitary, she thought. She could tell nobody, not even Septimus now, and looking back, she saw him sitting in his shabby overcoat alone, on the seat, hunched up, staring. And it was cowardly for a man to say he would kill himself, but Septimus had fought; he was brave; he was not Septimus now. She put on her lace collar. She put on her new hat and he never noticed; and he was happy without her. Nothing could make her happy without him! Nothing! He was selfish. So men are. For he was not ill. Dr. Holmes said there was nothing the matter with him. She spread her hand before her. Look! Her wedding ring slipped—she had grown so thin. It was she who suffered—but she had nobody to tell.

Far was Italy and the white houses and the room where her sisters sat making hats, and the streets crowded every evening with people walking, laughing out loud, not half alive like people here, huddled up in Bath chairs,[1] looking at a few ugly flowers stuck in pots!

"For you should see the Milan gardens," she said aloud. But to whom?

There was nobody. Her words faded. So a rocket fades. Its sparks, having grazed their way into the night, surrender to it, dark descends, pours over the outlines of houses and towers; bleak hill-sides soften and fall in. But though they are gone, the night is full of them; robbed of colour, blank of windows, they exist more ponderously, give out what the frank daylight fails to transmit—the trouble and suspense of things conglomerated there in the darkness; huddled together in the darkness; reft of the relief which dawn brings when, washing the walls white and grey, spotting each window-pane, lifting the mist from the fields, showing the red-brown cows peacefully grazing, all is once more decked out to the eye; exists again. I am alone; I am alone! she cried, by the fountain in Regent's Park (staring at the Indian and

---

1 A rolling chaise or wheelchair for invalids, usually with a folding hood.

his cross),[1] as perhaps at midnight, when all boundaries are lost, the country reverts to its ancient shape, as the Romans saw it, lying cloudy, when they landed, and the hills had no names and rivers wound they knew not where—such was her darkness; when suddenly, as if a shelf were shot forth and she stood on it, she said how she was his wife, married years ago in Milan, his wife, and would never, never tell that he was mad! Turning, the shelf fell; down, down she dropped. For he was gone, she thought—gone, as he threatened, to kill himself—to throw himself under a cart! But no; there he was; still sitting alone on the seat, in his shabby overcoat, his legs crossed, staring, talking aloud.

Men must not cut down trees. There is a God. (He noted such revelations on the backs of envelopes.) Change the world. No one kills from hatred. Make it known (he wrote it down). He waited. He listened. A sparrow perched on the railing opposite chirped Septimus, Septimus, four or five times over and went on, drawing its notes out, to sing freshly and piercingly in Greek words how there is no crime and, joined by another sparrow, they sang in voices prolonged and piercing in Greek words, from trees in the meadow of life beyond a river where the dead walk, how there is no death.[2]

There was his hand; there the dead. White things were assembling behind the railings opposite. But he dared not look. Evans was behind the railings!

"What are you saying?" said Rezia suddenly, sitting down by him.

Interrupted again! She was always interrupting.

Away from people—they must get away from people, he said (jumping up), right away over there, where there were chairs beneath a tree and the long slope of the park dipped like a length

---

1 Known as the "Ready Money" drinking fountain: "Given to the park in 1869 by Sir Cowasjee Jehangir, a wealthy Parsee industrialist from Bombay, whose nickname was Ready Money. It was his thank-you for the protection he and fellow Parsees received from British rule in India." See http://www.royalparks.org.uk/press/factsheets/factsheet_monuments inregentspark.cfm.

2 In this scene Woolf draws on symptoms she experienced during her second serious breakdown in 1904. In "Old Bloomsbury," a posthumously published memoir, she describes lying "in bed at the Dickinsons' house at Welwyn thinking that the birds were singing Greek choruses and that King Edward was using the foulest possible language among Ozzie Dickinson's azaleas" (*Moments of Being* 184).

of green stuff with a ceiling cloth of blue and pink smoke high above, and there was a rampart of far irregular houses, hazed in smoke, the traffic hummed in a circle, and on the right, dun-coloured animals stretched long necks over the Zoo palings, barking, howling. There they sat down under a tree.

"Look," she implored him, pointing at a little troop of boys carrying cricket stumps, and one shuffled, spun round on his heel and shuffled, as if he were acting a clown at the music hall.[1]

"Look," she implored him, for Dr. Holmes had told her to make him notice real things, go to a music hall, play cricket—that was the very game, Dr. Holmes said, a nice out-of-door game, the very game for her husband.

"Look," she repeated.

Look the unseen bade him, the voice which now communicated with him who was the greatest of mankind, Septimus, lately taken from life to death, the Lord who had come to renew society, who lay like a coverlet, a snow blanket smitten only by the sun, for ever unwasted, suffering for ever, the scapegoat, the eternal sufferer, but he did not want it, he moaned, putting from him with a wave of his hand that eternal suffering, that eternal loneliness.

"Look," she repeated, for he must not talk aloud to himself out of doors.

"Oh look," she implored him. But what was there to look at? A few sheep. That was all.

The way to Regent's Park Tube station—could they tell her the way to Regent's Park Tube station—Maisie Johnson wanted to know. She was only up from Edinburgh two days ago.

"Not this way—over there!" Rezia exclaimed, waving her aside, lest she should see Septimus.

Both seemed queer, Maisie Johnson thought. Everything seemed very queer. In London for the first time, come to take up a post at her uncle's in Leadenhall Street, and now walking through Regent's Park in the morning, this couple on the chairs gave her quite a turn; the young woman seeming foreign, the man looking queer; so that should she be very old she would still remember and make it jangle again among her memories how she had walked through Regent's Park on a fine summer's morning fifty years ago. For she was only nineteen and had got her way at last, to come to London; and now how queer it was, this couple

---

1 A form of British popular theatrical entertainment, similar to American vaudeville.

she had asked the way of, and the girl started and jerked her hand, and the man—he seemed awfully odd; quarrelling, perhaps; parting for ever, perhaps; something was up, she knew; and now all these people (for she returned to the Broad Walk), the stone basins, the prim flowers, the old men and women, invalids most of them in Bath chairs—all seemed, after Edinburgh, so queer. And Maisie Johnson, as she joined that gently trudging, vaguely gazing, breeze-kissed company—squirrels perching and preening, sparrow fountains fluttering for crumbs, dogs busy with the railings, busy with each other, while the soft warm air washed over them and lent to the fixed unsurprised gaze with which they received life something whimsical and mollified—Maisie Johnson positively felt she must cry Oh! (for that young man on the seat had given her quite a turn. Something was up, she knew).

Horror! horror! she wanted to cry. (She had left her people; they had warned her what would happen.)

Why hadn't she stayed at home? she cried, twisting the knob of the iron railing.

That girl, thought Mrs. Dempster (who saved crusts for the squirrels and often ate her lunch in Regent's Park), don't know a thing yet; and really it seemed to her better to be a little stout, a little slack, a little moderate in one's expectations. Percy drank. Well, better to have a son, thought Mrs. Dempster. She had had a hard time of it, and couldn't help smiling at a girl like that. You'll get married, for you're pretty enough, thought Mrs. Dempster. Get married, she thought, and then you'll know. Oh, the cooks, and so on. Every man has his ways. But whether I'd have chosen quite like that if I could have known, thought Mrs. Dempster, and could not help wishing to whisper a word to Maisie Johnson; to feel on the creased pouch of her worn old face the kiss of pity. For it's been a hard life, thought Mrs. Dempster. What hadn't she given to it? Roses; figure; her feet too. (She drew the knobbed lumps beneath her skirt.)

Roses, she thought sardonically. All trash, m'dear. For really, what with eating, drinking, and mating, the bad days and good, life had been no mere matter of roses, and what was more, let me tell you, Carrie Dempster had no wish to change her lot with any woman's in Kentish Town! But, she implored, pity. Pity, for the loss of roses. Pity she asked of Maisie Johnson, standing by the hyacinth beds.

Ah, but that aeroplane! Hadn't Mrs. Dempster always longed to see foreign parts? She had a nephew, a missionary. It soared and shot. She always went on the sea at Margate,[1] not out o' sight of land, but she had no patience with women who were afraid of water. It swept and fell. Her stomach was in her mouth. Up again. There's a fine young feller aboard of it, Mrs. Dempster wagered, and away and away it went, fast and fading, away and away the aeroplane shot; soaring over Greenwich and all the masts; over the little island of grey churches, St. Paul's[2] and the rest, till, on either side of London, fields spread out and dark brown woods where adventurous thrushes, hopping boldly, glancing quickly, snatched the snail and tapped him on a stone, once, twice, thrice.

Away and away the aeroplane shot, till it was nothing but a bright spark; an aspiration; a concentration; a symbol (so it seemed to Mr. Bentley, vigorously rolling his strip of turf at Greenwich) of man's soul; of his determination, thought Mr. Bentley, sweeping round the cedar tree, to get outside his body, beyond his house, by means of thought, Einstein, speculation, mathematics, the Mendelian theory[3]—away the aeroplane shot.

Then, while a seedy-looking nondescript man carrying a leather bag stood on the steps of St. Paul's Cathedral, and hesitated, for within was what balm, how great a welcome, how many tombs with banners waving over them, tokens of victories not over armies, but over, he thought, that plaguy spirit of truth seeking which leaves me at present without a situation, and more than that, the cathedral offers company, he thought, invites you to membership of a society; great men belong to it; martyrs have died for it; why not enter in, he thought, put this leather bag stuffed with pamphlets before an altar, a cross, the symbol of something which has soared beyond seeking and questing and knocking of words together and has become all spirit, disembodied, ghostly—why not enter in? he thought and while he hesitated out flew the aeroplane over Ludgate Circus.[4]

It was strange; it was still. Not a sound was to be heard above the traffic. Unguided it seemed; sped of its own free will. And

---

1 A seaside town in East Kent, England.

2 The famous domed St. Paul's Cathedral, designed by Sir Christopher Wren.

3 Foundational theory of modern genetics, based on the work of Gregor Mendel (1822-84).

4 A road junction where Farringdon Street and New Bridge Street cross Ludgate Hill and Fleet Street. In Britain, the word "circus" as part of a street name (Ludgate Circus, Piccadilly Circus) refers to a traffic roundabout or circle.

now, curving up and up, straight up, like something mounting in ecstasy, in pure delight, out from behind poured white smoke looping, writing a T, an O, an F.

"What are they looking at?" said Clarissa Dalloway to the maid who opened her door.

The hall of the house was cool as a vault. Mrs. Dalloway raised her hand to her eyes, and, as the maid shut the door to, and she heard the swish of Lucy's skirts, she felt like a nun who has left the world and feels fold round her the familiar veils and the response to old devotions. The cook whistled in the kitchen. She heard the click of the typewriter. It was her life, and, bending her head over the hall table, she bowed beneath the influence, felt blessed and purified, saying to herself, as she took the pad with the telephone message on it, how moments like this are buds on the tree of life, flowers of darkness they are, she thought (as if some lovely rose had blossomed for her eyes only); not for a moment did she believe in God; but all the more, she thought, taking up the pad, must one repay in daily life to servants, yes, to dogs and canaries, above all to Richard her husband, who was the foundation of it—of the gay sounds, of the green lights, of the cook even whistling, for Mrs. Walker was Irish and whistled all day long—one must pay back from this secret deposit of exquisite moments, she thought, lifting the pad, while Lucy stood by her, trying to explain how

"Mr. Dalloway, ma'am"—

Clarissa read on the telephone pad, "Lady Bruton wishes to know if Mr. Dalloway will lunch with her to-day."

"Mr. Dalloway, ma'am, told me to tell you he would be lunching out."

"Dear!" said Clarissa, and Lucy shared as she meant her to her disappointment (but not the pang); felt the concord between them; took the hint; thought how the gentry love; gilded her own future with calm; and, taking Mrs. Dalloway's parasol, handled it like a sacred weapon which a Goddess, having acquitted herself honourably in the field of battle, sheds, and placed it in the umbrella stand.

"Fear no more," said Clarissa. Fear no more the heat o' the sun; for the shock of Lady Bruton asking Richard to lunch without her made the moment in which she had stood shiver, as a plant on the river-bed feels the shock of a passing oar and shivers: so she rocked: so she shivered.

Millicent Bruton, whose lunch parties were said to be extraordinarily amusing, had not asked her. No vulgar jealousy could separate her from Richard. But she feared time itself, and read on Lady Bruton's face, as if it had been a dial cut in impassive stone, the dwindling of life; how year by year her share was sliced; how little the margin that remained was capable any longer of stretching, of absorbing, as in the youthful years, the colours, salts, tones of existence, so that she filled the room she entered, and felt often as she stood hesitating one moment on the threshold of her drawing-room, an exquisite suspense, such as might stay a diver before plunging while the sea darkens and brightens beneath him, and the waves which threaten to break, but only gently split their surface, roll and conceal and encrust as they just turn over the weeds with pearl.

She put the pad on the hall table. She began to go slowly upstairs, with her hand on the banisters, as if she had left a party, where now this friend now that had flashed back her face, her voice; had shut the door and gone out and stood alone, a single figure against the appalling night, or rather, to be accurate, against the stare of this matter-of-fact June morning; soft with the glow of rose petals for some, she knew, and felt it, as she paused by the open staircase window which let in blinds flapping, dogs barking, let in, she thought, feeling herself suddenly shrivelled, aged, breastless, the grinding, blowing, flowering of the day, out of doors, out of the window, out of her body and brain which now failed, since Lady Bruton, whose lunch parties were said to be extraordinarily amusing, had not asked her.

Like a nun withdrawing, or a child exploring a tower, she went, upstairs, paused at the window, came to the bathroom. There was the green linoleum and a tap dripping. There was an emptiness about the heart of life; an attic room. Women must put off their rich apparel. At midday they must disrobe. She pierced the pincushion and laid her feathered yellow hat on the bed. The sheets were clean, tight stretched in a broad white band from side to side. Narrower and narrower would her bed be. The candle was half burnt down and she had read deep in Baron Marbot's *Memoirs*.[1] She had read late at night of the retreat from Moscow.

---

1 Jean Baptiste Antoine Marcellin Marbot (1782-1854) served in the Napoleonic wars. His *Mémoires du général Bon de Marbot* (in three volumes), written for his family, were published posthumously in 1891 and translated into English in 1892.

For the House[1] sat so long that Richard insisted, after her illness, that she must sleep undisturbed. And really she preferred to read of the retreat from Moscow. He knew it. So the room was an attic; the bed narrow; and lying there reading, for she slept badly, she could not dispel a virginity preserved through childbirth which clung to her like a sheet. Lovely in girlhood, suddenly there came a moment—for example on the river beneath the woods at Clieveden[2]—when, through some contraction of this cold spirit, she had failed him. And then at Constantinople, and again and again. She could see what she lacked. It was not beauty; it was not mind. It was something central which permeated; something warm which broke up surfaces and rippled the cold contact of man and woman, or of women together. For *that* she could dimly perceive. She resented it, had a scruple picked up Heaven knows where, or, as she felt, sent by Nature (who is invariably wise); yet she could not resist sometimes yielding to the charm of a woman, not a girl, of a woman confessing, as to her they often did, some scrape, some folly. And whether it was pity, or their beauty, or that she was older, or some accident—like a faint scent, or a violin next door (so strange is the power of sounds at certain moments), she did undoubtedly then feel what men felt. Only for a moment; but it was enough. It was a sudden revelation, a tinge like a blush which one tried to check and then, as it spread, one yielded to its expansion, and rushed to the farthest verge and there quivered and felt the world come closer, swollen with some astonishing significance, some pressure of rapture, which split its thin skin and gushed and poured with an extraordinary alleviation over the cracks and sores! Then, for that moment, she had seen an illumination; a match burning in a crocus; an inner meaning almost expressed. But the close withdrew; the hard softened. It was over—the moment. Against such moments (with women too) there contrasted (as she laid her hat down) the bed and Baron Marbot and the candle half-burnt. Lying awake, the floor creaked; the lit house was suddenly darkened, and if she raised her head she could just hear the click of the handle released as gently as possible by Richard, who slipped upstairs in his socks and then, as often as not, dropped his hot-water bottle and swore! How she laughed!

---

1 The House of Commons. Richard Dalloway is a Conservative Member of Parliament.

2 Likely a variant spelling of Cliveden, an estate in Buckinghamshire above the River Thames.

But this question of love (she thought, putting her coat away), this falling in love with women. Take Sally Seton; her relation in the old days with Sally Seton. Had not that, after all, been love?

She sat on the floor—that was her first impression of Sally—she sat on the floor with her arms round her knees, smoking a cigarette. Where could it have been? The Mannings'? The Kinloch-Jones's? At some party (where, she could not be certain), for she had a distinct recollection of saying to the man she was with, "Who is *that*?" And he had told her, and said that Sally's parents did not get on (how that shocked her—that one's parents should quarrel!). But all that evening she could not take her eyes off Sally. It was an extraordinary beauty of the kind she most admired, dark, large-eyed, with that quality which, since she hadn't got it herself, she always envied—a sort of abandonment, as if she could say anything, do anything; a quality much commoner in foreigners than in English-women. Sally always said she had French blood in her veins, an ancestor had been with Marie Antoinette,[1] had his head cut off, left a ruby ring. Perhaps that summer she came to stay at Bourton, walking in quite unexpectedly without a penny in her pocket, one night after dinner, and upsetting poor Aunt Helena to such an extent that she never forgave her. There had been some awful quarrel at home. She literally hadn't a penny that night when she came to them—had pawned a brooch to come down. She had rushed off in a passion. They sat up till all hours of the night talking. Sally it was who made her feel, for the first time, how sheltered the life at Bourton was. She knew nothing about sex—nothing about social problems. She had once seen an old man who had dropped dead in a field—she had seen cows just after their calves were born. But Aunt Helena never liked discussion of anything (when Sally gave her William Morris,[2] it had to be wrapped in brown paper). There they sat, hour after hour, talking in her bedroom at the top of the house, talking about life, how they were to reform the world. They meant to found a society to abolish private property, and actually had a letter written, though not sent out. The ideas were Sally's, of course—but very soon she was just as excited—read

1 Austrian-born wife of Louis XVI of France, Marie Antoinette (1755-1793) became increasingly unpopular with the people and was guillotined during the French Revolution.

2 English artist, writer, and textile designer (1834-96). A member of the Pre-Raphaelite Brotherhood, Morris founded the Socialist League in 1884.

Plato[1] in bed before breakfast; read Morris; read Shelley[2] by the hour.

Sally's power was amazing, her gift, her personality. There was her way with flowers, for instance. At Bourton they always had stiff little vases all the way down the table. Sally went out, picked hollyhocks, dahlias—all sorts of flowers that had never been seen together—cut their heads off, and made them swim on the top of water in bowls. The effect was extraordinary—coming in to dinner in the sunset. (Of course Aunt Helena thought it wicked to treat flowers like that.) Then she forgot her sponge, and ran along the passage naked. That grim old housemaid, Ellen Atkins, went about grumbling—"Suppose any of the gentlemen had seen?" Indeed she did shock people. She was untidy, Papa said.

The strange thing, on looking back, was the purity, the integrity, of her feeling for Sally. It was not like one's feeling for a man. It was completely disinterested, and besides, it had a quality which could only exist between women, between women just grown up. It was protective, on her side; sprang from a sense of being in league together, a presentiment of something that was bound to part them (they spoke of marriage always as a catastrophe), which led to this chivalry, this protective feeling which was much more on her side than Sally's. For in those days she was completely reckless; did the most idiotic things out of bravado; bicycled round the parapet on the terrace; smoked cigars. Absurd, she was—very absurd. But the charm was overpowering, to her at least, so that she could remember standing in her bedroom at the top of the house holding the hot-water can in her hands and saying aloud, "She is beneath this roof.... She is beneath this roof!"

No, the words meant absolutely nothing to her now. She could not even get an echo of her old emotion. But she could remember going cold with excitement, and doing her hair in a kind of ecstasy (now the old feeling began to come back to her, as she took out her hairpins, laid them on the dressing-table, began to do her hair), with the rooks flaunting up and down in the pink evening light, and dressing, and going downstairs, and feeling as she crossed the hall "if it were now to die 'twere now to be most

---

1 Greek philosopher (c. 429-347 BCE).

2 Percy Bysshe Shelley (1792-1822), a major British Romantic poet and proponent of non-violence, vegetarianism, and social justice. These references call attention to the youthful idealism of Clarissa and Sally.

happy".[1] That was her feeling—Othello's feeling, and she felt it, she was convinced, as strongly as Shakespeare meant Othello to feel it, all because she was coming down to dinner in a white frock to meet Sally Seton!

She was wearing pink gauze—was that possible? She *seemed*, anyhow, all light, glowing, like some bird or air ball that has flown in, attached itself for a moment to a bramble. But nothing is so strange when one is in love (and what was this except being in love?) as the complete indifference of other people. Aunt Helena just wandered off after dinner; Papa read the paper. Peter Walsh might have been there, and old Miss Cummings; Joseph Breitkopf certainly was, for he came every summer, poor old man, for weeks and weeks, and pretended to read German with her, but really played the piano and sang Brahms without any voice.

All this was only a background for Sally. She stood by the fireplace talking, in that beautiful voice which made everything she said sound like a caress, to Papa, who had begun to be attracted rather against his will (he never got over lending her one of his books and finding it soaked on the terrace), when suddenly she said, "What a shame to sit indoors!" and they all went out on to the terrace and walked up and down. Peter Walsh and Joseph Breitkopf went on about Wagner. She and Sally fell a little behind. Then came the most exquisite moment of her whole life passing a stone urn with flowers in it. Sally stopped; picked a flower; kissed her on the lips. The whole world might have turned upside down! The others disappeared; there she was alone with Sally. And she felt that she had been given a present, wrapped up, which, as they walked (up and down, up and down), she uncovered, or the radiance burnt through, the revelation, the religious feeling!—when old Joseph and Peter faced them:

---

1 From *Othello*, II.i.185-95:

> It gives me wonder great as my content
> To see you here before me. O my soul's joy!
> If after every tempest come such calms,
> May the winds blow till they have waken'd death!
> And let the laboring bark climb hills of seas
> Olympus-high and duck again as low
> As hell's from heaven! If it were now to die,
> 'Twere now to be most happy; for, I fear,
> My soul hath her content so absolute
> That not another comfort like to this
> Succeeds in unknown fate.

See Wyatt.

"Star-gazing?" said Peter.

It was like running one's face against a granite wall in the darkness! It was shocking; it was horrible!

Not for herself. She felt only how Sally was being mauled already, maltreated; she felt his hostility; his jealousy; his determination to break into their companionship. All this she saw as one sees a landscape in a flash of lightning—and Sally (never had she admired her so much!) gallantly taking her way unvanquished. She laughed. She made old Joseph tell her the names of the stars, which he liked doing very seriously. She stood there: she listened. She heard the names of the stars.

"Oh this horror!" she said to herself, as if she had known all along that something would interrupt, would embitter her moment of happiness.

Yet, after all, how much she owed to him later. Always when she thought of him she thought of their quarrels for some reason—because she wanted his good opinion so much, perhaps. She owed him words: "sentimental," "civilised"; they started up every day of her life as if he guarded her. A book was sentimental; an attitude to life sentimental. "Sentimental," perhaps she was to be thinking of the past. What would he think, she wondered, when he came back?

That she had grown older? Would he say that, or would she see him thinking when he came back, that she had grown older? It was true. Since her illness she had turned almost white.

Laying her brooch on the table, she had a sudden spasm, as if, while she mused, the icy claws had had the chance to fix in her. She was not old yet. She had just broken into her fifty-second year. Months and months of it were still untouched. June, July, August! Each still remained almost whole, and, as if to catch the falling drop, Clarissa (crossing to the dressing-table) plunged into the very heart of the moment, transfixed it, there—the moment of this June morning on which was the pressure of all the other mornings, seeing the glass, the dressing-table, and all the bottles afresh, collecting the whole of her at one point (as she looked into the glass), seeing the delicate pink face of the woman who was that very night to give a party; of Clarissa Dalloway; of herself.

How many million times she had seen her face, and always with the same imperceptible contraction! She pursed her lips when she looked in the glass. It was to give her face point. That was her self—pointed; dartlike; definite. That was her self when some effort, some call on her to be her self, drew the parts together, she alone knew how different, how incompatible and composed so for the world only into one centre, one diamond, one woman who sat in her drawing-room and made a meeting-point, a radiancy no doubt in some dull lives, a refuge for the lonely to come to, perhaps; she had helped young people, who were grateful to her; had tried to be the same always, never showing a sign of all the other sides of her—faults, jealousies, vanities, suspicions, like this of Lady Bruton not asking her to lunch; which, she thought (combing her hair finally), is utterly base! Now, where was her dress?

Her evening dresses hung in the cupboard. Clarissa, plunging her hand into the softness, gently detached the green dress and carried it to the window. She had torn it. Some one had trod on the skirt. She had felt it give at the Embassy party at the top among the folds. By artificial light the green shone, but lost its colour now in the sun. She would mend it. Her maids had too much to do. She would wear it to-night. She would take her silks, her scissors, her—what was it?—her thimble, of course, down into the drawing-room, for she must also write, and see that things generally were more or less in order.

Strange, she thought, pausing on the landing, and assembling that diamond shape, that single person, strange how a mistress knows the very moment, the very temper of her house! Faint sounds rose in spirals up the well of the stairs; the swish of a mop; tapping; knocking; a loudness when the front door opened; a voice repeating a message in the basement; the chink of silver on a tray; clean silver for the party. All was for the party.

(And Lucy, coming into the drawing-room with her tray held out, put the giant candlesticks on the mantelpiece, the silver casket in the middle, turned the crystal dolphin towards the clock. They would come; they would stand; they would talk in the mincing tones which she could imitate, ladies and gentlemen. Of all, her mistress was loveliest—mistress of silver, of linen, of china, for the sun, the silver, doors off their hinges, Rumpelmayer's men, gave her a sense, as she laid the paper-knife on the inlaid table, of something achieved. Behold! Behold! she said, speaking to her old friends in the baker's shop, where she had first seen service at Caterham, prying into the glass. She was Lady Angela, attending Princess Mary, when in came Mrs. Dalloway.)

"Oh Lucy," she said, "the silver does look nice!"

"And how," she said, turning the crystal dolphin to stand upright, "how did you enjoy the play last night?" "Oh, they had to go before the end!" she said. "They had to be back at ten!" she said. "So they don't know what happened," she said. "That does seem hard luck," she said (for her servants stayed later, if they asked her). "That does seem rather a shame," she said, taking the old bald-looking cushion in the middle of the sofa and putting it in Lucy's arms, and giving her a little push, and crying:

"Take it away! Give it to Mrs. Walker with my compliments! Take it away!" she cried.

And Lucy stopped at the drawing-room door, holding the cushion, and said, very shyly, turning a little pink, Couldn't she help to mend that dress?

But, said Mrs. Dalloway, she had enough on her hands already, quite enough of her own to do without that.

"But, thank you, Lucy, oh, thank you," said Mrs. Dalloway, and thank you, thank you, she went on saying (sitting down on the sofa with her dress over her knees, her scissors, her silks), thank you, thank you, she went on saying in gratitude to her servants generally for helping her to be like this, to be what she wanted, gentle, generous-hearted. Her servants liked her. And then this dress of hers—where was the tear? and now her needle to be threaded. This was a favourite dress, one of Sally Parker's, the last almost she ever made, alas, for Sally had now retired, lived at Ealing,[1] and if ever I have a moment, thought Clarissa (but never would she have a moment any more), I shall go and see her at Ealing. For she was a character, thought Clarissa, a real artist. She thought of little out-of-the-way things; yet her dresses were never queer. You could wear them at Hatfield;[2] at Buckingham Palace. She had worn them at Hatfield; at Buckingham Palace.

Quiet descended on her, calm, content, as her needle, drawing the silk smoothly to its gentle pause, collected the green folds together and attached them, very lightly, to the belt. So on a summer's day waves collect, overbalance, and fall; collect and fall; and the whole world seems to be saying "that is all" more and more ponderously, until even the heart in the body which lies in the sun on the beach says too, That is all. Fear no more, says the heart. Fear no more, says the heart, committing its burden to some sea, which sighs collectively for all sorrows, and renews, begins, collects, lets fall. And the body alone listens to the passing bee; the wave breaking; the dog barking, far away barking and barking.

---

1 A suburban area in west London.

2 Hatfield House, a large country house in Hertfordshire, England, the family home of the Marquess of Salisbury.

"Heavens, the front-door bell!" exclaimed Clarissa, staying her needle. Roused, she listened.

"Mrs. Dalloway will see me," said the elderly man in the hall. "Oh yes, she will see *me*," he repeated, putting Lucy aside very benevolently, and running upstairs ever so quickly. "Yes, yes, yes," he muttered as he ran upstairs. "She will see me. After five years in India, Clarissa will see me."

"Who can—what can," asked Mrs. Dalloway (thinking it was outrageous to be interrupted at eleven o'clock on the morning of the day she was giving a party), hearing a step on the stairs. She heard a hand upon the door. She made to hide her dress, like a virgin protecting chastity, respecting privacy. Now the brass knob slipped. Now the door opened, and in came—for a single second she could not remember what he was called! so surprised she was to see him, so glad, so shy, so utterly taken aback to have Peter Walsh come to her unexpectedly in the morning! (She had not read his letter.)

"And how are you?" said Peter Walsh, positively trembling; taking both her hands; kissing both her hands. She's grown older, he thought, sitting down. I shan't tell her anything about it, he thought, for she's grown older. She's looking at me, he thought, a sudden embarrassment coming over him, though he had kissed her hands. Putting his hand into his pocket, he took out a large pocket-knife and half opened the blade.

Exactly the same, thought Clarissa; the same queer look; the same check suit; a little out of the straight his face is, a little thinner, dryer, perhaps, but he looks awfully well, and just the same.

"How heavenly it is to see you again!" she exclaimed. He had his knife out. That's so like him, she thought.

He had only reached town last night, he said; would have to go down into the country at once; and how was everything, how was everybody—Richard? Elizabeth?

"And what's all this?" he said, tilting his pen-knife towards her green dress.

He's very well dressed, thought Clarissa; yet he always criticizes *me*.

Here she is mending her dress; mending her dress as usual, he thought; here she's been sitting all the time I've been in India; mending her dress; playing about; going to parties; running to the House and back and all that, he thought, growing more and more irritated, more and more agitated, for there's nothing in the world so bad for some women as marriage, he thought; and politics; and having a Conservative husband, like the admirable Richard. So it is, so it is, he thought, shutting his knife with a snap.

"Richard's very well. Richard's at a Committee," said Clarissa.

And she opened her scissors, and said, did he mind her just finishing what she was doing to her dress, for they had a party that night?

"Which I shan't ask you to," she said. "My dear Peter!" she said.

But it was delicious to hear her say that—my dear Peter! Indeed, it was all so delicious—the silver, the chairs; all so delicious!

Why wouldn't she ask him to her party? he asked.

Now of course, thought Clarissa, he's enchanting! perfectly enchanting! Now I remember how impossible it was ever to make up my mind—and why did I make up my mind—not to marry him, she wondered, that awful summer?

"But it's so extraordinary that you should have come this morning!" she cried, putting her hands, one on top of another, down on her dress.

"Do you remember," she said, "how the blinds used to flap at Bourton?"

"They did," he said; and he remembered breakfasting alone, very awkwardly, with her father; who had died; and he had not written to Clarissa. But he had never got on well with old Parry, that querulous, weak-kneed old man, Clarissa's father, Justin Parry.

"I often wish I'd got on better with your father," he said.

"But he never liked any one who—our friends," said Clarissa; and could have bitten her tongue for thus reminding Peter that he had wanted to marry her.

Of course I did, thought Peter; it almost broke my heart too, he thought; and was overcome with his own grief, which rose like a moon looked at from a terrace, ghastly beautiful with light from the sunken day. I was more unhappy than I've ever been since, he thought. And as if in truth he were sitting there on the terrace he edged a little towards Clarissa; put his hand out; raised it; let it fall. There above them it hung, that moon. She too seemed to be sitting with him on the terrace, in the moonlight.

"Herbert has it now," she said. "I never go there now," she said.

Then, just as happens on a terrace in the moonlight, when one person begins to feel ashamed that he is already bored, and yet as the other sits silent, very quiet, sadly looking at the moon, does not like to speak, moves his foot, clears his throat, notices some iron scroll on a table leg, stirs a leaf, but says nothing—so Peter Walsh did now. For why go back like this to the past? he thought. Why make him think of it again? Why make him suffer, when she had tortured him so infernally? Why?

"Do you remember the lake?" she said, in an abrupt voice, under the pressure of an emotion which caught her heart, made the muscles of her throat stiff, and contracted her lips in a spasm as she said "lake." For she was a child, throwing bread to the ducks, between her parents, and at the same time a grown woman coming to her parents who stood by the lake, holding her life in her arms which, as she neared them, grew larger and larger in her arms, until it became a whole life, a complete life, which she put down by them and said, "This is what I have made of it! This!" And what had she made of it? What, indeed? sitting there sewing this morning with Peter.

She looked at Peter Walsh; her look, passing through all that time and that emotion, reached him doubtfully; settled on him tearfully; and rose and fluttered away, as a bird touches a branch and rises and flutters away. Quite simply she wiped her eyes.

"Yes," said Peter. "Yes, yes, yes," he said, as if she drew up to the surface something which positively hurt him as it rose. Stop! stop! he wanted to cry. For he was not old; his life was not over; not by any means. He was only just past fifty. Shall I tell her, he thought, or not? He would like to make a clean breast of it all. But she is too cold, he thought; sewing, with her scissors; Daisy would look ordinary beside Clarissa. And she would think me a failure, which I am in their sense, he thought; in the Dalloways sense. Oh yes, he had no doubt about that; he was a failure, compared with all this—the inlaid table, the mounted paper-knife, the dolphin and the candlesticks, the chair-covers and the old valuable English tinted prints—he was a failure! I detest the smugness of the whole affair, he thought; Richard's doing, not Clarissa's; save that she married him. (Here Lucy came into the room, carrying silver, more silver, but charming, slender, graceful she looked, he thought, as she stooped to put it down.) And this has been going on all the time! he thought; week after week; Clarissa's life; while I—he thought; and at once everything seemed to radiate from him; journeys; rides; quarrels; adventures; bridge parties; love affairs; work; work, work! and he took out his knife quite openly—his old horn-handled knife which Clarissa could swear he had had these thirty years—and clenched his fist upon it.

What an extraordinary habit that was, Clarissa thought; always playing with a knife. Always making one feel, too, frivolous; empty-minded; a mere silly chatterbox, as he used. But I too, she thought, and, taking up her needle, summoned, like a Queen whose guards have fallen asleep and left her unprotected (she had been quite taken aback by this visit—it had upset her) so that any one can stroll in and have a look at her where she lies with the brambles curving over her, summoned to her help the things she did; the things she liked; her husband; Elizabeth; her self, in short, which Peter hardly knew now, all to come about her and beat off the enemy.

"Well, and what's happened to you?" she said. So before a battle begins, the horses paw the ground; toss their heads; the light shines on their flanks; their necks curve. So Peter Walsh and Clarissa, sitting side by side on the blue sofa, challenged each other. His powers chafed and tossed in him. He assembled from different quarters all sorts of things; praise; his career at Oxford; his marriage, which she knew nothing whatever about; how he had loved; and altogether done his job.

"Millions of things!" he exclaimed, and, urged by the assembly of powers which were now charging this way and that and giving him the feeling at once frightening and extremely exhilarating of being rushed through the air on the shoulders of people he could no longer see, he raised his hands to his forehead.

Clarissa sat very upright; drew in her breath.

"I am in love," he said, not to her however, but to some one raised up in the dark so that you could not touch her but must lay your garland down on the grass in the dark.

"In love," he repeated, now speaking rather dryly to Clarissa Dalloway; "in love with a girl in India." He had deposited his garland. Clarissa could make what she would of it.

"In love!" she said. That he at his age should be sucked under in his little bow-tie by that monster! And there's no flesh on his neck; his hands are red; and he's six months older than I am! her eye flashed back to her; but in her heart she felt, all the same; he is in love. He has that, she felt; he is in love.

But the indomitable egotism which for ever rides down the hosts opposed to it, the river which says on, on, on; even though, it admits, there may be no goal for us whatever, still on, on; this indomitable egotism charged her cheeks with colour; made her look very young; very pink; very bright-eyed as she sat with her dress upon her knee, and her needle held to the end of green silk, trembling a little. He was in love! Not with her. With some younger woman, of course.

"And who is she?" she asked.

Now this statue must be brought from its height and set down between them.

"A married woman, unfortunately," he said; "the wife of a Major in the Indian Army."[1]

And with a curious ironical sweetness he smiled as he placed her in this ridiculous way before Clarissa.

(All the same, he is in love, thought Clarissa.)

"She has," he continued, very reasonably, "two small children; a boy and a girl; and I have come over to see my lawyers about the divorce."

There they are! he thought. Do what you like with them, Clarissa! There they are! And second by second it seemed to him that the wife of the Major in the Indian Army (his Daisy) and her two small children became more and more lovely as Clarissa looked at them; as if he had set light to a grey pellet on a plate and there had risen up a lovely tree in the brisk sea-salted air of their intimacy (for in some ways no one understood him, felt with him, as Clarissa did)—their exquisite intimacy.

She flattered him; she fooled him, thought Clarissa; shaping the woman, the wife of the Major in the Indian Army, with three strokes of a knife. What a waste! What a folly! All his life long Peter had been fooled like that; first getting sent down[2] from Oxford; next marrying the girl on the boat going out to India; now the wife of a Major—thank Heaven she had refused to marry him! Still, he was in love; her old friend, her dear Peter, he was in love.

"But what are you going to do?" she asked him. Oh the lawyers and solicitors, Messrs. Hooper and Grately of Lincoln's Inn,[3] they were going to do it, he said. And he actually pared his nails with his pocket-knife.

For Heaven's sake, leave your knife alone! she cried to herself in irrepressible irritation; it was his silly unconventionality, his weakness; his lack of the ghost of a notion what any one else was feeling that annoyed her, had always annoyed her; and now at his age, how silly!

---

1 A reference to the British Indian Army, the military arm of the British Raj or rule in India from 1858 until Indian independence in 1947.

2 Suspended or expelled.

3 One of the four Inns of Court, the four sets of buildings in London belonging to the four legal societies that hold the right to train and examine lawyers, and to admit them to the bar.

I know all that, Peter thought; I know what I'm up against, he thought, running his finger along the blade of his knife, Clarissa and Dalloway and all the rest of them; but I'll show Clarissa—and then to his utter surprise, suddenly thrown by those uncontrollable forces thrown through the air, he burst into tears; wept; wept without the least shame, sitting on the sofa, the tears running down his cheeks.

And Clarissa had leant forward, taken his hand, drawn him to her, kissed him,—actually had felt his face on hers before she could down the brandishing of silver-flashing plumes like pampas grass in a tropic gale in her breast, which, subsiding, left her holding his hand, patting his knee, and feeling as she sat back extraordinarily at her ease with him and light-hearted, all in a clap it came over her, If I had married him, this gaiety would have been mine all day!

It was all over for her. The sheet was stretched and the bed narrow. She had gone up into the tower alone and left them blackberrying in the sun. The door had shut, and there among the dust of fallen plaster and the litter of birds' nests how distant the view had looked, and the sounds came thin and chill (once on Leith Hill, she remembered), and Richard, Richard! she cried, as a sleeper in the night starts and stretches a hand in the dark for help. Lunching with Lady Bruton, it came back to her. He has left me; I am alone for ever, she thought, folding her hands upon her knee.

Peter Walsh had got up and crossed to the window and stood with his back to her, flicking a bandanna handkerchief from side to side. Masterly and dry and desolate he looked, his thin shoulder-blades lifting his coat slightly; blowing his nose violently. Take me with you, Clarissa thought impulsively, as if he were starting directly upon some great voyage; and then, next moment, it was as if the five acts of a play that had been very exciting and moving were now over and she had lived a lifetime in them and had run away, had lived with Peter, and it was now over.

Now it was time to move, and, as a woman gathers her things together, her cloak, her gloves, her opera-glasses, and gets up to go out of the theatre into the street, she rose from the sofa and went to Peter.

And it was awfully strange, he thought, how she still had the power, as she came tinkling, rustling, still had the power as she came across the room, to make the moon, which he detested, rise at Bourton on the terrace in the summer sky.

"Tell me," he said, seizing her by the shoulders. "Are you happy, Clarissa? Does Richard—"

The door opened.

"Here is my Elizabeth," said Clarissa, emotionally, histrionically, perhaps.

"How d'y do?" said Elizabeth coming forward.

The sound of Big Ben striking the half-hour struck out between them with extraordinary vigour, as if a young man, strong, indifferent, inconsiderate, were swinging dumb-bells this way and that.

"Hullo, Elizabeth!" cried Peter, stuffing his handkerchief into his pocket, going quickly to her, saying "Good-bye Clarissa" without looking at her, leaving the room quickly, and running downstairs and opening the hall door.

"Peter! Peter!" cried Clarissa, following him out on to the landing, "My party to-night! Remember my party to-night!" she cried, having to raise her voice against the roar of the open air, and, overwhelmed by the traffic and the sound of all the clocks striking, her voice crying "Remember my party to-night!" sounded frail and thin and very far away as Peter Walsh shut the door.

Remember my party, remember my party, said Peter Walsh as he stepped down the street, speaking to himself rhythmically, in time with the flow of the sound, the direct downright sound of Big Ben striking the half-hour. (The leaden circles dissolved in the air.) Oh these parties, he thought; Clarissa's parties. Why does she give these parties, he thought. Not that he blamed her or this effigy of a man in a tail-coat with a carnation in his button-hole coming towards him. Only one person in the world could be as he was, in love. And there he was, this fortunate man, himself, reflected in the plate-glass window of a motor-car manufacturer in Victoria Street. All India lay behind him; plains, mountains; epidemics of cholera; a district twice as big as Ireland; decisions he had come to alone—he, Peter Walsh; who was now really for the first time in his life, in love. Clarissa had grown hard, he thought; and a trifle sentimental into the bargain, he suspected, looking at the great motor-cars capable of doing—how many miles on how many gallons? For he had a turn for mechanics; had invented a plough in his district, had ordered wheel-barrows from England, but the coolies[1] wouldn't use them, all of which Clarissa knew nothing whatever about.

---

1 Native labourers in the Indian subcontinent; also applied to those in China and other Asian countries, now considered an offensive and derogatory term.

The way she said "Here is my Elizabeth!"—that annoyed him. Why not "Here's Elizabeth" simply? It was insincere. And Elizabeth didn't like it either. (Still the last tremors of the great booming voice shook the air around him; the half-hour; still early; only half-past eleven still.) For he understood young people; he liked them. There was always something cold in Clarissa, he thought. She had always, even as a girl, a sort of timidity, which in middle age becomes conventionality, and then it's all up, it's all up, he thought, looking rather drearily into the glassy depths, and wondering whether by calling at that hour he had annoyed her; overcome with shame suddenly at having been a fool; wept; been emotional; told her everything, as usual, as usual.

As a cloud crosses the sun, silence falls on London; and falls on the mind. Effort ceases. Time flaps on the mast. There we stop; there we stand. Rigid, the skeleton of habit alone upholds the human frame. Where there is nothing, Peter Walsh said to himself; feeling hollowed out, utterly empty within. Clarissa refused me, he thought. He stood there thinking, Clarissa refused me.

Ah, said St. Margaret's,[1] like a hostess who comes into her drawing-room on the very stroke of the hour and finds her guests there already. I am not late. No, it is precisely half-past eleven, she says. Yet, though she is perfectly right, her voice, being the voice of the hostess, is reluctant to inflict its individuality. Some grief for the past holds it back; some concern for the present. It is half-past eleven, she says, and the sound of St. Margaret's glides into the recesses of the heart and buries itself in ring after ring of sound, like something alive which wants to confide itself, to disperse itself, to be, with a tremor of delight, at rest—like Clarissa herself, thought Peter Walsh, coming downstairs on the stroke of the hour in white. It is Clarissa herself, he thought, with a deep emotion, and an extraordinarily clear, yet puzzling, recollection of her, as if this bell had come into the room years ago, where they sat at some moment of great intimacy, and had gone from one to the other and had left, like a bee with honey, laden with the moment. But what room? What moment? And why had he been so profoundly happy when the clock was striking? Then, as the sound of St. Margaret's languished, he thought, She has been ill, and the sound expressed languor and suffering. It was her heart, he remembered; and the sudden loudness of the final

---

1 Church located in the grounds of Westminster Abbey, the parish church of the House of Commons.

stroke tolled for death that surprised in the midst of life, Clarissa falling where she stood, in her drawing-room. No! No! he cried. She is not dead! I am not old, he cried, and marched up Whitehall, as if there rolled down to him, vigorous, unending, his future.

He was not old, or set, or dried in the least. As for caring what they said of him—the Dalloways, the Whitbreads, and their set, he cared not a straw—not a straw (though it was true he would have, some time or other, to see whether Richard couldn't help him to some job). Striding, staring, he glared at the statue of the Duke of Cambridge.[1] He had been sent down from Oxford—true. He had been a Socialist, in some sense a failure—true. Still the future of civilisation lies, he thought, in the hands of young men like that; of young men such as he was, thirty years ago; with their love of abstract principles; getting books sent out to them all the way from London to a peak in the Himalayas; reading science; reading philosophy. The future lies in the hands of young men like that, he thought.

A patter like the patter of leaves in a wood came from behind, and with it a rustling, regular thudding sound, which as it overtook him drummed his thoughts, strict in step, up Whitehall, without his doing. Boys in uniform, carrying guns, marched with their eyes ahead of them, marched, their arms stiff, and on their faces an expression like the letters of a legend written round the base of a statue praising duty, gratitude, fidelity, love of England.

It is, thought Peter Walsh, beginning to keep step with them, a very fine training. But they did not look robust. They were weedy for the most part, boys of sixteen, who might, to-morrow, stand behind bowls of rice, cakes of soap on counters. Now they wore on them unmixed with sensual pleasure or daily preoccupations the solemnity of the wreath which they had fetched from Finsbury Pavement[2] to the empty tomb. They had taken their vow. The traffic respected it; vans were stopped.

I can't keep up with them, Peter Walsh thought, as they marched up Whitehall, and sure enough, on they marched, past

---

1 Prince George, Duke of Cambridge (1819-1904), grandson of King George III and commander-in-chief of the British Army, 1856-95. His statue is in Whitehall, Westminster, London.

2 A street connecting Moorgate with City Road in Islington, London. The "boys in uniform" are marching from Islington to the Cenotaph in Whitehall. A war memorial, the Cenotaph (the word means "empty tomb") was unveiled by George V on 11 November 1920.

him, past every one, in their steady way, as if one will worked legs and arms uniformly, and life, with its varieties, its irreticences, had been laid under a pavement of monuments and wreaths and drugged into a stiff yet staring corpse by discipline. One had to respect it; one might laugh; but one had to respect it, he thought. There they go, thought Peter Walsh, pausing at the edge of the pavement; and all the exalted statues, Nelson, Gordon, Havelock, the black, the spectacular images of great soldiers stood looking ahead of them, as if they too had made the same renunciation (Peter Walsh felt he, too, had made it the great renunciation), trampled under the same temptations, and achieved at length a marble stare.[1] But the stare Peter Walsh did not want for himself in the least; though he could respect it in others. He could respect it in boys. They don't know the troubles of the flesh yet, he thought, as the marching boys disappeared in the direction of the Strand—all that I've been through, he thought, crossing the road, and standing under Gordon's statue, Gordon whom as a boy he had worshipped; Gordon standing lonely with one leg raised and his arms crossed,—poor Gordon, he thought.

And just because nobody yet knew he was in London, except Clarissa, and the earth, after the voyage, still seemed an island to him, the strangeness of standing alone, alive, unknown, at half-past eleven in Trafalgar Square overcame him. What is it? Where am I? And why, after all, does one do it? he thought, the divorce seeming all moonshine. And down his mind went flat as a marsh, and three great emotions bowled over him; understanding; a vast philanthropy; and finally, as if the result of the others, an irrepressible, exquisite delight; as if inside his brain by another hand strings were pulled, shutters moved, and he, having nothing to do with it, yet stood at the opening of endless avenues, down

---

1 Peter Walsh has arrived at Trafalgar Square where he observes the monuments to Britain's great military and, especially, imperial heroes. These include Nelson's Column, in honour of Horatio Nelson, a naval hero of the Napoleonic Wars, who was killed at the Battle of Trafalgar in 1805; the statue of Sir Henry Havelock, who recaptured Cawnpore (now Kanpur) during the so-called Indian Rebellion of 1857; and the statue of General Charles George Gordon (also known as "Chinese Gordon" or "Gordon of Khartoum"), best remembered for campaigns in China and north Africa. Gordon's statue was moved from Trafalgar Square in 1943 and later installed on the Victoria Embankment. (See Cohen.) "The black" may refer to a figure, a member of Nelson's crew, in one of four bronze relief panels, "The Death of Nelson" (by John Edward Carew), at the foot of Nelson's Column.

which if he chose he might wander. He had not felt so young for years.

He had escaped! was utterly free—as happens in the downfall of habit when the mind, like an unguarded flame, bows and bends and seems about to blow from its holding. I haven't felt so young for years! thought Peter, escaping (only of course for an hour or so) from being precisely what he was, and feeling like a child who runs out of doors, and sees, as he runs, his old nurse waving at the wrong window. But she's extraordinarily attractive, he thought, as walking across Trafalgar Square in the direction of the Haymarket,[1] came a young woman who, as she passed Gordon's statue, seemed, Peter Walsh thought (susceptible as he was), to shed veil after veil, until she became the very woman he had always had in mind; young, but stately; merry, but discreet; black, but enchanting.

Straightening himself and stealthily fingering his pocket-knife he started after her to follow this woman, this excitement, which seemed even with its back turned to shed on him a light which connected them, which singled him out, as if the random uproar of the traffic had whispered through hollowed hands his name, not Peter, but his private name which he called himself in his own thoughts. "You," she said, only "you," saying it with her white gloves and her shoulders. Then the thin long cloak which the wind stirred as she walked past Dent's shop in Cockspur Street[2] blew out with an enveloping kindness, a mournful tenderness, as of arms that would open and take the tired—

But she's not married; she's young; quite young, thought Peter, the red carnation he had seen her wear as she came across Trafalgar Square burning again in his eyes and making her lips red. But she waited at the kerbstone. There was a dignity about her. She was not worldly, like Clarissa; not rich, like Clarissa. Was she, he wondered as she moved, respectable? Witty, with a lizard's flickering tongue, he thought (for one must invent, must allow oneself a little diversion), a cool waiting wit, a darting wit; not noisy.

She moved; she crossed; he followed her. To embarrass her was the last thing he wished. Still if she stopped he would say "Come

---

1 A street that runs south from Piccadilly Circus to Pall Mall. Originally near a market for hay and straw (see *LE*), the Haymarket is associated with theatrical entertainment.

2 E. Dent & Co., Ltd., the watch and clockmakers who made "Big Ben" (see p. 46, n. 1) had a shop at 34 Cockspur Street.

and have an ice," he would say, and she would answer, perfectly simply, "Oh yes."

But other people got between them in the street, obstructing him, blotting her out. He pursued; she changed. There was colour in her cheeks; mockery in her eyes; he was an adventurer, reckless, he thought, swift, daring, indeed (landed as he was last night from India) a romantic buccaneer, careless of all these damned proprieties, yellow dressing-gowns, pipes, fishing-rods, in the shop windows; and respectability and evening parties and spruce old men wearing white slips beneath their waistcoats. He was a buccaneer. On and on she went, across Piccadilly, and up Regent Street, ahead of him, her cloak, her gloves, her shoulders combining with the fringes and the laces and the feather boas in the windows to make the spirit of finery and whimsy which dwindled out of the shops on to the pavement, as the light of a lamp goes wavering at night over hedges in the darkness.

Laughing and delightful, she had crossed Oxford Street and Great Portland Street and turned down one of the little streets, and now, and now, the great moment was approaching, for now she slackened, opened her bag, and with one look in his direction, but not at him, one look that bade farewell, summed up the whole situation and dismissed it triumphantly, for ever, had fitted her key, opened the door, and gone! Clarissa's voice saying, Remember my party, Remember my party, sang in his ears. The house was one of those flat red houses with hanging flower-baskets of vague impropriety. It was over.

Well, I've had my fun; I've had it, he thought, looking up at the swinging baskets of pale geraniums. And it was smashed to atoms—his fun, for it was half made up, as he knew very well; invented, this escapade with the girl; made up, as one makes up the better part of life, he thought—making oneself up; making her up; creating an exquisite amusement, and something more. But odd it was, and quite true; all this one could never share—it smashed to atoms.

He turned; went up the street, thinking to find somewhere to sit, till it was time for Lincoln's Inn—for Messrs. Hooper and Grateley. Where should he go? No matter. Up the street, then, towards Regent's Park. His boots on the pavement struck out "no matter"; for it was early, still very early.

It was a splendid morning too. Like the pulse of a perfect heart, life struck straight through the streets. There was no fumbling—no hesitation. Sweeping and swerving, accurately, punctually, noiselessly, there, precisely at the right instant, the motor-car stopped at the door. The girl, silk-stockinged, feathered, evanescent, but not to him particularly attractive (for he had had his fling), alighted. Admirable butlers, tawny chow dogs, halls laid in black and white lozenges with white blinds blowing, Peter saw through the opened door and approved of. A splendid achievement in its own way, after all, London; the season; civilisation. Coming as he did from a respectable Anglo-Indian[1] family which for at least three generations had administered the affairs of a continent (it's strange, he thought, what a sentiment I have about that, disliking India, and empire, and army as he did), there were moments when civilisation, even of this sort, seemed dear to him as a personal possession; moments of pride in England; in butlers; chow dogs; girls in their security. Ridiculous enough, still there it is, he thought. And the doctors and men of business and capable women all going about their business, punctual, alert, robust, seemed to him wholly admirable, good fellows, to whom one would entrust one's life, companions in the art of living, who would see one through. What with one thing and another, the show was really very tolerable; and he would sit down in the shade and smoke.

There was Regent's Park. Yes. As a child he had walked in Regent's Park—odd, he thought, how the thought of childhood keeps coming back to me—the result of seeing Clarissa, perhaps; for women live much more in the past than we do, he thought. They attach themselves to places; and their fathers—a woman's always proud of her father. Bourton was a nice place, a very nice place, but I could never get on with the old man, he thought. There was quite a scene one night—an argument about something or other, what, he could not remember. Politics presumably.

Yes, he remembered Regent's Park; the long straight walk; the little house where one bought air-balls[2] to the left; an absurd statue with an inscription somewhere or other. He looked for an empty seat. He did not want to be bothered (feeling a little drowsy as he did) by people asking him the time. An elderly grey nurse, with a baby asleep in its perambulator—that was the best he could do for himself; sit down at the far end of the seat by that nurse.

---

1 Although the term Anglo-Indian now refers to a person of mixed British and Indian descent, when *Mrs. Dalloway* was published it referred to a person (or family) of British descent born or living in India.

2 Balloons.

She's a queer-looking girl, he thought, suddenly remembering Elizabeth as she came into the room and stood by her mother. Grown big; quite grown-up, not exactly pretty; handsome rather; and she can't be more than eighteen. Probably she doesn't get on with Clarissa. "There's my Elizabeth"—that sort of thing—why not "Here's Elizabeth" simply?—trying to make out, like most mothers, that things are what they are not. She trusts to her charm too much, he thought. She overdoes it.

The rich benignant cigar smoke eddied coolly down his throat; he puffed it out again in rings which breasted the air bravely for a moment; blue, circular—I shall try and get a word alone with Elizabeth to-night, he thought—then began to wobble into hourglass shapes and taper away; odd shapes they take, he thought. Suddenly he closed his eyes, raised his hand with an effort, and threw away the heavy end of his cigar. A great brush swept smooth across his mind, sweeping across it moving branches, children's voices, the shuffle of feet, and people passing, and humming traffic, rising and falling traffic. Down, down he sank into the plumes and feathers of sleep, sank, and was muffled over.

The grey nurse resumed her knitting as Peter Walsh, on the hot seat beside her, began snoring. In her grey dress, moving her hands indefatigably yet quietly, she seemed like the champion of the rights of sleepers, like one of those spectral presences which rise in twilight in woods made of sky and branches. The solitary traveller, haunter of lanes, disturber of ferns, and devastator of great hemlock plants, looking up suddenly, sees the giant figure at the end of the ride.

By conviction an atheist perhaps, he is taken by surprise with moments of extraordinary exaltation. Nothing exists outside us except a state of mind, he thinks; a desire for solace, for relief, for something outside these miserable pigmies, these feeble, these ugly, these craven men and women. But if he can conceive of her, then in some sort she exists, he thinks, and advancing down the path with his eyes upon sky and branches he rapidly endows them with womanhood; sees with amazement how grave they become; how majestically, as the breeze stirs them, they dispense with a dark flutter of the leaves charity, comprehension, absolution, and then, flinging themselves suddenly aloft, confound the piety of their aspect with a wild carouse.

Such are the visions which proffer great cornucopias full of fruit to the solitary traveller, or murmur in his ear like sirens lolloping away on the green sea waves, or are dashed in his face like bunches of roses, or rise to the surface like pale faces which fishermen flounder through floods to embrace.

Such are the visions which ceaselessly float up, pace beside, put their faces in front of, the actual thing; often overpowering the solitary traveller and taking away from him the sense of the earth, the wish to return, and giving him for substitute a general peace, as if (so he thinks as he advances down the forest ride) all this fever of living were simplicity itself; and myriads of things merged in one thing; and this figure, made of sky and branches as it is, had risen from the troubled sea (he is elderly, past fifty now) as a shape might be sucked up out of the waves to shower down from her magnificent hands compassion, comprehension, absolution. So, he thinks, may I never go back to the lamplight; to the sitting-room; never finish my book; never knock out my pipe; never ring for Mrs. Turner to clear away; rather let me walk straight on to this great figure, who will, with a toss of her head, mount me on her streamers and let me blow to nothingness with the rest.

Such are the visions. The solitary traveller is soon beyond the wood; and there, coming to the door with shaded eyes, possibly to look for his return, with hands raised, with white apron blowing, is an elderly woman who seems (so powerful is this infirmity) to seek, over the desert, a lost son; to search for a rider destroyed; to be the figure of the mother whose sons have been killed in the battles of the world. So, as the solitary traveller advances down the village street where the women stand knitting and the men dig in the garden, the evening seems ominous; the figures still; as if some august fate, known to them, awaited without fear, were about to sweep them into complete annihilation.

Indoors among ordinary things, the cupboard, the table, the window-sill with its geraniums, suddenly the outline of the landlady, bending to remove the cloth, becomes soft with light, an adorable emblem which only the recollection of cold human contacts forbids us to embrace. She takes the marmalade; she shuts it in the cupboard.

"There is nothing more to-night, sir?"

But to whom does the solitary traveller make reply?

So the elderly nurse knitted over the sleeping baby in Regent's Park. So Peter Walsh snored. He woke with extreme suddenness, saying to himself, "The death of the soul."

"Lord, Lord!" he said to himself out loud, stretching and opening his eyes. "The death of the soul." The words attached themselves to some scene, to some room, to some past he had been dreaming of. It became clearer; the scene, the room, the past he had been dreaming of.

It was at Bourton that summer, early in the 'nineties, when he was so passionately in love with Clarissa. There were a great many people there, laughing and talking, sitting round a table after tea, and the room was bathed in yellow light and full of cigarette smoke. They were talking about a man who had married his housemaid, one of the neighbouring squires, he had forgotten his name. He had married his housemaid, and she had been brought to Bourton to call—an awful visit it had been. She was absurdly overdressed, "like a cockatoo," Clarissa had said, imitating her, and she never stopped talking. On and on she went, on and on. Clarissa imitated her. Then somebody said—Sally Seton it was—did it make any real difference to one's feelings to know that before they'd married she had had a baby? (In those days, in mixed company, it was a bold thing to say.) He could see Clarissa now, turning bright pink; somehow contracting; and saying, "Oh, I shall never be able to speak to her again!" Whereupon the whole party sitting round the tea-table seemed to wobble. It was very uncomfortable.

He hadn't blamed her for minding the fact, since in those days a girl brought up as she was, knew nothing, but it was her manner that annoyed him; timid; hard; arrogant; prudish. "The death of the soul." He had said that instinctively, ticketing the moment as he used to do—the death of her soul.

Every one wobbled; every one seemed to bow, as she spoke, and then to stand up different. He could see Sally Seton, like a child who has been in mischief, leaning forward, rather flushed, wanting to talk, but afraid, and Clarissa did frighten people. (She was Clarissa's greatest friend, always about the place, an attractive creature, handsome, dark, with the reputation in those days of great daring, and he used to give her cigars, which she smoked in her bedroom, and she had either been engaged to somebody or quarrelled with her family, and old Parry disliked them both equally, which was a great bond.) Then Clarissa, still with an air of being offended with them all, got up, made some excuse, and went off, alone. As she opened the door, in came that great shaggy dog which ran after sheep. She flung herself upon him, went into raptures. It was as if she said to Peter—it was all aimed at him, he knew—"I know you thought me absurd about that woman just now; but see how extraordinarily sympathetic I am; see how I love my Rob!"

They had always this queer power of communicating without words. She knew directly he criticised her. Then she would do something quite obvious to defend herself, like this fuss with the dog—but it never took him in, he always saw through Clarissa. Not that he said anything, of course; just sat looking glum. It was the way their quarrels often began.

She shut the door. At once he became extremely depressed. It all seemed useless—going on being in love; going on quarrelling; going on making it up, and he wandered off alone, among outhouses, stables, looking at the horses. (The place was quite a humble one; the Parrys were never very well off; but there were always grooms and stable-boys about—Clarissa loved riding—and an old coachman—what was his name?—an old nurse, old Moody, old Goody, some such name they called her, whom one was taken to visit in a little room with lots of photographs, lots of bird-cages.)

It was an awful evening! He grew more and more gloomy, not about that only; about everything. And he couldn't see her; couldn't explain to her; couldn't have it out. There were always people about—she'd go on as if nothing had happened. That was the devilish part of her—this coldness, this woodenness, something very profound in her, which he had felt again this morning talking to her; an impenetrability. Yet Heaven knows he loved her. She had some queer power of fiddling on one's nerves, turning one's nerves to fiddle-strings, yes.

He had gone into dinner rather late, from some idiotic idea of making himself felt, and had sat down by old Miss Parry—Aunt Helena—Mr. Parry's sister, who was supposed to preside. There she sat in her white Cashmere shawl, with her head against the window—a formidable old lady, but kind to him, for he had found her some rare flower, and she was a great botanist, marching off in thick boots with a black tin collecting box slung between her shoulders. He sat down beside her, and couldn't speak. Everything seemed to race past him; he just sat there, eating. And then half-way through dinner he made himself look across at Clarissa for the first time. She was talking to a young man on her right. He had a sudden revelation. "She will marry that man," he said to himself. He didn't even know his name.

For of course it was that afternoon, that very afternoon, that Dalloway had come over; and Clarissa called him "Wickham"; that was the beginning of it all. Somebody had brought him over;

and Clarissa got his name wrong. She introduced him to everybody as Wickham. At last he said "My name is Dalloway!"—that was his first view of Richard—a fair young man, rather awkward, sitting on a deck-chair, and blurting out "My name is Dalloway!" Sally got hold of it; always after that she called him "My name is Dalloway!"

He was a prey to revelations at that time. This one—that she would marry Dalloway—was blinding—overwhelming at the moment. There was a sort of—how could he put it?—a sort of ease in her manner to him; something maternal; something gentle. They were talking about politics. All through dinner he tried to hear what they were saying.

Afterwards he could remember standing by old Miss Parry's chair in the drawing-room. Clarissa came up, with her perfect manners, like a real hostess, and wanted to introduce him to some one—spoke as if they had never met before, which enraged him. Yet even then he admired her for it. He admired her courage; her social instinct; he admired her power of carrying things through. "The perfect hostess," he said to her, whereupon she winced all over. But he meant her to feel it. He would have done anything to hurt her, after seeing her with Dalloway. So she left him. And he had a feeling that they were all gathered together in a conspiracy against him—laughing and talking—behind his back. There he stood by Miss Parry's chair as though he had been cut out of wood, talking about wild flowers. Never, never had he suffered so infernally! He must have forgotten even to pretend to listen; at last he woke up; he saw Miss Parry looking rather disturbed, rather indignant, with her prominent eyes fixed. He almost cried out that he couldn't attend because he was in Hell! People began going out of the room. He heard them talking about fetching cloaks; about its being cold on the water, and so on. They were going boating on the lake by moonlight—one of Sally's mad ideas. He could hear her describing the moon. And they all went out. He was left quite alone.

"Don't you want to go with them?" said Aunt Helena—poor old lady!—she had guessed. And he turned round and there was Clarissa again. She had come back to fetch him. He was overcome by her generosity—her goodness.

"Come along," she said. "They're waiting."

He had never felt so happy in the whole of his life! Without a word they made it up. They walked down to the lake. He had twenty minutes of perfect happiness. Her voice, her laugh, her dress (something floating, white, crimson), her spirit, her adventurousness; she made them all disembark and explore the island; she startled a hen; she laughed; she sang. And all the time, he knew perfectly well, Dalloway was falling in love with her; she was falling in love with Dalloway; but it didn't seem to matter. Nothing mattered. They sat on the ground and talked—he and Clarissa. They went in and out of each other's minds without any effort. And then in a second it was over. He said to himself as they were getting into the boat, "She will marry that man," dully, without any resentments; but it was an obvious thing. Dalloway would marry Clarissa.

Dalloway rowed them in. He said nothing. But somehow as they watched him start, jumping on to his bicycle to ride twenty miles through the woods, wobbling off down the drive, waving his hand and disappearing, he obviously did feel, instinctively, tremendously, strongly, all that; the night; the romance; Clarissa. He deserved to have her.

For himself, he was absurd. His demands upon Clarissa (he could see it now) were absurd. He asked impossible things. He made terrible scenes. She would have accepted him still, perhaps, if he had been less absurd. Sally thought so. She wrote him all that summer long letters; how they had talked of him; how she had praised him, how Clarissa burst into tears! It was an extraordinary summer—all letters, scenes, telegrams—arriving at Bourton early in the morning, hanging about till the servants were up; appalling *têtes-à-têtes* with old Mr. Parry at breakfast; Aunt Helena formidable but kind; Sally sweeping him off for talks in the vegetable garden; Clarissa in bed with headaches.

The final scene, the terrible scene which he believed had mattered more than anything in the whole of his life (it might be an exaggeration—but still, so it did seem now), happened at three o'clock in the afternoon of a very hot day. It was a trifle that led up to it—Sally at lunch saying something about Dalloway, and calling him "My name is Dalloway"; whereupon Clarissa suddenly stiffened, coloured, in a way she had, and rapped out sharply, "We've had enough of that feeble joke." That was all; but for him it was as if she had said, "I'm only amusing myself with you; I've an understanding with Richard Dalloway." So he took it. He had not slept for nights. "It's got to be finished one way or the other," he said to himself. He sent a note to her by Sally asking her to meet him by the fountain at three. "Something very important has happened," he scribbled at the end of it.

The fountain was in the middle of a little shrubbery, far from the house, with shrubs and trees all round it. There she came, even before the time, and they stood with the fountain between them, the spout (it was broken) dribbling water incessantly. How sights fix themselves upon the mind! For example, the vivid green moss.

She did not move. "Tell me the truth, tell me the truth," he kept saying. He felt as if his forehead would burst. She seemed contracted, petrified. She did not move. "Tell me the truth," he repeated, when suddenly that old man Breitkopf popped his head in carrying the *Times*; stared at them; gaped; and went away. They neither of them moved. "Tell me the truth," he repeated. He felt that he was grinding against something physically hard; she was unyielding. She was like iron, like flint, rigid up the backbone. And when she said, "It's no use. It's no use. This is the end"—after he had spoken for hours, it seemed, with the tears running down his cheeks—it was as if she had hit him in the face. She turned, she left him, she went away.

"Clarissa!" he cried. "Clarissa!" But she never came back. It was over. He went away that night. He never saw her again.

It was awful, he cried, awful! awful!

Still, the sun was hot. Still, one got over things. Still, life had a way of adding day to day. Still, he thought, yawning and beginning to take notice—Regent's Park had changed very little since he was a boy, except for the squirrels[1]—still, presumably there were compensations—when little Elise Mitchell, who had been picking up pebbles to add to the pebble collection which she and her brother were making on the nursery mantelpiece, plumped her handful down on the nurse's knee and scudded off again full tilt into a lady's legs. Peter Walsh laughed out loud.

But Lucrezia Warren Smith was saying to herself, It's wicked; why should I suffer? she was asking, as she walked down the broad path. No; I can't stand it any longer, she was saying, having left Septimus, who wasn't Septimus any longer, to say hard, cruel, wicked things, to talk to himself, to talk to a dead man, on the seat over there; when the child ran full tilt into her, fell flat, and burst out crying.

---

1 Perhaps a reference to the fact that the native British red squirrel was being inadvertently supplanted by the introduced American grey squirrel in many parts of Britain, including Regent's Park, during this period. (See B.C.R. Bertram and D.-P. Moltu, "Reintroducing Red Squirrels into Regent's Park," *Mammal Rev.* 16.2 [1986]: 81-88.)

That was comforting rather. She stood her upright, dusted her frock, kissed her.

But for herself she had done nothing wrong; she had loved Septimus; she had been happy; she had had a beautiful home, and there her sisters lived still, making hats. Why should *she* suffer?

The child ran straight back to its nurse, and Rezia saw her scolded, comforted, taken up by the nurse who put down her knitting, and the kind-looking man gave her his watch to blow open to comfort her—but why should *she* be exposed? Why not left in Milan? Why tortured? Why?

Slightly waved by tears the broad path, the nurse, the man in grey, the perambulator, rose and fell before her eyes. To be rocked by this malignant torturer was her lot. But why? She was like a bird sheltering under the thin hollow of a leaf, who blinks at the sun when the leaf moves; starts at the crack of a dry twig. She was exposed; she was surrounded by the enormous trees, vast clouds of an indifferent world, exposed; tortured; and why should she suffer? Why?

She frowned; she stamped her foot. She must go back again to Septimus since it was almost time for them to be going to Sir William Bradshaw. She must go back and tell him, go back to him sitting there on the green chair under the tree, talking to himself, or to that dead man Evans, whom she had only seen once for a moment in the shop. He had seemed a nice quiet man; a great friend of Septimus's, and he had been killed in the War. But such things happen to every one. Every one has friends who were killed in the War. Every one gives up something when they marry. She had given up her home. She had come to live here, in this awful city. But Septimus let himself think about horrible things, as she could too, if she tried. He had grown stranger and stranger. He said people were talking behind the bedroom walls. Mrs. Filmer thought it odd. He saw things too—he had seen an old woman's head in the middle of a fern. Yet he could be happy when he chose. They went to Hampton Court[1] on top of a bus, and they were perfectly happy. All the little red and yellow flowers were out on the grass, like floating lamps he said, and talked and chattered and laughed, making up stories. Suddenly he said,

---

1 Hampton Court Palace, on the banks of the Thames 15 miles southwest of London; now, and in 1923, a popular day trip. Originally built by Cardinal Wolsey who later gifted it to Henry VIII, the palace was opened to the public by Queen Victoria in 1838.

"Now we will kill ourselves," when they were standing by the river, and he looked at it with a look which she had seen in his eyes when a train went by, or an omnibus—a look as if something fascinated him; and she felt he was going from her and she caught him by the arm. But going home he was perfectly quiet—perfectly reasonable. He would argue with her about killing themselves; and explain how wicked people were; how he could see them making up lies as they passed in the street. He knew all their thoughts, he said; he knew everything. He knew the meaning of the world, he said.

Then when they got back he could hardly walk. He lay on the sofa and made her hold his hand to prevent him from falling down, down, he cried, into the flames! and saw faces laughing at him, calling him horrible disgusting names, from the walls, and hands pointing round the screen. Yet they were quite alone. But he began to talk aloud, answering people, arguing, laughing, crying, getting very excited and making her write things down. Perfect nonsense it was; about death; about Miss Isabel Pole. She could stand it no longer. She would go back.

She was close to him now, could see him staring at the sky, muttering, clasping his hands. Yet Dr. Holmes said there was nothing the matter with him. What, then, had happened—why had he gone, then, why, when she sat by him, did he start, frown at her, move away, and point at her hand, take her hand, look at it terrified?

Was it that she had taken off her wedding ring? "My hand has grown so thin," she said; "I have put it in my purse," she told him.

He dropped her hand. Their marriage was over, he thought, with agony, with relief. The rope was cut; he mounted; he was free, as it was decreed that he, Septimus, the lord of men, should be free; alone (since his wife had thrown away her wedding ring; since she had left him), he, Septimus, was alone, called forth in advance of the mass of men to hear the truth, to learn the meaning, which now at last, after all the toils of civilisation—Greeks, Romans, Shakespeare, Darwin,[1] and now himself—was to be given whole to.... "To whom?" he asked aloud, "To the Prime Minister," the voices which rustled above his head replied. The supreme secret must be told to the Cabinet; first, that trees are alive; next, there is no crime; next, love, universal love, he mut-

1 Charles Darwin (1809-82), scientist and author of *On the Origin of Species* (1859) which presented the evidence for natural selection and established the foundation of evolutionary theory.

tered, gasping, trembling, painfully drawing out these profound truths which needed, so deep were they, so difficult, an immense effort to speak out, but the world was entirely changed by them for ever.

No crime; love; he repeated, fumbling for his card and pencil, when a Skye terrier snuffed his trousers and he started in an agony of fear. It was turning into a man! He could not watch it happen! It was horrible, terrible to see a dog become a man! At once the dog trotted away.

Heaven was divinely merciful, infinitely benignant. It spared him, pardoned his weakness. But what was the scientific explanation (for one must be scientific above all things)? Why could he see through bodies, see into the future, when dogs will become men? It was the heat wave presumably, operating upon a brain made sensitive by eons of evolution. Scientifically speaking, the flesh was melted off the world. His body was macerated until only the nerve fibres were left. It was spread like a veil upon a rock.

He lay back in his chair, exhausted but upheld. He lay resting, waiting, before he again interpreted, with effort, with agony, to mankind. He lay very high, on the back of the world. The earth thrilled beneath him. Red flowers grew through his flesh; their stiff leaves rustled by his head. Music began clanging against the rocks up here. It is a motor horn down in the street, he muttered; but up here it cannoned from rock to rock, divided, met in shocks of sound which rose in smooth columns (that music should be visible was a discovery) and became an anthem, an anthem twined round now by a shepherd boy's piping (That's an old man playing a penny whistle by the public-house, he muttered) which, as the boy stood still, came bubbling from his pipe, and then, as he climbed higher, made its exquisite plaint while the traffic passed beneath. This boy's elegy is played among the traffic, thought Septimus. Now he withdraws up into the snows, and roses hang about him—the thick red roses which grow on my bedroom wall, he reminded himself. The music stopped. He has his penny, he reasoned it out, and has gone on to the next public house.

But he himself remained high on his rock, like a drowned sailor on a rock. I leant over the edge of the boat and fell down, he thought. I went under the sea. I have been dead, and yet am now alive, but let me rest still, he begged (he was talking to himself again—it was awful, awful!); and as, before waking, the voices of birds and the sound of wheels chime and chatter in a queer harmony, grown louder and louder, and the sleeper feels himself drawing to the shores of life, so he felt himself drawing towards life, the sun growing hotter, cries sounding louder, something tremendous about to happen.

He had only to open his eyes; but a weight was on them; a fear. He strained; he pushed; he looked; he saw Regent's Park before him. Long streamers of sunlight fawned at his feet. The trees waved, brandished. We welcome, the world seemed to say; we accept; we create. Beauty, the world seemed to say. And as if to prove it (scientifically) wherever he looked, at the houses, at the railings, at the antelopes stretching over the palings, beauty sprang instantly. To watch a leaf quivering in the rush of air was an exquisite joy. Up in the sky swallows swooping, swerving, flinging themselves in and out, round and round, yet always with perfect control as if elastics held them; and the flies rising and falling; and the sun spotting now this leaf, now that, in mockery, dazzling it with soft gold in pure good temper; and now and again some chime (it might be a motor horn) tinkling divinely on the grass stalks—all of this, calm and reasonable as it was, made out of ordinary things as it was, was the truth now; beauty, that was the truth now. Beauty was everywhere.

"It is time," said Rezia.

The word "time" split its husk; poured its riches over him; and from his lips fell like shells, like shavings from a plane, without his making them, hard, white, imperishable, words, and flew to attach themselves to their places in an ode to Time; an immortal ode to Time. He sang. Evans answered from behind the tree. The dead were in Thessaly,[1] Evans sang, among the orchids. There they waited until the War was over, and now the dead, now Evans himself—

"For God's sake don't come!" Septimus cried out. For he could not look upon the dead.

But the branches parted. A man in grey was actually walking towards them. It was Evans! But no mud was on him; no wounds; he was not changed. I must tell the whole world, Septimus cried, raising his hand (as the dead man in the grey suit came nearer), raising his hand like some colossal figure who has lamented the

---

1 A region in central Greece. It is unclear why Woolf has chosen to allude to this region specifically, though Greece in general was associated in her mind with her brother Thoby, who died of typhoid fever in 1906 shortly after the four Stephen siblings (Vanessa, Thoby, Virginia and Adrian), and their family friend, Violet Dickinson, returned from a trip to Greece.

fate of man for ages in the desert alone with his hands pressed to his forehead, furrows of despair on his cheeks, and now sees light on the desert's edge which broadens and strikes the iron-black figure (and Septimus half rose from his chair), and with legions of men prostrate behind him he, the giant mourner, receives for one moment on his face the whole—

"But I am so unhappy, Septimus," said Rezia, trying to make him sit down.

The millions lamented; for ages they had sorrowed. He would turn round, he would tell them in a few moments, only a few moments more, of this relief, of this joy, of this astonishing revelation—

"The time, Septimus," Rezia repeated. "What is the time?"

He was talking, he was starting, this man must notice him. He was looking at them.

"I will tell you the time," said Septimus, very slowly, very drowsily, smiling mysteriously at the dead man in the grey suit. As he sat smiling, the quarter struck—the quarter to twelve.

And that is being young, Peter Walsh thought, as he passed them. To be having an awful scene—the poor girl looked absolutely desperate—in the middle of the morning. But what was it about, he wondered; what had the young man in the overcoat been saying to her to make her look like that; what awful fix had they got themselves into, both to look so desperate as that on a fine summer morning? The amusing thing about coming back to England, after five years, was the way it made, anyhow the first days, things stand out as if one had never seen them before; lovers squabbling under a tree; the domestic family life of the parks. Never had he seen London look so enchanting—the softness of the distances; the richness; the greenness; the civilisation, after India, he thought, strolling across the grass.

This susceptibility to impressions had been his undoing, no doubt. Still at his age he had, like a boy or a girl even, these alternations of mood; good days, bad days, for no reason whatever, happiness from a pretty face, downright misery at the sight of a frump. After India of course one fell in love with every woman one met. There was a freshness about them; even the poorest dressed better than five years ago surely; and to his eye the fashions had never been so becoming; the long black cloaks; the slimness; the elegance; and then the delicious and apparently universal habit of paint. Every woman, even the most respectable, had roses blooming under glass; lips cut with a knife; curls of Indian ink; there was design, art, everywhere; a change of some sort had undoubtedly taken place. What did the young people think about? Peter Walsh asked himself.

Those five years—1918 to 1923—had been, he suspected, somehow very important. People looked different. Newspapers seemed different. Now, for instance, there was a man writing quite openly in one of the respectable weeklies about water-closets.[1] That you couldn't have done ten years ago—written quite openly about water-closets in a respectable weekly. And then this taking out a stick of rouge, or a powder-puff, and making up in public. On board ship coming home there were lots of young men and girls—Betty and Bertie he remembered in particular—carrying on quite openly; the old mother sitting and watching them with her knitting, cool as a cucumber. The girl would stand still and powder her nose in front of every one. And they weren't engaged; just having a good time; no feelings hurt on either side. As hard as nails she was—Betty Whatshername—but a thorough good sort. She would make a very good wife at thirty—she would marry when it suited her to marry; marry some rich man and live in a large house near Manchester.

Who was it now who had done that? Peter Walsh asked himself, turning into the Broad Walk—married a rich man and lived in a large house near Manchester? Somebody who had written him a long, gushing letter quite lately about "blue hydrangeas." It was seeing blue hydrangeas that made her think of him and the old days—Sally Seton, of course! It was Sally Seton—the last person in the world one would have expected to marry a rich man and live in a large house near Manchester, the wild, the daring, the romantic Sally!

But of all that ancient lot, Clarissa's friends—Whitbreads, Kindersleys, Cunninghams, Kinlock Jones's[2]—Sally was probably the best. She tried to get hold of things by the right end anyhow. She saw through Hugh Whitbread anyhow—the admirable Hugh—when Clarissa and the rest were at his feet.

"The Whitbreads?" he could hear her saying. "Who are the Whitbreads? Coal merchants. Respectable tradespeople."

Hugh she detested for some reason. He thought of nothing but his own appearance, she said. He ought to have been a Duke. He would be certain to marry one of the Royal Princesses. And of course Hugh had the most extraordinary, the most natural, the

---

1 Small rooms containing a flush toilet.

2 One of the small errors that appears in the first Hogarth Press edition—earlier in the novel the name is spelled Kinloch-Jones.

most sublime respect for the British aristocracy of any human being he had ever come across. Even Clarissa had to own that. Oh, but he was such a dear, so unselfish, gave up shooting to please his old mother—remembered his aunts' birthdays, and so on.

Sally, to do her justice, saw through all that. One of the things he remembered best was an argument one Sunday morning at Bourton about women's rights (that antediluvian topic), when Sally suddenly lost her temper, flared up, and told Hugh that he represented all that was most detestable in British middle-class life. She told him that she considered him responsible for the state of "those poor girls in Piccadilly"[1]—Hugh, the perfect gentleman, poor Hugh!—never did a man look more horrified! She did it on purpose, she said afterwards (for they used to get together in the vegetable garden and compare notes). "He's read nothing, thought nothing, felt nothing," he could hear her saying in that very emphatic voice which carried so much farther than she knew. The stable boys had more life in them than Hugh, she said. He was a perfect specimen of the public school type, she said. No country but England could have produced him. She was really spiteful, for some reason; had some grudge against him. Something had happened—he forgot what—in the smoking-room. He had insulted her—kissed her? Incredible! Nobody believed a word against Hugh, of course. Who could? Kissing Sally in the smoking-room! If it had been some Honourable Edith or Lady Violet, perhaps; but not that ragamuffin Sally without a penny to her name, and a father or a mother gambling at Monte Carlo. For of all the people he had ever met Hugh was the greatest snob—the most obsequious—no, he didn't cringe exactly. He was too much of a prig for that. A first-rate valet was the obvious comparison—somebody who walked behind carrying suit cases; could be trusted to send telegrams—indispensable to hostesses. And he'd found his job—married his Honourable Evelyn; got some little post at Court, looked after the King's cellars, polished the Imperial shoe-buckles, went about in knee-breeches and lace ruffles. How remorseless life is! A little job at Court!

He had married this lady, the Honourable Evelyn, and they lived hereabouts, so he thought (looking at the pompous houses overlooking the Park), for he had lunched there once in a house which had, like all Hugh's possessions, something that no other house could possibly have—linen cupboards it might have been.

1 A reference to prostitutes in Piccadilly Circus.

You had to go and look at them—you had to spend a great deal of time always admiring whatever it was—linen cupboards, pillow-cases, old oak furniture, pictures, which Hugh had picked up for an old song. But Mrs. Hugh sometimes gave the show away. She was one of those obscure mouse-like little women who admire big men. She was almost negligible. Then suddenly she would say something quite unexpected—something sharp. She had the relics of the grand manner, perhaps. The steam coal was a little too strong for her—it made the atmosphere thick. And so there they lived, with their linen cupboards and their old masters and their pillow-cases fringed with real lace, at the rate of five or ten thousand a year presumably, while he, who was two years older than Hugh, cadged for a job.

At fifty-three he had to come and ask them to put him into some secretary's office, to find him some usher's job teaching little boys Latin, at the beck and call of some mandarin in an office, something that brought in five hundred a year;[1] for if he married Daisy, even with his pension, they could never do on less. Whitbread could do it presumably; or Dalloway. He didn't mind what he asked Dalloway. He was a thorough good sort; a bit limited; a bit thick in the head; yes; but a thorough good sort. Whatever he took up he did in the same matter-of-fact sensible way; without a touch of imagination, without a spark of brilliancy, but with the inexplicable niceness of his type. He ought to have been a country gentleman—he was wasted on politics. He was at his best out of doors, with horses and dogs—how good he was, for instance, when that great shaggy dog of Clarissa's got caught in a trap and had its paw half torn off, and Clarissa turned faint and Dalloway did the whole thing; bandaged, made splints; told Clarissa not to be a fool. That was what she liked him for, perhaps—that was what she needed. "Now, my dear, don't be a fool. Hold this—fetch that," all the time talking to the dog as if it were a human being.

But how could she swallow all that stuff about poetry? How could she let him hold forth about Shakespeare? Seriously and solemnly Richard Dalloway got on his hind legs and said that no decent man ought to read Shakespeare's sonnets because it was

---

1 In *A Room of One's Own*, Woolf estimated that a woman who wanted to be a writer needed an independent income of £500 a year. While it is difficult to calculate exactly how much £500 would be worth in 2012, one measure (average earnings) puts it at £84,100. See http://www.measuringworth.com/. See also p. 127, n. 1; p. 180, n. 1, and p. 195, n. 2.

like listening at keyholes (besides, the relationship was not one that he approved). No decent man ought to let his wife visit a deceased wife's sister.[1] Incredible! The only thing to do was to pelt him with sugared almonds—it was at dinner. But Clarissa sucked it all in; thought it so honest of him; so independent of him; Heaven knows if she didn't think him the most original mind she'd ever met!

That was one of the bonds between Sally and himself. There was a garden where they used to walk, a walled-in place, with rose-bushes and giant cauliflowers—he could remember Sally tearing off a rose, stopping to exclaim at the beauty of the cabbage leaves in the moonlight (it was extraordinary how vividly it all came back to him, things he hadn't thought of for years), while she implored him, half laughing of course, to carry off Clarissa, to save her from the Hughs and the Dalloways and all the other "perfect gentlemen" who would "stifle her soul" (she wrote reams of poetry in those days), make a mere hostess of her, encourage her worldliness. But one must do Clarissa justice. She wasn't going to marry Hugh anyhow. She had a perfectly clear notion of what she wanted. Her emotions were all on the surface. Beneath, she was very shrewd—a far better judge of character than Sally, for instance, and with it all, purely feminine; with that extraordinary gift, that woman's gift, of making a world of her own wherever she happened to be. She came into a room; she stood, as he had often seen her, in a doorway with lots of people round her. But it was Clarissa one remembered. Not that she was striking; not beautiful at all; there was nothing picturesque about her; she never said anything specially clever; there she was, however; there she was.

No, no, no! He was not in love with her any more! He only felt, after seeing her that morning, among her scissors and silks, making ready for the party, unable to get away from the thought of her; she kept coming back and back like a sleeper jolting against him in a railway carriage; which was not being in love, of course; it was thinking of her, criticising her, starting again, after thirty years, trying to explain her. The obvious thing to say of her was that she was worldly; cared too much for rank and society and getting on in the world—which was true in a sense; she had admitted it to him. (You could always get her to own up if you

---

1 The Deceased Wife's Sister's Marriage Act (1907) amended British law to permit a man to marry his deceased wife's sister. The Marriage Act of 1835 had prohibited such a union.

took the trouble; she was honest.) What she would say was that she hated frumps, fogies, failures, like himself presumably; thought people had no right to slouch about with their hands in their pockets; must do something, be something; and these great swells, these Duchesses, these hoary old Countesses one met in her drawing-room, unspeakably remote as he felt them to be from anything that mattered a straw, stood for something real to her. Lady Bexborough, she said once, held herself upright (so did Clarissa herself; she never lounged in any sense of the word; she was straight as a dart, a little rigid in fact). She said they had a kind of courage which the older she grew the more she respected. In all this there was a great deal of Dalloway, of course; a great deal of the public-spirited, British Empire, tariff-reform,[1] governing-class spirit, which had grown on her, as it tends to do. With twice his wits, she had to see things through his eyes—one of the tragedies of married life. With a mind of her own, she must always be quoting Richard—as if one couldn't know to a tittle what Richard thought by reading the *Morning Post*[2] of a morning! These parties, for example, were all for him, or for her idea of him (to do Richard justice he would have been happier farming in Norfolk). She made her drawing-room a sort of meeting-place; she had a genius for it. Over and over again he had seen her take some raw youth, twist him, turn him, wake him up; set him going. Infinite numbers of dull people conglomerated round her, of course. But odd unexpected people turned up; an artist sometimes; sometimes a writer; queer fish in that atmosphere. And behind it all was that network of visiting, leaving cards, being kind to people; running about with bunches of flowers, little presents; So-and-so was going to France—must have an air-cushion; a real drain on her strength; all that interminable traffic that women of her sort keep up; but she did it genuinely, from a natural instinct.

Oddly enough, she was one of the most thorough-going sceptics he had ever met, and possibly (this was a theory he used to make up to account for her, so transparent in some ways, so inscrutable in others), possible she said to herself, As we are a doomed race, chained to a sinking ship (her favourite reading as

---

1 In 1923 tariff reform, intended to protect the British manufacturing sector, was a central tenet of the Conservative Party under Prime Minister Stanley Baldwin. See Introduction, p. 33; and Appendix C4.

2 A conservative daily newspaper published in London from 1772 to 1937.

a girl was Huxley and Tyndall,[1] and they were fond of these nautical metaphors), as the whole thing is a bad joke, let us, at any rate, do our part; mitigate the sufferings of our fellow-prisoners (Huxley again); decorate the dungeon with flowers and air-cushions; be as decent as we possibly can. Those ruffians, the Gods, shan't have it all their own way—her notion being that the Gods, who never lost a chance of hurting, thwarting and spoiling human lives, were seriously put out if, all the same, you behaved like a lady. That phase came directly after Sylvia's death—that horrible affair. To see your own sister killed by a falling tree (all Justin Parry's fault—all his carelessness) before your very eyes, a girl too on the verge of life, the most gifted of them, Clarissa always said, was enough to turn one bitter. Later she wasn't so positive, perhaps; she thought there were no Gods; no one was to blame; and so she evolved this atheist's religion of doing good for the sake of goodness.

And of course she enjoyed life immensely. It was her nature to enjoy (though, goodness only knows, she had her reserves; it was a mere sketch, he often felt, that even he, after all these years, could make of Clarissa). Anyhow there was no bitterness in her; none of that sense of moral virtue which is so repulsive in good women. She enjoyed practically everything. If you walked with her in Hyde Park[2] now it was a bed of tulips, now a child in a perambulator, now some absurd little drama she made up on the spur of the moment. (Very likely she would have talked to those lovers, if she had thought them unhappy.) She had a sense of comedy that was really exquisite, but she needed people, always people, to bring it out, with the inevitable result that she frittered her time away, lunching, dining, giving these incessant parties of hers, talking nonsense, saying things she didn't mean, blunting the edge of her mind, losing her discrimination. There she would sit at the head of the table taking infinite pains with some old buffer who might be useful to Dalloway—they knew the most appalling bores in Europe—or in came Elizabeth and every thing

---

1 References to Thomas Henry Huxley (1825-95), biologist, self-described agnostic, and defender of Darwin's theory of evolution by natural selection; and John Tyndall (1820-93), physicist, mountaineer, and scientific educator. Lifelong friends, both Huxley and Tyndall were committed to the separation of science and religion.

2 The largest of the eight Royal Parks, Hyde Park is bounded by Bayswater Road in the north, Knightsbridge in the south, and Park Lane in the east; it merges with Kensington Gardens in the west.

must give way to *her*. She was at a High School, at the inarticulate stage last time he was over, a round-eyed, pale-faced girl, with nothing of her mother in her, a silent stolid creature, who took it all as a matter of course, let her mother make a fuss of her, and then said "May I go now?" like a child of four; going off, Clarissa explained, with that mixture of amusement and pride which Dalloway himself seemed to rouse in her, to play hockey. And now Elizabeth was "out,"[1] presumably; thought him an old fogy, laughed at her mother's friends. Ah well, so be it. The compensation of growing old, Peter Walsh thought, coming out of Regent's Park, and holding his hat in his hand, was simply this; that the passions remain as strong as ever, but one has gained—at last!—the power which adds the supreme flavour to existence—the power of taking hold of experience, of turning it round, slowly, in the light.

A terrible confession it was (he put his hat on again), but now, at the age of fifty-three, one scarcely needed people any more. Life itself, every moment of it, every drop of it, here, this instant, now, in the sun, in Regent's Park, was enough. Too much, indeed. A whole lifetime was too short to bring out, now that one had acquired the power, the full flavour; to extract every ounce of pleasure, every shade of meaning; which both were so much more solid than they used to be, so much less personal. It was impossible that he should ever suffer again as Clarissa had made him suffer. For hours at a time (pray God that one might say these things without being overheard!), for hours and days he never thought of Daisy.

Could it be that he was in love with her, then, remembering the misery, the torture, the extraordinary passion of those days? It was a different thing altogether—a much pleasanter thing—the truth being, of course, that now *she* was in love with *him*. And that perhaps was the reason why, when the ship actually sailed, he felt an extraordinary relief, wanted nothing so much as to be alone; was annoyed to find all her little attentions—cigars, notes, a rug for the voyage—in his cabin. Every one if they were honest would say the same; one doesn't want people after fifty; one doesn't want to go on telling women they are pretty; that's what most men of fifty would say, Peter Walsh thought, if they were honest.

---

1 Upper-class young women "came out" or made their debut in society (often by being presented at court), signalling their availability for marriage.

But then these astonishing accesses of emotion—bursting into tears this morning, what was all that about? What could Clarissa have thought of him? thought him a fool presumably, not for the first time. It was jealousy that was at the bottom of it—jealousy which survives every other passion of mankind, Peter Walsh thought, holding his pocket-knife at arm's length. She had been meeting Major Orde, Daisy said in her last letter; said it on purpose, he knew; said it to make him jealous; he could see her wrinkling her forehead as she wrote, wondering what she could say to hurt him; and yet it made no difference; he was furious! All this pother of coming to England and seeing lawyers wasn't to marry her, but to prevent her from marrying someone else. That was what tortured him, that was what came over him when he saw Clarissa so calm, so cold, so intent on her dress or whatever it was; realising what she might have spared him, what she had reduced him to—a whimpering, snivelling old ass. But women, he thought, shutting his pocket-knife, don't know what passion is. They don't know the meaning of it to men. Clarissa was as cold as an icicle. There she would sit on the sofa by his side, let him take her hand, give him one kiss on the cheek—Here he was at the crossing.

A sound interrupted him; a frail quivering sound, a voice bubbling up without direction, vigour, beginning or end, running weakly and shrilly and with an absence of all human meaning into

> ee um fah um so
> foo swee too eem oo—[1]

the voice of no age or sex, the voice of an ancient spring spouting from the earth; which issued, just opposite Regent's Park Tube Station, from a tall quivering shape, like a funnel, like a rusty pump, like a wind-beaten tree for ever barren of leaves which lets the wind run up and down its branches singing

---

1 J. Hillis Miller has identified this as "a song by Richard Strauss, 'Allerseelen,' with words by Hermann von Gilm." *Allerseelen* translates loosely as All Souls' Day, "the day of a collective resurrection of spirits. On this day the bereaved lover can hope that the beloved will return from the grave" (Miller 190). Miller translates the words of the song, in part, as follows: "One day in the year is free to the dead / Come to my heart that I may have you again, / As once in May" (Miller 177).

ee um fah um so
foo swee too eem oo,

and rocks and creaks and moans in the eternal breeze.

Through all ages—when the pavement was grass, when it was swamp, through the age of tusk and mammoth, through the age of silent sunrise—the battered woman—for she wore a skirt—with her right hand exposed, her left clutching at her side, stood singing of love—love which has lasted a million years, she sang, love which prevails, and millions of years ago, her lover, who had been dead these centuries, had walked, she crooned, with her in May; but in the course of ages, long as summer days, and flaming, she remembered, with nothing but red asters, he had gone; death's enormous sickle had swept those tremendous hills, and when at last she laid her hoary and immensely aged head on the earth, now become a mere cinder of ice, she implored the gods to lay by her side a bunch of purple heather, there on her high burial place which the last rays of the last sun caressed; for then the pageant of the universe would be over.

As the ancient song bubbled up opposite Regent's Park Tube Station, still the earth seemed green and flowery; still, though it issued from so rude a mouth, a mere hole in the earth, muddy too, matted with root fibres and tangled grasses, still the old bubbling burbling song, soaking through the knotted roots of infinite ages, and skeletons and treasure, streamed away in rivulets over the pavement and all along the Marylebone Road, and down towards Euston, fertilising, leaving a damp stain.

Still remembering how once in some primeval May she had walked with her lover, this rusty pump, this battered old woman with one hand exposed for coppers, the other clutching her side, would still be there in ten million years, remembering how once she had walked in May, where the sea flows now, with whom it did not matter—he was a man, oh yes, a man who had loved her. But the passage of ages had blurred the clarity of that ancient May day; the bright petalled flowers were hoar and silver frosted; and she no longer saw, when she implored him (as she did now quite clearly) "look in my eyes with thy sweet eyes intently," she no longer saw brown eyes, black whiskers or sunburnt face, but only a looming shape, a shadow shape, to which, with the bird-like freshness of the very aged, she still twittered "give me your hand and let me press it gently" (Peter Walsh couldn't help giving the poor creature a coin as he stepped into his taxi), "and if some one should see, what matter they?" she demanded; and her fist clutched at her side, and she smiled, pocketing her shilling, and all peering inquisitive eyes seemed blotted out, and the passing generations—the pavement was crowded with bustling middle-class people—vanished, like leaves, to be trodden under, to be soaked and steeped and made mould of by that eternal spring—

ee um fah um so
foo swee too eem oo.

"Poor old woman," said Rezia Warren Smith.

Oh poor old wretch! she said, waiting to cross.

Suppose it was a wet night? Suppose one's father, or somebody who had known one in better days had happened to pass, and saw one standing there in the gutter? And where did she sleep at night?

Cheerfully, almost gaily, the invincible thread of sound wound up into the air like the smoke from a cottage chimney, winding up clean beech trees and issuing in a tuft of blue smoke among the topmost leaves. "And if some one should see, what matter they?"

Since she was so unhappy, for weeks and weeks now, Rezia had given meanings to things that happened, almost felt sometimes that she must stop people in the street, if they looked good, kind people, just to say to them "I am unhappy"; and this old woman singing in the street "if someone should see, what matter they?" made her suddenly quite sure that everything was going to be right. They were going to Sir William Bradshaw; she thought his name sounded nice; he would cure Septimus at once. And then there was a brewer's cart, and the grey horses had upright bristles of straw in their tails; there were newspaper placards. It was a silly, silly dream, being unhappy.

So they crossed, Mr. and Mrs. Septimus Warren Smith, and was there, after all, anything to draw attention to them, anything to make a passer-by suspect here is a young man who carries in him the greatest message in the world, and is, moreover, the happiest man in the world, and the most miserable? Perhaps they walked more slowly than other people, and there was something hesitating, trailing, in the man's walk, but what more natural for a clerk, who has not been in the West End on a week-day at this hour for years, than to keep looking at the sky, looking at this, that and the other, as if Portland Place were a room he had come into when the family are away, the chandeliers being hung in holland bags,[1] and the caretaker, as she lets in long shafts of dusty light upon deserted, queer-looking arm-chairs, lifting one corner of the long blinds, explains to the visitors what a wonderful place it is; how wonderful, but at the same time, he thinks, how strange.

To look at, he might have been a clerk, but of the better sort; for he wore brown boots;[2] his hands were educated; so, too, his profile—his angular, big-nosed, intelligent, sensitive profile; but not his lips altogether, for they were loose; and his eyes (as eyes tend to be), eyes merely; hazel, large; so that he was, on the whole, a border case, neither one thing nor the other; might end with a house at Purley[3] and a motor car, or continue renting apartments in back streets all his life; one of those half-educated, self-educated men whose education is all learnt from books borrowed from public libraries, read in the evening after the day's work, on the advice of well-known authors consulted by letter.

As for the other experiences, the solitary ones, which people go through alone, in their bedrooms, in their offices, walking the fields and the streets of London, he had them; had left home, a mere boy, because of his mother; she lied; because he came down to tea for the fiftieth time with his hands unwashed; because he could see no future for a poet in Stroud; and so, making a confidant of his little sister, had gone to London leaving an absurd note behind him, such as great men have written, and the world has read later when the story of their struggles has become famous.

London has swallowed up many millions of young men called Smith; thought nothing of fantastic Christian names like Septimus with which their parents have thought to distinguish them. Lodging off the Euston Road, there were experiences, again experiences, such as change a face in two years from a pink innocent oval to a face lean, contracted, hostile. But of all this what could the most observant of friends have said except what a gardener says when he opens the conservatory door in

---

1 Protective coverings made of unbleached linen.

2 In an earlier manuscript version of *Mrs. Dalloway*, this passage includes the explanation that "the working classes do not wear brown shoes" (Wussow 103). Septimus's brown boots indicate his social aspirations just as his reading indicates his intellectual aspirations.

3 A suburb in south London.

the morning and finds a new blossom on his plant:—It has flowered; flowered from vanity, ambition, idealism, passion, loneliness, courage, laziness, the usual seeds, which all muddled up (in a room off the Euston Road), made him shy, and stammering, made him anxious to improve himself, made him fall in love with Miss Isabel Pole, lecturing in the Waterloo Road upon Shakespeare.[1]

Was he not like Keats?[2] she asked; and reflected how she might give him a taste of *Antony and Cleopatra*[3] and the rest; lent him books; wrote him scraps of letters; and lit in him such a fire as burns only once in a lifetime, without heat, flickering a red gold flame infinitely ethereal and insubstantial over Miss Pole; *Antony and Cleopatra*; and the Waterloo Road. He thought her beautiful, believed her impeccably wise; dreamed of her, wrote poems to her, which, ignoring the subject, she corrected in red ink; he saw her, one summer evening, walking in a green dress in a square. "It has flowered," the gardener might have said, had he opened the door; had he come in, that is to say, any night about this time, and found him writing; found him tearing up his writing; found him finishing a masterpiece at three o'clock in the morning and running out to pace the streets, and visiting churches, and fasting one day, drinking another, devouring

---

1 Although Woolf does not identify the college, it is clear that, prior to the war, Septimus was a student at Morley College, a college "for working men and women," which had its origins in a series of weekly evening lectures at the Royal Victoria Theatre (the Old Vic) at the corner of The Cut and Waterloo Road in the Lambeth area of London. (See Appendices E1 and E2, and Kelly 193-94.) Morley College was formally established in 1889; and from 1905 to 1907 Virginia Woolf, then Virginia Stephen, taught courses there on English composition, literature, and history. Hermione Lee suggests that one of one of her students, Cyril Zeldwyn, served as the model for Septimus Warren Smith (Lee 219). Woolf's July 1905 "Report on Teaching at Morley College" is reproduced as Appendix B in Quentin Bell's *Virginia Woolf: A Biography* (1972), vol. 1, 202-04.

2 John Keats (1795-1821), a major English Romantic poet and the son of an ostler (or stableman) who died when Keats was only eight. Keats left school at 14 to apprentice with a surgeon and apothecary, determining at 21 to commit himself to poetry instead. He remained under financial stress until his death of tuberculosis only five years later.

3 As with *Cymbeline* and *Othello*, references to Shakespeare's *Antony and Cleopatra* recur in the novel.

Shakespeare, Darwin, *The History of Civilisation*,[1] and Bernard Shaw.[2]

Something was up, Mr. Brewer knew; Mr. Brewer, managing clerk at Sibleys and Arrowsmiths, auctioneers, valuers, land and estate agents; something was up, he thought, and, being paternal with his young men, and thinking very highly of Smith's abilities, and prophesying that he would, in ten or fifteen years, succeed to the leather arm-chair in the inner room under the skylight with the deed-boxes round him, "if he keeps his health," said Mr. Brewer, and that was the danger—he looked weakly; advised football, invited him to supper and was seeing his way to consider recommending a rise of salary, when something happened which threw out many of Mr. Brewer's calculations, took away his ablest young fellows, and eventually, so prying and insidious were the fingers of the European War, smashed a plaster cast of Ceres,[3] ploughed a hole in the geranium beds, and utterly ruined the cook's nerves at Mr. Brewer's establishment at Muswell Hill.

Septimus was one of the first to volunteer. He went to France to save an England which consisted almost entirely of Shakespeare's plays and Miss Isabel Pole in a green dress walking in a square. There in the trenches the change which Mr. Brewer desired when he advised football was produced instantly; he developed manliness; he was promoted; he drew the attention, indeed the affection of his officer, Evans by name. It was a case of two dogs playing on a hearth-rug; one worrying a paper screw, snarling, snapping, giving a pinch, now and then, at the old dog's

---

1 Morris Beja suggests that this may refer to François Pierre Guillaume Guizot's *The History of Civilization: From the Fall of the Roman Empire to the French Revolution* (1828; trans. W. Hazlitt, 1846), while David Bradshaw suggests that it refers to Henry Thomas Buckle's two-volume *History of Civilisation in England* (1857-61). See Bradshaw 541. It is also possible that *The History of Civilisation* is an invented title, perhaps a spoof of H.G. Wells's *The Outline of History* (1920).

2 George Bernard Shaw (1856-1950), Irish playwright, socialist, and co-founder of the Fabian Society and the London School of Economics.

3 Roman goddess of agriculture and fertility. This reference may have been inspired by the second part of Ezra Pound's long modernist poem *Hugh Selwyn Mauberley* (1920), in which the poet denounces mass produced art: "The 'age demanded' chiefly a mould in plaster" (II, l. 9). Woolf's claim to "hate [Pound's] works" in a 1923 letter to Ottoline Morrell is evidence that she had read him, and was thinking of him while working on *Mrs. Dalloway* (*Letters* III, 71).

ear; the other lying somnolent, blinking at the fire, raising a paw, turning and growling good-temperedly. They had to be together, share with each other, fight with each other, quarrel with each other. But when Evans (Rezia, who had only seen him once, called him "a quiet man," a sturdy red-haired man, undemonstrative in the company of women), when Evans was killed, just before the Armistice, in Italy, Septimus, far from showing any emotion or recognising that here was the end of a friendship, congratulated himself upon feeling very little and very reasonably. The War had taught him. It was sublime. He had gone through the whole show, friendship, European War, death, had won promotion, was still under thirty and was bound to survive. He was right there. The last shells missed him. He watched them explode with indifference. When peace came he was in Milan, billeted in the house of an innkeeper with a courtyard, flowers in tubs, little tables in the open, daughters making hats, and to Lucrezia, the younger daughter, he became engaged one evening when the panic was on him—that he could not feel.

For now that it was all over, truce signed, and the dead buried, he had, especially in the evening, these sudden thunder-claps of fear. He could not feel. As he opened the door of the room where the Italian girls sat making hats, he could see them; could hear them; they were rubbing wires among coloured beads in saucers; they were turning buckram shapes this way and that; the table was all strewn with feathers, spangles, silks, ribbons; scissors were rapping on the table; but something failed him; he could not feel. Still, scissors rapping, girls laughing, hats being made protected him; he was assured of safety; he had a refuge. But he could not sit there all night. There were moments of waking in the early morning. The bed was falling; he was falling. Oh for the scissors and the lamplight and the buckram shapes! He asked Lucrezia to marry him, the younger of the two, the gay, the frivolous, with those little artist's fingers that she would hold up and say "It is all in them." Silk, feathers, what not were alive to them.

"It is the hat that matters most," she would say, when they walked out together. Every hat that passed, she would examine; and the cloak and the dress and the way the woman held herself. Ill-dressing, over-dressing she stigmatised, not savagely, rather with impatient movements of the hands, like those of a painter who puts from him some obvious well-meant glaring imposture; and then, generously, but always critically, she would welcome a shop-girl who had turned her little bit of stuff gallantly, or praise, wholly, with enthusiastic and professional understanding, a

French lady descending from her carriage, in chinchilla, robes, pearls.

"Beautiful!" she would murmur, nudging Septimus, that he might see. But beauty was behind a pane of glass. Even taste (Rezia liked ices, chocolates, sweet things) had no relish to him. He put down his cup on the little marble table. He looked at people outside; happy they seemed, collecting in the middle of the street, shouting, laughing, squabbling over nothing. But he could not taste, he could not feel. In the tea-shop among the tables and the chattering waiters the appalling fear came over him—he could not feel. He could reason; he could read, Dante for example, quite easily ("Septimus, do put down your book," said Rezia, gently shutting the *Inferno*),[1] he could add up his bill; his brain was perfect; it must be the fault of the world then—that he could not feel.

"The English are so silent," Rezia said. She liked it, she said. She respected these Englishmen, and wanted to see London, and the English horses, and the tailor-made suits, and could remember hearing how wonderful the shops were, from an Aunt who had married and lived in Soho.

It might be possible, Septimus thought, looking at England from the train window, as they left Newhaven;[2] it might be possible that the world itself is without meaning.

At the office they advanced him to a post of considerable responsibility. They were proud of him; he had won crosses. "You have done your duty; it is up to us—" began Mr. Brewer; and could not finish, so pleasurable was his emotion. They took admirable lodgings off the Tottenham Court Road.

Here he opened Shakespeare once more. That boy's business of the intoxication of language—*Antony and Cleopatra*—had shrivelled utterly. How Shakespeare loathed humanity—the putting on of clothes, the getting of children, the sordidity of the mouth and the belly! This was now revealed to Septimus; the message hidden in the beauty of words. The secret signal which one generation passes, under disguise, to the next is loathing,

1 The first part of the *Divine Comedy* by Italian poet Dante Alighieri (1265-1321). It describes the poet's journey through the nine circles of Hell, guided by the Roman poet Virgil.

2 A town and ferry port in the Lewes District of East Sussex at the mouth of the River Ouse. Septimus and Rezia have taken the ferry from Dieppe to Newhaven, and are now en route to London. The River Ouse was the site of Woolf's 1941 suicide.

hatred, despair. Dante the same. Aeschylus[1] (translated) the same. There Rezia sat at the table trimming hats. She trimmed hats for Mrs. Filmer's friends; she trimmed hats by the hour. She looked pale, mysterious, like a lily, drowned, under water, he thought.

"The English are so serious," she would say, putting her arms round Septimus, her cheeks against his.

Love between man and woman was repulsive to Shakespeare. The business of copulation was filth to him before the end. But, Rezia said, she must have children. They had been married five years.

They went to the Tower[2] together; to the Victoria and Albert Museum;[3] stood in the crowd to see the King open Parliament. And there were the shops—hat shops, dress shops, shops with leather bags in the window, where she would stand staring. But she must have a boy.

She must have a son like Septimus, she said. But nobody could be like Septimus; so gentle; so serious; so clever. Could she not read Shakespeare too? Was Shakespeare a difficult author? she asked.

One cannot bring children into a world like this. One cannot perpetuate suffering, or increase the breed of these lustful animals, who have no lasting emotions, but only whims and vanities, eddying them now this way, now that.

He watched her snip, shape, as one watches a bird hop, flit in the grass, without daring to move a finger. For the truth is (let her ignore it) that human beings have neither kindness, nor faith, nor charity beyond what serves to increase the pleasure of the moment. They hunt in packs. Their packs scour the desert and vanish screaming into the wilderness. They desert the fallen. They are plastered over with grimaces. There was Brewer at the office, with his waxed moustache, coral tie-pin, white slip, and pleasurable emotions—all coldness and clamminess within,—his gerani-

---

1 Greek dramatist (c. 525-456 BCE), author of *The Oresteia* trilogy outlining the tragic history of the family of Agamemnon, King of Argos. The fact that Septimus has read Aeschylus in translation is an allusion to his class and self-education: men of Clarissa's class would have received a classical education and read it in Greek.

2 Tower of London, a medieval fortress and historic castle on the north bank of the Thames. Variously a royal residence, a prison, an armoury, and more, the Tower was by 1923 a major tourist attraction.

3 A museum of decorative arts and design established in 1852.

ums ruined in the War—his cook's nerves destroyed; or Amelia Whatshername, handing round cups of tea punctually at five—a leering, sneering obscene little harpy; and the Toms and Berties in their starched shirt fronts oozing thick drops of vice. They never saw him drawing pictures of them naked at their antics in his notebook. In the street, vans roared past him; brutality blared out on placards; men were trapped in mines; women burnt alive; and once a maimed file of lunatics being exercised or displayed for the diversion of the populace (who laughed aloud), ambled and nodded and grinned past him, in the Tottenham Court Road, each half apologetically, yet triumphantly, inflicting his hopeless woe. And would *he* go mad?

At tea Rezia told him that Mrs. Filmer's daughter was expecting a baby. *She* could not grow old and have no children! She was very lonely, she was very unhappy! She cried for the first time since they were married. Far away he heard her sobbing; he heard it accurately, he noticed it distinctly; he compared it to a piston thumping. But he felt nothing.

His wife was crying, and he felt nothing; only each time she sobbed in this profound, this silent, this hopeless way, he descended another step into the pit.

At last, with a melodramatic gesture which he assumed mechanically and with complete consciousness of its insincerity, he dropped his head on his hands. Now he had surrendered; now other people must help him. People must be sent for. He gave in.

Nothing could rouse him. Rezia put him to bed. She sent for a doctor—Mrs. Filmer's Dr. Holmes. Dr. Holmes examined him. There was nothing whatever the matter, said Dr. Holmes. Oh, what a relief! What a kind man, what a good man! thought Rezia. When he felt like that he went to the Music Hall, said Dr. Holmes. He took a day off with his wife and played golf. Why not try two tabloids of bromide[1] dissolved in a glass of water at bedtime? These old Bloomsbury houses, said Dr. Holmes, tapping the wall, are often full of very fine panelling, which the landlords have the folly to paper over. Only the other day, visiting a patient, Sir Somebody Something, in Bedford Square—

So there was no excuse; nothing whatever the matter, except the sin for which human nature had condemned him to death; that he did not feel. He had not cared when Evans was killed; that was worst; but all the other crimes raised their heads and shook their fingers and jeered and sneered over the rail of the bed in the

---

1 Potassium bromide, usually taken as a sedative.

early hours of the morning at the prostrate body which lay realising its degradation; how he had married his wife without loving her; had lied to her; seduced her; outraged Miss Isabel Pole, and was so pocked and marked with vice that women shuddered when they saw him in the street. The verdict of human nature on such a wretch was death.

Dr. Holmes came again. Large, fresh-coloured, handsome, flicking his boots, looking in the glass, he brushed it all aside—headaches, sleeplessness, fears, dreams—nerve symptoms and nothing more, he said. If Dr. Holmes found himself even half a pound below eleven stone six, he asked his wife for another plate of porridge at breakfast. (Rezia would learn to cook porridge.) But, he continued, health is largely a matter in our own control. Throw yourself into outside interests; take up some hobby. He opened Shakespeare—*Antony and Cleopatra*; pushed Shakespeare aside. Some hobby, said Dr. Holmes, for did he not owe his own excellent health (and he worked as hard as any man in London) to the fact that he could always switch off from his patients on to old furniture? And what a very pretty comb, if he might say so, Mrs. Warren Smith was wearing!

When the damned fool came again, Septimus refused to see him. Did he indeed? said Dr. Holmes, smiling agreeably. Really he had to give that charming little lady, Mrs. Smith, a friendly push before he could get past her into her husband's bedroom.

"So you're in a funk," he said agreeably, sitting down by his patient's side. He had actually talked of killing himself to his wife, quite a girl, a foreigner, wasn't she? Didn't that give her a very odd idea of English husbands? Didn't one owe perhaps a duty to one's wife? Wouldn't it be better to do something instead of lying in bed? For he had had forty years' experience behind him; and Septimus could take Dr. Holmes's word for it—there was nothing whatever the matter with him. And next time Dr. Holmes came he hoped to find Smith out of bed and not making that charming little lady his wife anxious about him.

Human nature, in short, was on him—the repulsive brute, with the blood-red nostrils. Holmes was on him. Dr. Holmes came quite regularly every day. Once you stumble, Septimus wrote on the back of a postcard, human nature is on you. Holmes is on you. Their only chance was to escape, without letting Holmes know; to Italy—anywhere, anywhere, away from Dr. Holmes.

But Rezia could not understand him. Dr. Holmes was such a kind man. He was so interested in Septimus. He only wanted to help them, he said. He had four little children and he had asked her to tea, she told Septimus.

So he was deserted. The whole world was clamouring: Kill yourself, kill yourself, for our sakes. But why should he kill himself for their sakes? Food was pleasant; the sun hot; and this killing oneself, how does one set about it, with a table knife, uglily, with floods of blood,—by sucking a gaspipe? He was too weak; he could scarcely raise his hand. Besides, now that he was quite alone, condemned, deserted, as those who are about to die are alone, there was a luxury in it, an isolation full of sublimity; a freedom which the attached can never know. Holmes had won of course; the brute with the red nostrils had won. But even Holmes himself could not touch this last relic straying on the edge of the world, this outcast, who gazed back at the inhabited regions, who lay, like a drowned sailor, on the shore of the world.

It was at that moment (Rezia had gone shopping) that the great revelation took place. A voice spoke from behind the screen. Evans was speaking. The dead were with him.

"Evans, Evans!" he cried.

Mr. Smith was talking aloud to himself, Agnes the servant girl cried to Mrs. Filmer in the kitchen. "Evans, Evans!" he had said as she brought in the tray. She jumped, she did. She scuttled downstairs.

And Rezia came in, with her flowers, and walked across the room, and put the roses in a vase, upon which the sun struck directly, and went laughing, leaping round the room.

She had had to buy the roses, Rezia said, from a poor man in the street. But they were almost dead already, she said, arranging the roses.

So there was a man outside; Evans presumably; and the roses, which Rezia said were half dead, had been picked by him in the fields of Greece. Communication is health; communication is happiness. Communication, he muttered.

"What are you saying, Septimus?" Rezia asked, wild with terror, for he was talking to himself.

She sent Agnes running for Dr. Holmes. Her husband, she said, was mad. He scarcely knew her.

"You brute! You brute!" cried Septimus, seeing human nature, that is Dr. Holmes, enter the room.

"Now what's all this about," said Dr. Holmes in the most amiable way in the world. "Talking nonsense to frighten your wife?" But he would give him something to make him sleep. And if they were rich people, said Dr. Holmes, looking ironically round the room, by all means let them go to Harley Street;[1] if they had no confidence in him, said Dr. Holmes, looking not quite so kind.

It was precisely twelve o'clock; twelve by Big Ben; whose stroke was wafted over the northern part of London; blent with that of other clocks, mixed in a thin ethereal way with the clouds and wisps of smoke and died up there among the seagulls—twelve o'clock struck as Clarissa Dalloway laid her green dress on her bed, and the Warren Smiths walked down Harley Street. Twelve was the hour of their appointment. Probably, Rezia thought, that was Sir William Bradshaw's house with the grey motor car in front of it. (The leaden circles dissolved in the air.)

Indeed it was—Sir William Bradshaw's motor car; low, powerful, grey with plain initials interlocked on the panel, as if the pomps of heraldry were incongruous, this man being the ghostly helper, the priest of science; and, as the motor car was grey, so to match its sober suavity, grey furs, silver grey rugs were heaped in it, to keep her ladyship warm while she waited. For often Sir William would travel sixty miles or more down into the country to visit the rich, the afflicted, who could afford the very large fee which Sir William very properly charged for his advice. Her ladyship waited with the rugs about her knees an hour or more, leaning back, thinking sometimes of the patient, sometimes, excusably, of the wall of gold, mounting minute by minute while she waited; the wall of gold that was mounting between them and all shifts and anxieties (she had borne them bravely; they had had their struggles) until she felt wedged on a calm ocean, where only spice winds blow; respected, admired, envied, with scarcely anything left to wish for, though she regretted her stoutness; large dinner-parties every Thursday night to the profession; an occasional bazaar to be opened; Royalty greeted; too little time, alas, with her husband, whose work grew and grew; a boy doing well at Eton;[2] she would have liked a daughter too; interests she had, however, in plenty; child welfare; the after-care of the epileptic, and photography, so that if there was a church building, or a church decaying, she bribed the sexton, got the key and took

1 In the Westminster area of London, a centre for medical specialists, surgeons, professional medical organizations since the mid-nineteenth century.

2 A prestigious British boys' public (or independent) school established in 1440.

photographs, which were scarcely to be distinguished from the work of professionals, while she waited.

Sir William himself was no longer young. He had worked very hard; he had won his position by sheer ability (being the son of a shopkeeper); loved his profession; made a fine figurehead at ceremonies and spoke well—all of which had by the time he was knighted given him a heavy look, a weary look (the stream of patients being so incessant, the responsibilities and privileges of his profession so onerous), which weariness, together with his grey hairs, increased the extraordinary distinction of his presence and gave him the reputation (of the utmost importance in dealing with nerve cases) not merely of lightning skill and almost infallible accuracy in diagnosis, but of sympathy; tact; understanding of the human soul. He could see the first moment they came into the room (the Warren Smiths they were called); he was certain directly he saw the man; it was a case of extreme gravity. It was a case of complete breakdown—complete physical and nervous breakdown, with every symptom in an advanced stage, he ascertained in two or three minutes (writing answers to questions, murmured discreetly, on a pink card).

How long had Dr. Holmes been attending him?

Six weeks.

Prescribed a little bromide? Said there was nothing the matter? Ah yes (these general practitioners! thought Sir William. It took half his time to undo their blunders. Some were irreparable).

"You served with great distinction in the War?"

The patient repeated the word "war" interrogatively.

He was attaching meanings to words of a symbolical kind. A serious symptom to be noted on the card.

"The War?" the patient asked. The European War—that little shindy of schoolboys with gunpowder? Had he served with distinction? He really forgot. In the War itself he had failed.

"Yes, he served with the greatest distinction," Rezia assured the doctor; "he was promoted."

"And they have the very highest opinion of you at your office?" Sir William murmured, glancing at Mr. Brewer's very generously worded letter. "So that you have nothing to worry you, no financial anxiety, nothing?"

He had committed an appalling crime and been condemned to death by human nature.

"I have—I have," he began, "committed a crime—"

"He has done nothing wrong whatever," Rezia assured the doctor. If Mr. Smith would wait, said Sir William, he would speak to Mrs. Smith in the next room. Her husband was very seriously ill, Sir William said. Did he threaten to kill himself?

Oh, he did, she cried. But he did not mean it, she said. Of course not. It was merely a question of rest, said Sir William; of rest, rest, rest; a long rest in bed.[1] There was a delightful home down in the country where her husband would be perfectly looked after. Away from her? she asked. Unfortunately, yes; the people we care for most are not good for us when we are ill. But he was not mad, was he? Sir William said he never spoke of "madness"; he called it not having a sense of proportion. But her husband did not like doctors. He would refuse to go there. Shortly and kindly Sir William explained to her the state of the case. He had threatened to kill himself. There was no alternative. It was a question of law. He would lie in bed in a beautiful house in the country. The nurses were admirable. Sir William would visit him once a week. If Mrs. Warren Smith was quite sure she had no more questions to ask—he never hurried his patients—they would return to her husband. She had nothing more to ask—not of Sir William.

So they returned to the most exalted of mankind; the criminal who faced his judges; the victim exposed on the heights; the fugitive; the drowned sailor; the poet of the immortal ode; the Lord who had gone from life to death; to Septimus Warren Smith, who sat in the arm-chair under the skylight staring at a photograph of Lady Bradshaw in Court dress, muttering messages about beauty.

"We have had our little talk," said Sir William.

"He says you are very, very ill," Rezia cried.

"We have been arranging that you should go into a home," said Sir William.

"One of Holmes's homes?" sneered Septimus.

The fellow made a distasteful impression. For there was in Sir William, whose father had been a tradesman, a natural respect for breeding and clothing, which shabbiness nettled; again, more profoundly, there was in Sir William, who had never had time for reading, a grudge, deeply buried, against cultivated people who came into his room and intimated that doctors, whose profession

---

1 As biographer Hermione Lee points out, Woolf's physicians typically prescribed rest cures to treat her breakdowns: "All her doctors recommended rest cures, milk and meat diets for weight gain, fresh air, avoidance of excitement and early nights. All prescribed sedatives like bromides" (183).

is a constant strain upon all the highest faculties, are not educated men.

"One of *my* homes, Mr. Warren Smith," he said, "where we will teach you to rest."

And there was just one thing more.

He was quite certain that when Mr. Warren Smith was well he was the last man in the world to frighten his wife. But he had talked of killing himself.

"We all have our moments of depression," said Sir William.

Once you fall, Septimus repeated to himself, human nature is on you. Holmes and Bradshaw are on you. They scour the desert. They fly screaming into the wilderness. The rack and the thumbscrew are applied. Human nature is remorseless.

"Impulses came upon him sometimes?" Sir William asked, with his pencil on a pink card.

That was his own affair, said Septimus.

"Nobody lives for himself alone," said Sir William, glancing at the photograph of his wife in Court dress.

"And you have a brilliant career before you," said Sir William. There was Mr. Brewer's letter on the table. "An exceptionally brilliant career."

But if he confessed? If he communicated? Would they let him off then, Holmes Bradshaw?

"I—I—" he stammered.

But what was his crime? He could not remember it.

"Yes?" Sir William encouraged him. (But it was growing late.)

Love, trees, there is no crime—what was his message?

He could not remember it.

"I—I—" Septimus stammered.

"Try to think as little about yourself as possible," said Sir William kindly. Really, he was not fit to be about.

Was there anything else they wished to ask him? Sir William would make all arrangements (he murmured to Rezia) and he would let her know between five and six that evening.

"Trust everything to me," he said, and dismissed them.

Never, never had Rezia felt such agony in her life! She had asked for help and been deserted! He had failed them! Sir William Bradshaw was not a nice man.

The upkeep of that motor car alone must cost him quite a lot, said Septimus, when they got out into the street.

She clung to his arm. They had been deserted.

But what more did she want?

To his patients he gave three-quarters of an hour; and if in this exacting science which has to do with what, after all, we know nothing about—the nervous system, the human brain—a doctor loses his sense of proportion, as a doctor he fails. Health we must have; and health is proportion; so that when a man comes into your room and says he is Christ (a common delusion), and has a message, as they mostly have, and threatens, as they often do, to kill himself, you invoke proportion; order rest in bed; rest in solitude; silence and rest; rest without friends, without books, without messages; six months' rest; until a man who went in weighing seven stone six[1] comes out weighing twelve.

Proportion, divine proportion, Sir William's goddess, was acquired by Sir William walking hospitals, catching salmon, begetting one son in Harley Street by Lady Bradshaw, who caught salmon herself and took photographs scarcely to be distinguished from the work of professionals. Worshipping proportion, Sir William not only prospered himself but made England prosper, secluded her lunatics, forbade childbirth, penalised despair, made it impossible for the unfit to propagate their views until they, too, shared his sense of proportion—his, if they were men, Lady Bradshaw's if they were women (she embroidered, knitted, spent four nights out of seven at home with her son), so that not only did his colleagues respect him, his subordinates fear him, but the friends and relations of his patients felt for him the keenest gratitude for insisting that these prophetic Christs and Christesses, who prophesied the end of the world, or the advent of God, should drink milk in bed, as Sir William ordered; Sir William with his thirty years' experience of these kinds of cases, and his infallible instinct, this is madness, this sense; his sense of proportion.

But Proportion has a sister, less smiling, more formidable, a Goddess even now engaged—in the heat and sands of India, the mud and swamp of Africa, the purlieus of London, wherever in short the climate or the devil tempts men to fall from the true belief which is her own—is even now engaged in dashing down shrines, smashing idols, and setting up in their place her own stern countenance. Conversion is her name and she feasts on the wills of the weakly, loving to impress, to impose, adoring her own features stamped on the face of the populace. At Hyde Park

---

1 I.e., 104 pounds. One stone is equivalent to 14 pounds or 6.36 kilograms.

Corner[1] on a tub she stands preaching; shrouds herself in white and walks penitentially disguised as brotherly love through factories and parliaments; offers help, but desires power; smites out of her way roughly the dissentient, or dissatisfied; bestows her blessing on those who, looking upward, catch submissively from her eyes the light of their own. This lady too (Rezia Warren Smith divined it) had her dwelling in Sir William's heart, though concealed, as she mostly is, under some plausible disguise; some venerable name; love, duty, self-sacrifice. How he would work—how toil to raise funds, propagate reforms, initiate institutions! But conversion, fastidious Goddess, loves blood better than brick, and feasts most subtly on the human will. For example, Lady Bradshaw. Fifteen years ago she had gone under. It was nothing you could put your finger on; there had been no scene, no snap; only the slow sinking, water-logged, of her will into his. Sweet was her smile, swift her submission; dinner in Harley Street, numbering eight or nine courses, feeding ten or fifteen guests of the professional classes, was smooth and urbane. Only as the evening wore on a very slight dulness, or uneasiness perhaps, a nervous twitch, fumble, stumble and confusion indicated, what it was really painful to believe—that the poor lady lied. Once, long ago, she had caught salmon freely: now, quick to minister to the craving which lit her husband's eye so oilily for dominion, for power, she cramped, squeezed, pared, pruned, drew back, peeped through; so that without knowing precisely what made the evening disagreeable, and caused this pressure on the top of the head (which might well be imputed to the professional conversation, or the fatigue of a great doctor whose life, Lady Bradshaw said, "is not his own but his patient's"), disagreeable it was: so that guests, when the clock struck ten, breathed in the air of Harley Street even with rapture; which relief, however, was denied to his patients.

There in the grey room, with the pictures on the wall, and the valuable furniture, under the ground glass skylight, they learnt the extent of their transgressions; huddled up in arm-chairs, they watched him go through, for their benefit, a curious exercise with the arms, which he shot out, brought sharply back to his hip, to prove (if the patient was obstinate) that Sir William was master of

---

1 In the southeast corner of Hyde Park. However, this is likely intended as a reference to Speaker's Corner in the northeast corner of Hyde Park, a traditional location for speeches and protest, by serious debaters and cranks alike.

his own actions, which the patient was not. There some weakly broke down; sobbed, submitted; others, inspired by Heaven knows what intemperate madness, called Sir William to his face a damnable humbug; questioned, even more impiously, life itself. Why live? they demanded. Sir William replied that life was good. Certainly Lady Bradshaw in ostrich feathers hung over the mantelpiece, and as for his income it was quite twelve thousand a year.[1] But to us, they protested, life has given no such bounty. He acquiesced. They lacked a sense of proportion. And perhaps, after all, there is no God? He shrugged his shoulders. In short, this living or not living is an affair of our own? But there they were mistaken. Sir William had a friend in Surrey where they taught, what Sir William frankly admitted was a difficult art—a sense of proportion. There were, moreover, family affection; honour; courage; and a brilliant career. All of these had in Sir William a resolute champion. If they failed, he had to support him police and the good of society, which, he remarked very quietly, would take care, down in Surrey, that these unsocial impulses, bred more than anything by the lack of good blood, were held in control. And then stole out from her hiding-place and mounted her throne that Goddess whose lust is to override opposition, to stamp indelibly in the sanctuaries of others the image of herself. Naked, defenceless, the exhausted, the friendless received the impress of Sir William's will. He swooped; he devoured. He shut people up. It was this combination of decision and humanity that endeared Sir William so greatly to the relations of his victims.

But Rezia Warren Smith cried, walking down Harley Street, that she did not like that man.

Shredding and slicing, dividing and subdividing, the clocks of Harley Street nibbled at the June day, counselled submission, upheld authority, and pointed out in chorus the supreme advan-

---

1 It is difficult to calculate the relative value of a British pound sterling in 1923 and today. Using the retail price index, Sir William Bradshaw's income of £12,000 a year would be worth well over half a million pounds today; using an average earnings index, his £12,000 would be worth well over two million pounds. See the Measuring Worth website, http://www.measuringworth.com/. An additional way of placing Dr. Bradshaw's income in context is to remember that Peter Walsh is hoping to gain a position that would bring him £500 a year, the same amount that Virginia Woolf identified in *A Room of One's Own* as necessary to support an independent life as a writer. See p. 104, n. 1; p. 180, n. 1; and p. 195, n. 2.

tages of a sense of proportion, until the mound of time was so far diminished that a commercial clock, suspended above a shop in Oxford Street, announced, genially and fraternally, as if it were a pleasure to Messrs. Rigby and Lowndes to give the information gratis, that it was half-past one.

Looking up, it appeared that each letter of their names stood for one of the hours; subconsciously one was grateful to Rigby and Lowndes for giving one time ratified by Greenwich;[1] and this gratitude (so Hugh Whitbread ruminated, dallying there in front of the shop window) naturally took the form later of buying off Rigby and Lowndes socks or shoes. So he ruminated. It was his habit. He did not go deeply. He brushed surfaces; the dead languages, the living, life in Constantinople, Paris, Rome; riding, shooting, tennis, it had been once. The malicious asserted that he now kept guard at Buckingham Palace, dressed in silk stockings and knee-breeches, over what nobody knew. But he did it extremely efficiently. He had been afloat on the cream of English society for fifty-five years. He had known Prime Ministers. His affections were understood to be deep. And if it were true that he had not taken part in any of the great movements of the time or held important office, one or two humble reforms stood to his credit; an improvement in public shelters was one; the protection of owls in Norfolk another; servant girls had reason to be grateful to him; and his name at the end of letters to the *Times*, asking for funds, appealing to the public to protect, to preserve, to clear up litter, to abate smoke, and stamp out immorality in parks, commanded respect.

A magnificent figure he cut too, pausing for a moment (as the sound of the half-hour died away) to look critically, magisterially, at socks and shoes; impeccable, substantial, as if he beheld the world from a certain eminence, and dressed to match; but realised the obligations which size, wealth, health entail, and observed punctiliously even when not absolutely necessary, little courtesies, old-fashioned ceremonies which gave a quality to his manner, something to imitate, something to remember him by, for he would never lunch, for example, with Lady Bruton, whom he had known these twenty years, without bringing her in his outstretched hand a bunch of carnations and asking Miss Brush, Lady Bruton's secretary, after her brother in South Africa, which, for some reason, Miss Brush, deficient though she was in every

---

1 Greenwich Mean Time, the official time standard calculated by the Royal Observatory in Greenwich, London.

attribute of female charm, so much resented that she said "Thank you, he's doing very well in South Africa," when, for half-a-dozen years, he had been doing badly in Portsmouth.[1]

Lady Bruton herself preferred Richard Dalloway, who arrived at the same moment. Indeed they met on the doorstep.

Lady Bruton preferred Richard Dalloway of course. He was made of much finer material. But she wouldn't let them run down her poor dear Hugh. She could never forget his kindness—he had been really remarkably kind—she forgot precisely upon what occasion. But he had been—remarkably kind. Anyhow, the difference between one man and another does not amount to much. She had never seen the sense of cutting people up, as Clarissa Dalloway did—cutting them up and sticking them together again; not at any rate when one was sixty-two. She took Hugh's carnations with her angular grim smile. There was nobody else coming, she said. She had got them there on false pretences, to help her out of a difficulty—

"But let us eat first," she said.

And so there began a soundless and exquisite passing to and fro through swing doors of aproned white-capped maids, handmaidens not of necessity, but adepts in a mystery or grand deception practised by hostesses in Mayfair[2] from one-thirty to two, when, with a wave of the hand, the traffic ceases, and there rises instead this profound illusion in the first place about food—how it is not paid for; and then that the table spreads itself voluntarily with glass and silver, little mats, saucers of red fruit; films of brown cream mask turbot; in casseroles severed chickens swim; coloured, undomestic, the fire burns; and with the wine and the coffee (not paid for) rise jocund visions before musing eyes; gently speculative eyes; eyes to whom life appears musical, mysterious; eyes now kindled to observe genially the beauty of the red carnations which Lady Bruton (whose movements were always angular) had laid beside her plate, so that Hugh Whitbread, feeling at peace with the entire universe and at the same time completely sure of his standing, said, resting his fork:

"Wouldn't they look charming against your lace?"

Miss Brush resented this familiarity intensely. She thought him an underbred fellow. She made Lady Bruton laugh.

Lady Bruton raised the carnations, holding them rather stiffly with much the same attitude with which the General held the

---

1 City on the south coast of England.

2 A fashionable and wealthy district in west London.

scroll in the picture behind her; she remained fixed, tranced. Which was she now, the General's great-grand-daughter? great-great grand-daughter? Richard Dalloway asked himself. Sir Roderick, Sir Miles, Sir Talbot—that was it. It was remarkable how in that family the likeness persisted in the women. She should have been a general of dragoons[1] herself. And Richard would have served under her, cheerfully; he had the greatest respect for her; he cherished these romantic views about well-set-up old women of pedigree, and would have liked, in his good-humoured way, to bring some young hot-heads of his acquaintance to lunch with her; as if a type like hers could be bred of amiable tea-drinking enthusiasts! He knew her country. He knew her people. There was a vine, still bearing, which either Lovelace or Herrick[2]—she never read a word of poetry herself, but so the story ran—had sat under. Better wait to put before them the question that bothered her (about making an appeal to the public; if so, in what terms and so on), better wait until they have had their coffee, Lady Bruton thought; and so laid the carnations down beside her plate.

"How's Clarissa?" she asked abruptly.

Clarissa always said that Lady Bruton did not like her. Indeed, Lady Bruton had the reputation of being more interested in politics than people; of talking like a man; of having had a finger in some notorious intrigue of the eighties, which was now beginning to be mentioned in memoirs. Certainly there was an alcove in her drawing-room, and a table in that alcove, and a photograph upon that table of General Sir Talbot Moore, now deceased, who had written there (one evening in the eighties) in Lady Bruton's presence, with her cognisance, perhaps advice, a telegram ordering the British troops to advance upon an historical occasion. (She kept the pen and told the story.) Thus, when she said in her off-hand way "How's Clarissa?" husbands had difficulty in persuading their wives and indeed, however devoted, were secretly doubtful themselves, of her interest in women who often got in their husbands' way, prevented them from accepting posts abroad, and had to be taken to the seaside in the middle of the session to recover from influenza. Nevertheless her inquiry, "How's

---

1 Armed cavalry or horse soldiers.

2 Richard Lovelace (1618-57) and Robert Herrick (1591-1674), both lyric cavalier poets (supporting King Charles I during the English Civil War). Herrick is best remembered for his poem "To the Virgins, to Make Much of Time," which begins: "Gather ye rosebuds while ye may."

Clarissa?" was known by women infallibly to be a signal from a well-wisher, from an almost silent companion, whose utterances (half a dozen perhaps in the course of a lifetime) signified recognition of some feminine comradeship which went beneath masculine lunch parties and united Lady Bruton and Mrs. Dalloway, who seldom met, and appeared when they did meet indifferent and even hostile, in a singular bond.

"I met Clarissa in the Park this morning," said Hugh Whitbread, diving into the casserole, anxious to pay himself this little tribute, for he had only to come to London and he met everybody at once; but greedy, one of the greediest men she had ever known, Milly Brush thought, who observed men with unflinching rectitude, and was capable of everlasting devotion, to her own sex in particular, being knobbed, scraped, angular, and entirely without feminine charm.

"D'you know who's in town?" said Lady Bruton, suddenly bethinking her. "Our old friend, Peter Walsh."

They all smiled. Peter Walsh! And Mr. Dalloway was genuinely glad, Milly Brush thought; and Mr. Whitbread thought only of his chicken.

Peter Walsh! All three, Lady Bruton, Hugh Whitbread, and Richard Dalloway, remembered the same thing—how passionately Peter had been in love; been rejected; gone to India; come a cropper; made a mess of things; and Richard Dalloway had a very great liking for the dear old fellow too. Milly Brush saw that; saw a depth in the brown of his eyes; saw him hesitate; consider; which interested her, as Mr. Dalloway always interested her, for what was he thinking, she wondered, about Peter Walsh?

That Peter Walsh had been in love with Clarissa; that he would go back directly after lunch and find Clarissa; that he would tell her, in so many words, that he loved her. Yes, he would say that.

Milly Brush once might almost have fallen in love with these silences; and Mr. Dalloway was always so dependable; such a gentleman too. Now, being forty, Lady Bruton had only to nod, or turn her head a little abruptly, and Milly Brush took the signal, however deeply she might be sunk in these reflections of a detached spirit, of an uncorrupted soul whom life could not bamboozle, because life had not offered her a trinket of the slightest value; not a curl, smile, lip, cheek, nose; nothing whatever; Lady Bruton had only to nod, and Perkins was instructed to quicken the coffee.

"Yes; Peter Walsh has come back," said Lady Bruton. It was vaguely flattering to them all. He had come back, battered, unsuccessful, to their secure shores. But to help him, they reflected, was impossible; there was some flaw in his character. Hugh Whitbread said one might of course mention his name to So-and-so. He wrinkled lugubriously, consequentially, at the thought of the letters he would write to the heads of Government offices about "my old friend, Peter Walsh," and so on. But it wouldn't lead to anything—not to anything permanent, because of his character.

"In trouble with some woman," said Lady Bruton. They had all guessed that *that* was at the bottom of it.

"However," said Lady Bruton, anxious to leave the subject, "we shall hear the whole story from Peter himself."

(The coffee was very slow in coming.)

"The address?" murmured Hugh Whitbread; and there was at once a ripple in the grey tide of service which washed round Lady Bruton day in, day out, collecting, intercepting, enveloping her in a fine tissue which broke concussions, mitigated interruptions, and spread round the house in Brook Street a fine net where things lodged and were picked out accurately, instantly, by grey-haired Perkins, who had been with Lady Bruton these thirty years and now wrote down the address; handed it to Mr. Whitbread, who took out his pocket-book, raised his eyebrows, and slipping it in among documents of the highest importance, said that he would get Evelyn to ask him to lunch.

(They were waiting to bring the coffee until Mr. Whitbread has finished.)

Hugh was very slow, Lady Bruton thought. He was getting fat, she noticed. Richard always kept himself in the pink of condition. She was getting impatient; the whole of her being was setting positively, undeniably, domineeringly brushing aside all this unnecessary trifling (Peter Walsh and his affairs) upon that subject which engaged her attention, and not merely her attention, but that fibre which was the ramrod of her soul, that essential part of her without which Millicent Bruton would not have been Millicent Bruton; that project for emigrating young people of both sexes born of respectable parents and setting them up with a fair prospect of doing well in Canada.[1] She exaggerated. She had per-

---

1 On 13 June 1923, *The Times* reported a conference in London, convened by the Empire League for Training and Overseas Settlement, "to consider the question of Empire employment and development." "Resolutions will be submitted embodying proposals for cooperation between the Imperial Government and local authorities at home and the Governments of the overseas Dominions" (9).

haps lost her sense of proportion. Emigration was not to others the obvious remedy, the sublime conception. It was not to them (not to Hugh, or Richard, or even to devoted Miss Brush) the liberator of the pent egotism, which a strong martial woman, well nourished, well descended, of direct impulses, downright feelings, and little introspective power (broad and simple—why could not every one be broad and simple? she asked) feels rise within her, once youth is past, and must eject upon some object—it may be Emigration, it may be Emancipation; but whatever it be, this object round which the essence of her soul is daily secreted becomes inevitably prismatic, lustrous, half looking-glass, half precious stone; now carefully hidden in case people should sneer at it; now proudly displayed. Emigration had become, in short, largely Lady Bruton.

But she had to write. And one letter to the *Times*, she used to say to Miss Brush, cost her more than to organise an expedition to South Africa (which she had done in the war). After a morning's battle beginning, tearing up, beginning again, she used to feel the futility of her own womanhood as she felt it on no other occasion, and would turn gratefully to the thought of Hugh Whitbread who possessed—no one could doubt it—the art of writing letters to the *Times*.

A being so differently constituted from herself, with such a command of language; able to put things as editors liked them put; had passions which one could not call simply greed. Lady Bruton often suspended judgement upon men in deference to the mysterious accord in which they, but no woman, stood to the laws of the universe; knew how to put things; knew what was said; so that if Richard advised her, and Hugh wrote for her, she was sure of being somehow right. So she let Hugh eat his soufflé; asked after poor Evelyn; waited until they were smoking, and then said,

"Milly, would you fetch the papers?"

And Miss Brush went out, came back; laid papers on the table; and Hugh produced his fountain pen; his silver fountain pen, which had done twenty years' service, he said, unscrewing the cap. It was still in perfect order; he had shown it to the makers; there was no reason, they said, why it should ever wear out; which was somehow to Hugh's credit, and to the credit of the sentiments which his pen expressed (so Richard Dalloway felt) as Hugh began carefully writing capital letters with rings round them in the margin, and thus marvellously reduced Lady Bruton's tangles to sense, to grammar such as the editor of the *Times*,

Lady Bruton felt, watching the marvellous transformation, must respect. Hugh was slow. Hugh was pertinacious. Richard said one must take risks. Hugh proposed modifications in deference to people's feelings, which, he said rather tartly when Richard laughed, "had to be considered," and read out "how, therefore, we are of opinion that the times are ripe ... the superfluous youth of our ever-increasing population ... what we owe to the dead ..." which Richard thought all stuffing and bunkum, but no harm in it, of course, and Hugh went on drafting sentiments in alphabetical order of the highest nobility, brushing the cigar ash from his waistcoat, and summing up now and then the progress they had made until, finally, he read out the draft of a letter which Lady Bruton felt certain was a masterpiece. Could her own meaning sound like that?

Hugh could not guarantee that the editor would put it in; but he would be meeting somebody at luncheon.

Whereupon Lady Bruton, who seldom did a graceful thing, stuffed all Hugh's carnations into the front of her dress, and flinging her hands out called him "My Prime Minister!" What she would have done without them both she did not know. They rose. And Richard Dalloway strolled off as usual to have a look at the General's portrait, because he meant, whenever he had a moment of leisure, to write a history of Lady Bruton's family.

And Millicent Bruton was very proud of her family. But they could wait, they could wait, she said, looking at the picture; meaning that her family, of military men, administrators, admirals, had been men of action, who had done their duty; and Richard's first duty was to his country, but it was a fine face, she said; and all the papers were ready for Richard down at Aldmixton whenever the time came; the Labour Government she meant.[1] "Ah, the news from India!" she cried.

And then, as they stood in the hall taking yellow gloves from the bowl on the malachite table[2] and Hugh was offering Miss Brush with quite unnecessary courtesy some discarded ticket or other compliment, which she loathed from the depths of her heart and blushed brick red, Richard turned to Lady Bruton, with his hat in his hand, and said,

---

1 Lady Bruton's political instincts are sound: the Labour Party, under J. Ramsay MacDonald, would form Britain's first Labour Government only six months after the events of the novel take place.

2 A green-coloured stone table top made from a copper carbonate hydroxide mineral.

"We shall see you at our party to-night?" whereupon Lady Bruton resumed the magnificence which letter-writing had shattered. She might come; or she might not come. Clarissa had wonderful energy. Parties terrified Lady Bruton. But then, she was getting old. So she intimated, standing at her doorway; handsome; very erect; while her chow stretched behind her, and Miss Brush disappeared into the background with her hands full of papers.

And Lady Bruton went ponderously, majestically, up to her room, lay, one arm extended, on the sofa. She sighed, she snored, not that she was asleep, only drowsy and heavy, drowsy and heavy, like a field of clover in the sunshine this hot June day, with the bees going round and about and the yellow butterflies. Always she went back to those fields down in Devonshire, where she had jumped the brooks on Patty, her pony, with Mortimer and Tom, her brothers. And there were the dogs; there were the rats; there were her father and mother on the lawn under the trees, with the tea-things out, and the beds of dahlias, the hollyhocks, the pampas grass; and they, little wretches, always up to some mischief! stealing back through the shrubbery, so as not to be seen, all bedraggled from some roguery. What old nurse used to say about her frocks!

Ah dear, she remembered—it was Wednesday in Brook Street. Those kind good fellows, Richard Dalloway, Hugh Whitbread, had gone this hot day through the streets whose growl came up to her lying on the sofa. Power was hers, position, income. She had lived in the forefront of her time. She had had good friends; known the ablest men of her day. Murmuring London flowed up to her, and her hand, lying on the sofa back, curled upon some imaginary baton such as her grandfathers might have held, holding which she seemed, drowsy and heavy, to be commanding battalions marching to Canada, and those good fellows walking across London, that territory of theirs, that little bit of carpet, Mayfair.

And they went further and further from her, being attached to her by a thin thread (since they had lunched with her) which would stretch and stretch, get thinner and thinner as they walked across London; as if one's friends were attached to one's body, after lunching with them, by a thin thread, which (as she dozed there) became hazy with the sound of bells, striking the hour or ringing to service, as a single spider's thread is blotted with raindrops, and, burdened, sags down. So she slept.

And Richard Dalloway and Hugh Whitbread hesitated at the corner of Conduit Street at the very moment that Millicent Bruton, lying on the sofa, let the thread snap; snored. Contrary winds buffeted at the street corner. They looked in at a shop window; they did not wish to buy or to talk but to part, only with contrary winds buffeting the street corner, with some sort of lapse in the tides of the body, two forces meeting in a swirl, morning and afternoon, they paused. Some newspaper placard went up in the air, gallantly, like a kite at first, then paused, swooped, fluttered; and a lady's veil hung. Yellow awnings trembled. The speed of the morning traffic slackened, and single carts rattled carelessly down half-empty streets. In Norfolk, of which Richard Dalloway was half thinking, a soft warm wind blew back the petals; confused the waters; ruffled the flowering grasses. Haymakers, who had pitched beneath hedges to sleep away the morning toil, parted curtains of green blades; moved trembling globes of cow parsley to see the sky; the blue, the steadfast, the blazing summer sky.

Aware that he was looking at a silver two-handled Jacobean[1] mug, and that Hugh Whitbread admired condescendingly, with airs of connoisseurship, a Spanish necklace which he thought of asking the price of in case Evelyn might like it—still Richard was torpid; could not think or move. Life had thrown up this wreckage; shop windows full of coloured paste, and one stood stark with the lethargy of the old, stiff with the rigidity of the old, looking in. Evelyn Whitbread might like to buy this Spanish necklace—so she might. Yawn he must. Hugh was going into the shop.

"Right you are!" said Richard, following.

Goodness knows he didn't want to go buying necklaces with Hugh. But there are tides in the body. Morning meets afternoon. Borne like a frail shallop[2] on deep, deep floods, Lady Bruton's great-grandfather and his memoir and his campaigns in North America were whelmed and sunk. And Millicent Bruton too. She went under. Richard didn't care a straw what became of Emigration; about that letter, whether the editor put it in or not. The necklace hung stretched between Hugh's admirable fingers. Let him give it to a girl, if he must buy jewels—any girl, any girl in the street. For the worthlessness of this life did strike Richard pretty forcibly—buying necklaces for Evelyn. If he'd had a boy he'd have said, Work, work. But he had his Elizabeth; he adored his Elizabeth.

"I should like to see Mr. Dubonnet," said Hugh in his curt worldly way. It appeared that this Dubonnet had the measure-

1 From the time of James I (reigned 1603-25).

2 A boat for use in shallow waters.

ments of Mrs. Whitbread's neck, or, more strangely still, knew her views upon Spanish jewellery and the extent of her possessions in that line (which Hugh could not remember). All of which seemed to Richard Dalloway awfully odd. For he never gave Clarissa presents, except a bracelet two or three years ago, which had not been a success. She never wore it. It pained him to remember that she never wore it. And as a single spider's thread after wavering here and there attaches itself to the point of a leaf, so Richard's mind, recovering from its lethargy, set now on his wife, Clarissa, whom Peter Walsh had loved so passionately; and Richard had had a sudden vision of her there at luncheon; of himself and Clarissa; of their life together; and he drew the tray of old jewels towards him, and taking up first this brooch then that ring, "How much is that?" he asked, but doubted his own taste. He wanted to open the drawing-room door and come in holding out something; a present for Clarissa. Only what? But Hugh was on his legs again. He was unspeakably pompous. Really, after dealing here for thirty-five years he was not going to be put off by a mere boy who did not know his business. For Dubonnet, it seemed, was out, and Hugh would not buy anything until Mr. Dubonnet chose to be in; at which the youth flushed and bowed his correct little bow. It was all perfectly correct. And yet Richard couldn't have said that to save his life! Why these people stood that damned insolence he could not conceive. Hugh was becoming an intolerable ass. Richard Dalloway could not stand more than an hour of his society. And, flicking his bowler hat by way of farewell, Richard turned at the corner of Conduit Street eager, yes, very eager, to travel that spider's thread of attachment between himself and Clarissa; he would go straight to her, in Westminster.

But he wanted to come in holding something. Flowers? Yes, flowers, since he did not trust his taste in gold; any number of flowers, roses, orchids, to celebrate what was, reckoning things as you will, an event; this feeling about her when they spoke of Peter Walsh at luncheon; and they never spoke of it; not for years had they spoken of it; which, he thought, grasping his red and white roses together (a vast bunch in tissue paper), is the greatest mistake in the world. The time comes when it can't be said; one's too shy to say it, he thought, pocketing his sixpence or two of change, setting off with his great bunch held against his body to Westminster to say straight out in so many words (whatever she might think of him), holding out his flowers, "I love you." Why not? Really it was a miracle thinking of the war, and thousands of poor chaps, with all their lives before them, shovelled together, already half forgotten; it was a miracle. Here he was walking across London to say to Clarissa in so many words that he loved her. Which one never does say, he thought. Partly one's lazy; partly one's shy. And Clarissa—it was difficult to think of her; except in starts, as at luncheon, when he saw her quite distinctly; their whole life. He stopped at the crossing; and repeated—being simple by nature, and undebauched, because he had tramped, and shot; being pertinacious and dogged, having championed the down-trodden and followed his instincts in the House of Commons; being preserved in his simplicity yet at the same time grown rather speechless, rather stiff—he repeated that it was a miracle, that he should have married Clarissa; a miracle—his life had been a miracle, he thought; hesitating to cross. But it did make his blood boil to see little creatures of five or six crossing Piccadilly alone. The Police ought to have stopped the traffic at once. He had no illusions about the London police. Indeed, he was collecting evidence of their malpractices; and those costermongers,[1] not allowed to stand their barrows in the streets; and prostitutes, good Lord, the fault wasn't in them, nor in young men either, but in our detestable social system and so forth; all of which he considered, could be seen considering, grey, dogged, dapper, clean, as he walked across the Park to tell his wife that he loved her.

For he would say it in so many words, when he came into the room. Because it is a thousand pities never to say what one feels, he thought, crossing the Green Park and observing with pleasure how in the shade of the trees whole families, poor families, were sprawling; children kicking up their legs; sucking milk; paper bags thrown about, which could easily be picked up (if people objected) by one of those fat gentlemen in livery; for he was of opinion that every park, and every square, during the summer months should be open to children (the grass of the park flushed and faded, lighting up the poor mothers of Westminster and their crawling babies, as if a yellow lamp were moved beneath). But what could be done for female vagrants like that poor creature, stretched on her elbow (as if she had flung herself on the earth, rid of all ties, to observe curiously, to speculate boldly, to consider the whys and the wherefores, impudent, loose-lipped, humorous), he did not know. Bearing his flowers like a weapon, Richard Dalloway approached her; intent he passed her; still there was time for a spark between them—she laughed at the

---

1 Independent retailers who sell fruit, vegetables, fish, etc., in the street from a barrow.

sight of him, he smiled good-humouredly, considering the problem of the female vagrant; not that they would ever speak. But he would tell Clarissa that he loved her, in so many words. He had, once upon a time, been jealous of Peter Walsh; jealous of him and Clarissa. But she had often said to him that she had been right not to marry Peter Walsh; which, knowing Clarissa, was obviously true; she wanted support. Not that she was weak; but she wanted support.

As for Buckingham Palace (like an old prima donna facing the audience all in white) you can't deny it a certain dignity, he considered, nor despise what does, after all, stand to millions of people (a little crowd was waiting at the gate to see the King drive out) for a symbol, absurd though it is; a child with a box of bricks could have done better, he thought; looking at the memorial to Queen Victoria (whom he could remember in her horn spectacles driving through Kensington),[1] its white mound, its billowing motherliness; but he liked being ruled by the descendant of Horsa;[2] he liked continuity; and the sense of handing on the traditions of the past. It was a great age in which to have lived. Indeed, his own life was a miracle; let him make no mistake about it; here he was, in the prime of life, walking to his house in Westminster to tell Clarissa that he loved her. Happiness is this he thought.

It is this, he said, as he entered Dean's Yard. Big Ben was beginning to strike, first the warning, musical; then the hour, irrevocable. Lunch parties waste the entire afternoon, he thought, approaching his door.

The sound of Big Ben flooded Clarissa's drawing-room, where she sat, ever so annoyed, at her writing-table; worried; annoyed. It was perfectly true that she had not asked Ellie Henderson to her party; but she had done it on purpose. Now Mrs. Marsham wrote: "She had told Ellie Henderson she would ask Clarissa—Ellie so much wanted to come."

But why should she invite all the dull women in London to her parties? Why should Mrs. Marsham interfere? And there was Elizabeth closeted all this time with Doris Kilman. Anything more nauseating she could not conceive. Prayer at this hour with that woman. And the sound of the bell flooded the room with its

---

1 A fashionable residential area in central London.

2 In Anglo-Saxon legend, one of two Germanic brothers (the other is Hengist) who led armies conquering the first territories of Britain in the fifth century.

melancholy wave; which receded, and gathered itself together to fall once more, when she heard, distractingly, something fumbling, something scratching at the door. Who at this hour? Three, good Heavens! Three already! For with overpowering directness and dignity the clock struck three; and she heard nothing else; but the door handle slipped round and in came Richard! What a surprise! In came Richard, holding out flowers. She had failed him, once at Constantinople; and Lady Bruton, whose lunch parties were said to be extraordinarily amusing, had not asked her. He was holding out flowers—roses, red and white roses. (But he could not bring himself to say he loved her; not in so many words.)

But how lovely, she said, taking his flowers. She understood; she understood without his speaking; his Clarissa. She put them in vases on the mantelpiece. How lovely they looked! she said. And was it amusing, she asked? Had Lady Bruton asked after her? Peter Walsh was back. Mrs. Marsham had written. Must she ask Ellie Henderson? That woman Kilman was upstairs.

"But let us sit down for five minutes," said Richard.

It all looked so empty. All the chairs were against the wall. What had they been doing? Oh, it was for the party; no, he had not forgotten the party. Peter Walsh was back. Oh yes; she had had him. And he was going to get a divorce; and he was in love with some woman out there. And he hadn't changed in the slightest. There she was, mending her dress....

"Thinking of Bourton," she said.

"Hugh was at lunch," said Richard. She had met him too! Well, he was getting absolutely intolerable. Buying Evelyn necklaces; fatter than ever; an intolerable ass.

"And it came over me, 'I might have married you'," she said, thinking of Peter sitting there in his little bow-tie; with that knife, opening it, shutting it. "Just as he always was, you know."

They were talking about him at lunch, said Richard. (But he could not tell her he loved her. He held her hand. Happiness is this, he thought.) They had been writing a letter to the *Times* for Millicent Bruton. That was about all Hugh was fit for.

"And our dear Miss Kilman?" he asked. Clarissa thought the roses absolutely lovely; first bunched together; now of their own accord starting apart.

"Kilman arrives just as we've done lunch," she said. "Elizabeth turns pink. They shut themselves up. I suppose they're praying."

Lord! He didn't like it; but these things pass over if you let them.

"In a mackintosh with an umbrella," said Clarissa.

He had not said "I love you"; but he held her hand. Happiness is this, is this, he thought.

"But why should I ask all the dull women in London to my parties?" said Clarissa. And if Mrs. Marsham gave a party, did *she* invite her guests?

"Poor Ellie Henderson," said Richard—it was a very odd thing how much Clarissa minded about her parties, he thought.

But Richard had no notion of the look of a room. However—what was he going to say?

If she worried about these parties he would not let her give them. Did she wish she had married Peter? But he must go.

He must be off, he said, getting up. But he stood for a moment as if he were about to say something; and she wondered what? Why? There were the roses.

"Some Committee?" she asked, as he opened the door.

"Armenians," he said; or perhaps it was "Albanians."[1]

And there is a dignity in people; a solitude; even between husband and wife a gulf; and that one must respect, thought Clarissa, watching him open the door; for one would not part with it oneself, or take it, against his will, from one's husband, without losing one's independence, one's self-respect—something, after all, priceless.

He returned with a pillow and a quilt.

"An hour's complete rest after luncheon," he said. And he went.

How like him! He would go on saying "An hour's complete rest after luncheon" to the end of time, because a doctor had ordered it once. It was like him to take what doctors said literally; part of his adorable, divine simplicity, which no one had to the same extent; which made him go and do the thing while she and Peter frittered their time away bickering. He was already halfway

---

1 Richard Dalloway would almost certainly have been serving on a parliamentary committee on the "Armenian Question" as it was called at the time. Trudi Tate argues that Clarissa's confusion of the Armenians and the Albanians is an indication of her complicity with "those who managed the social and economic aspects of the war and kept its victims under control afterwards" (470). As Tate points out, the Armenian people "had been colonized and expelled by various imperial powers since the eleventh century," the most recent massacres occurring during World War I in 1915 (Tate 472-73). The need for an Armenian national home was widely reported in the British press during 1922 and 1923.

to the House of Commons, to his Armenians, his Albanians, having settled her on the sofa, looking at his roses. And people would say, "Clarissa Dalloway is spoilt." She cared much more for her roses than for the Armenians. Hunted out of existence, maimed, frozen, the victims of cruelty and injustice (she had heard Richard say so over and over again)—no, she could feel nothing for the Albanians, or was it the Armenians? but she loved her roses (didn't that help the Armenians?)—the only flowers she could bear to see cut. But Richard was already at the House of Commons; at his Committee, having settled all her difficulties. But no; alas, that was not true. He did not see the reasons against asking Ellie Henderson. She would do it, of course, as he wished it. Since he had brought the pillows, she would lie down.... But—but—why did she suddenly feel, for no reason that she could discover, desperately unhappy? As a person who has dropped some grain of pearl or diamond into the grass and parts the tall blades very carefully, this way and that, and searches here and there vainly, and at last spies it there at the roots, so she went through one thing and another; no, it was not Sally Seton saying that Richard would never be in the Cabinet because he had a second-class brain (it came back to her); no, she did not mind that; nor was it to do with Elizabeth either and Doris Kilman; those were facts. It was a feeling, some unpleasant feeling, earlier in the day perhaps; something that Peter had said, combined with some depression of her own, in her bedroom, taking off her hat; and what Richard had said had added to it, but what had he said? There were his roses. Her parties! That was it! Her parties! Both of them had criticised her very unfairly, laughed at her very unjustly, for her parties. That was it! That was it!

Well, how was she going to defend herself? Now that she knew what it was, she felt perfectly happy. They thought, or Peter at any rate thought, that she enjoyed imposing herself; liked to have famous people about her; great names; was simply a snob in short. Well, Peter might think so. Richard merely thought it foolish of her to like excitement when she knew it was bad for her heart. It was childish, he thought. And both were quite wrong. What she liked was simply life.

"That's what I do it for," she said, speaking aloud, to life.

Since she was lying on the sofa, cloistered, exempt, the presence of this thing which she felt to be so obvious became physically existent; with robes of sound from the street, sunny, with hot breath, whispering, blowing out the blinds. But suppose Peter said to her, "Yes, yes, but your parties—what's the sense of your parties?" all she could say was (and nobody could be expected to understand): They're an offering; which sounded horribly vague. But who was Peter to make out that life was all plain sailing?—Peter always in love, always in love with the wrong woman? What's your love? she might say to him. And she knew his answer; how it is the most important thing in the world and no woman possibly understood it. Very well. But could any man understand what she meant either? about life? She could not imagine Peter or Richard taking the trouble to give a party for no reason whatsoever.

But to go deeper, beneath what people said (and these judgements, how superficial, how fragmentary they are!) in her own mind now, what did it mean to her, this thing she called life? Oh, it was very queer. Here was So-and-so in South Kensington; some one up in Bayswater; and somebody else, say, in Mayfair. And she felt quite continuously a sense of their existence; and she felt what a waste; and she felt what a pity; and she felt if only they could be brought together; so she did it. And it was an offering; to combine, to create; but to whom?

An offering for the sake of offering, perhaps. Anyhow, it was her gift. Nothing else had she of the slightest importance; could not think, write, even play the piano. She muddled Armenians and Turks; loved success; hated discomfort; must be liked; talked oceans of nonsense: and to this day, ask her what the Equator was, and she did not know.

All the same, that one day should follow another; Wednesday, Thursday, Friday, Saturday; that one should wake up in the morning; see the sky; walk in the park; meet Hugh Whitbread; then suddenly in came Peter; then these roses; it was enough. After that, how unbelievable death was!—that it must end; and no one in the whole world would know how she had loved it all; how, every instant ...

The door opened. Elizabeth knew that her mother was resting. She came in very quietly. She stood perfectly still. Was it that some Mongol had been wrecked on the coast of Norfolk (as Mrs. Hilbery said), had mixed with the Dalloway ladies, perhaps a hundred years ago? For the Dalloways, in general, were fair-haired; blue-eyed; Elizabeth, on the contrary, was dark; had Chinese eyes in a pale face; an Oriental mystery; was gentle, considerate, still. As a child, she had had a perfect sense of humour; but now at seventeen, why, Clarissa could not in the least understand, she had become very serious; like a hyacinth sheathed in glossy green, with buds just tinted, a hyacinth which has had no sun.

She stood quite still and looked at her mother; but the door was ajar, and outside the door was Miss Kilman, as Clarissa knew; Miss Kilman in her mackintosh, listening to whatever they said.

Yes, Miss Kilman stood on the landing, and wore a mackintosh; but had her reasons. First, it was cheap; second, she was over forty; and did not, after all, dress to please. She was poor, moreover; degradingly poor. Otherwise she would not be taking jobs from people like the Dalloways; from rich people, who liked to be kind. Mr. Dalloway, to do him justice, had been kind. But Mrs. Dalloway had not. She had been merely condescending. She came from the most worthless of all classes—the rich, with a smattering of culture. They had expensive things everywhere; pictures, carpets, lots of servants. She considered that she had a perfect right to anything that the Dalloways did for her.

She had been cheated. Yes, the word was no exaggeration, for surely a girl has a right to some kind of happiness? And she had never been happy, what with being so clumsy and so poor. And then, just as she might have had a chance at Miss Dolby's school, the war came; and she had never been able to tell lies. Miss Dolby thought she would be happier with people who shared her views about the Germans. She had had to go. It was true that the family name was of German origin; spelt the name Kiehlman in the eighteenth century; but her brother had been killed. They turned her out because she would not pretend that the Germans were all villains—when she had German friends, when the only happy days of her life had been spent in Germany! And after all, she could read history. She had had to take whatever she could get. Mr. Dalloway had come across her working for the Friends.[1] He had allowed her (and that was really generous of him) to teach his daughter history. Also she did a little Extension lecturing[2] and so

---

1 The Quakers, also known as the Religious Society of Friends. It's possible that Miss Kilman was working for the Friends Emergency Committee for the Assistance of Germans, Austrians, and Hungarians in Distress (see Appendix C2).

2 The University Extension Movement in England began at Cambridge University in the late 1860s. The intention was twofold: to connect "the old English universities ... with the growing life of the nation" by teaching adults who were not formally enrolled in a university, and to provide teaching work to "the young men [who] were sent out every year by *alma mater* for whom there was no place in the teaching system of the university itself" (Browning 61). Like Septimus Warren Smith's attendance at Morley College, Miss Kilman's extension lecturing is evidence of Woolf's commitment to the issue of access to higher education.

on. Then Our Lord had come to her (and here she always bowed her head). She had seen the light two years and three months ago. Now she did not envy women like Clarissa Dalloway; she pitied them.

She pitied and despised them from the bottom of her heart, as she stood on the soft carpet, looking at the old engraving of a little girl with a muff. With all this luxury going on, what hope was there for a better state of things? Instead of lying on a sofa—"My mother is resting," Elizabeth had said—she should have been in a factory; behind a counter; Mrs. Dalloway and all the other fine ladies!

Bitter and burning, Miss Kilman had turned into a church two years three months ago. She had heard the Rev. Edward Whittaker preach; the boys sing; had seen the solemn lights descend, and whether it was the music, or the voices (she herself when alone in the evening found comfort in a violin; but the sound was excruciating; she had no ear), the hot and turbulent feelings which boiled and surged in her had been assuaged as she sat there, and she had wept copiously, and gone to call on Mr. Whittaker at his private house in Kensington. It was the hand of God, he said. The Lord had shown her the way. So now, whenever the hot and painful feelings boiled within her, this hatred of Mrs. Dalloway, this grudge against the world, she thought of God. She thought of Mr. Whittaker. Rage was succeeded by calm. A sweet savour filled her veins, her lips parted, and, standing formidable upon the landing in her mackintosh, she looked with steady and sinister serenity at Mrs. Dalloway, who came out with her daughter.

Elizabeth said she had forgotten her gloves. That was because Miss Kilman and her mother hated each other. She could not bear to see them together. She ran upstairs to find her gloves.

But Miss Kilman did not hate Mrs. Dalloway. Turning her large gooseberry-coloured eyes upon Clarissa, observing her small pink face, her delicate body, her air of freshness and fashion, Miss Kilman felt, Fool! Simpleton! You who have known neither sorrow nor pleasure; who have trifled your life away! And there rose in her an overmastering desire to overcome her; to unmask her. If she could have felled her it would have eased her. But it was not the body; it was the soul and its mockery that she wished to subdue; make feel her mastery. If only she could make her weep; could ruin her; humiliate her; bring her to her knees crying, You are right! But this was God's will, not Miss Kilman's. It was to be a religious victory. So she glared; so she glowered.

Clarissa was really shocked. This a Christian—this woman! This woman had taken her daughter from her! She in touch with invisible presences! Heavy, ugly, commonplace, without kindness or grace, she know the meaning of life!

"You are taking Elizabeth to the Stores?" Mrs. Dalloway said.

Miss Kilman said she was. They stood there. Miss Kilman was not going to make herself agreeable. She had always earned her living. Her knowledge of modern history was thorough in the extreme. She did out of her meagre income set aside so much for causes she believed in; whereas this woman did nothing, believed nothing; brought up her daughter—but here was Elizabeth, rather out of breath, the beautiful girl.

So they were going to the Stores. Odd it was, as Miss Kilman stood there (and stand she did, with the power and taciturnity of some prehistoric monster armoured for primeval warfare), how, second by second, the idea of her diminished, how hatred (which was for ideas, not people) crumbled, how she lost her malignity, her size, became second by second merely Miss Kilman, in a mackintosh, whom Heaven knows Clarissa would have liked to help.

At this dwindling of the monster, Clarissa laughed. Saying good-bye, she laughed.

Off they went together, Miss Kilman and Elizabeth, downstairs.

With a sudden impulse, with a violent anguish, for this woman was taking her daughter from her, Clarissa leant over the banisters and cried out, "Remember the party! Remember our party to-night!"

But Elizabeth had already opened the front door; there was a van passing; she did not answer.

Love and religion! thought Clarissa, going back into the drawing-room, tingling all over. How detestable, how detestable they are! For now that the body of Miss Kilman was not before her, it overwhelmed her—the idea. The cruellest things in the world, she thought, seeing them clumsy, hot, domineering, hypocritical, eavesdropping, jealous, infinitely cruel and unscrupulous dressed in a mackintosh coat, on the landing; love and religion. Had she ever tried to convert any one herself? Did she not wish everybody merely to be themselves? And she watched out of the window the old lady opposite climbing upstairs. Let her climb upstairs if she wanted to; let her stop; then let her, as Clarissa had often seen her, gain her bedroom, part her curtains, and disappear again into the background. Somehow one respected that—that old woman looking out of the window, quite unconscious that she was being watched. There was something solemn in it—but love and religion would destroy that, whatever it was, the privacy of the soul. The odious Kilman would destroy it. Yet it was a sight that made her want to cry.

Love destroyed too. Everything that was fine, everything that was true went. Take Peter Walsh now. There was a man, charming, clever, with ideas about everything. If you wanted to know about Pope,[1] say, or Addison,[2] or just to talk nonsense, what people were like, what things meant, Peter knew better than any one. It was Peter who had helped her; Peter who had lent her books. But look at the women he loved—vulgar, trivial, commonplace. Think of Peter in love—he came to see her after all these years, and what did he talk about? Himself. Horrible passion! she thought. Degrading passion! she thought, thinking of Kilman and her Elizabeth walking to the Army and Navy Stores.[3]

Big Ben struck the half-hour.

How extraordinary it was, strange, yes touching to see the old lady (they had been neighbours ever so many years) move away from the window, as if she were attached to that sound, that string. Gigantic as it was, it had something to do with her. Down, down, into the midst of ordinary things the finger fell making the moment solemn. She was forced, so Clarissa imagined, by that sound, to move, to go—but where? Clarissa tried to follow her as she turned and disappeared, and could still just see her white cap moving at the back of the bedroom. She was still there moving about at the other end of the room. Why creeds and prayers and mackintoshes? when, thought Clarissa, that's the miracle, that's the mystery; that old lady, she meant, whom she could see going from chest of drawers to dressing-table. She could still see her. And the supreme mystery which Kilman might say she had solved, or Peter might say he had solved, but Clarissa didn't believe either of them had the ghost of an idea of solving, was

---

1 See p. 49, n. 2.

2 Joseph Addison (1672-1719), English poet, playwright, essayist, and politician.

3 Originally founded in 1872 as a kind of cooperative, with membership "restricted to officers and non-commissioned officers, their families and friends introduced by them, together with officials of various service organizations and clubs" (Abbott 205). By the 1920s, the Army and Navy Stores had evolved to become normal department stores, serving "a loyal but generally unfashionable clientele" (Abbott 205).

simply this: here was one room; there another. Did religion solve that, or love?

Love—but here the other clock, the clock which always struck two minutes after Big Ben, came shuffling in with its lap full of odds and ends, which it dumped down as if Big Ben were all very well with his majesty laying down the law, so solemn, so just, but she must remember all sorts of little things besides—Mrs. Marsham, Ellie Henderson, glasses for ices—all sorts of little things came flooding and lapping and dancing in on the wake of that solemn stroke which lay flat like a bar of gold on the sea. Mrs. Marsham, Ellie Henderson, glasses for ices. She must telephone now at once.

Volubly, troublously, the late clock sounded, coming in on the wake of Big Ben, with its lap full of trifles. Beaten up, broken up by the assault of carriages, the brutality of vans, the eager advance of myriads of angular men, of flaunting women, the domes and spires of offices and hospitals, the last relics of this lap full of odds and ends seemed to break, like the spray of an exhausted wave, upon the body of Miss Kilman standing still in the street for a moment to mutter "It is the flesh."

It was the flesh that she must control. Clarissa Dalloway had insulted her. That she expected. But she had not triumphed; she had not mastered the flesh. Ugly, clumsy, Clarissa Dalloway had laughed at her for being that; and had revived the fleshly desires, for she minded looking as she did beside Clarissa. Nor could she talk as she did. But why wish to resemble her? Why? She despised Mrs. Dalloway from the bottom of her heart. She was not serious. She was not good. Her life was a tissue of vanity and deceit. Yet Doris Kilman had been overcome. She had, as a matter of fact, very nearly burst into tears when Clarissa Dalloway laughed at her. "It is the flesh, it is the flesh," she muttered (it being her habit to talk aloud), trying to subdue this turbulent and painful feeling as she walked down Victoria Street. She prayed to God. She could not help being ugly; she could not afford to buy pretty clothes. Clarissa Dalloway had laughed—but she would concentrate her mind upon something else until she had reached the pillar-box.[1] At any rate she had got Elizabeth. But she would think of something else; she would think of Russia; until she reached the pillar-box.

How nice it must be, she said, in the country, struggling, as Mr. Whittaker had told her, with that violent grudge against the

---

1 A mailbox shaped like a pillar.

world which had scorned her, sneered at her, cast her off, beginning with this indignity—the infliction of her unlovable body which people could not bear to see. Do her hair as she might, her forehead remained like an egg, bald, white. No clothes suited her. She might buy anything. And for a woman, of course, that meant never meeting the opposite sex. Never would she come first with any one. Sometimes lately it had seemed to her that, except for Elizabeth, her food was all that she lived for; her comforts; her dinner, her tea; her hot-water bottle at night. But one must fight; vanquish; have faith in God. Mr. Whittaker had said she was there for a purpose. But no one knew the agony! He said, pointing to the crucifix, that God knew. But why should she have to suffer when other women, like Clarissa Dalloway, escaped? Knowledge comes through suffering, said Mr. Whittaker.

She had passed the pillar-box, and Elizabeth had turned into the cool brown tobacco department of the Army and Navy Stores while she was still muttering to herself what Mr. Whittaker had said about knowledge coming through suffering and the flesh. "The flesh," she muttered.

What department did she want? Elizabeth interrupted her.

"Petticoats," she said abruptly, and stalked straight on to the lift.

Up they went. Elizabeth guided her this way and that; guided her in her abstraction as if she had been a great child, an unwieldy battleship. There were the petticoats, brown, decorous, striped, frivolous, solid, flimsy; and she chose, in her abstraction, portentously, and the girl serving thought her mad.

Elizabeth rather wondered, as they did up the parcel, what Miss Kilman was thinking. They must have their tea, said Miss Kilman, rousing, collecting herself. They had their tea.

Elizabeth rather wondered whether Miss Kilman could be hungry. It was her way of eating, eating with intensity, then looking, again and again, at a plate of sugared cakes on the table next them; then, when a lady and a child sat down and the child took the cake, could Miss Kilman really mind it? Yes, Miss Kilman did mind it. She had wanted that cake—the pink one. The pleasure of eating was almost the only pure pleasure left her, and then to be baffled even in that!

When people are unhappy they have a reserve, she had told Elizabeth, upon which to draw, whereas she was like a wheel without a tyre (she was fond of such metaphors), jolted by every pebble—so she would say staying on after the lesson, standing by the fire-place with her bag of books, her "satchel," she called it, on a Tuesday morning, after the lesson was over. And she talked too about the war. After all, there were people who did not think the English invariably right. There were books. There were meetings. There were other points of view. Would Elizabeth like to come with her to listen to So-and-so? (a most extraordinary-looking old man). Then Miss Kilman took her to some church in Kensington and they had tea with a clergyman. She had lent her books. Law, medicine, politics, all professions are open to women of your generation, said Miss Kilman.[1] But for herself, her career was absolutely ruined, and was it her fault? Good gracious, said Elizabeth, no.

And her mother would come calling to say that a hamper had come from Bourton and would Miss Kilman like some flowers? To Miss Kilman she was always very, very nice, but Miss Kilman squashed the flowers all in a bunch, and hadn't any small talk, and what interested Miss Kilman bored her mother, and Miss Kilman and she were terrible together; and Miss Kilman swelled and looked very plain, but Miss Kilman was frightfully clever. Elizabeth had never thought about the poor. They lived with everything they wanted,—her mother had breakfast in bed every day; Lucy carried it up; and she liked old women because they were Duchesses, and being descended from some Lord. But Miss Kilman said (one of those Tuesday mornings when the lesson was over), "My grandfather kept an oil and colour shop in Kensington." Miss Kilman was quite different from any one she knew; she made one feel so small.

Miss Kilman took another cup of tea. Elizabeth, with her oriental bearing, her inscrutable mystery, sat perfectly upright; no, she did not want anything more. She looked for her gloves—her white gloves. They were under the table. Ah, but she must not go! Miss Kilman could not let her go! this youth, that was so beautiful; this girl, whom she genuinely loved! Her large hand opened and shut on the table.

But perhaps it was a little flat somehow, Elizabeth felt. And really she would like to go.

But said Miss Kilman, "I've not quite finished yet."

Of course, then, Elizabeth would wait. But it was rather stuffy in here.

---

1 The Sex Disqualification (Removal) Act, which made it illegal to bar women from participation in the professions (e.g., law, the civil service), was passed in 1919. It did, however, allow universities to decide for themselves whether they would admit women. (See Appendix E3.)

"Are you going to the party to-night?" Miss Kilman said. Elizabeth supposed she was going; her mother wanted her to go. She must not let parties absorb her, Miss Kilman said, fingering the last two inches of a chocolate éclair.

She did not much like parties, Elizabeth said. Miss Kilman opened her mouth, slightly projected her chin, and swallowed down the last inches of the chocolate éclair, then wiped her fingers, and washed the tea round in her cup.

She was about to split asunder, she felt. The agony was so terrific. If she could grasp her, if she could clasp her, if she could make her hers absolutely and for ever and then die; that was all she wanted. But to sit here, unable to think of anything to say; to see Elizabeth turning against her; to be felt repulsive even by her—it was too much; she could not stand it. The thick fingers curled inwards.

"I never go to parties," said Miss Kilman, just to keep Elizabeth from going. "People don't ask me to parties"—and she knew as she said it that it was this egotism that was her undoing; Mr. Whittaker had warned her; but she could not help it. She had suffered so horribly. "Why should they ask me?" she said. "I'm plain, I'm unhappy." She knew it was idiotic. But it was all those people passing—people with parcels who despised her—who made her say it. However, she was Doris Kilman. She had her degree. She was a woman who had made her way in the world. Her knowledge of modern history was more than respectable.

"I don't pity myself," she said. "I pity"—she meant to say "your mother," but no, she could not, not to Elizabeth. "I pity other people much more."

Like some dumb creature who has been brought up to a gate for an unknown purpose, and stands there longing to gallop away, Elizabeth Dalloway sat silent. Was Miss Kilman going to say anything more?

"Don't quite forget me," said Doris Kilman; her voice quivered. Right away to the end of the field the dumb creature galloped in terror.

The great hand opened and shut.

Elizabeth turned her head. The waitress came. One had to pay at the desk, Elizabeth said, and went off, drawing out, so Miss Kilman felt, the very entrails in her body, stretching them as she crossed the room, and then, with a final twist, bowing her head very politely, she went.

She had gone. Miss Kilman sat at the marble tale among the éclairs, stricken once, twice, thrice by shocks of suffering. She had gone. Mrs. Dalloway had triumphed. Elizabeth had gone. Beauty had gone; youth had gone.

So she sat. She got up, blundered off among the little tables, rocking slightly from side to side, and somebody came after her with her petticoat, and she lost her way, and was hemmed in by trunks specially prepared for taking to India; next got among the accouchement sets and baby linen; through all the commodities of the world, perishable and permanent, hams, drugs, flowers, stationery, variously smelling, now sweet, now sour, she lurched; saw herself thus lurching with her hat askew, very red in the face, full length in a looking-glass; and at last came out into the street.

The tower of Westminster Cathedral[1] rose in front of her, the habitation of God. In the midst of the traffic, there was the habitation of God. Doggedly she set off with her parcel to that other sanctuary, the Abbey,[2] where, raising her hands in a tent before her face, she sat beside those driven into shelter too; the variously assorted worshippers, now divested of social rank, almost of sex, as they raised their hands before their faces; but once they removed them, instantly reverent, middle-class, English men and women, some of them desirous of seeing the wax works.[3]

But Miss Kilman held her tent before her face. Now she was deserted; now rejoined. New worshippers came in from the street to replace the strollers, and still, as people gazed round and shuffled past the tomb of the Unknown Warrior,[4] still she barred her eyes with her fingers and tried in this double darkness, for the light in the Abbey was bodiless, to aspire above the vanities, the desires, the commodities, to rid herself both of hatred and of love. Her hands twitched. She seemed to struggle. Yet to others God was accessible and the path to Him smooth. Mr. Fletcher,

---

1 A Roman Catholic cathedral, the largest Catholic church in England and Wales.

2 The Collegiate Church of St. Peter at Westminster, popularly known as Westminster Abbey, the traditional site of coronation and burial for British monarchs.

3 The funeral effigies contained in the Abbey's museum. These include effigies of Edward III, Henry VII, Charles II, William III, Prime Minister William Pitt, and Horatio Nelson.

4 Located in the west end of the nave of Westminster Abbey, it contains the body of an unidentified British soldier killed in battle during World War I. The body was repatriated from France and interred on 11 November 1920.

retired, of the Treasury, Mrs. Gorham, widow of the famous K.C.,[1] approached Him simply, and having done their praying, leant back, enjoyed the music (the organ pealed sweetly), and saw Miss Kilman at the end of the row, praying, praying, and, being still on the threshold of their underworld, thought of her sympathetically as a soul haunting the same territory; a soul cut out of immaterial substance; not a woman, a soul.

But Mr. Fletcher had to go. He had to pass her, and being himself neat as a new pin, could not help being a little distressed by the poor lady's disorder; her hair down; her parcel on the floor. She did not at once let him pass. But, as he stood gazing about him, at the white marbles, grey window panes, and accumulated treasures (for he was extremely proud of the Abbey), her largeness, robustness, and power as she sat there shifting her knees from time to time (it was so rough the approach to her God—so tough her desires) impressed him, as they had impressed Mrs. Dalloway (she could not get the thought of her out of her mind that afternoon), the Rev. Edward Whittaker, and Elizabeth too.

And Elizabeth waited in Victoria Street for an omnibus. It was so nice to be out of doors. She thought perhaps she need not go home just yet. It was so nice to be out in the air. So she would get on to an omnibus. And already, even as she stood there, in her very well-cut clothes, it was beginning.... People were beginning to compare her to poplar trees, early dawn, hyacinths, fawns, running water, and garden lilies; and it made her life a burden to her, for she so much preferred being left alone to do what she liked in the country, but they would compare her to lilies, and she had to go to parties, and London was so dreary compared to being alone in the country with her father and the dogs.

Buses swooped, settled, were off—garish caravans, glistening with red and yellow varnish. But which should she get on to? She had no preferences. Of course, she would not push her way. She inclined to be passive. It was expression she needed, but her eyes were fine, Chinese, oriental, and, as her mother said, with such nice shoulders and holding herself so straight, she was always charming to look at; and lately, in the evening especially, when

---

1 The designation King's Counsel (or Queen's Counsel during the reign of a female monarch), an honour accorded to distinguished lawyers on the recommendation of the Lord Chancellor.

she was interested, for she never seemed excited, she looked almost beautiful, very stately, very serene. What could she be thinking? Every man fell in love with her, and she was really awfully bored. For it was beginning. Her mother could see that—the compliments were beginning. That she did not care more about it—for instance for her clothes—sometimes worried Clarissa, but perhaps it was as well with all those puppies and guinea pigs about having distemper, and it gave her a charm. And now there was this odd friendship with Miss Kilman. Well, thought Clarissa about three o'clock in the morning, reading Baron Marbot for she could not sleep, it proves she has a heart.

Suddenly Elizabeth stepped forward and most competently boarded the omnibus, in front of everybody. She took a seat on top. The impetuous creature—a pirate—started forward, sprang away; she had to hold the rail to steady herself, for a pirate it was, reckless, unscrupulous, bearing down ruthlessly, circumventing dangerously, boldly snatching a passenger, or ignoring a passenger, squeezing eel-like and arrogant in between, and then rushing insolently all sails spread up Whitehall. And did Elizabeth give one thought to poor Miss Kilman who loved her without jealousy, to whom she had been a fawn in the open, a moon in a glade? She was delighted to be free. The fresh air was so delicious. It had been so stuffy in the Army and Navy Stores. And now it was like riding, to be rushing up Whitehall; and to each movement of the omnibus the beautiful body in the fawn-coloured coat responded freely like a rider, like the figure-head of a ship, for the breeze slightly disarrayed her; the heat gave her cheeks the pallor of white painted wood; and her fine eyes, having no eyes to meet, gazed ahead, blank, bright, with the staring incredible innocence of sculpture.

It was always talking about her own sufferings that made Miss Kilman so difficult. And was she right? If it was being on committees and giving up hours and hours every day (she hardly ever saw him in London) that helped the poor, her father did that, goodness knows—if that was what Miss Kilman meant about being a Christian; but it was so difficult to say. Oh, she would like to go a little farther. Another penny was it to the Strand? Here was another penny, then. She would go up to the Strand.

She liked people who were ill. And every profession is open to women of your generation, said Miss Kilman. So she might be a doctor. She might be a farmer. Animals are often ill. She might own a thousand acres and have people under her. She would go and see them in their cottages. This was Somerset House.[1] One might be a very good farmer—and that, strangely enough, though Miss Kilman had her share in it, was almost entirely due to Somerset House. It looked so splendid, so serious, that great grey building. And she liked the feeling of people working. She liked those churches, like shapes of grey paper, breasting the stream of the Strand. It was quite different here from Westminster, she thought, getting off at Chancery Lane.[2] It was so serious; it was so busy. In short, she would like to have a profession. She would become a doctor, a farmer, possibly go into Parliament if she found it necessary, all because of the Strand.

The feet of those people busy about their activities, hands putting stone to stone, minds eternally occupied not with trivial chatterings (comparing women to poplars—which was rather exciting, of course, but very silly), but with thoughts of ships, of business, of law, of administration, and with it all so stately (she was in the Temple),[3] gay (there was the river), pious (there was the Church),[4] made her quite determined, whatever her mother might say, to become either a farmer or a doctor. But she was, of course, rather lazy.

And it was much better to say nothing about it. It seemed so silly. It was the sort of thing that did sometimes happen, when one was alone—buildings without architects' names, crowds of people coming back from the city having more power than single clergymen in Kensington, than any of the books Miss Kilman had lent her, to stimulate what lay slumbrous, clumsy, and shy on the mind's sandy floor, to break surface, as a child suddenly stretches its arms; it was just that, perhaps, a sigh, a stretch of the arms, an impulse, a revelation, which has its effects for ever, and then down again it went to the sandy floor. She must go home.

---

1 Located in the Strand, the first Renaissance palace in England, later the home of the Royal Academy (1771-1836), the Royal Society (1780-1857), and the Board of Inland Revenue (1849). In 1923 it contained the offices of the General Register of Births, Deaths, and Marriages. See *LE*.

2 Associated primarily with the legal profession.

3 An area of central London associated primarily with the law. Two of the four Inns of Court, the Inner and Middle Temple, are located here.

4 Temple Church, the church of the Inner and Middle Temple, built in the late twelfth century by the Knights Templar.

She must dress for dinner. But what was the time?—where was a clock?

She looked up Fleet Street.[1] She walked just a little way towards St. Paul's, shyly, like some one penetrating on tiptoe, exploring a strange house by night with a candle, on edge lest the owner should suddenly fling wide his bedroom door and ask her business, nor did she dare wander off into queer alleys, tempting by-streets, any more than in a strange house open doors which might be bedroom doors, or sitting-room doors, or lead straight to the larder. For no Dalloways came down the Strand daily; she was a pioneer, a stray, venturing, trusting.

In many ways, her mother felt, she was extremely immature, like a child still, attached to dolls, to old slippers; a perfect baby; and that was charming. But then, of course, there was in the Dalloway family the tradition of public service. Abbesses, principals, head mistresses, dignitaries, in the republic of women—without being brilliant, any of them, they were that. She penetrated a little farther in the direction of St. Paul's. She liked the geniality, sisterhood, motherhood, brotherhood of this uproar. It seemed to her good. The noise was tremendous; and suddenly there were trumpets (the unemployed) blaring, rattling about in the uproar; military music; as if people were marching; yet had they been dying—had some woman breathed her last, and whoever was watching, opening the window of the room where she had just brought off that act of supreme dignity, looked down on Fleet Street, that uproar, that military music would have come triumphing up to him, consolatory, indifferent.

It was not conscious. There was no recognition in it of one's fortune, or fate, and for that very reason even to those dazed with watching for the last shivers of consciousness on the faces of the dying, consoling.

Forgetfulness in people might wound, their ingratitude corrode, but this voice, pouring endlessly, year in year out, would take whatever it might be; this vow; this van; this life; this procession, would wrap them all about and carry them on, as in the rough stream of a glacier the ice holds a splinter of bone, a blue petal, some oak trees, and rolls them on.

But it was later than she thought. Her mother would not like her to be wandering off alone like this. She turned back down the Strand.

---

1 Associated primarily with printing, publishing, and especially journalism.

A puff of wind (in spite of the heat, there was quite a wind) blew a thin black veil over the sun and over the Strand. The faces faded; the omnibuses suddenly lost their glow. For although the clouds were of mountainous white so that one could fancy hacking hard chips off with a hatchet, with broad golden slopes, lawns of celestial pleasure gardens, on their flanks, and had all the appearance of settled habitations assembled for the conference of gods above the world, there was a perpetual movement among them. Signs were interchanged, when, as if to fulfil some scheme arranged already, now a summit dwindled, now a whole block of pyramidal size which had kept its station inalterably advanced into the midst or gravely led the procession to fresh anchorage. Fixed though they seemed at their posts, at rest in perfect unanimity, nothing could be fresher, freer, more sensitive superficially than the snow-white or gold-kindled surface; to change, to go, to dismantle the solemn assemblage was immediately possible; and in spite of the grave fixity, the accumulated robustness and solidity, now they struck light to the earth, now darkness.

Calmly and competently, Elizabeth Dalloway mounted the Westminster omnibus.

Going and coming, beckoning, signalling, so the light and shadow, which now made the wall grey, now the bananas bright yellow, now made the Strand grey, now made the omnibuses bright yellow, seemed to Septimus Warren Smith lying on the sofa in the sitting-room; watching the watery gold glow and fade with the astonishing sensibility of some live creature on the roses, on the wall-paper. Outside the trees dragged their leaves like nets through the depths of the air; the sound of water was in the room, and through the waves came the voices of birds singing. Every power poured its treasures on his head, and his hand lay there on the back of the sofa, as he had seen his hand lie when he was bathing, floating, on the top of the waves, while far away on shore he heard dogs barking and barking far away. Fear no more, says the heart in the body; fear no more.

He was not afraid. At every moment Nature signified by some laughing hint like that gold spot which went round the wall—there, there, there—her determination to show, by brandishing her plumes, shaking her tresses, flinging her mantle this way and that, beautifully, always beautifully, and standing close up to breathe through her hollowed hands Shakespeare's words, her meaning.

Rezia, sitting at the table twisting a hat in her hands, watched him; saw him smiling. He was happy then. But she could not bear to see him smiling. It was not marriage; it was not being one's husband to look strange like that, always to be starting, laughing, sitting hour after hour silent, or clutching her and telling her to write. The table drawer was full of those writings; about war; about Shakespeare; about great discoveries; how there is no death. Lately he had become excited suddenly for no reason (and both Dr. Holmes and Sir William Bradshaw said excitement was the worst thing for him), and waved his hands and cried out that he knew the truth! He knew everything! That man, his friend who was killed, Evans, had come, he said. He was singing behind the screen. She wrote it down just as he spoke it. Some things were very beautiful; others sheer nonsense. And he was always stopping in the middle, changing his mind; wanting to add something; hearing something new; listening with his hand up. But she heard nothing.

And once they found the girl who did the room reading one of these papers in fits of laughter. It was a dreadful pity. For that made Septimus cry out about human cruelty—how they tear each other to pieces. The fallen, he said, they tear to pieces. "Holmes is on us," he would say, and he would invent stories about Holmes; Holmes eating porridge; Holmes reading Shakespeare—making himself roar with laughter or rage, for Dr. Holmes seemed to stand for something horrible to him. "Human nature," he called him. Then there were the visions. He was drowned, he used to say, and lying on a cliff with the gulls screaming over him. He would look over the edge of the sofa down into the sea. Or he was hearing music. Really it was only a barrel organ or some man crying in the street. But "Lovely!" he used to cry, and the tears would run down his cheeks, which was to her the most dreadful thing of all, to see a man like Septimus, who had fought, who was brave, crying. And he would lie listening until suddenly he would cry that he was falling down, down into the flames! Actually she would look for flames, it was so vivid. But there was nothing. They were alone in the room. It was a dream, she would tell him, and so quiet him at last, but sometimes she was frightened too. She sighed as she sat sewing.

Her sigh was tender and enchanting, like the wind outside a wood in the evening. Now she put down her scissors; now she turned to take something from the table. A little stir, a little crinkling, a little tapping built up something on the table there, where she sat sewing. Through his eyelashes he could see her blurred outline; her little black body; her face and hands; her turning movements at the table, as she took up a reel, or looked (she was apt to lose things) for her silk. She was making a hat for Mrs. Filmer's married daughter, whose name was—he had forgotten her name.

"What is the name of Mrs. Filmer's married daughter?" he asked.

"Mrs. Peters," said Rezia. She was afraid it was too small, she said, holding it before her. Mrs. Peters was a big woman; but she did not like her. It was only because Mrs. Filmer had been so good to them—"She gave me grapes this morning," she said—that Rezia wanted to do something to show that they were grateful. She had come into the room the other evening and found Mrs. Peters, who thought they were out, playing the gramophone.

"Was it true?" he asked. She was playing the gramophone? Yes; she had told him about it at the time; she had found Mrs. Peters playing the gramophone.

He began, very cautiously, to open his eyes, to see whether a gramophone was really there. But real things—real things were too exciting. He must be cautious. He would not go mad. First he looked at the fashion papers on the lower shelf, then gradually at the gramophone with the green trumpet. Nothing could be more exact. And so, gathering courage, he looked at the sideboard; the plate of bananas; the engraving of Queen Victoria and the Prince Consort;[1] at the mantelpiece, with the jar of roses. None of these things moved. All were still; all were real.

"She is a woman with a spiteful tongue," said Rezia.

"What does Mr. Peters do?" Septimus asked.

"Ah," said Rezia, trying to remember. She thought Mrs. Filmer had said that he travelled for some company. "Just now he is in Hull," she said.

"Just now!" She said that with her Italian accent. She said that herself. He shaded his eyes so that he might see only a little of her face at a time, first the chin, then the nose, then the forehead, in case it were deformed, or had some terrible mark on it. But no, there she was, perfectly natural, sewing, with the pursed lips that women have, the set, the melancholy expression, when sewing. But there was nothing terrible about it, he assured himself, looking a second time, a third time at her face, her hands, for what was frightening or disgusting in her as she sat there in broad daylight, sewing? Mrs. Peters had a spiteful tongue. Mr. Peters was

---

1 Prince Albert of Saxe-Coburg and Gotha (1819-61), the husband of Queen Victoria.

in Hull. Why then rage and prophesy? Why fly scourged and outcast? Why be made to tremble and sob by the clouds? Why seek truths and deliver messages when Rezia sat sticking pins into the front of her dress, and Mr. Peters was in Hull? Miracles, revelations, agonies, loneliness, falling through the sea, down, down into the flames, all were burnt out, for he had a sense, as he watched Rezia trimming the straw hat for Mrs. Peters, of a coverlet of flowers.

"It's too small for Mrs. Peters," said Septimus.

For the first time for days he was speaking as he used to do! Of course it was—absurdly small, she said. But Mrs. Peters had chosen it.

He took it out of her hands. He said it was an organ grinder's monkey's hat.

How it rejoiced her that! Not for weeks had they laughed like this together, poking fun privately like married people. What she meant was that if Mrs. Filmer had come in, or Mrs. Peters or anybody, they would not have understood what she and Septimus were laughing at.

"There," she said, pinning a rose to one side of the hat. Never had she felt so happy! Never in her life!

But that was still more ridiculous, Septimus said. Now the poor woman looked like a pig at a fair. (Nobody ever made her laugh as Septimus did.)

What had she got in her work-box? She had ribbons and beads, tassels, artificial flowers. She tumbled them out on the table. He began putting odd colours together—for though he had no fingers, could not even do up a parcel, he had a wonderful eye, and often he was right, sometimes absurd, of course, but sometimes wonderfully right.

"She shall have a beautiful hat!" he murmured, taking up this and that, Rezia kneeling by his side, looking over his shoulder. Now it was finished—that is to say the design; she must stitch it together. But she must be very, very careful, he said, to keep it just as he had made it.

So she sewed. When she sewed, he thought, she made a sound like a kettle on the hob; bubbling, murmuring, always busy, her strong little pointed fingers pinching and poking; her needle flashing straight. The sun might go in and out, on the tassels, on the wall-paper, but he would wait, he thought, stretching out his feet, looking at his ringed sock at the end of the sofa; he would wait in this warm place, this pocket of still air, which ones comes on at the edge of a wood sometimes in the evening, when, because of a fall in the ground, or some arrangement of the trees (one must be scientific above all, scientific), warmth lingers, and the air buffets the cheek like the wing of a bird.

"There it is," said Rezia, twirling Mrs. Peters' hat on the tips of her fingers. "That'll do for the moment. Later ..." her sentence bubbled away drip, drip, drip, like a contented tap left running.

It was wonderful. Never had he done anything which made him feel so proud. It was so real, it was so substantial, Mrs. Peters' hat.

"Just look at it," he said.

Yes, it would always make her happy to see that hat. He had become himself then, he had laughed then. They had been alone together. Always she would like that hat.

He told her to try it on.

"But I must look so queer!" she cried, running over to the glass and looking first this side, then that. Then she snatched it off again, for there was a tap at the door. Could it be Sir William Bradshaw? Had he sent already?

No! it was only the small girl with the evening paper.

What always happened, then happened—what happened every night of their lives. The small girl sucked her thumb at the door; Rezia went down on her knees; Rezia cooed and kissed; Rezia got a bag of sweets out of the table drawer. For so it always happened. First one thing, then another. So she built it up, first one thing and then another. Dancing, skipping, round and round the room they went. He took the paper. Surrey was all out, he read.[1] There was a heat wave. Rezia repeated: Surrey was all out. There was a heat wave, making it part of the game she was playing with Mrs. Filmer's grandchild, both of them laughing, chattering at the same time, at their game. He was very tired. He was very happy. He would sleep. He shut his eyes. But directly he saw nothing the sounds of the game became fainter and stranger and sounded like the cries of people seeking and not finding, and passing farther and farther away. They had lost him!

He started up in terror. What did he see? The plate of bananas on the sideboard. Nobody was there (Rezia had taken the child to its mother; it was bedtime). That was it: to be alone for ever. That was the doom pronounced in Milan when he came into the

---

1 A newspaper story indicating that the Surrey cricket team is out because ten of its eleven batsmen have been dismissed. On the significance of cricket in *Mrs. Dalloway* see Bateman 83-84.

room and saw them cutting out buckram shapes with their scissors; to be alone for ever.

He was alone with the sideboard and the bananas. He was alone, exposed on this bleak eminence, stretched out—but not on a hill-top; not on a crag; on Mrs. Filmer's sitting-room sofa. As for the visions, the faces, the voices of the dead, where were they? There was a screen in front of him, with black bulrushes and blue swallows. Where he had once seen mountains, where he had seen faces, where he had seen beauty, there was a screen.

"Evans!" he cried. There was no answer. A mouse had squeaked, or a curtain rustled. Those were the voices of the dead. The screen, the coal-scuttle, the sideboard remained him. Let him then face the screen, the coal-scuttle and the sideboard ... but Rezia burst into the room chattering.

Some letter had come. Everybody's plans were changed. Mrs. Filmer would not be able to go to Brighton[1] after all. There was no time to let Mrs. Williams know, and really Rezia thought it very, very annoying, when she caught sight of the hat and thought ... perhaps ... she ... might just make a little.... Her voice died out in contented melody.

"Ah, damn!" she cried (it was a joke of theirs, her swearing); the needle had broken. Hat, child, Brighton, needle. She built it up; first one thing, then another, she built it up, sewing.

She wanted him to say whether by moving the rose she had improved the hat. She sat on the end of the sofa.

They were perfectly happy now, she said suddenly, putting the hat down. For she could say anything to him now. She could say whatever came into her head. That was almost the first thing she had felt about him, that night in the café when he had come in with his English friends. He had come in, rather shyly, looking round him, and his hat had fallen when he hung it up. That she could remember. She knew he was English, though not one of the large Englishmen her sister admired, for he was always thin; but he had a beautiful fresh colour; and with his big nose, his bright eyes, his way of sitting a little hunched, made her think, she had often told him, of a young hawk, that first evening she saw him, when they were playing dominoes, and he had come in—of a young hawk; but with her he was always very gentle. She had never seen him wild or drunk, only suffering sometimes through this terrible war, but even so, when she came in, he would put it all away. Anything, anything in the whole world, any little bother

1 Popular seaside resort town in southeast England.

with her work, anything that struck her to say she would tell him, and he understood at once. Her own family even were not the same. Being older than she was and being so clever—how serious he was, wanting her to read Shakespeare before she could even read a child's story in English!—being so much more experienced, he could help her. And she, too, could help him.

But this hat now. And then (it was getting late) Sir William Bradshaw.

She held her hands to her head, waiting for him to say did he like the hat or not, and as she sat there, waiting, looking down, he could feel her mind, like a bird, falling from branch to branch, and always alighting, quite rightly; he could follow her mind, as she sat there in one of those loose lax poses that came to her naturally, and, if he should say anything, at once she smiled, like a bird alighting with all its claws firm upon the bough.

But he remembered. Bradshaw said, "The people we are most fond of are not good for us when we are ill." Bradshaw said he must be taught to rest. Bradshaw said they must be separated.

"Must," "must," why "must"? What power had Bradshaw over him? "What right has Bradshaw to say 'must' to me?" he demanded.

"It is because you talked of killing yourself," said Rezia. (Mercifully, she could now say anything to Septimus.)

So he was in their power! Holmes and Bradshaw were on him! The brute with the red nostrils was snuffing into every secret place! "Must" it could say! Where were his papers? the things he had written?

She brought him his papers, the things he had written, things she had written for him. She tumbled them out on to the sofa. They looked at them together. Diagrams, designs, little men and women brandishing sticks for arms, with wings—were they?—on their backs; circles traced round shillings and sixpences—the suns and stars; zigzagging precipices with mountaineers ascending roped together, exactly like knives and forks; sea pieces with little faces laughing out of what might perhaps be waves: the map of the world. Burn them! he cried. Now for his writings; how the dead sing behind rhododendron bushes; odes to Time; conversations with Shakespeare; Evans, Evans, Evans—his messages from the dead; do not cut down trees; tell the Prime Minister. Universal love: the meaning of the world. Burn them! he cried.

But Rezia laid her hands on them. Some were very beautiful, she thought. She would tie them up (for she had no envelope) with a piece of silk.

Even if they took him, she said, she would go with him. They could not separate them against their wills, she said.

Shuffling the edges straight, she did up the papers, and tied the parcel almost without looking, sitting close, sitting beside him, he thought, as if all her petals were about her. She was a flowering tree; and through her branches looked out the face of a lawgiver, who had reached a sanctuary where she feared no one; not Holmes; not Bradshaw; a miracle, a triumph, the last and greatest. Staggering he saw her mount the appalling staircase, laden with Holmes and Bradshaw, men who never weighed less than eleven stone six, who sent their wives to court, men who made ten thousand a year and talked of proportion; who differed in their verdicts (for Holmes said one thing, Bradshaw another), yet judges they were; who mixed the vision and the sideboard; saw nothing clear, yet ruled, yet inflicted. Over them she triumphed.

"There!" she said. The papers were tied up. No one should get at them. She would put them away.

And, she said, nothing should separate them. She sat down beside him and called him by the name of that hawk or crow which being malicious and a great destroyer of crops was precisely like him. No one could separate them, she said.

Then she got up to go into the bedroom to pack their things, but hearing voices downstairs and thinking that Dr. Holmes had perhaps called, ran down to prevent him coming up.

Septimus could hear her talking to Holmes on the staircase.

"My dear lady, I have come as a friend," Holmes was saying.

"No. I will not allow you to see my husband," she said.

He could see her, like a little hen, with her wings spread barring his passage. But Holmes persevered.

"My dear lady, allow me ..." Holmes said, putting her aside (Holmes was a powerfully built man).

Holmes was coming upstairs. Holmes would burst open the door. Holmes would say, "In a funk, eh?" Holmes would get him. But no; not Holmes; not Bradshaw. Getting up rather unsteadily, hopping indeed from foot to foot, he considered Mrs. Filmer's nice clean bread-knife with "Bread" carved on the handle. Ah, but one mustn't spoil that. The gas fire? But it was too late now. Holmes was coming. Razors he might have got, but Rezia, who always did that sort of thing, had packed them. There remained only the window, the large Bloomsbury lodging-house window; the tiresome, the troublesome, and rather melodramatic business of opening the window and throwing himself out. It was their idea of tragedy, not his or Rezia's (for she was with him). Holmes and Bradshaw like that sort of thing. (He sat on the sill.) But he would wait till the very last moment. He did not want to die. Life was good. The sun hot. Only human beings? Coming down the staircase opposite an old man stopped and stared at him. Holmes was at the door. "I'll give it you!" he cried, and flung himself vigorously, violently down on to Mrs. Filmer's area railings.

"The coward!" cried Dr. Holmes, bursting the door open. Rezia ran to the window, she saw; she understood. Dr. Holmes and Mrs. Filmer collided with each other. Mrs. Filmer flapped her apron and made her hide her eyes in the bedroom. There was a great deal of running up and down stairs. Dr. Holmes came in—white as a sheet, shaking all over, with a glass in his hand. She must be brave and drink something, he said (What was it? Something sweet), for her husband was horribly mangled, would not recover consciousness, she must not see him, must be spared as much as possible, would have the inquest to go through, poor young woman. Who could have foretold it? A sudden impulse, no one was in the least to blame (he told Mrs. Filmer). And why the devil he did it, Dr. Holmes could not conceive.

It seemed to her as she drank the sweet stuff that she was opening long windows, stepping out into some garden. But where? The clock was striking—one, two, three: how sensible the sound was; compared with all this thumping and whispering; like Septimus himself. She was falling asleep. But the clock went on striking, four, five, six and Mrs. Filmer waving her apron (they wouldn't bring the body in here, would they?) seemed part of that garden; or a flag. She had once seen a flag slowly rippling out from a mast when she stayed with her aunt at Venice. Men killed in battle were thus saluted, and Septimus had been through the War. Of her memories, most were happy.

She put on her hat, and ran through cornfields—where could it have been?—on to some hill, somewhere near the sea, for there were ships, gulls, butterflies; they sat on a cliff. In London, too, there they sat, and, half dreaming, came to her through the bedroom door, rain falling, whisperings, stirrings among dry corn, the caress of the sea, as it seemed to her, hollowing them in its arched shell and murmuring to her laid on shore, strewn she felt, like flying flowers over some tomb.

"He is dead," she said, smiling at the poor old woman who guarded her with her honest light-blue eyes fixed on the door. (They wouldn't bring him in here, would they?) But Mrs. Filmer pooh-poohed. Oh no, oh no! They were carrying him away now.

Ought she not to be told? Married people ought to be together, Mrs. Filmer thought. But they must do as the doctor said.

"Let her sleep," said Dr. Holmes, feeling her pulse. She saw the large outline of his body dark against the window. So that was Dr. Holmes.

One of the triumphs of civilisation, Peter Walsh thought. It is one of the triumphs of civilisation, as the light high bell of the ambulance sounded. Swiftly, cleanly, the ambulance sped to the hospital, having picked up instantly, humanely, some poor devil; some one hit on the head, struck down by disease, knocked over perhaps a minute or so ago at one of these crossings, as might happen to oneself. That was civilisation. It struck him coming back from the East—the efficiency, the organisation, the communal spirit of London. Every cart or carriage of its own accord drew aside to let the ambulance pass. Perhaps it was morbid; or was it not touching rather, the respect which they showed this ambulance with its victim inside—busy men hurrying home, yet instantly bethinking them as it passed of some wife; or presumably how easily it might have been them there, stretched on a shelf with a doctor and a nurse ... Ah, but thinking became morbid, sentimental, directly one began conjuring up doctors, dead bodies; a little glow of pleasure, a sort of lust, too, over the visual impression warned one not to go on with that sort of thing any more—fatal to art, fatal to friendship. True. And yet, thought Peter Walsh, as the ambulance turned the corner, though the light high bell could be heard down the next street and still farther as it crossed the Tottenham Court Road, chiming constantly, it is the privilege of loneliness; in privacy one may do as one chooses. One might weep if no one saw. It had been his undoing—this susceptibility—in Anglo-Indian society; not weeping at the right time, or laughing either. I have that in me, he thought, standing by the pillar-box, which could now dissolve in tears. Why, heaven knows. Beauty of some sort probably, and the weight of the day, which, beginning with that visit to Clarissa, had exhausted him with its heat, its intensity, and the drip, drip of one impression after another down into that cellar where they stood, deep, dark, and no one would ever know. Partly for that reason, its secrecy, complete and inviolable, he had found life like an unknown garden, full of turns and corners, surprising, yes; really it took one's breath away, these moments; there coming to him by the pillar-box opposite the British Museum[1] one of them, a moment, in which things came together; this ambulance; and life and death. It was as if he were sucked up to some very high roof by that rush of emotion, and the rest of him, like a white shell-sprinkled beach, left bare. It had been his undoing in Anglo-Indian society—this susceptibility.

Clarissa once, going on top of an omnibus with him somewhere, Clarissa superficially at least, so easily moved, now in despair, now in the best of spirits, all aquiver in those days and such good company, spotting queer little scenes, names, people from the top of a bus, for they used to explore London and bring back bags full of treasures from the Caledonian market[2]—Clarissa had a theory in those days—they had heaps of theories, always theories, as young people have. It was to explain the feeling they had of dissatisfaction; not knowing people; not being known. For how could they know each other? You met every day; then not for six months, or years. It was unsatisfactory, they agreed, how little one knew people. But she said, sitting on the bus going up Shaftesbury Avenue, she felt herself everywhere; not "here, here, here"; and she tapped the back of the seat; but everywhere. She waved her hand, going up Shaftesbury Avenue. She was all that. So that to know her, or any one, one must seek out the people who completed them; even the places. Odd affinities she had with people she had never spoken to, some woman in the street, some man behind a counter—even trees, or barns. It ended in a transcendental theory which, with her horror of death, allowed her to believe, or say that she believed (for all her scepticism), that since our apparitions, the part of us which appears, are so momentary compared with the other, the unseen part of us, which spreads wide, the unseen might survive, be recovered somehow attached to this person or that, or even haunting certain places, after death. Perhaps—perhaps.

Looking back over that long friendship of almost thirty years her theory worked to this extent. Brief, broken, often painful as their actual meetings had been, what with his absences and interruptions (this morning, for instance, in came Elizabeth, like a long-legged colt, handsome, dumb, just as he was beginning to

---

1 National museum established in 1753 and opened to the public in 1759, containing a monumental collection of art and antiquities. Until 1997 it also contained the British Library.

2 An antique market specializing in silverware.

talk to Clarissa), the effect of them on his life was immeasurable. There was a mystery about it. You were given a sharp, acute, uncomfortable grain—the actual meeting; horribly painful as often as not; yet in absence, in the most unlikely places, it would flower out, open, shed its scent, let you touch, taste, look about you, get the whole feel of it and understanding, after years of lying lost. Thus she had come to him; on board ship; in the Himalayas; suggested by the oddest things (so Sally Seton, generous, enthusiastic goose! thought of *him* when she saw blue hydrangeas). She had influenced him more than any person he had ever known. And always in this way coming before him without his wishing it, cool, lady-like, critical; or ravishing, romantic, recalling some field or English harvest. He saw her most often in the country, not in London. One scene after another at Bourton....

He had reached his hotel. He crossed the hall, with its mounds of reddish chairs and sofas, its spike-leaved, withered-looking plants. He got his key off the hook. The young lady handed him some letters. He went upstairs—he saw her most often at Bourton, in the late summer, when he stayed there for a week, or fortnight even, as people did in those days. First on top of some hill there she would stand, hands clapped to her hair, her cloak blowing out, pointing, crying to them—She saw the Severn[1] beneath. Or in a wood, making the kettle boil—very ineffective with her fingers; the smoke curtseying, blowing in their faces; her little pink face showing through; begging water from an old woman in a cottage, who came to the door to watch them go. They walked always; the others drove. She was bored driving, disliked all animals, except that dog. They tramped miles along roads. She would break off to get her bearings, pilot him back across country; and all the time they argued, discussed poetry, discussed people, discussed politics (she was a Radical then); never noticing a thing except when she stopped, cried out at a view or a tree, and made him look with her; and so on again, through stubble fields, she walking ahead, with a flower for her aunt, never tired of walking for all her delicacy; to drop down on Bourton in the dusk. Then, after dinner, old Breitkopf would open the piano and sing without any voice, and they would lie sunk in arm-chairs, trying not to laugh, but always breaking

1 The longest river in Great Britain, which begins in Wales and flows through the English counties of Shropshire, Worcestershire, and Gloucestershire.

down and laughing, laughing—laughing at nothing. Breitkopf was supposed not to see. And then in the morning, flirting up and down like a wagtail[1] in front of the house....

Oh it was a letter from her! This blue envelope; that was her hand. And he would have to read it. Here was another of those meetings, bound to be painful! To read her letter needed the devil of an effort. "How heavenly it was to see him. She must tell him that." That was all.

But it upset him. It annoyed him. He wished she hadn't written it. Coming on top of his thoughts, it was like a nudge in the ribs. Why couldn't she let him be? After all, she had married Dalloway, and lived with him in perfect happiness all these years.

These hotels are not consoling places. Far from it. Any number of people had hung up their hats on those pegs. Even the flies, if you thought of it, had settled on other people's noses. As for the cleanliness which hit him in the face, it wasn't cleanliness, so much as bareness, frigidity; a thing that had to be. Some arid matron made her rounds at dawn sniffing, peering, causing blue-nosed maids to scour, for all the world as if the next visitor were a joint of meat to be served on a perfectly clean platter. For sleep, one bed; for sitting in, one arm-chair; for cleaning one's teeth and shaving one's chin, one tumbler, one looking-glass. Books, letters, dressing-gown, slipped about on the impersonality of the horsehair like incongruous impertinences. And it was Clarissa's letter that made him see all this. "Heavenly to see you. She must say so!" He folded the paper; pushed it away; nothing would induce him to read it again!

To get that letter to him by six o'clock she must have sat down and written it directly he left her; stamped it; sent somebody to the post.[2] It was, as people say, very like her. She was upset by his visit. She had felt a great deal; had for a moment, when she kissed his hand, regretted, envied him even, remembered possibly (for he saw her look it) something he had said—how they would change the world if she married him perhaps; whereas, it was this; it was middle age; it was mediocrity; then forced herself with her indomitable vitality to put all that aside, there being in her a thread of life which for toughness, endurance, power to overcome obstacles, and carry her triumphantly through he had never known the like of. Yes; but there would come a reaction directly he left the room. She would be frightfully sorry for him; she

1 A long-tailed songbird.

2 In 1923 there were a minimum of six postal deliveries a day in London.

would think what in the world she could do to give him pleasure (short always of the one thing), and he could see her with the tears running down her cheeks going to her writing-table and dashing off that one line which he was to find greeting him.... "Heavenly to see you!" And she meant it.

Peter Walsh had now unlaced his boots.

But it would not have been a success, their marriage. The other thing, after all, came so much more naturally.

It was odd; it was true; lots of people felt it. Peter Walsh, who had done just respectably, filled the usual posts adequately, was liked, but thought a little cranky, gave himself airs—it was odd that *he* should have had, especially now that his hair was grey, a contented look; a look of having reserves. It was this that made him attractive to women, who liked the sense that he was not altogether manly. There was something unusual about him, or something behind him. It might be that he was bookish—never came to see you without taking up the book on the table (he was now reading, with his bootlaces trailing on the floor); or that he was a gentleman, which showed itself in the way he knocked the ashes out of his pipe, and in his manners of course to women. For it was very charming and quite ridiculous how easily some girl without a grain of sense could twist him round her finger. But at her own risk. That is to say, though he might be ever so easy, and indeed with his gaiety and good-breeding fascinating to be with, it was only up to a point. She said something—no, no; he saw through that. He wouldn't stand that—no, no. Then he could shout and rock and hold his sides together over some joke with men. He was the best judge of cooking in India. He was a man. But not the sort of man one had to respect—which was a mercy; not like Major Simmons, for instance; not in the least, Daisy thought, when in spite of her two small children, she used to compare them.

He pulled off his boots. He emptied his pockets. Out came with his pocket-knife a snapshot of Daisy on the verandah; Daisy all in white, with a fox-terrier on her knee; very charming, very dark; the best he had ever seen of her. It did come, after all, so naturally; so much more naturally than Clarissa. No fuss. No bother. No finicking and fidgeting. All plain sailing. And the dark, adorably pretty girl on the verandah exclaimed (he could hear her) Of course, of course she would give him everything! she cried (she had no sense of discretion), everything he wanted! she cried, running to meet him, whoever might be looking. And she was only twenty-four. And she had two children. Well, well!

Well indeed he had got himself into a mess at his age. And it came over him when he woke in the night pretty forcibly. Suppose they did marry? For him it would be all very well, but what about her? Mrs. Burgess, a good sort and no chatterbox, in whom he had confided, thought this absence of his in England, ostensibly to see lawyers, might serve to make Daisy reconsider, think what it meant. It was a question of her position, Mrs. Burgess said; the social barrier; giving up her children. She'd be a widow with a past one of these days, draggling about in the suburbs, or more likely, indiscriminate (you know, she said, what such women get like, with too much paint). But Peter Walsh pooh-poohed all that. He didn't mean to die yet. Anyhow, she must settle for herself; judge for herself, he thought, padding about the room in his socks, smoothing out his dress-shirt, for he might go to Clarissa's party, or he might go to one of the Halls,[1] or he might settle in and read an absorbing book written by a man he used to know at Oxford. And if he did retire, that's what he'd do—write books. He would go to Oxford and poke about in the Bodleian.[2] Vainly the dark, adorably pretty girl ran to the end of the terrace; vainly waved her hand; vainly cried she didn't care a straw what people said. There he was, the man she thought the world of, the perfect gentleman, the fascinating, the distinguished (and his age made not the least difference to her), padding about a room in an hotel in Bloomsbury, shaving, washing, continuing, as he took up cans, put down razors, to poke about in the Bodleian, and get at the truth about one or two little matters that interested him. And he would have a chat with whoever it might be, and so come to disregard more and more precise hours for lunch, and miss engagements; and when Daisy asked him, as she would, for a kiss, a scene, fail to come up to the scratch (though he was genuinely devoted to her)—in short it might be happier, as Mrs. Burgess said, that she should forget him, or merely remember him as he was in August 1922, like a figure standing at the cross roads at dusk, which grows more and more remote as the dog-cart[3] spins away, carrying her securely fastened to the back seat, though her arms are outstretched, and as she sees the figure dwindle and disappear, still she cries out how she would do anything in the world, anything, anything, anything....

---

1 I.e., music halls. See p. 65, n. 1.

2 The main research library at the University of Oxford.

3 A two-wheeled horsedrawn cart.

He never knew what people thought. It became more and more difficult for him to concentrate. He became absorbed; he became busied with his own concerns; now surly, now gay; dependent on women, absent-minded, moody, less and less able (so he thought as he shaved) to understand why Clarissa couldn't simply find them a lodging and be nice to Daisy; introduce her. And then he could just—just do what? just haunt and hover (he was at the moment actually engaged in sorting out various keys, papers), swoop and taste, be alone, in short, sufficient to himself; and yet nobody of course was more dependent upon others (he buttoned his waistcoat); it had been his undoing. He could not keep out of smoking-rooms, liked colonels, liked golf, liked bridge, and above all women's society, and the fineness of their companionship, and their faithfulness and audacity and greatness in loving which, though it had its drawbacks, seemed to him (and the dark, adorably pretty face was on top of the envelopes) so wholly admirable, so splendid a flower to grow on the crest of human life, and yet he could not come up to the scratch, being always apt to see round things (Clarissa had sapped something in him permanently), and to tire very easily of mute devotion and to want variety in love, though it would make him furious if Daisy loved anybody else, furious! for he was jealous, uncontrollably jealous by temperament. He suffered tortures! But where was his knife; his watch; his seals, his note-case, and Clarissa's letter which he would not read again but liked to think of, and Daisy's photograph? And now for dinner.

They were eating.

Sitting at little tables round vases, dressed or not dressed, with their shawls and bags laid beside them, with their air of false composure, for they were not used to so many courses at dinner; and confidence, for they were able to pay for it; and strain, for they had been running about London all day shopping, sightseeing; and their natural curiosity, for they looked round and up as the nice-looking gentleman in horn-rimmed spectacles came in; and their good nature, for they would have been glad to do any little service, such as lend a time-table or impart useful information; and their desire, pulsing in them, tugging at them subterraneously, somehow to establish connections if it were only a birthplace (Liverpool, for example), in common or friends of the same name; with their furtive glances, odd silences, and sudden withdrawals into family jocularity and isolation; there they sat eating dinner when Mr. Walsh came in and took his seat at a little table by the curtain.

It was not that he said anything, for being solitary he could only address himself to the waiter; it was his way of looking at the menu, of pointing his forefinger to a particular wine, of hitching himself up to the table, of addressing himself seriously, not gluttonously to dinner, that won him their respect; which, having to remain unexpressed for the greater part of the meal, flared up at the table where the Morrises sat when Mr. Walsh was heard to say at the end of the meal, "Bartlett pears." Why he should have spoken so moderately yet firmly, with the air of a disciplinarian well within his rights which are founded upon justice, neither young Charles Morris, nor old Charles, neither Miss Elaine nor Mrs. Morris knew. But when he said, "Bartlett pears," sitting alone at his table, they felt that he counted on their support in some lawful demand; was champion of a cause which immediately became their own, and when they all reached the smoking-room simultaneously, a little talk between them became inevitable.

It was not very profound—only to the effect that London was crowded; had changed in thirty years; that Mr. Morris preferred Liverpool; that Mrs. Morris had been to the Westminster flower-show, and that they had all seen the Prince of Wales. Yet, thought Peter Walsh, no family in the world can compare with the Morrises; none whatever; and their relations to each other are perfect, and they don't care a hang for the upper classes, and they like what they like, and Elaine is training for the family business, and the boy has won a scholarship at Leeds, and the old lady (who is about his own age) has three more children at home; and they have two motor cars, but Mr. Morris still mends the boots on Sunday: it is superb, it is absolutely superb, thought Peter Walsh, swaying a little backwards and forwards with his liqueur glass in his hand among the hairy red chairs and ash-trays, feeling very well pleased with himself, for the Morrises liked him. Yes, they liked a man who said "Bartlett pears." They liked him, he felt.

He would go to Clarissa's party. (The Morrises moved off; but they would meet again.) He would go to Clarissa's party, because he wanted to ask Richard what they were doing in India—the conservative duffers. And what's being acted? And music.... Oh yes, and mere gossip.

For this is the truth about our soul, he thought, our self, who fish-like inhabits deep seas and plies among obscurities threading her way between the boles of giant weeds, over sun-flickered spaces and on and on into gloom, cold, deep, inscrutable; suddenly she shoots to the surface and sports on the wind-wrinkled waves; that is, has a positive need to brush, scrape, kindle herself, gossiping. What did the Government mean—Richard Dalloway would know—to do about India?

Since it was a very hot night and the paper boys went by with placards proclaiming in huge red letters that there was a heat-wave, wicker chairs were placed on the hotel steps and there, sipping, smoking, detached gentlemen sat. Peter Walsh sat there. One might fancy that day, the London day, was just beginning. Like a woman who has slipped off her print dress and white apron to array herself in blue and pearls, the day changed, put off stuff, took gauze, changed to evening, and with the same sigh of exhilaration that a woman breathes, tumbling petticoats on the floor, it too shed dust, heat, colour; the traffic thinned; motor cars, tinkling, darting, succeeded the lumber of vans; and here and there among the thick foliage of the squares an intense light hung. I resign, the evening seemed to say, as it paled and faded above the battlements and prominences, moulded, pointed, of hotel, flat, and block of shops, I fade, she was beginning, I disappear, but London would have none of it, and rushed her bayonets into the sky, pinioned her, constrained her to partnership in her revelry.

For the great revolution of Mr. Willett's summer time had taken place since Peter Walsh's last visit to England.[1] The prolonged evening was new to him. It was inspiriting, rather. For as the young people went by with their despatch-boxes, awfully glad to be free, proud too, dumbly, of stepping this famous pavement, joy of a kind, cheap, tinselly, if you like, but all the same rapture, flushed their faces. They dressed well too; pink stockings; pretty shoes. They would now have two hours at the pictures. It sharpened, it refined them, the yellow-blue evening light; and on the leaves in the square shone lurid, livid—they looked as if dipped in sea water—the foliage of a submerged city. He was astonished by the beauty; it was encouraging too, for where the returned Anglo-Indian sat by rights (he knew crowds of them) in the Oriental Club[2] biliously summing up the ruin of the world, here was

---

1 Daylight Saving Time, or Summer Time as it is known in Britain, was initially proposed by William Willett (1857-1915), a builder, in 1907 in a pamphlet titled *The Waste of Daylight.* It was first introduced in Britain in April 1916 as a wartime economy.

2 A men's club founded in 1824 by members of the East India Company and other officials in public service in India. In 1923 the clubhouse was located in Hanover Square.

he, as young as ever; envying young people their summer time and the rest of it, and more than suspecting from the words of a girl, from a housemaid's laughter—intangible things you couldn't lay your hands on—that shift in the whole pyramidal accumulation which in his youth had seemed immovable. On top of them it had pressed; weighed them down, the women especially, like those flowers Clarissa's Aunt Helena used to press between sheets of grey blotting-paper with Littré's dictionary on top, sitting under the lamp after dinner. She was dead now. He had heard of her, from Clarissa, losing the sight of one eye. It seemed so fitting—one of nature's masterpieces—that old Miss Parry should turn to glass. She would die like some bird in a frost gripping her perch. She belonged to a different age, but being so entire, so complete, would always stand up on the horizon, stone-white, eminent, like a lighthouse marking some past stage on this adventurous, long, long voyage, this interminable—(he felt for a copper to buy a paper and read about Surrey and Yorkshire (he had held out that copper millions of times) Surrey was all out once more)[1]—this interminable life. But cricket was no mere game. Cricket was important. He could never help reading about cricket. He read the scores in the stop press first, then how it was a hot day; then about a murder case. Having done things millions of times enriched them, though it might be said to take the surface off. The past enriched, and experience, and having cared for one or two people, and so having acquired the power which the young lack, of cutting short, doing what one likes, not caring a rap what people say and coming and going without any very great expectations (he left his paper on the table and moved off), which however (and he looked for his hat and coat) was not altogether true of him, not to-night, for here he was starting to go to a party, at his age, with the belief upon him, that he was about to have an experience. But what?

Beauty anyhow. Not the crude beauty of the eye. It was not beauty pure and simple—Bedford Place leading into Russell Square. It was straightness and emptiness of course; the symmetry of a corridor; but it was also windows lit up, a piano, a gramophone sounding; a sense of pleasure making hidden, but now and again emerging when, through the uncurtained window, the window left open, one saw parties sitting over tables, young people slowly circling, conversations between men and women, maids

---

1 See p. 161, n. 1. Peter Walsh is reading about the same cricket match as Septimus Warren Smith.

idly looking out (a strange comment theirs, when work was done), stockings drying on top ledges, a parrot, a few plants. Absorbing, mysterious, of infinite richness, this life. And in the large square where the cabs shot and swerved so quick, there were loitering couples, dallying, embracing, shrunk up under the shower of a tree; that was moving; so silent, so absorbed, that one passed, discreetly, timidly, as if in the presence of some sacred ceremony to interrupt which would have been impious. That was interesting. And so on into the flare and glare.

His light overcoat blew open, he stepped with indescribable idiosyncrasy, leant a little forward, tripped, with his hands behind his back and his eyes still a little hawk-like; he tripped through London, towards Westminster, observing.

Was everybody dining out, then? Doors were being opened here by a footman to let issue a high-stepping old dame, in buckled shoes, with three purple ostrich feathers in her hair. Doors were being opened for ladies wrapped like mummies in shawls with bright flowers on them, ladies with bare heads. And in respectable quarters with stucco pillars through small front gardens, lightly swathed, with combs in their hair (having run up to see the children), women came; men waited for them, with their coats blowing open, and the motor started. Everybody was going out. What with these doors being opened, and the descent and the start, it seemed as if the whole of London were embarking in little boats moored to the bank, tossing on the waters, as if the whole place were floating off in carnival. And Whitehall was skated over, silver beaten as it was, skated over by spiders, and there was a sense of midges round the arc lamps; it was so hot that people stood about talking. And here in Westminster was a retired Judge, presumably, sitting four square at his house door dressed all in white. An Anglo-Indian presumably.

And here a shindy of brawling women, drunken women; here only a policeman and looming houses, high houses, domed houses, churches, parliaments, and the hoot of a steamer on the river, a hollow misty cry. But it was her street, this, Clarissa's; cabs were rushing round the corner, like water round the piers of a bridge, drawn together, it seemed to him because they bore people going to her party, Clarissa's party.

The cold stream of visual impressions failed him now as if the eye were a cup that overflowed and let the rest run down its china walls unrecorded. The brain must wake now. The body must contract now, entering the house, the lighted house, where the door stood open, where the motor cars were standing, and bright women descending: the soul must brave itself to endure. He opened the big blade of his pocket-knife.

Lucy came running full tilt downstairs, having just nipped in to the drawing-room to smooth a cover, to straighten a chair, to pause a moment and feel whoever came in must think how clean, how bright, how beautifully cared for, when they saw the beautiful silver, the brass fire-irons, the new chair-covers, and the curtains of yellow chintz: she appraised each; heard a roar of voices; people already coming up from dinner; she must fly!

The Prime Minister was coming, Agnes said: so she had heard them say in the dining-room, she said, coming in with a tray of glasses. Did it matter, did it matter in the least, one Prime Minister more or less? It made no difference at this hour of the night to Mrs. Walker among the plates, saucepans, cullenders, frying-pans, chicken in aspic, ice-cream freezers, pared crusts of bread, lemons, soup tureens, and pudding basins which, however hard they washed up in the scullery, seemed to be all on top of her, on the kitchen table, on chairs, while the fire blared and roared, the electric lights glared, and still supper had to be laid. All she felt was, one Prime Minister more or less made not a scrap of difference to Mrs. Walker.

The ladies were going upstairs already, said Lucy; the ladies were going up, one by one, Mrs. Dalloway walking last and almost always sending back some message to the kitchen, "My love to Mrs. Walker," that was it one night. Next morning they would go over the dishes—the soup, the salmon; the salmon, Mrs. Walker knew, as usual underdone, for she always got nervous about the pudding and left it to Jenny; so it happened, the salmon was always underdone. But some lady with fair hair and silver ornaments had said, Lucy said, about the entrée, was it really made at home? But it was the salmon that bothered Mrs. Walker, as she spun the plates round and round, and pushed in dampers and pulled out dampers; and there came a burst of laughter from the dining-room; a voice speaking; then another burst of laughter—the gentlemen enjoying themselves when the ladies had gone. The tokay,[1] said Lucy running in. Mr. Dalloway had sent for the tokay, from the Emperor's cellars, the Imperial Tokay.

---

1 A sweet wine made near Tokaj in Hungary.

It was borne through the kitchen. Over her shoulder Lucy reported how Miss Elizabeth looked quite lovely; she couldn't take her eyes off her; in her pink dress, wearing the necklace Mr. Dalloway had given her. Jenny must remember the dog, Miss Elizabeth's fox-terrier, which, since it bit had to be shut up and might, Elizabeth thought, want something. Jenny must remember the dog. But Jenny was not going upstairs with all those people about. There was a motor at the door already! There was a ring at the bell—and the gentlemen still in the dining-room, drinking tokay!

There, they were going upstairs; that was the first to come, and now they would come faster and faster, so that Mrs. Parkinson (hired for parties) would leave the hall door ajar, and the hall would be full of gentlemen waiting (they stood waiting, sleeking down their hair) while the ladies took their cloaks off in the room along the passage; where Mrs. Barnet helped them, old Ellen Barnet, who had been with the family for forty years, and came every summer to help the ladies, and remembered mothers when they were girls, and though very unassuming did shake hands; said "milady" very respectfully, yet had a humorous way with her, looking at the young ladies, and ever so tactfully helping Lady Lovejoy, who had some trouble with her underbodice. And they could not help feeling, Lady Lovejoy and Miss Alice, that some little privilege in the matter of brush and comb, was awarded them having known Mrs. Barnet—"thirty years, milady," Mrs. Barnet supplied her. Young ladies did not use to rouge, said Lady Lovejoy, when they stayed at Bourton in the old days. And Miss Alice didn't need rouge, said Mrs. Barnet, looking at her fondly. There Mrs. Barnet would sit, in the cloakroom, patting down the furs, smoothing out the Spanish shawls, tidying the dressing-table, and knowing perfectly well, in spite of the furs and the embroideries, which were nice ladies, which were not. The dear old body, said Lady Lovejoy, mounting the stairs, Clarissa's old nurse.

And then Lady Lovejoy stiffened. "Lady and Miss Lovejoy," she said to Mr. Wilkins (hired for parties). He had an admirable manner, as he bent and straightened himself, bent and straightened himself and announced with perfect impartiality "Lady and Miss Lovejoy ... Sir John and Lady Needham ... Miss Weld ... Mr. Walsh." His manner was admirable; his family life must be irreproachable, except that it seemed impossible that a being with greenish lips and shaven cheeks could ever have blundered into the nuisance of children.

"How delightful to see you!" said Clarissa. She said it to every one. How delightful to see you! She was at her worst—effusive, insincere. It was a great mistake to have come. He should have stayed at home and read his book, thought Peter Walsh; should have gone to a music hall; he should have stayed at home, for he knew no one.

Oh dear, it was going to be a failure; a complete failure, Clarissa felt it in her bones as dear old Lord Lexham stood there apologising for his wife who had caught cold at the Buckingham Palace garden party. She could see Peter out of the tail of her eye, criticising her, there, in that corner. Why, after all, did she do these things? Why seek pinnacles and stand drenched in fire? Might it consume her anyhow! Burn her to cinders! Better anything, better brandish one's torch and hurl it to earth than taper and dwindle away like some Ellie Henderson! It was extraordinary how Peter put her into these states just by coming and standing in a corner. He made her see herself; exaggerate. It was idiotic. But why did he come, then, merely to criticise? Why always take, never give? Why not risk one's one little point of view? There he was wandering off, and she must speak to him. But she would not get the chance. Life was that—humiliation, renunciation. What Lord Lexham was saying was that his wife would not wear her furs at the garden party because "my dear, you ladies are all alike"—Lady Lexham being seventy-five at least! It was delicious, how they petted each other, that old couple. She did like old Lord Lexham. She did think it mattered, her party, and it made her feel quite sick to know that it was all going wrong, all falling flat. Anything, any explosion, any horror was better than people wandering aimlessly, standing in a bunch at a corner like Ellie Henderson, not even caring to hold themselves upright.

Gently the yellow curtain with all the birds of Paradise blew out and it seemed as if there were a flight of wings into the room, right out, then sucked back. (For the windows were open.) Was it draughty, Ellie Henderson wondered? She was subject to chills. But it did not matter that she should come down sneezing tomorrow; it was the girls with their naked shoulders she thought of, being trained to think of others by an old father, an invalid, late vicar of Bourton, but he was dead now; and her chills never went to her chest, never. It was the girls she thought of, the young girls with their bare shoulders, she herself having always been a wisp of a creature, with her thin hair and meagre profile; though now, past fifty, there was beginning to shine through some mild beam, something purified into distinction by years of self-abnegation but obscured again, perpetually, by her distressing gentility, her panic fear, which arose from three hundred pounds income,[1] and her weaponless state (she could not earn a penny) and it made her timid, and more and more disqualified year by year to meet well-dressed people who did this sort of thing every night of the season, merely telling their maids "I'll wear so and so," whereas Ellie Henderson ran out nervously and bought cheap pink flowers, half-a-dozen, and then threw a shawl over her old black dress. For her invitation to Clarissa's party had come at the last moment. She was not quite happy about it. She had a sort of feeling that Clarissa had not meant to ask her this year.

Why should she? There was no reason really, except that they had always known each other. Indeed, they were cousins. But naturally they had rather drifted apart, Clarissa being so sought after. It was an event to her, going to a party. It was quite a treat just to see the lovely clothes. Wasn't that Elizabeth, grown up, with her hair done in the fashionable way, in the pink dress? Yet she could not be more than seventeen. She was very, very handsome. But girls when they first came out didn't seem to wear white as they used. (She must remember everything to tell Edith.) Girls wore straight frocks, perfectly tight, with skirts well above the ankles. It was not becoming, she thought.

So, with her weak eyesight, Ellie Henderson craned rather forward, and it wasn't so much she who minded not having any one to talk to (she hardly knew anybody there), for she felt that they were all such interesting people to watch; politicians presumably; Richard Dalloway's friends; but it was Richard himself who felt that he could not let the poor creature go on standing there all the evening by herself.

"Well, Ellie, and how's the world treating *you*?" he said in his genial way, and Ellie Henderson, getting nervous and flushing and feeling that it was extraordinarily nice of him to come and talk to her, said that many people really felt the heat more than the cold.

"Yes, they do," said Richard Dalloway. "Yes."

But what more did one say?

"Hullo, Richard," said somebody, taking him by the elbow, and, good Lord, there was old Peter, old Peter Walsh. He was delighted to see him—ever so pleased to see him! He hadn't

---

1 With regard to the value of incomes in 1923 relative to today, see p. 104, n. 1; p. 127, n. 1; and p. 195, n. 2.

changed a bit. And off they went together walking right across the room, giving each other little pats, as if they hadn't met for a long time, Ellie Henderson thought, watching them go, certain she knew that man's face. A tall man, middle aged, rather fine eyes, dark, wearing spectacles, with a look of John Burrows. Edith would be sure to know.

The curtain with its flight of birds of Paradise blew out again. And Clarissa saw—she saw Ralph Lyon beat it back, and go on talking. So it wasn't a failure after all! it was going to be all right now—her party. It had begun. It had started. But it was still touch and go. She must stand there for the present. People seemed to come in a rush.

Colonel and Mrs. Garrod ... Mr. Hugh Whitbread ... Mr. Bowley ... Mrs. Hilbery ... Lady Mary Maddox ... Mr. Quin ... intoned Wilkin.[1] She had six or seven words with each, and they went on, they went into the rooms; into something now, not nothing, since Ralph Lyon had beat back the curtain.

And yet for her own part, it was too much of an effort. She was not enjoying it. It was too much like being—just anybody, standing there; anybody could do it; yet this anybody she did a little admire, couldn't help feeling that she had, anyhow, made this happen, that it marked a stage, this post that she felt herself to have become, for oddly enough she had quite forgotten what she looked like, but felt herself a stake driven in at the top of her stairs. Every time she gave a party she had this feeling of being something not herself, and that every one was unreal in one way; much more real in another. It was, she thought, partly their clothes, partly being taken out of their ordinary ways, partly the background; it was possible to say things you couldn't say anyhow else, things that needed an effort; possible to go much deeper. But not for her; not yet anyhow.

"How delightful to see you!" she said. Dear old Sir Harry! He would know every one.

And what was so odd about it was the sense one had as they came up the stairs one after another, Mrs. Mount and Celia, Herbert Ainsty, Mrs. Dakers—oh, and Lady Bruton!

"How awfully good of you to come!" she said, and she meant it—it was odd how standing there one felt them going on, going on, some quite old, some ...

---

1 Elsewhere in the novel, the butler's name appears as Wilkins—another of the small errors that found its way into the first Hogarth Press edition.

What name? Lady Rosseter? But who on earth was Lady Rosseter?

"Clarissa!" That voice! It was Sally Seton! Sally Seton! after all these years! She loomed through a mist. For she hadn't looked like *that*, Sally Seton, when Clarissa grasped the hot water can. To think of her under this roof, under this roof! Not like that!

All on top of each other, embarrassed, laughing, words tumbled out—passing through London; heard from Clara Haydon; what a chance of seeing you! So I thrust myself in—without an invitation....

One might put down the hot water can quite composedly. The lustre had left her. Yet it was extraordinary to see her again, older, happier, less lovely. They kissed each other, first this cheek, then that, by the drawing room door, and Clarissa turned, with Sally's hand in hers, and saw her rooms full, heard the roar of voices, saw the candlesticks, the blowing curtains, and the roses which Richard had given her.

"I have five enormous boys," said Sally.

She had the simplest egotism, the most open desire to be thought first always, and Clarissa loved her for being still like that. "I can't believe it!" she cried, kindling all over with pleasure at the thought of the past.

But alas, Wilkins; Wilkins wanted her; Wilkins was emitting in a voice of commanding authority, as if the whole company must be admonished and the hostess reclaimed from frivolity, one name:

"The Prime Minister," said Peter Walsh.

The Prime Minister? Was it really? Ellie Henderson marvelled. What a thing to tell Edith!

One couldn't laugh at him. He looked so ordinary. You might have stood him behind a counter and bought biscuits—poor chap, all rigged up in gold lace. And to be fair, as he went his rounds, first with Clarissa, then with Richard escorting him, he did it very well. He tried to look somebody. It was amusing to watch. Nobody looked at him. They just went on talking, yet it was perfectly plain that they all knew, felt to the marrow of their bones, this majesty passing; this symbol of what they all stood for, English society. Old Lady Bruton, and she looked very fine too, very stalwart in her lace, swam up, and they withdrew into a little room which at once became spied upon, guarded, and a sort of stir and rustle rippled through every one openly: the Prime Minister!

Lord, lord, the snobbery of the English! thought Peter Walsh, standing in the corner. How they loved dressing up in gold lace and doing homage! There! That must be—by Jove it was—Hugh Whitbread, snuffing round the precincts of the great, grown rather fatter, rather whiter, the admirable Hugh!

He looked always as if he were on duty, thought Peter, a privileged but secretive being, hoarding secrets which he would die to defend, though it was only some little piece of tittle-tattle dropped by a court footman which would be in all the papers tomorrow. Such were his rattles, his baubles, in playing with which he had grown white, come to the verge of old age, enjoying the respect and affection of all who had the privilege of knowing this type of the English public school man. Inevitably one made up things like that about Hugh; that was his style; the style of those admirable letters which Peter had read thousands of miles across the sea in the *Times*, and had thanked God he was out of that pernicious hubble-bubble if it were only to hear baboons chatter and coolies beat their wives. An olive-skinned youth from one of the Universities stood obsequiously by. Him he would patronise, initiate, teach how to get on. For he liked nothing better than doing kindnesses, making the hearts of old ladies palpitate with the joy of being thought of in their age, their affliction, thinking themselves quite forgotten, yet here was dear Hugh driving up and spending an hour talking of the past, remembering trifles, praising the home-made cake, though Hugh might eat cake with a Duchess any day of his life, and, to look at him, probably did spend a good deal of time in that agreeable occupation. The All-judging, the All-merciful, might excuse. Peter Walsh had no mercy. Villains there must be, and, God knows, the rascals who get hanged for battering the brains of a girl out in a train do less harm on the whole than Hugh Whitbread and his kindness! Look at him now, on tiptoe, dancing forward, bowing and scraping, as the Prime Minister and Lady Bruton emerged, intimating for all the world to see that he was privileged to say something, something private, to Lady Bruton as she passed. She stopped. She wagged her fine old head. She was thanking him presumably for some piece of servility. She had her toadies, minor officials in Government offices who ran about putting through little jobs on her behalf, in return for which she gave them luncheon. But she derived from the eighteenth century. She was all right.

And now Clarissa escorted her Prime Minister down the room, prancing, sparkling, with the stateliness of her grey hair. She wore ear-rings, and a silver-green mermaid's dress. Lolloping on the waves and braiding her tresses she seemed, having that gift still; to be; to exist; to sum it all up in the moment as she passed;

turned, caught her scarf in some other woman's dress, unhitched it, laughed, all with the most perfect ease and air of a creature floating in its element. But age had brushed her; even as a mermaid might behold in her glass the setting sun on some very clear evening over the waves. There was a breath of tenderness; her severity, her prudery, her woodenness were all warmed through now, and she had about her as she said good-bye to the thick gold-laced man who was doing his best, and good luck to him, to look important, an inexpressible dignity; an exquisite cordiality; as if she wished the whole world well, and must now, being on the very verge and rim of things, take her leave. So she made him think. (But he was not in love.)

Indeed, Clarissa felt, the Prime Minister had been good to come. And, walking down the room with him, with Sally there and Peter there and Richard very pleased, with all those people rather inclined, perhaps, to envy, she had felt that intoxication of the moment, that dilatation of the nerves of the heart itself till it seemed to quiver, steeped, upright;—yes, but after all it was what other people felt, that; for, though she loved it and felt it tingle and sting, still these semblances, these triumphs (dear old Peter, for example, thinking her so brilliant), had a hollowness; at arm's length they were, not in the heart; and it might be that she was growing old, but they satisfied her no longer as they used; and suddenly, as she saw the Prime Minister go down the stairs, the gilt rim of the Sir Joshua picture[1] of the little girl with a muff brought back Kilman with a rush; Kilman her enemy. That was satisfying; that was real. Ah, how she hated her—hot, hypocritical, corrupt; with all that power; Elizabeth's seducer; the woman who had crept in to steal and defile (Richard would say, What nonsense!). She hated her: she loved her. It was enemies one wanted, not friends—not Mrs. Durrant and Clara, Sir William and Lady Bradshaw, Miss Truelock and Eleanor Gibson (whom she saw coming upstairs). They must find her if they wanted her. She was for the party!

There was her old friend Sir Harry.

"Dear Sir Harry!" she said, going up to the fine old fellow who had produced more bad pictures than any other two Academicians[2]

---

1 Sir Joshua Reynolds (1723-92), a leading English portrait painter of the eighteenth century.

2 Members of the Royal Academy of Arts, established 1768. Sir Joshua Reynolds was one of the founders and the first President of the Academy.

in the whole of St. John's Wood[1] (they were always of cattle, standing in sunset pools absorbing moisture, or signifying, for he had a certain range of gesture, by the raising of one foreleg and the toss of the antlers, "the Approach of the Stranger"—all his activities, dining out, racing, were founded on cattle standing absorbing moisture in sunset pools).

"What are you laughing at?" she asked him. For Willie Titcomb and Sir Harry and Herbert Ainsty were all laughing. But no. Sir Harry could not tell Clarissa Dalloway (much though he liked her; of her type he thought her perfect, and threatened to paint her) his stories of the music hall stage. He chaffed her about her party. He missed his brandy. These circles, he said, were above him. But he liked her; respected her, in spite of her damnable, difficult, upper-class refinement, which made it impossible to ask Clarissa Dalloway to sit on his knee. And up came that wandering will-o'-the-wisp, that vagous[2] phosphorescence, old Mrs. Hilbery, stretching her hands to the blaze of his laughter (about the Duke and the Lady), which, as she heard it across the room, seemed to reassure her on a point which sometimes bothered her if she woke early in the morning and did not like to call her maid for a cup of tea: how it is certain we must die.

"They won't tell us their stories," said Clarissa.

"Dear Clarissa!" exclaimed Mrs. Hilbery. She looked to-night, she said, so like her mother as she first saw her walking in a garden in a grey hat.

And really Clarissa's eyes filled with tears. Her mother, walking in a garden! But alas, she must go.

For there was Professor Brierly, who lectured on Milton,[3] talking to little Jim Hutton (who was unable even for a party like this to compass both tie and waistcoat or make his hair lie flat), and even at this distance they were quarrelling, she could see. For Professor Brierly was a very queer fish. With all those degrees, honours, lectureships between him and the scribblers, he suspected instantly an atmosphere not favourable to his queer com-

---

1 A district in northwest London, and the location of Lord's Cricket Ground. In the nineteenth century it was home to numerous writers and artists, including the novelist George Eliot, the painter Edwin Landseer, and the sculptor Onslow Ford (see *LE*).

2 Wandering, unsettled.

3 John Milton (1608-74), English poet and pamphleteer, author of the epic poem *Paradise Lost*.

pound; his prodigious learning and timidity; his wintry charm without cordiality; his innocence blent with snobbery; he quivered if made conscious, by a lady's unkempt hair, a youth's boots, of an underworld, very creditable doubtless, of rebels, of ardent young people; of would-be geniuses, and intimated with a little toss of the head, with a sniff—Humph!—the value of moderation; of some slight training in the classics in order to appreciate Milton. Professor Brierly (Clarissa could see) wasn't hitting it off with little Jim Hutton (who wore red socks, his black being at the laundry) about Milton. She interrupted.

She said she loved Bach.[1] So did Hutton. That was the bond between them, and Hutton (a very bad poet) always felt that Mrs. Dalloway was far the best of the great ladies who took an interest in art. It was odd how strict she was. About music she was purely impersonal. She was rather a prig. But how charming to look at! She made her house so nice, if it weren't for her Professors. Clarissa had half a mind to snatch him off and set him down at the piano in the back room. For he played divinely.

"But the noise!" she said. "The noise!"

"The sign of a successful party." Nodding urbanely, the Professor stepped delicately off.

"He knows everything in the whole world about Milton," said Clarissa.

"Does he indeed?" said Hutton, who would imitate the Professor throughout Hampstead:[2] the Professor on Milton; the Professor on moderation; the Professor stepping delicately off.

But she must speak to that couple, said Clarissa, Lord Gayton and Nancy Blow.

Not that *they* added perceptibly to the noise of the party. They were not talking (perceptibly) as they stood side by side by the yellow curtains. They would soon be off elsewhere, together; and never had very much to say in any circumstances. They looked; that was all. That was enough. They looked so clean, so sound, she with an apricot bloom of powder and paint, but he scrubbed, rinsed, with the eyes of a bird, so that no ball could pass him or stroke surprise him. He struck, he leapt, accurately, on the spot.

---

1 Johann Sebastian Bach (1685-1750), German composer of the Baroque period.

2 An area of London that attracted numerous writers, artists, and intellectuals including H.G. Wells, Rabindranath Tagore, Robert Louis Stevenson, D.H. Lawrence, Katherine Mansfield, Henry Moore, and others (see *LE*).

Ponies' mouths quivered at the end of his reins. He had his honours, ancestral monuments, banners hanging in the church at home. He had his duties; his tenants; a mother and sisters; had been all day at Lords, and that was what they were talking about—cricket, cousins, the movies—when Mrs. Dalloway came up. Lord Gayton liked her most awfully. So did Miss Blow. She had such charming manners.

"It is angelic—it is delicious of you to have come!" she said. She loved Lords; she loved youth, and Nancy, dressed at enormous expense by the greatest artists in Paris, stood there looking as if her body had merely put forth, of its own accord, a green frill.

"I had meant to have dancing," said Clarissa.

For the young people could not talk. And why should they? Shout, embrace, swing, be up at dawn; carry sugar to ponies; kiss and caress the snouts of adorable chows; and then, all tingling and streaming, plunge and swim. But the enormous resources of the English language, the power it bestows, after all, of communicating feelings (at their age, she and Peter would have been arguing all the evening), was not for them. They would solidify young. They would be good beyond measure to the people on the estate, but alone, perhaps, rather dull.

"What a pity!" she said. "I had hoped to have dancing."

It was so extraordinarily nice of them to have come! But talk of dancing! The rooms were packed.

There was old Aunt Helena in her shawl. Alas, she must leave them—Lord Gayton and Nancy Blow. There was old Miss Parry, her aunt.

For Miss Helena Parry was not dead: Miss Parry was alive. She was past eighty. She ascended staircases slowly with a stick. She was placed in a chair (Richard had seen to it). People who had known Burma in the 'seventies were always led up to her.[1] Where had Peter got to? They used to be such friends. For at the mention of India, or even Ceylon,[2] her eyes (only one was glass) slowly deepened, became blue, beheld, not human beings—she had no tender memories, no proud illusions about Viceroys,[3] Generals,

1 Burma, now the Republic of the Union of Myanmar, fell under British rule over the course of three wars, beginning in 1824. It achieved independence in 1948.

2 Since 1972 known as Sri Lanka.

3 British governors of colonial territories; those appointed to act on behalf of the king.

Mutinies[1]—it was orchids she saw, and mountain passes, and herself carried on the backs of coolies in the 'sixties over solitary peaks; or descending to uproot orchids (startling blossoms, never beheld before) which she painted in water-colour; an indomitable Englishwoman, fretful if disturbed by the war, say, which dropped a bomb at her very door, from her deep meditation over orchids and her own figure journeying in the 'sixties in India—but here was Peter.

"Come and talk to Aunt Helena about Burma," said Clarissa.

And yet he had not had a word with her all the evening!

"We will talk later," said Clarissa, leading him up to Aunt Helena, in her white shawl, with her stick.

"Peter Walsh," said Clarissa.

That meant nothing.

Clarissa had asked her. It was tiring; it was noisy; but Clarissa had asked her. So she had come. It was a pity that they lived in London—Richard and Clarissa. If only for Clarissa's health it would have been better to live in the country. But Clarissa had always been fond of society.

"He has been in Burma," said Clarissa.

Ah! She could not resist recalling what Charles Darwin had said about her little book on the orchids of Burma.

(Clarissa must speak to Lady Bruton.)

No doubt it was forgotten now, her book on the orchids of Burma, but it went into three editions before 1870, she told Peter. She remembered him now. He had been at Bourton (and he had left her, Peter Walsh remembered, without a word in the drawing-room that night when Clarissa had asked him to come boating).

"Richard so much enjoyed his lunch party," said Clarissa to Lady Bruton.

"Richard was the greatest possible help," Lady Bruton replied. "He helped me to write a letter. And how are you?"

"Oh, perfectly well!" said Clarissa. (Lady Bruton detested illness in the wives of politicians.)

"And there's Peter Walsh!" said Lady Bruton (for she could never think of anything to say to Clarissa; though she liked her. She had lots of fine qualities; but they had nothing in common—she and Clarissa. It might have been better if Richard had married a woman with less charm, who could have helped him more

---

1 A reference to the Indian Rebellion of 1857, referred to in Britain in 1923 as the Indian Mutiny.

in his work. He had lost his chance of the Cabinet). "There's Peter Walsh!" she said, shaking hands with that agreeable sinner, that very able fellow who should have made a name for himself but hadn't (always in difficulties with women), and, of course, old Miss Parry. Wonderful old lady!

Lady Bruton stood by Miss Parry's chair, a spectral grenadier, draped in black, inviting Peter Walsh to lunch; cordial; but without small talk, remembering nothing whatever about the flora or fauna of India. She had been there, of course; had stayed with three Viceroys; thought some of the Indian civilians uncommonly fine fellows; but what a tragedy it was—the state of India! The Prime Minister had just been telling her (old Miss Parry, huddled up in her shawl, did not care what the Prime Minister had just been telling her), and Lady Bruton would like to have Peter Walsh's opinion, he being fresh from the centre, and she would get Sir Sampson to meet him, for really it prevented her from sleeping at night, the folly of it, the wickedness she might say, being a soldier's daughter. She was an old woman now, not good for much. But her house, her servants, her good friend Milly Brush—did he remember her?—were all there only asking to be used if—if they could be of help, in short. For she never spoke of England, but this isle of men, this dear, dear land,[1] was in her blood (without reading Shakespeare), and if ever a woman could have worn the helmet and shot the arrow, could have led troops to attack, ruled with indomitable justice barbarian hordes and lain under a shield noseless in a church or made a green grass mound on some primeval hillside, that woman was Millicent Bruton. Debarred by her sex, and some truancy, too, of the logical faculty (she found it impossible to write a letter to the *Times*), she had the thought of Empire always at hand, and had acquired from her association with that armoured goddess her ramrod bearing, her robustness of demeanour, so that one could not figure her even in death parted from the earth or roaming territories over which, in some spiritual shape, the Union Jack had ceased to fly. To be not English even among the dead—no, no! Impossible!

But was it Lady Bruton? (whom she used to know). Was it Peter Walsh grown grey? Lady Rosseter asked herself (who had been Sally Seton). It was old Miss Parry certainly—the old aunt

---

1 Paraphrased from John of Gaunt's speech in Shakespeare's *Richard II*—"This royal throne of kings, this scepter'd isle ... this dear dear land" (II.i.722-39).

who used to be so cross when she stayed at Bourton. Never should she forget running along the passage naked, and being sent for by Miss Parry! And Clarissa! oh Clarissa! Sally caught her by the arm.

Clarissa stopped beside them.

"But I can't stay," she said. "I shall come later. Wait," she said, looking at Peter and Sally. They must wait, she meant, until all these people had gone.

"I shall come back," she said, looking at her old friends, Sally and Peter, who were shaking hands, and Sally, remembering the past no doubt, was laughing.

But her voice was wrung of its old ravishing richness; her eyes not aglow as they used to be, when she smoked cigars, when she ran down the passage to fetch her sponge bag without a stitch of clothing on her, and Ellen Atkins asked, What if the gentlemen had met her? But everybody forgave her. She stole a chicken from the larder because she was hungry in the night; she smoked cigars in her bedroom; she left a priceless book in the punt. But everybody adored her (except perhaps Papa). It was her warmth; her vitality—she would paint, she would write. Old women in the village never to this day forgot to ask after "your friend in the red cloak who seemed so bright." She accused Hugh Whitbread, of all people (and there he was, her old friend Hugh, talking to the Portuguese Ambassador), of kissing her in the smoking-room to punish her for saying that women should have votes. Vulgar men did, she said. And Clarissa remembered having to persuade her not to denounce him at family prayers—which she was capable of doing with her daring, her recklessness, her melodramatic love of being the centre of everything and creating scenes, and it was bound, Clarissa used to think, to end in some awful tragedy; her death; her martyrdom; instead of which she had married, quite unexpectedly, a bald man with a large buttonhole who owned, it was said, cotton mills at Manchester. And she had five boys!

She and Peter had settled down together. They were talking: it seemed so familiar—that they should be talking. They would discuss the past. With the two of them (more even than with Richard) she shared her past; the garden; the trees; old Joseph Breitkopf singing Brahms without any voice; the drawing-room wallpaper; the smell of the mats. A part of this Sally must always be; Peter must always be. But she must leave them. There were the Bradshaws, whom she disliked.

She must go up to Lady Bradshaw (in grey and silver, balancing like a sea-lion at the edge of its tank, barking for invitations,

Duchesses, the typical successful man's wife), she must go up to Lady Bradshaw and say ...

But Lady Bradshaw anticipated her.

"We are shockingly late, dear Mrs. Dalloway; we hardly dared to come in," she said.

And Sir William, who looked very distinguished, with his grey hair and blue eyes, said yes; they had not been able to resist the temptation. He was talking to Richard about that Bill probably, which they wanted to get through the Commons.[1] Why did the sight of him, talking to Richard, curl her up? He looked what he was, a great doctor. A man absolutely at the head of his profession, very powerful, rather worn. For think what cases came before him—people in the uttermost depths of misery; people on the verge of insanity; husbands and wives. He had to decide questions of appalling difficulty. Yet—what she felt was, one wouldn't like Sir William to see one unhappy. No; not that man.

"How is your son at Eton?" she asked Lady Bradshaw.

He had just missed his eleven,[2] said Lady Bradshaw, because of the mumps. His father minded even more than he did, she thought, "being," she said, "nothing but a great boy himself."

Clarissa looked at Sir William, talking to Richard. He did not look like a boy—not in the least like a boy.

She had once gone with some one to ask his advice. He had been perfectly right; extremely sensible. But Heavens—what a relief to get out to the street again! There was some poor wretch sobbing, she remembered, in the waiting-room. But she did not know what it was about Sir William; what exactly she disliked. Only Richard agreed with her, "didn't like his taste, didn't like his smell." But he was extraordinarily able. They were talking about this Bill. Some case Sir William was mentioning, lowering his voice. It had its bearing upon what he was saying about the deferred effects of shell shock. There must be some provision in the Bill.

Sinking her voice, drawing Mrs. Dalloway into the shelter of a common femininity, a common pride in the illustrious qualities of husbands and their sad tendency to overwork, Lady Bradshaw (poor goose—one didn't dislike her) murmured how, "just as we were starting, my husband was called up on the telephone, a very

---

1 Probably referring to legislation arising from the 1922 "Report of the War Office Committee of Enquiry into 'Shell-shock'"; see Thomas and Appendix D2.

2 A cricket team, consisting of eleven players.

sad case. A young man (that is what Sir William is telling Mr. Dalloway) had killed himself. He had been in the army." Oh! thought Clarissa, in the middle of my party, here's death, she thought.

She went on, into the little room where the Prime Minister had gone with Lady Bruton. Perhaps there was somebody there. But there was nobody. The chairs still kept the impress of the Prime Minister and Lady Bruton, she turned deferentially, he sitting four-square, authoritatively. They had been talking about India. There was nobody. The party's splendour fell to the floor, so strange it was to come in alone in her finery.

What business had the Bradshaws to talk of death at her party? A young man had killed himself. And they talked of it at her party—the Bradshaws talked of death. He had killed himself—but how? Always her body went through it, when she was told, first, suddenly, of an accident; her dress flamed, her body burnt. He had thrown himself from a window. Up had flashed the ground; through him, blundering, bruising, went the rusty spikes. There he lay with a thud, thud, thud in his brain, and then a suffocation of blackness. So she saw it. But why had he done it? And the Bradshaws talked of it at her party!

She had once thrown a shilling into the Serpentine, never anything more. But he had flung it away. They went on living (she would have to go back; the rooms were still crowded; people kept on coming). They (all day she had been thinking of Bourton, of Peter, of Sally), they would grow old. A thing there was that mattered; a thing, wreathed about with chatter, defaced, obscured in her own life, let drop every day in corruption, lies, chatter. This he had preserved. Death was defiance. Death was an attempt to communicate, people feeling the impossibility of reaching the centre which, mystically, evaded them; closeness drew apart; rapture faded; one was alone. There was an embrace in death.

But this young man who had killed himself—had he plunged holding his treasure? "If it were now to die, 'twere now to be most happy,"[1] she had said to herself once, coming down, in white.

Or there were the poets and thinkers. Suppose he had had that passion, and had gone to Sir William Bradshaw, a great doctor, yet to her obscurely evil, without sex or lust, extremely polite to women, but capable of some indescribable outrage—forcing your soul, that was it—if this young man had gone to him, and Sir William had impressed him, like that, with his power, might he

---

1 See p. 73, n. 1.

not then have said (indeed she felt it now), Life is made intolerable; they make life intolerable, men like that?

Then (she had felt it only this morning) there was the terror; the overwhelming incapacity, one's parents giving it into one's hands, this life, to be lived to the end, to be walked with serenely; there was in the depths of her heart an awful fear. Even now, quite often if Richard had not been there reading the *Times*, so that she could crouch like a bird and gradually revive, send roaring up that immeasurable delight, rubbing stick to stick, one thing with another, she must have perished. She had escaped. But that young man had killed himself.

Somehow it was her disaster—her disgrace. It was her punishment to see sink and disappear here a man, there a woman, in this profound darkness, and she forced to stand here in her evening dress. She had schemed; she had pilfered. She was never wholly admirable. She had wanted success, Lady Bexborough and the rest of it. And once she had walked on the terrace at Bourton.

Odd, incredible; she had never been so happy. Nothing could be slow enough; nothing last too long. No pleasure could equal, she thought, straightening the chairs, pushing in one book on the shelf, this having done with the triumphs of youth, lost herself in the process of living, to find it, with a shock of delight, as the sun rose, as the day sank. Many a time had she gone, at Bourton when they were all talking, to look at the sky; or seen it between people's shoulders at dinner; seen it in London when she could not sleep. She walked to the window.

It held, foolish as the idea was, something of her own in it, this country sky, this sky above Westminster. She parted the curtains; she looked. Oh, but how surprising!—in the room opposite the old lady stared straight at her! She was going to bed. And the sky. It will be a solemn sky, she had thought, it will be a dusky sky, turning away its cheek in beauty. But there it was—ashen pale, raced over quickly by tapering vast clouds. It was new to her. The wind must have risen. She was going to bed, in the room opposite. It was fascinating to watch her, moving about, that old lady, crossing the room, coming to the window. Could she see her? It was fascinating, with people still laughing and shouting in the drawing-room, to watch that old woman, quite quietly, going to bed alone. She pulled the blind now. The clock began striking. The young man had killed himself; but she did not pity him; with the clock striking the hour, one, two, three, she did not pity him, with all this going on. There! the old lady had put out her light! the whole house was dark now with this going on, she repeated, and the words came to her, Fear no more the heat of the sun. She must go back to them. But what an extraordinary night! She felt somehow very like him—the young man who had killed himself. She felt glad that he had done it; thrown it away while they went on living. The clock was striking. The leaden circles dissolved in the air. But she must go back. She must assemble. She must find Sally and Peter. And she came in from the little room.

"But where is Clarissa?" said Peter. He was sitting on the sofa with Sally. (After all these years he really could not call her "Lady Rosseter.") "Where's the woman gone to?" he asked. "Where's Clarissa?"

Sally supposed, and so did Peter for the matter of that, that there were people of importance, politicians, whom neither of them knew unless by sight in the picture papers, whom Clarissa had to be nice to, had to talk to. She was with them. Yet there was Richard Dalloway not in the Cabinet. He hadn't been a success, Sally supposed? For herself, she scarcely ever read the papers. She sometimes saw his name mentioned. But then—well, she lived a very solitary life, in the wilds, Clarissa would say, among great merchants, great manufacturers, men, after all, who did things. She had done things too!

"I have five sons!" she told him.

Lord, lord, what a change had come over her! the softness of motherhood; its egotism too. Last time they met, Peter remembered, had been among the cauliflowers in the moonlight, the leaves "like rough bronze" she had said, with her literary turn; and she had picked a rose. She had marched him up and down that awful night, after the scene by the fountain; he was to catch the midnight train. Heavens, he had wept!

That was his old trick, opening a pocket-knife, thought Sally, always opening and shutting a knife when he got excited. They had been very, very intimate, she and Peter Walsh, when he was in love with Clarissa, and there was that dreadful, ridiculous scene over Richard Dalloway at lunch. She had called Richard "Wickham." Why not call Richard "Wickham"? Clarissa had flared up! and indeed they had never seen each other since, she and Clarissa, not more than half-a-dozen times perhaps in the last ten years. And Peter Walsh had gone off to India, and she had heard vaguely that he had made an unhappy marriage, and she didn't know whether he had any children, and she couldn't ask him, for he had changed. He was rather shrivelled-looking, but kinder, she felt, and she had a real affection for him, for he was connected with her youth, and she still had a little Emily Brontë[1] he had given her, and he was to write, surely? In those days he was to write.

"Have you written?" she asked him, spreading her hand, her firm and shapely hand, on her knee in a way he recalled.

"Not a word!" said Peter Walsh, and she laughed.

She was still attractive, still a personage, Sally Seton. But who was this Rosseter? He wore two camellias on his wedding day—that was all Peter knew of him. "They have myriads of servants, miles of conservatories," Clarissa wrote; something like that. Sally owned it with a shout of laughter.

"Yes, I have ten thousand a year"[2]—whether before the tax was paid or after, she couldn't remember, for her husband, "whom you must meet," she said, "whom you would like," she said, did all that for her.

And Sally used to be in rags and tatters. She had pawned her great-grandfather's ring which Marie Antoinette had given him—had he got it right?—to come to Bourton.

Oh yes, Sally remembered; she had it still, a ruby ring which Marie Antoinette had given her great-grandfather. She never had a penny to her name in those days, and going to Bourton always meant some frightful pinch. But going to Bourton had meant so much to her—had kept her sane, she believed, so unhappy had she been at home. But that was all a thing of the past—all over now, she said. And Mr. Parry was dead; and Miss Parry was still alive. Never had he had such a shock in his life! said Peter. He had been quite certain she was dead. And the marriage had been, Sally supposed, a success? And that very handsome, very self-possessed young woman was Elizabeth, over there, by the curtains, in red.[3]

(She was like a poplar, she was like a river, she was like a hyacinth, Willie Titcomb was thinking. Oh how much nicer to be in the country and do what she liked! She could hear her poor dog howling, Elizabeth was certain.) She was not a bit like Clarissa, Peter Walsh said.

"Oh, Clarissa!" said Sally.

---

1 English novelist (1818-48), author of *Wuthering Heights* (1847).

2 Sally is referring to her income of ten thousand pounds a year. See p. 104, n. 1; p. 127, n. 1; and p. 180, n. 2.

3 Another small error in the first Hogarth Press edition: elsewhere in the novel, Elizabeth's dress is described as pink.

What Sally felt was simply this. She had owed Clarissa an enormous amount. They had been friends, not acquaintances, friends, and she still saw Clarissa all in white going about the house with her hands full of flowers—to this day tobacco plants made her think of Bourton. But—did Peter understand?—she lacked something. Lacked what was it? She had charm; she had extraordinary charm. But to be frank (and she felt that Peter was an old friend, a real friend—did absence matter? did distance matter? She had often wanted to write to him, but torn it up, yet felt he understood, for people understand without things being said, as one realises growing old, and old she was, had been that afternoon to see her sons at Eton, where they had the mumps), to be quite frank, then, how could Clarissa have done it?—married Richard Dalloway? a sportsman, a man who cared only for dogs. Literally, when he came into the room he smelt of the stables. And then all this? She waved her hand.

Hugh Whitbread it was, strolling past in his white waistcoat, dim, fat, blind, past everything he looked, except self-esteem and comfort.

"He's not going to recognise *us*," said Sally, and really she hadn't the courage—so that was Hugh! the admirable Hugh!

"And what does he do?" she asked Peter.

He blacked the King's boots or counted bottles at Windsor, Peter told her. Peter kept his sharp tongue still! But Sally must be frank, Peter said. That kiss now, Hugh's.

On the lips, she assured him, in the smoking-room one evening. She went straight to Clarissa in a rage. Hugh didn't do such things! Clarissa said, the admirable Hugh! Hugh's socks were without exception the most beautiful she had ever seen—and now his evening dress. Perfect! And had he children?

"Everybody in the room has six sons at Eton," Peter told her, except himself. He, thank God, had none. No sons, no daughters, no wife. Well, he didn't seem to mind, said Sally. He looked younger, she thought, than any of them.

But it had been a silly thing to do, in many ways, Peter said, to marry like that; "a perfect goose she was," he said, but, he said, "we had a splendid time of it," but how could that be? Sally wondered; what did he mean? and how odd it was to know him and yet not know a single thing that had happened to him. And did he say it out of pride? Very likely, for after all it must be galling for him (though he was an oddity, a sort of sprite, not at all an ordinary man), it must be lonely at his age to have no home, nowhere to go to. But he must stay with them for weeks and weeks. Of course he would; he would love to stay with them, and that was how it came out. All these years the Dalloways had never been once. Time after time they had asked them. Clarissa (for it was Clarissa of course) would not come. For, said Sally, Clarissa was at heart a snob—one had to admit it, a snob. And it was that that was between them, she was convinced. Clarissa thought she had married beneath her, her husband being—she was proud of it—a miner's son. Every penny they had he had earned. As a little boy (her voice trembled) he had carried great sacks.

(And so she would go on, Peter felt, hour after hour; the miner's son; people thought she had married beneath her; her five sons; and what was the other thing—plants, hydrangeas, syringas, very very rare hybiscus lilies that never grow north of the Suez Canal, but she, with one gardener in a suburb near Manchester, had beds of them, positively beds! Now all that Clarissa had escaped, unmaternal as she was.)

A snob was she? Yes, in many ways. Where was she, all this time? It was getting late.

"Yet," said Sally, "when I heard Clarissa was giving a party, I felt I couldn't *not* come—must see her again (and I'm staying in Victoria Street, practically next door). So I just came without an invitation. But," she whispered, "tell me, do. Who is this?"

It was Mrs. Hilbery, looking for the door. For how late it was getting! And, she murmured, as the night grew later, as people went, one found old friends; quiet nooks and corners; and the loveliest views. Did they know, she asked, that they were surrounded by an enchanted garden? Lights and trees and wonderful gleaming lakes and the sky. Just a few fairy lamps, Clarissa Dalloway had said, in the back garden! But she was a magician! It was a park.... And she didn't know their names, but friends she knew they were, friends without names, songs without words, always the best. But there were so many doors, such unexpected places, she could not find her way.

"Old Mrs. Hilbery," said Peter; but who was that? that lady standing by the curtain all the evening, without speaking? He knew her face; connected her with Bourton. Surely she used to cut up underclothes at the large table in the window? Davidson, was that her name?

"Oh, that is Ellie Henderson," said Sally. Clarissa was really very hard on her. She was a cousin, very poor. Clarissa *was* hard on people.

She was rather, said Peter. Yet, said Sally, in her emotional way, with a rush of that enthusiasm which Peter used to love her for, yet dreaded a little now, so effusive she might become—how generous to her friends Clarissa was! and what a rare quality one found it, and how sometimes at night or on Christmas Day, when she counted up her blessings, she put that friendship first. They were young; that was it. Clarissa was pure-hearted; that was it. Peter would think her sentimental. So she was. For she had come to feel that it was the only thing worth saying—what one felt. Cleverness was silly. One must say simply what one felt.

"But I do not know," said Peter Walsh, "what I feel."

Poor Peter, thought Sally. Why did not Clarissa come and talk to them? That was what he was longing for. She knew it. All the time he was thinking only of Clarissa, and was fidgeting with his knife.

He had not found life simple, Peter said. His relations with Clarissa had not been simple. It had spoilt his life, he said. (They had been so intimate—he and Sally Seton, it was absurd not to say it.) One could not be in love twice, he said. And what could she say? Still it is better to have loved (but he would think her sentimental—he used to be so sharp). He must come and stay with them in Manchester. That is all very true, he said. All very true. He would love to come and stay with them, directly he had done what he had to do in London.

And Clarissa had cared for him more than she had ever cared for Richard, Sally was positive of that.

"No, no, no!" said Peter (Sally should not have said that—she went too far). That good fellow—there he was at the end of the room, holding forth, the same as ever, dear old Richard. Who was he talking to? Sally asked, that very distinguished-looking man? Living in the wilds as she did, she had an insatiable curiosity to know who people were. But Peter did not know. He did not like his looks, he said, probably a Cabinet Minister. Of them all, Richard seemed to him the best, he said—the most disinterested.

"But what has he done?" Sally asked. Public work, she supposed. And were they happy together? Sally asked (she herself was extremely happy); for, she admitted, she knew nothing about them, only jumped to conclusions, as one does, for what can one know even of the people one lives with every day? she asked. Are we not all prisoners? She had read a wonderful play about a man who scratched on the wall of his cell, and she had felt that was true of life—one scratched on the wall. Despairing of human relationships (people were so difficult), she often went into her garden and got from her flowers a peace which men and women never gave her. But no; he did not like cabbages; he preferred human beings, Peter said. Indeed, the young are beautiful, Sally said, watching Elizabeth cross the room. How unlike Clarissa at her age! Could he make anything of her? She would not open her lips. Not much, not yet, Peter admitted. She was like a lily, Sally said, a lily by the side of a pool. But Peter did not agree that we know nothing. We know everything, he said; at least he did.

But these two, Sally whispered, these two coming now (and really she must go, if Clarissa did not come soon), this distinguished-looking man and his rather common-looking wife who had been talking to Richard—what could one know about people like that?

"That they're damnable humbugs," said Richard,[1] looking at them casually. He made Sally laugh.

But Sir William Bradshaw stopped at the door to look at a picture. He looked in the corner for the engraver's name. His wife looked too. Sir William Bradshaw was so interested in art.

When one was young, said Peter, one was too much excited to know people. Now that one was old, fifty-two[2] to be precise (Sally was fifty-five, in body, she said, but her heart was like a girl's of twenty); now that one was mature then, said Peter, one could watch, one could understand, and one did not lose the power of feeling, he said. No, that is true, said Sally. She felt more deeply, more passionately, every year. It increased, he said, alas, perhaps, but one should be glad of it—it went on increasing in his experience. There was some one in India. He would like to tell Sally about her. He would like Sally to know her. She was married, he said. She had two small children. They must all come to Manchester, said Sally—he must promise before they left.

"There's Elizabeth," he said, "she feels not half what we feel, not yet." "But," said Sally, watching Elizabeth go to her father, "one can see they are devoted to each other." She could feel it by the way Elizabeth went to her father.

For her father had been looking at her, as he stood talking to the Bradshaws, and he had thought to himself who is that lovely girl? And suddenly he realised that it was his Elizabeth, and he had not recognised her, she looked so lovely in her pink frock! Elizabeth had felt him looking at her as she talked to Willie Titcomb. So she went to him and they stood together, now that the

---

1 Perhaps the most serious of the errors appearing in the first Hogarth Press edition: the speaker here is, of course, Peter Walsh.

2 Another small error in the first Hogarth Press edition: elsewhere in the novel Peter Walsh is described as fifty-three years old.

party was almost over, looking at the people going, and the rooms getting emptier and emptier, with things scattered on the floor. Even Ellie Henderson was going, nearly last of all, though no one had spoken to her, but she had wanted to see everything, to tell Edith. And Richard and Elizabeth were rather glad it was over, but Richard was proud of his daughter. And he had not meant to tell her, but he could not help telling her. He had looked at her, he said, and he had wondered, who is that lovely girl? and it was his daughter! That did make her happy. But her poor dog was howling.

"Richard has improved. You are right," said Sally. "I shall go and talk to him. I shall say good-night. What does the brain matter," said Lady Rosseter, getting up, "compared with the heart?"

"I will come," said Peter, but he sat on for a moment. What is this terror? what is this ecstasy? he thought to himself. What is it that fills me with extraordinary excitement?

It is Clarissa, he said.

For there she was.

THE END

Appendix A: Contemporary Reviews

1. From John W. Crawford, "One Day in London the Subject of Mrs. Woolf's New Novel," *The New York Times Book Review* (10 May 1925): 10

One day in the life of Clarissa Dalloway, a June day in London, punctuated accurately, impersonally, unfeelingly, by the chimes of Big Ben and a fashionable party to end it, is the complete story of Mrs. Woolf's new novel, "Mrs. Dalloway," yet she contrives to enmesh all the inflections of Mrs. Dalloway's personality, and many of the implications of modern civilization in the account of those twenty-four hours. The trees in full leaf are a festival, and Mrs. Dalloway's greeting of socially prominent friends, as she meets them in the street, is a progress of quick and bird-like inquisitiveness and ever youthful, sterile zest. Mrs. Dalloway is more than fifty and the mother of a daughter, who is not fashionable, who is even serious. Yet she is "a charming woman," and somehow untouched, with something "of the bird about her...." Mrs. Dalloway in her own home is "the perfect hostess," even to her servants, to her daughter, her husband and her rejected suitor of long ago, who cannot free his mind of her. It is almost a perfect being that Mrs. Dalloway enjoys, but there is a resentfulness in her, some paucity of spiritual graces, or rather some positive hideousness: "It rasped in her, though, to have stirring about in her this brutal monster, to hear twigs cracking and feel hooves planted down in the depths of that leaf-encumbered forest, the soul...."

Those amazing ziggurat[1] towers of phrase that would be Babel[2] under a less skilful guidance than Mrs. Woolf's, carry a subtle cadence which, in the rich orchestration of the prose, comes to be identified with the sudden, calculated enthusiasms, the artful graciousness and the inveigling ways of Clarissa, and become, in effect, her very leitmotiv. Mrs. Woolf elects an Olympian license in assembling contributions to the moods of Clarissa: she follows them with apparent willfulness, selecting them out of a crowd, making them individuals, investing them with situations and bringing them elusively and obliquely to bear upon Clarissa. Each of these has a personal leitmotiv. There is, indeed,

1 "A staged tower of pyramid form in which each successive storey is smaller than that below it, so as to leave a terrace all round; an Assyrian or Babylonian temple-tower" (*OED* online).

2 A confusion of sound or noise, derived from the biblical story of the Tower of Babel, Genesis 11:1-9.

in any congruence of two or more of these elements in the synthesis of Clarissa, a sense of ascending excitement, of mounting and counter-balancing, frictionful impulsions of rhythm, as of accessions of instruments to the development of a symphony. It is incredible that this could be done with English prose....

Mrs. Woolf has set free a new clarity of thought and rendered possible a more precise and more evocative agglutination of complicated ideas in simplicity of expression. Her design, in effect, is no more than another of those fashionable pictures of an attractive, pretty woman, who is selfish and worldly, and preternaturally fearful.... The latent irony that attends upon Clarissa rather follows upon the contradictions and incongruities of Clarissa, than grows out of Mrs. Woolf's "conscious superiority"; this brand of cheap sneer does not concern Mrs. Woolf. Her detachment is beautiful and complete, yet there is a sense that she is present, improvising fastidiously, yet concretely, those involutions which are to produce that ultimate effect upon Clarissa's old lover and upon the reader ...

Clarissa's day, the impressions she gives and receives, the memories and recognitions which stir in her, the events which are initiated remotely and engineered almost to touching distance of the impervious Clarissa, capture in a definitive matrix the drift of thought and feeling in a period, the point of view of a class, and seem almost to indicate the strength and weakness of an entire civilization. Mrs. Woolf is concerned with those governing classes of England which Ford Madox Ford[1] demolished in "Some Do Not." Her dissociations, instead of being bludgeoned directly, almost specifically, contrive insidiously and unobtrusively to disintegrate accepted values.

It is not only that Clarissa is giving, in fact does give, one of those parties at which the successful, the titled and the important pay a tacit homage to the political prestige of her husband, a member of the Parliament, and an overt tribute to the fascinations of Clarissa herself. It is not alone that Clarissa's snobberies and exclusions, her hatred of ugliness and excess, her dainty wrapping of herself in cotton wool and her "tender superfluous probing into all that pollutes" are unerringly depicted. The whole progress of the circumstances of Clarissa's day, from the passing of a "somebody" in a closed motor car to the ignoring of a nobody at her party, make for a vivid interaction and interrelation of the social forces and personal tendencies which act upon and proceed from Clarissa.

---

1 English novelist, critic, and editor (1873-1939). *Some Do Not* (1924) was the first in what would become a four-volume series of World War I novels, *Parade's End*, published between 1924 and 1928.

Clarissa might almost be one of those figures of high society which Mrs. Humphry Ward[1] delighted in. She is as callous and vain as any of those earlier portraits. Clarissa is, however, conceived so brilliantly, dimensioned so thoroughly and documented so absolutely that her type, in the words of Constantin Stanislavsky,[2] might be said to have been done "inviolably and for all time." Clarissa carries a conviction of the feeling of truth and inner justification.

2. From Richard Hughes, "A Day in London Life," *Saturday Review of Literature* (16 May 1925): 755

[Then in his mid-20s, British novelist, playwright and poet Richard Hughes (1900-76) was to become an important literary figure in his own right, perhaps best known for his novel *A High Wind in Jamaica* (1929; originally titled *The Innocent Voyage*). This review appeared in an American weekly magazine.]

... In Mrs. Woolf's new novel, "Mrs. Dalloway," the visible world exists with a brilliance, a luminous clarity. In particular, it is London: to the reader, London is made, for the first time (this will probably surprise him) to exist. It emerges, shining like crystal, out of the fog in which all the merely material universe is ordinarily enveloped in his mind: it emerges and stays. The present writer has "known" London all his life: but Mrs. Woolf's evocation of it is of a very different quality from his own memories: a quality which answers the farmer's question, when he was puzzled as to why folk should pay five hundred guineas for a painting of his farm, when they could have the house itself for two hundred. To Mrs. Woolf London exists, and to Mrs. Woolf's readers anywhere and at any time London will exist with a reality it can never have for those who merely live there.

Vividness alone, of course, is not art: it is only the material of art. But Mrs. Woolf has, I think, a finer sense of form than any but the oldest living English novelist. As well as the power of brilliant evocation she has that creative faculty of form which differs from what is ordinarily called construction in the same way that life differs from

1 Mary Augusta Ward (1851-1920), a prolific and best-selling British novelist who published as Mrs. Humphry Ward. Although in 1908 she was one of the founding members of the Women's National Anti-Suffrage League, her work overall was reformist in character.

2 Russian actor and theatre director (1863-1938), whose "system" of acting influenced the development of American "method" acting.

mechanism: the same quality as Cézanne.[1] In the case of the painter, of course, this "form" is purely visual; the synthesis—relation—rhythm—whatever you call it, is created on this side the eye; while in the case of the poet the pattern is a mental one, created behind the eye of the reader, composed directly of mental processes, ideas, sensory evocation—not of external agents (not of the words used, I mean). So, in the case of Mrs. Woolf, and of the present novel, it is not by its vividness that her writing ultimately stays in the mind, but by the coherent and processional form which is composed of, and transcends, that vividness.

Philosophy as much as the smell of violets is grist to the artist's mill: in actual practice, it is generally more so. Here, Mrs. Woolf touches all the time the verge of the problem of reality: not directly, like Pirandello,[2] but by implication. (She is not so prone to emphasis as Pirandello.) In contrast to the solidity of her visible world there rises throughout the book in a delicate crescendo *fear*. The most notable feature of contemporary thought is the wide recognition by the human mind of its own limitation; *i.e.*, that it is itself not a microcosm (as men used to think) but the macrocosm: that it cannot "find out" anything about the universe because the terms both of question and answer are terms purely relative to itself: that even the key-words, *being* and *not-being*, bear no relation to anything except the mind which formulates them.... In short, that logical and associative thinking do not differ in ultimate value—or even perhaps in kind. So, in this book each of the very different characters—Clarissa Dalloway herself, the slightly more speculative Peter, the Blakeian[3] "lunatic," Septimus Warren Smith, each with their own more or less formulated hypothesis of the meaning of life—together are an unanswerable illustration of that bottomlessness on which all spiritual values are based. This is what I mean by fear.

To come to the matter of chronicle, this novel is an account of a single day in London life; its sole principal event is the return from India of Mrs. Dalloway's rejected suitor; the other characters are in many

---

1 Paul Cézanne (1839-1906), a French Post-Impressionist painter. Cézanne was among the painters introduced to London at "Manet and the Post-Impressionists," the 1910 exhibition organized at the Grafton Galleries by Roger Fry, artist, art critic, and member of the Bloomsbury Group. Fry coined the term "post-impressionism" for this exhibit.

2 Luigi Pirandello (1867-1936), Italian playwright, novelist, and poet, probably best known in English-speaking countries for his 1921 play *Six Characters in Search of an Author*.

3 A reference to William Blake (1757-1827), the visionary British poet, artist, and political radical of the early Romantic period.

cases not even acquainted with the principals—sometimes simply people they pass in the street, or even people who merely see the same aeroplane in the sky. Towards the end, one of these strangers flings himself from a window; and Mrs. Dalloway, after spending most of the morning wandering about Bond Street, gives a party in the evening. But then, Chronicle is an ass; this is an unusually coherent, lucid, and enthralling book, whatever he may suggest to the contrary.

3. From [Arthur Sydney McDowall,] "A Novelist's Experiment," *Times Literary Supplement* (21 May 1925): 349

All Mrs. Woolf's fiction shows such an instinct for experiment that we may have to show cause why this new book should be called peculiarly experimental. "Jacob's Room,"[1] too, was an adventure. But there is one obvious difference between that novel and "Mrs. Dalloway." While the other, however innovating in its method, observed the usual time-span of a novel, this one describes the passage of a single day. The idea, though new enough to be called an experiment, may not be unique in modern fiction. There was a precedent in "Ulysses."[2] But Mrs. Woolf's vision escapes disaster and produces something of her own. People and events here have a peculiar, almost ethereal transparency, as though bathed in a medium where one thing permeates another. Undoubtedly our world is less solid than it was, and our novels may have to shake themselves a little free of matter. Here, Mrs. Woolf seems to say, is the stream of life, but reflected always in a mental vision.

Life itself, with the first cool radiance of a June morning in London, is wafted to Clarissa Dalloway as she goes out to buy flowers for her party in the evening—the same Clarissa who made a brief irruption into "The Voyage Out," so exquisitely there and brightly, almost excessively, interested; and now, at fifty-one, a little wiser, more pensive, but adoring life. An hour or two later, and Peter Walsh, whimsically sympathetic, who had been Clarissa's suitor years ago and has just returned from India, is falling asleep on a bench in Regent's Park to dream of memories, and will awake to think them out. Near him is a young couple, who seem to be having a grim quarrel; but the man is a war victim who has gone out of his mind, and we shall read the last page of his tragedy before dusk falls. We shall be also at luncheon with Lady Bruton, at tea in the Army and Navy Stores, where Miss Kilman is making her last tense effort to snatch Clarissa's lovely daughter from her mother. But how often these lives and doings seem to distil them-

1 Novel by Woolf, first published in 1922.

2 Novel by James Joyce, first published serially in *The Little Review* from March 1918 to December 1920, and then in its entirety in 1922. See Richter.

selves in something as immaterial as the passing of sunlight or the sound of a clock striking the hour. Distances gleam in the liquid clearness of that drop or bubble. For Mrs. Woolf's sensitiveness can retain those wayward flashes as well as the whole chain of mixed images and feelings that unwinds from some tiny coil of memory. If in "Jacob's Room" she suggested the simultaneousness of life, here she paints not only this but its stream-like continuity.

Outwardly, however, the book is a cross-section of life. It does not simplify and concentrate as a play would do, nor does it thread everything on a single mind's experience. On the contrary, Mrs. Woolf expands her view with the fullest freedom of a novelist, although she has the briefest limit as regards time; and the fusion of these opposing tendencies into one is a thrilling and hazardous enterprise. Only through sheer vision can it have form and life; and here the finely imaginative substance into which Mrs. Woolf has woven it all is certainly reassuring. Moreover, while delineating processes she does not efface persons; on them all the threads depend, and theirs are the values. Theirs too, that final riddle of separateness, of otherness in the midst of the continuous ...

Watching Mrs. Woolf's experiment, certainly one of the hardest and very subtly planned, one reckons up its cost. To get the whole value of the present you must enhance it, perhaps, with the past. And with her two chief figures, Clarissa and Peter, meeting after a long severance, Mrs. Woolf has a full scope for the use of memories. They are amusing and they illuminate; yet either because of the rest of the design, or one's sense of the probable, or both, one fancies that sometimes these remembrances stretch almost too far. And the tragedy of poor Septimus, the war victim, although poignant in contrast, makes a block in the tideway now and then.

Although there is a surprising characterization in the process, characters must necessarily be shown with the tantalising fluidness of life itself. Lesser figures like Richard Dalloway or Lady Bruton or Miss Kilman, that grimly pathetic vampire, do well enough in outline; but as soon as we are shown more of a character, like Clarissa's or Peter's, we want more still, craving a further dimension that we cannot get. Also the cinema-like speed of the picture robs us of a great deal of the delight in Mrs. Woolf's style. It has to be a little clipped, a little breathless; and the reading of her book is not so easy as it seems. Her wit is irresistible when it can escape a little way, as in the vision of those rival goddesses, Proportion and Conversion. In the end no one will complain of her for using all the freedom that she can. All her technical suppleness is needed to cope with the new form. It remains experimental in so far as we are uncertain what more can be done with it, and whether it can give the author's rare gifts full play. But something real has been achieved; for, having the courage of her theme and setting free her vision, Mrs. Woolf steeps it in an emotion and irony and delicate imagination which enhance the consciousness and the zest of living.

4. From Gerald Bullett, "New Fiction," *The Saturday Review* (30 May 1925): 588

[Gerald Bullett (1893-1958) was a British novelist, short story writer, poet, and critic, known especially for his fantasy fiction. This review appeared in a London weekly newspaper.]

... Mrs. Woolf is a brilliant experimentalist ... The searchlight of [her] suggestive art passes zigzag over the minds of men and women, illuminating those dark interiors with the light of an extraordinarily subtle vision. It rests, this penetrating ray, longest upon Peter Walsh himself, who is just returned from long exile in India.

Peter calls on Clarissa in the morning; he attends her party at night. With this second meeting the book closes. In the interval we have watched minutely the quivering activity of his cerebrum. And not his alone, but Clarissa's and Septimus Smith's and Miss Kilman's and Elizabeth's, to name but a few others. It is to be noted that we watch these intimate experiences rather than share them, that the emotions which we know, by inference, must accompany this cerebral activity do not always communicate themselves to us; we remain a little more than usually detached. We are moved, when we are moved at all, less by the particular emotions of these people than by the poetry of thought and phrase (seldom of rhythm), and by that curious sensation which is the book's continuous effect: the sensation of seeing and feeling the very stream of life, the undeviating tide of time, flowing luminously by, with all the material phenomena, streets and stars, bicycles and human bodies, floating like straws upon its surface. Whether to communicate this sense of the incessant flux was part of Mrs. Woolf's intention I cannot undertake to say: I can only record my own reaction to her book. To add that there are very definite limitations to the scope of this curious technique is hardly necessary, for there is no form of writing to which the same remark would not in some degree apply. Highly impressionistic work such as this lacks external drama, for its intellectual and technical bias provides that the most startling action—a young man's throwing himself out of the window, for example—shall seem trivial compared with the bright ferment of consciousness. Mrs. Woolf's is an inversion of the ordinary method of narration ... The fact that the life of the mind is more significant than the movement of the body is reflected in the very texture of the narrative, action being treated throughout as a mere parenthesis ... And even when the action is not apparently subordinate it is actually so. One part of this method's general effect on the reader is to make him feel that he is observing, from a great height, a world of disembodied spirits. It is not so much that the picture lacks definition as that it lacks stability; its outlines are incessantly flowing into new, bright patterns. Nothing for a moment stands still; the flying landscape daubs across our vision a myriad bright streaks of changing colour; shapes are perpetually disintegrating and resolving into new shapes. To those who desire a static universe, in which they can examine things at their leisure, this speed, this insubstantiality, this exhilarating deluge of impressions, will be perhaps unpleasing....

5. From "New Novels," *New Statesman* (6 June 1925): 229

[The *New Statesman* was founded in 1913 by prominent members of the Fabian Society. Its literary editor in 1925 was Desmond MacCarthy, Virginia Woolf's friend and a member of the Bloomsbury Group. He held that position from 1920 to 1928, writing a weekly column under the *nom de plume* "Affable Hawk."]

... *Mrs. Dalloway* is in many ways beautiful; but I think it sets out to be, and continues to the end to pretend to be, what it is not. I think it quite sincerely claims to employ a new method, and I think it employs an old one. Personally, I see no reason for trying to escape the old one, which I believe will still answer all purposes of subtlety and excitement; but, if one sets out to escape, one should succeed in escaping. People will tell you, with a face of praise, that the whole action of *Mrs. Dalloway* passes in one day. But it doesn't pass in one day. In order to create that impression, Mrs. Woolf makes her characters move about London, and when two of them come into purely fortuitous and external contact, she gives you the history of each backwards. She might just as well—better—have given it forwards. The novelty is not a novelty. It is a device that is used constantly, especially [in] the "pictures," when the hero closes his eyes, a blur crawls across the screen, and the heroine is seen in short skirts and ringlets, as he knew her in the old home-village before she was betrayed. Seven years elapse between Parts I and II; and the hero is still dreaming; but no one would say that the action of the film passes in one day. Mrs. Woolf has really imposed on several quite different stories a purely artificial unity. But, it may be said, the threads are knit at the close. They are indeed—the more's the pity. Peter Walsh, home from India, has all his life loved Clarissa, who has married Richard Dalloway and borne a daughter, Elizabeth. Clarissa goes for a walk, and sees a motor-car containing a Personage.

A crowd gathers outside Buckingham Palace; it sees an aeroplane writing on the sky; the same portent is seen by Lucrezia Warren Smith, sitting with her husband in Regent's Park. First connection. A slender one, you will admit; those smoky tendrils might bind anything to anything; an eye sufficiently remote could see everything at once. Peter calls upon Clarissa. They are still, after all these years, uncomfortable. They are middle-aged, reminiscent, critical, resentful; they part. Peter goes for a walk; he is still reminiscent; he hears an old woman singing opposite Regent's Park Tube Station; the same old woman is heard by the Warren Smiths; connection number two. Smith is a "shell-shocked" soldier; he has moments of vision, of certainty, of the kind that is called illusion; he goes to a specialist; he kills himself; the specialist attends Clarissa Dalloway's party in the evening and talks about death. Connection number three! One sees the significance of it.... But any tragedy would have served for that contrast; the artificial link is purely redundant, purely improbable, purely pointless. It is the sort of coincidence which mars the conventional novel; but it is less distracting there, because there it at any rate serves a purpose.

Mrs. Woolf, too, has—or so it seems to me—a purpose: and a genuinely splendid one. The whole trouble is the incongruity between the apparent purpose and the distracting method. I take it (and, though there is always a certain impertinence in attempting to say, or even to see, what anybody else means, the critic cannot avoid it)—I take it that Mrs. Woolf means to show us the kaleidoscope of life shaken into a momentary plan; the vagueness, the casualness, the chaos, suffering the compulsion which gives order and makes order. And that, I repeat, is splendid. All art aims, consciously or unconsciously, at that. But all the novelty of Mrs. Woolf's technique simply distracts from it. And if, as I suspect, she has the subsidiary but still vital purpose of stressing the incoherence, of catching the bubble, the spark, the half-dream, the inexplicable memory, the doubt, the snare, the joke, the dread, the come-and-go of the moment on the wing—then again the needless links, the coincidences, distract.

Mrs. Woolf has extraordinary gifts; the only doubt is whether they are the specific gifts of the novelist. She excels in description of mood or sudden scene; but the mood might always be anybody's; anybody might occupy the scene. In all this brilliant novel (and the brilliance is at times quite dazzling) there are no people. It is like that ghostly world of Mr. Bertrand Russell's philosophy,[1] in which

1 British analytic philosopher, mathematician, and anti-war activist (1872-1970); co-author, with Alfred North Whitehead (his former tutor at Cambridge University), of *Principia Mathematica* (published in 3 volumes, 1911-13).

there are lots of sensations but no one to have them. If Mrs. Woolf had created a single character, I cannot conceive that she would have *wanted* to deviate from the ordinary manner of the novelist; who, after all, could want a better or a bigger job than to tell us about a real person, about what happened to him or to her? But Mrs. Woolf's masterly and masterful intellect is critical (I don't use the word in opposition to "creative"—there is, of course, creation in criticism, in page after page of Mrs. Woolf's delicately hurrying prose). She understands a mood; she analyses it; she presents it; she catches its finer implications; but she never moves me with it, because she never makes me feel that the person credited with it is other than an object of the keenest and most skilful study. She uses the words "terror," "ecstasy," "excitement," with perfect justice; but it isn't justice they want. I hope I have made it clear that my admiration for what Mrs. Woolf has achieved outweighs my dislike of the fetters she has put on her achievement. Call *Mrs. Dalloway* an intellectual triumph, and I agree. I could quote scores of fine and profound things from it ... But I want to weep with Peter Walsh and leap to death with poor Septimus Warren Smith; and my trouble is that I can't....

6. From J.F. Holms, *The Calendar of Modern Letters* 1 (July 1925): 404-05

[*The Calendar of Modern Letters* was a modernist "little magazine" published monthly in London from March 1925 until February 1926, and then quarterly as *The Calendar* from April 1926 to July 1927.]

... "Mrs. Dalloway" is considerably the best book she has written; in it her gifts achieve their full effect, and her capacity to say what she wants to is almost complete. How then, one asks, as the tide rises through her pages, can such talent coexist with a sentimentality that would be remarkable in a stockbroker, and inconceivable among educated people. Sentimentality is an interesting term, more liable to misconstruction than most; and it is perhaps clearer to say of this novel that it is impossible to believe that if its author were asked directly whether the thoughts that pass during an hour through the head of any man of fifty bear any resemblance whatever to the soliloquies of Peter Walsh and other characters that fill her pages, her answer could differ from our own. This, however, is what we have to believe, with the result that in spite of, or on account of Mrs. Woolf's talent, her writing conveys an effect of automatism[1] that is curious, and aesthetically corrupt. "Mrs. Dalloway" has the design, apparent intensity, and immediate aspect of a work of art, and it is an interesting problem of aesthetic psychology to explain so self-subsistent a mirage entirely unconnected with reality. This is not to say that falsity is inherent throughout Mrs. Woolf's writing. Her natural and unvitiated talent springs immediately from sensation, and her sensibility of this kind is rare and valuable. When she resists the virtuoso's temptation to expanded bravura pieces, her transcriptions of immediate sensation have the freshness, delicacy and vitality of direct perception, a quality that is not relative, and is sufficient in itself to distinguish her work from intelligent novel-writing. But here Mrs. Woolf's talent stops, in more senses than one. For this quality of direct sensational perception is precisely that of a child's, undisturbed by thought, feeling and other functions to be acquired in the course of its development as a social organism. And Mrs. Woolf is by no means entirely a child; she is thoroughly involved in human relationships, which form moreover her subject matter as a novelist. But her essential reactions to them are a child's automatic reactions, who believes what he reads in a book, who believes life is what he is told it is, that some people are good and others bad—though bad ones are not to be found among persons he knows—who believes, in short, in the absoluteness of his first social impressions as a group member. Together with this more essential Mrs. Woolf exists an intelligent, experienced and sensitive adult, whose business it is to justify her to the world. But these are unhallowed partnerships whose offspring, as I have said, are sentimentality and aesthetic corruption. When she leaves immediate impressions of experience, Mrs. Woolf's treatment of character and human relations is almost ludicrously devoid of psychological and aesthetic truth; as soon as she touches them she is as false as her rendering of impressions is true. The motives, thoughts and emotions she attributes to her characters have precisely as much and as little relation to the truth of life as the motives, thought and emotions postulated of the ideal person who forms its public by the daily paper. There are one or two exceptions to this, in particular the character of Septimus Warren Smith, where Mrs. Woolf rather shakily approaches imaginative truths; but most of the book, despite its pure and brilliant impressionism, is sentimental in conception and texture, and is accordingly aesthetically

1 "The theory, belief, or doctrine that living organisms act purely mechanically, like automata, and are motivated by physical causes, rather than consciousness, intelligence, or will. Also: the condition or state of being so motivated" (*OED* online).

worthless. Such judgments, as is evident in this review, cannot be expressed in terms of purely literary criticism, which, indeed, is an instrument not applicable to the valuation of contemporary literature, as should be clear from experience and history.

7. From E.M. Forster, "The Novels of Virginia Woolf," *The Criterion* IV.2 (April 1926): 277-86

[Edward Morgan Forster (1879-1970) was a member of the Bloomsbury Group, and author of such major novels as *A Room with a View* (1908), *Howard's End* (1910), and *A Passage to India* (1924).]

... Three years after *Jacob's Room* comes another novel in the same style, or slight modification of the style: *Mrs. Dalloway*. It is perhaps her masterpiece, but difficult, and I am not altogether sure about every detail ... Here is London at all events—so much is certain, London chorussing with all its clocks and shops and sunlit parks, and writing texts with an aeroplane across God's heaven. Here is Clarissa Dalloway, elderly, kind, graceful, rather hard and superficial, and a terrible snob. How she loves London! And there is Septimus Warren Smith—she never meets him—a case of shell shock—very sad—who hears behind the chorus the voices of the dead singing, and sees his own apotheosis or damnation in the sky. That dreadful war! Sir William Bradshaw of Harley Street, himself in perfect health, very properly arranges for Septimus Warren Smith to go to a lunatic asylum. Septimus is ungrateful and throws himself out of the window. 'Coward,' cries the doctor, but it is too late. News of which comes to Clarissa as she is giving an evening party. Does she likewise commit suicide? I thought she did the first time I read the book; not at my second reading, nor is the physical act important, for she is certainly left with the full knowledge—inside knowledge—of what suicide is. The societified lady and the obscure maniac are in a sense the same person. His foot has slipped through the gay surface on which she still stands—that is all the difference between them. She returns (it would seem) to her party and to the man she loves, and a hint of her new knowledge comes through to him as the London clocks strike three. Such apparently is the outline of this exquisite and superbly constructed book, and having made that outline one must rub it out at once. For emphasis is fatal to the understanding of this author's work.... As far as her work has a message, it seems to be ... Here is one room, there another. Required like most authors to choose between the surface and the depths as the basis of her operations, she chooses the surface and then burrows in as far as she can....

But what of the subject that she regards as of the highest importance: human beings as a whole and as wholes? She tells us (in her essays) that human beings are the permanent material of fiction, that it is only the method of presenting them which changes and ought to change, that to capture their inner life presents a different problem to each generation of novelists; the great Victorians solved it in their way; the Edwardians shelved it by looking outwards at relatives and houses; the Georgians must solve it anew, and if they succeed a new age of fiction will begin. Has she herself succeeded? Do her own characters live?

I feel that they do live, but not continuously ... [T]he problem before her—the problem that she has set herself, and that certainly would inaugurate a new literature if solved—is to retain her own wonderful new method and form, and yet allow her readers to inhabit each character with Victorian thoroughness. Think how difficult this is. If you work in a storm of atoms and seconds, if your highest joy is 'life; London; this moment in June' and your deepest mystery 'here is one room; there another,' then how can you construct your human beings so that each shall be not a movable monument but an abiding home, how can you build between them any permanent roads of love and hate? ...

8. From Edwin Muir, "Contemporary Writers: Virginia Woolf," *Nation and Athenaeum* (17 April 1926): 70-72

[Edwin Muir (1887-1959) was a British poet, novelist, and notable translator of the works of Franz Kafka. *Nation and Athenaeum* was a left-liberal weekly newsletter formed in 1921 through a merger of the *Athenaeum* (founded 1828) and *The Nation*. In 1923 John Maynard Keynes, economist and member of the Bloomsbury Group, became its chairman, and Leonard Woolf served as literary editor from 1923 to 1930.]

... "Mrs. Dalloway" is the most characteristic work Mrs. Woolf has written.... As a piece of expressive writing there is nothing in contemporary English fiction to rival it. Shades of an evanescence which one might have thought uncapturable, visual effects so fine that the eye does not take them in, that only in the memory are guessed at from the impression they leave in passing, exquisitely graded qualities of sound, of emotion, of reverie, are in Mrs. Woolf's prose not merely dissected, but imaginatively reconstructed. All that in the earlier novels was analyzed is resolved in "Mrs. Dalloway" into evocative images. There is nothing left of the stubborn explanatory machinery of the analytical novel; the material upon which the author works is the same as before, but it has all been sublimated, and, although the psychology is subtle and exact, no trace remains of the psychologist.

> And Clarissa had leant forward, taken his hand, drawn him to her, kissed him—actually had felt his face on hers before she could down the brandishing of silver-flashing plumes like pampas grass in a tropic gale in her breast, which, subsiding, left her holding his hand, patting his knee, and feeling, as she sat back, extraordinarily at ease with him and light-hearted—all in a clap it came over her, If I had married him, this gaiety would have been mine all day!

How much more exact that is than analysis could be! It is more exact, for the ebb and flow of the imagery, the rhythm of the sentence, follow the course of the emotion. First we have Clarissa's effusion of uncontrolled, blind emotion evoking the image, "the brandishing of silver-flashing plumes"; then the emergence from it to a recognition of diurnal reality, reported rather than described, "leaving her holding his hand, patting his knee"; and finally in the accelerating pace with which the sentence ends, the sudden thought that if she had married him! It is exquisitely done....

In a novel like "Mrs. Dalloway," where the sensory impressions are so concretely evoked and are so much more immediate than they were before, a sort of rearrangement of the elements of experience insensibly takes place. In the traditional novel we have on the one hand the characters and on the other the background, each existing in a separate dimension, and the one generally more solid than the other.... But in "Mrs. Dalloway" they are more intimately connected; the one merges into the other; the character is suffused with the emanations of the things he sees, hears, feels; and almost inevitably what is presented is a complex of life of which character and background are elements and are both animate, rather than the living characters stalking among inanimate things. The characters in "Mrs. Dalloway" are real; they have their drama; but the day and the properties of the day move with them, have their drama too; and we do not know which is the more real where all is real—whether the characters are bathed in the emanations of the day, or the day coloured by the minds of the characters. The result is less akin to anything else attempted in the novel than to certain kinds of poetry, to poetry such as Wordsworth's,[1] which records not so much a general judgment on life as a moment of serene illumination, a state of soul. What nature is in "The Excursion," London is in "Mrs. Dalloway," a living presence, a source of deep pleasure....

---

1 William Wordsworth (1770-1850), a major British poet of the Romantic period. His long poem *The Excursion* (1814) was intended to be the second of a three-part series, *The Recluse*, never fully completed.

Appendix B: Literary Context

[As discussed in the Introduction to this edition (see p. 18), the characters of Clarissa and Richard Dalloway passed through several iterations before Woolf completed *Mrs. Dalloway*. Indeed, Clarissa haunted Woolf's imagination for many years. Her first appearance was in Woolf's first novel, *The Voyage Out*, published a full ten years before *Mrs. Dalloway*. In *The Voyage Out* (see Appendix B1) the characters of both Clarissa and Richard are one-dimensional, or "flat" (to use E.M. Forster's term[1]). Clarissa is more superficial, less death-haunted, with a less fully realized feeling for poetry. Richard is more forceful, more closely connected with the "humming oily centre" of imperial power, and more physically threatening. Their wealth is emphasized. By the time Woolf wrote her 1923 short story "Mrs. Dalloway in Bond Street" (see Appendix B2), which focuses solely on Clarissa, she had arrived at many of the themes and motifs that would dominate the novel: the omnipresence of time, indicated through Big Ben's striking of the hours; the centrality and specificity of Woolf's beloved London; the lingering effects of war; and Clarissa's apprehension of mortality.

Mrs. Dalloway is, of course, the fully realized vision and it stands as one of the great novels of the twentieth century. But in addition to being a great novelist, Woolf was an important theorist and critic of the modernist novel. In "Mr. Bennett and Mrs. Brown" (Appendix B3) and "Modern Fiction" (Appendix B4) she argues for new forms of realism to meet the demands of a new age, an age in which class barriers are falling (as the cook enters the drawing-room "to borrow *The Daily Herald*," p. 227), and women's issues move from the background to the foreground of politics and literature; an age in which, as Woolf says, "the accent falls differently from of old; the moment of importance came not here but there" (p. 232).]

1. From Virginia Woolf, *The Voyage Out* (London: Hogarth Press, Uniform Edition, 1929; originally published London: Duckworth & Co., 1915): 40-48

... Their arrival, of course, created some stir, and it was seen by several pairs of eyes that Mrs. Dalloway was a tall slight woman, her body wrapped in furs, her head in veils, while Mr. Dalloway appeared to be a middle-sized man of sturdy build, dressed like a sportsman on an autumnal moor. Many solid leather bags of a rich brown hue soon sur-

1 In *Aspects of the Novel* (New York: Harcourt, Brace & Company, 1927), *passim*.

rounded them, in addition to which Mr. Dalloway carried a despatch box,[1] and his wife a dressing-case[2] suggestive of a diamond necklace and bottles with silver tops.

...

[Mrs. Ambrose] suddenly recollected that [Mr. Dalloway] had been in Parliament.

"Don't you ever find it rather dull?" she asked, not knowing exactly what to say.

Richard spread his hands before him, as if inscriptions were to be read in the palms of them.

"If you ask me whether I ever find it rather dull," he said, "I am bound to say yes; on the other hand, if you ask me what career do you consider on the whole, taking the good with the bad, the most enjoyable and enviable, not to speak of its more serious side, of all careers, for a man, I am bound to say, 'The Politician's.'"

"The Bar or politics, I agree," said Willoughby. "You get more run for your money."

"All one's faculties have their play," said Richard. "I may be treading on dangerous ground; but what I feel about poets and artists in general is this: on your own lines, you can't be beaten—granted; but off your own lines—puff—one has to make allowances. Now, I shouldn't like to think that any one had to make allowances for me."

"I don't quite agree, Richard," said Mrs. Dalloway. "Think of Shelley.[3] I feel that there's almost everything one wants in 'Adonais.'"

"Read 'Adonais' by all means," Richard conceded. "But whenever I hear of Shelley I repeat to myself the words of Matthew Arnold,[4] 'What a set! What a set!'"

This roused Ridley's attention. "Matthew Arnold? A detestable prig!" he snapped.

---

1 Box containing official documents, here relating to Richard Dalloway's career as a Member of Parliament.

2 Small case containing toiletries.

3 Percy Bysshe Shelley (1792-1822), major British poet of the Romantic period. *Adonais* (1821) is his elegy on the death by tuberculosis of fellow poet John Keats (1795-1821).

4 British poet and critic (1822-88), author of *Culture and Anarchy* (1869). Arnold was famously critical of Shelley's personal life, describing him as "not entirely sane." In 1814 Shelley abandoned his wife, Harriet (who committed suicide two years later) to run away with Mary Godwin, the daughter of Mary Wollstonecraft and William Godwin. Mary Godwin is now better known as Mary Shelley, author of *Frankenstein* (1818).

"A prig—granted," said Richard; "but, I think, a man of the world. That's where my point comes in. We politicians doubtless seem to you" (he grasped somehow that Helen was the representative of the arts) "a gross commonplace set of people; but we see both sides; we may be clumsy, but we do our best to get a grasp of things. Now your artists *find* things in a mess, shrug their shoulders, turn aside to their visions—which I grant may be very beautiful—and *leave* things in a mess. Now that seems to me to be evading one's responsibilities. Besides we aren't all born with the artistic faculty."

"It's dreadful," said Mrs. Dalloway, who, while her husband spoke, had been thinking. "When I'm with artists I feel so intensely the delights of shutting oneself up in a little world of one's own, with pictures and music and everything beautiful, and then I go out into the streets and the first child I meet with its poor, hungry, dirty little face makes me turn round and say, 'No, I *can't* shut myself up—I *won't* live in a world of my own. I should like to stop all the painting and writing and music until this kind of thing exists no longer.' Don't you feel," she wound up, addressing Helen, "that life's a perpetual conflict?"

Helen considered for a moment. "No," she said. "I don't think I do."

There was a pause, which was decidedly uncomfortable. Mrs. Dalloway then gave a little shiver, and asked whether she might have her fur cloak brought to her.

...

[Rachel] had taken no part in the talk; no one had spoken to her; but she had listened to every word that was said. She had looked from Mrs. Dalloway to Mr. Dalloway, and from Mr. Dalloway back again. Clarissa, indeed, was a fascinating spectacle. She wore a white dress and a long glittering necklace. What with her clothes, and her arch delicate face, which showed exquisitely pink beneath hair turning grey, she was astonishingly like an eighteenth-century masterpiece—a Reynolds or a Romney.[1] She made Helen and the others look coarse and slovenly beside her. Sitting lightly upright she seemed to be dealing with the world as she chose; the enormous solid globe spun round this way and that beneath her fingers. And her husband! Mr. Dalloway rolling that rich deliberate voice was even more impressive. He seemed to come from the humming oily centre of the machine where the polished rods are sliding, and the pistons thumping; he grasped thing so firmly but so loosely; he made the others appear like old maids cheap-

1 Joshua Reynolds (1723-92) and George Romney (1734-1802), both celebrated English portrait painters.

ening remnants. Rachel followed in the wake of the matrons, as if in a trance; a curious scent of violets came back from Mrs. Dalloway, mingling with the soft rustling of her skirts, and the tinkling of her chains....

2. Virginia Woolf, "Mrs. Dalloway in Bond Street," *The Dial*[1] 75.1 (July 1923): 20-27

[This story can be compared to the text of *Mrs. Dalloway*, pp. 45-55 above. Explanatory footnotes that appear there are not repeated below.]

Mrs. Dalloway said she would buy the gloves herself.

Big Ben was striking as she stepped out into the street. It was eleven o'clock and the unused hour was fresh as if issued to children on a beach. But there was something solemn in the deliberate swing of the repeated strokes; something stirring in the murmur of wheels and the shuffle of footsteps.

No doubt they were not all bound on errands of happiness. There is much more to be said about us than that we walk the streets of Westminster. Big Ben too is nothing but steel rods consumed by rust were it not for the care of H.M.'s Office of Works.[2] Only for Mrs. Dalloway the moment was complete; for Mrs. Dalloway June was fresh. A happy childhood—and it was not to his daughters only that Justin Parry had seemed a fine fellow (weak of course on the Bench);[3] flowers at evening, smoking rising; the caw of rooks falling from ever so high, down down through the October air—there is nothing to take the place of childhood. A leaf of mint brings it back: or a cup with a blue ring.

Poor little wretches, she sighed, and pressed forward. Oh, right under the horses' noses, you little demon! and there she was left on the kerb stretching her hand out, while Jimmy Dawes grinned on the further side.

---

1 Published in Chicago, and edited from 1920 to 1926 by Scofield Thayer, *The Dial* was an important and influential modernist literary magazine, publishing work by W.B. Yeats, Ezra Pound, T.S. Eliot, Djuna Barnes, Marianne Moore, and Hart Crane, among many others.

2 His Majesty's Office of Works, originally established in 1378 to oversee the building of royal residences, later expanded to include woods, forests, land revenues, works, and buildings, and, in 1851, brought under control of Parliament.

3 I.e., as a judge.

A charming woman, poised, eager, strangely white-haired for her pink cheeks, so Scope Purvis, C.B.,[1] saw her as he hurried to his office. She stiffened a little, waiting for Durtnall's van to pass. Big Ben struck the tenth; struck the eleventh stroke. The leaden circles dissolved in the air. Pride held her erect, inheriting, handing on, acquainted with discipline and with suffering. How people suffered, how they suffered, she thought, thinking of Mrs. Foxcroft at the Embassy last night decked out with jewels, eating her heart out, because that nice boy was dead, and now the old Manor House (Durtnall's van passed) must go to a cousin.

"Good morning to you!" said Hugh Whitbread raising his hat rather extravagantly by the china shop, for they had known each other as children. "Where are you off to?"

"I love walking in London" said Mrs. Dalloway. "Really it's better than walking in the country!"

"We've just come up," said Hugh Whitbread. "Unfortunately to see doctors."

"Milly?" said Mrs. Dalloway, instantly compassionate.

"Out of sorts," said Hugh Whitbread. "That sort of thing. Dick all right?"

"First rate!" said Clarissa.

Of course, she thought, walking on, Milly is about my age—fifty—fifty-two. So it is probably *that.* Hugh's manner had said so, said it perfectly—dear old Hugh, thought Mrs. Dalloway, remembering with amusement, with gratitude, with emotion, how shy, like a brother—one would rather die than speak to one's brother—Hugh had always been, when he was at Oxford, and came over, and perhaps one of them (drat the thing!) couldn't ride. How then could women sit in Parliament? How could they do things with men? For there is this extraordinarily deep instinct, something inside one; you can't get over it; it's no use trying; and men like Hugh respect it without our saying it, which is what one loves, thought Clarissa, in dear old Hugh.

She had passed through the Admiralty Arch[2] and saw at the end of the empty road with its thin trees Victoria's white mound, Victoria's billowing motherliness, amplitude and homeliness, always ridiculous,

---

1 Companion of the Most Honourable Order of the Bath, an order of chivalry founded by George I in 1725. Recipients are usually senior military officers or senior civil servants.

2 Large office building commissioned by King Edward VII in memory of his mother Queen Victoria, completed in 1911 and originally used for offices and residences for leaders of the Royal Navy. The five arches that comprise the Admiralty Arch lead from Trafalgar Square to the Mall, looking toward Buckingham Palace.

yet how sublime, thought Mrs. Dalloway, remembering Kensington Gardens[1] and the old lady in horn spectacles and being told by Nanny to stop dead still and bow to the Queen.[2] The flag flew above the Palace.[3] The King and Queen were back then. Dick had met her at lunch the other day—a thoroughly nice woman. It matters so much to the poor, thought Clarissa, and to the soldiers. A man in bronze stood heroically on a pedestal with a gun on her left hand side—the South African war. It matters, thought Mrs. Dalloway walking towards Buckingham Palace. There it stood four-square, in the broad sunshine, uncompromising, plain. But it was character she thought; something inborn in the race; what Indians respected. The Queen went to hospitals, opened bazaars—the Queen of England, thought Clarissa, looking at the Palace. Already at this hour a motor car passed out at the gates; soldiers saluted; the gates were shut. And Clarissa, crossing the road, entered the Park, holding herself upright.

June had drawn out every leaf on the trees. The mothers of Westminster with mottled breasts gave suck to their young. Quite respectable girls lay stretched on the grass. An elderly man, stooping very stiffly, picked up a crumpled paper, spread it out flat and flung it away. How horrible! Last night at the Embassy Sir Dighton had said "If I want a fellow to hold my horse, I have only to put up my hand." But the religious question is far more serious than the economic, Sir Dighton had said, which she thought extraordinarily interesting, from a man like Sir Dighton. "Oh, the country will never know what it has lost" he had said, talking, of his own accord, about dear Jack Stewart.

She mounted the little hill lightly. The air stirred with energy. Messages were passing from the Fleet to the Admiralty. Piccadilly and Arlington Street and the Mall seemed to chafe the very air in the Park and lift its leaves hotly, brilliantly, upon waves of that divine vitality which Clarissa loved. To ride; to dance; she had adored all that. Or going long walks in the country, talking, about books, what to do with one's life, for young people were amazingly priggish—oh, the things one had said! But one had conviction. Middle age is the devil. People like Jack'll never know that, she thought; for he never once thought of death, never, they said, knew he was dying. And now can never mourn—how did it go?—a head grown grey.... From the contagion of the world's slow stain ... have drunk their cup a round or two

1 One of the eight Royal Parks of London, lying immediately to the west of Hyde Park.

2 Queen Victoria (1819-1901), who reigned from 1837 until her death.

3 Buckingham Palace. The Royal Standard ("the flag") is flown when the monarch is in residence.

before.... From the contagion of the world's slow stain![1] She held herself upright.

But how Jack would have shouted! Quoting Shelley, in Piccadilly! "You want a pin," he would have said. He hated frumps. "My God Clarissa! My God Clarissa!"—she could hear him now at the Devonshire House party, about poor Sylvia Hunt in her amber necklace and that dowdy old silk. Clarissa held herself upright for she had spoken aloud and now she was in Piccadilly, passing the house with the slender green columns, and the balconies; passing club windows full of newspapers; passing old Lady Burdett Coutts' house where the glazed white parrot used to hang; and Devonshire House, without its gilt leopards; and Claridge's,[2] where she must remember Dick wanted her to leave a card[3] on Mrs. Jepson or she would be gone. Rich Americans can be very charming. There was St James Palace; like a child's game with bricks; and now—she had passed Bond Street—she was by Hatchard's book shop. The stream was endless—endless—endless. Lords, Ascot, Hurlingham[4]—what was it? What a duck, she thought, looking at the frontispiece of some book of memoirs spread wide in the bow window, Sir Joshua perhaps or Romney;[5] arch, bright, demure; the sort of girl—like her own Elizabeth—the only *real* sort of girl. And there was that absurd book, Soapy Sponge, which Jim used to quote by the yard; and Shakespeare's Sonnets. She knew them by heart. Phil and she had argued all day about the Dark Lady,[6] and Dick had said straight out at dinner that night that he had never heard of

---

1 Clarissa Dalloway is recalling stanza 40 of Shelley's poem *Adonais*:

He has outsoared the shadow of our night.
Envy and calumny and hate and pain,
And that unrest which men miscall delight,
Can touch him not and torture not again.
From the contagion of the world's slow stain
He is secure; and now can never mourn
A heart grown cold, a head grown grey in vain—
Nor, when the spirit's self has ceased to burn,
With sparkless ashes load an unlamented urn.

See also p. 72, n. 2.

2 Claridge's Hotel in the Westminster area of London.

3 A calling card, which contained a person's name and address and was left in lieu or in advance of a visit.

4 See *Mrs. Dalloway*, p. 47, n. 1.

5 See p. 184, n. 1.

6 Reference to Shakespeare's Dark Lady sequence, sonnets 127-52 of his 154 sonnets. The Dark Lady sonnets are distinguished by their addressee, a woman with black hair and dark skin, and by their (sometimes bawdy) theme of sexual longing.

her. Really, she had married him for that! He had never read Shakespeare! There must be some little cheap book she could buy for Milly—Cranford[1] of course! Was there ever anything so enchanting as the cow in petticoats? If only people had that sort of humour, that sort of self-respect now, thought Clarissa, for she remembered the broad pages; the sentences ending; the characters—how one talked about them as if they were real. For all the great things must go to the past, she thought. From the contagion of the world's slow stain.... Fear no more the heat o' the sun ... And now can never mourn, can never mourn, she repeated, her eyes straying over the window; for it ran in her head; the test of great poetry; the moderns had never written anything one wanted to read about death, she thought; and turned.

Omnibuses joined motor cars; motor cars vans; vans taxicabs; taxicabs motor cars—here was an open motor car with a girl, alone. Up till four, her feet tingling, I know, thought Clarissa, for the girl looked washed out, half asleep, in the corner of the car after the dance. And another car came; and another. No! No! No! Clarissa smiled good-naturedly. The fat lady had taken every sort of trouble, but diamonds! orchids! at this hour of the morning! No! No! No! The excellent policeman would, when the time came, hold up his hand. Another motor car passed. How utterly unattractive! Why should a girl of that age paint black round her eyes? And a young man, with a girl, at this hour, when the country—The admirable policeman raised his hand and Clarissa acknowledging his sway, taking her time, crossed, walked towards Bond Street; saw the narrow crooked street, the yellow banners; the thick notched telegraph wires stretched across the sky.

A hundred years ago her great-great-grandfather, Seymour Parry, who ran away with Conway's daughter, had walked down Bond Street. Down Bond Street the Parrys had walked for a hundred years, and might have met the Dalloways (Leighs on the mother's side) going up. Her father got his clothes from Hill's. There was a roll of cloth in the window, and here just one jar on a black table, incredibly expensive; like the thick pink salmon on the ice block at the fishmonger's. The jewels were exquisite—pink and orange stars, paste, Spanish, she thought, and chains of old gold; starry buckles, little brooches which had been worn on sea green satin by ladies with high head-dresses. But no good looking! One must economize. She must go on past the picture dealer's where one of the odd French pictures hung, as if people had thrown confetti—pink and blue—for a joke. If you had lived with pictures (and it's the same with books and music)

---

1 Elizabeth Gaskell's novel *Cranford*, published serially in 1851 in *Household Words* and in volume form two years later.

thought Clarissa, passing the Aeolian Hall,[1] you can't be taken in by a joke.

The river of Bond Street was clogged. There, like a queen at a tournament, raised, regal, was Lady Bexborough. She sat in her carriage, upright, alone, looking through her glasses. The white glove was loose at her wrist. She was in black, quite shabby, yet, thought Clarissa, how extraordinarily it tells, breeding, self-respect, never saying a word too much or letting people gossip; an astonishing friend; no one can pick a hole in her after all these years, and now, there she is, thought Clarissa, passing the Countess who waited powdered, perfectly still, and Clarissa would have given anything to be like that, the mistress of Clarefield, talking politics, like a man. But she never goes anywhere, thought Clarissa, and it's quite useless to ask her, and the carriage went on and Lady Bexborough was borne past like a Queen at a tournament, though she had nothing to live for and the old man is failing and they say she is sick of it all, thought Clarissa and the tears actually rose to her eyes as she entered the shop.

"Good morning," said Clarissa in her charming voice. "Gloves," she said with her exquisite friendliness and putting her bag on the counter began, very slowly, to undo the buttons. "White gloves," she said, "Above the elbow" and she looked straight into the shopwoman's face—but this was not the girl she remembered? She looked quite old. "These really don't fit" said Clarissa. The shop girl looked at them. "Madame wears bracelets?" Clarissa spread out her fingers. "Perhaps it's my rings." And the girl took the grey gloves with her to the end of the counter.

Yes, thought Clarissa, if it's the girl I remember she's twenty years older.... There was only one other customer, sitting sideways at the counter, her elbow poised, her bare hand drooping, vacant; like a figure on a Japanese fan, though Clarissa, too vacant perhaps, yet some men would adore her. The lady shook her head sadly. Again the gloves were too large. She turned round the glass. "Above the wrist" she reproached the grey-headed woman; who looked and agreed.

They waited; a clock ticked; Bond Street hummed, dulled, distant; the woman went away holding gloves. "Above the wrist" said the lady, mournfully, raising her voice. And she would have to order chairs, ices, flowers, and cloak-room tickets, thought Clarissa. The people she didn't want would come; the others wouldn't. She would stand by the door. They sold stockings—silk stockings. A lady is known by her

---

1 Originally the Grosvenor Gallery on Bond Street, the building was sold to an American manufacturer of musical instruments who converted the space into offices, showrooms, and a performance hall.

gloves and her shoes, old Uncle William used to say. And through the hanging silk stockings quivering silver she looked at the lady, sloping shouldered, her hand drooping, her bag slipping, her eyes vacantly on the floor. It would be intolerable if dowdy women came to her party! Would one have liked Keats if he had worn red socks? Oh, at last—she drew into the counter and it flashed into her mind:

"Do you remember before the war you had gloves with pearl buttons?"

"French gloves, Madame?"

"Yes, they were French" said Clarissa. The other lady rose very sadly and took her bag, and looked at the gloves on the counter. But they were all too large—always too large at the wrist.

"With pearl buttons," said the shop-girl, who looked ever so much older. She split the lengths of tissue paper apart on the counter. With pearl buttons, thought Clarissa, perfectly simple—how French!

"Madame's hands are so slender" said the shop-girl, drawing the glove firmly, smoothly down over her rings. And Clarissa looked at her arm in the looking glass. The glove hardly came to her elbow. Were there others half an inch longer? Still it seemed tiresome to bother her—perhaps the one day in the month, thought Clarissa, when it's agony to stand. "Oh, don't bother," she said. But the gloves were brought.

"Don't you get fearfully tired" she said in her charming voice, "standing? When d'you get your holiday?"

"In September, Madame, when we're not so busy."

When we're in the country thought Clarissa. Or shooting. She has a fortnight at Brighton. In some stuffy lodging. The landlady takes the sugar. Nothing would be easier than to send her to Mrs. Lumley's right in the country (and it was on the tip of her tongue). But then she remembered how on their honeymoon Dick had shown her the folly of giving impulsively. It was much more important, he said, to get trade with China. Of course he was right. And she could feel the girl wouldn't like to be given things. There she was in her place. So was Dick. Selling gloves was her job. She had her own sorrows quite separate, "and now can never mourn, can never mourn" the words ran in her head, "From the contagion of the world's slow stain" thought Clarissa holding her arm stiff, for there are moments when it seems utterly futile (the glove was drawn off leaving her arm flecked with powder)—simply one doesn't believe, thought Clarissa, any more in God.

The traffic suddenly roared; the silk stockings brightened. A customer came in.

"White gloves," she said, with some ring in her voice that Clarissa remembered.

It used, thought Clarissa, to be so simple. Down down through the air came the caw of the rooks. When Sylvia died, hundreds of years ago, the yew hedges looked so lovely with the diamond webs in the mist before early church. But if Dick were to die to-morrow as for believing in God—no, she would let the children choose, but for herself, like Lady Bexborough, who opened the bazaar, they say, with the telegram in her hand—Roden, her favourite, killed—she would go on. But why, if one doesn't believe? For the sake of others, she thought, taking the glove in her hand. This girl would be much more unhappy if she didn't believe.

"Thirty shillings" said the shopwoman. "No, pardon me Madame, thirty-five. The French gloves are more."

For one doesn't live for oneself, thought Clarissa.

And then the other customer took a glove, tugged it, and it split.

"There!" she exclaimed.

"A fault of the skin," said the grey-headed woman hurriedly. "Sometimes a drop of acid in tanning. Try this pair, Madame."

"But it's an awful swindle to ask two pound ten!"

Clarissa looked at the lady; the lady looked at Clarissa.

"Gloves have never been quite so reliable since the war" said the shop-girl, apologizing, to Clarissa.

But where had she seen the other lady?—elderly, with a frill under her chin; wearing a black ribbon for gold eyeglasses; sensual, clever, like a Sargent[1] drawing. How one can tell from a voice when people are in the habit, thought Clarissa, of making other people—"It's a shade too tight" she said—obey. The shopwoman went off again. Clarissa was left waiting. Fear no more, she repeated, playing her finger on the counter. Fear no more the heat o' the sun. Fear no more she repeated. There were little brown spots on her arm. And the girl crawled like a snail. Thou thy worldly task hast done. Thousands of young men had died that things might go on. At last! Half an inch above the elbow; pearl buttons; five and a quarter. My dear slow coach, thought Clarissa, do you think I can sit here the whole morning? Now you'll take twenty-five minutes to bring me my change!

There was a violent explosion in the street outside. The shopwomen cowered behind the counters. But Clarissa, sitting very upright, smiled at the other lady. "Miss Anstruther!" she exclaimed.

---

1 John Singer Sargent (1856-1925), American portrait painter and water colourist.

3. From Virginia Woolf, *Mr. Bennett and Mrs. Brown* (London: Hogarth Press, 1924)

[This essay, the first in the Hogarth Essays series of short critical pamphlets, was originally a paper read to the Heretics Society, Cambridge, on 18 May 1924. It continues the debate between Woolf and Arnold Bennett (1867-1931), English journalist, essayist, and author of *The Old Wives' Tale* (1908) and several other realist novels about life in the West Midland area of England. See Introduction, p. 16.]

It seems to me possible, perhaps desirable, that I may be the only person in this room who has committed the folly of writing, trying to write, or failing to write, a novel. And when I asked myself, as your invitation to speak to you about modern fiction made me ask myself, what demon whispered in my ear and urged me to my doom, a little figure rose before me—the figure of a man, or of a woman, who said, "My name is Brown. Catch me if you can."

Most novelists have the same experience. Some Brown, Smith, or Jones comes before them and says in the most seductive and charming way in the world, "Come and catch me if you can." And so, led on by this will-o'-the-wisp, they flounder through volume after volume, spending the best years of their lives in the pursuit, and receiving for the most part very little cash in exchange. Few catch the phantom; most have to be content with a scrap of her dress or a wisp of her hair.

My belief that men and women write novels because they are lured on to create some character which has thus imposed itself upon them has the sanction of Mr. Arnold Bennett. In an article from which I will quote he says: "The foundation of good fiction is character-creating and nothing else.... Style counts; plot counts; originality of outlook counts. But none of these counts anything like so much as the convincingness of the characters. If the characters are real the novel will have a chance; if they are not, oblivion will be its portion...." And he goes on to draw the conclusion that we have no young novelists of first-rate importance at the present moment, because they are unable to create characters that are real, true, and convincing.

These are the questions that I want with greater boldness than discretion to discuss to-night. I want to make out what we mean when we talk about "character" in fiction; to say something about the question of reality which Mr. Bennett raises; and to suggest some reasons why the younger novelists fail to create characters, if, as Mr. Bennett asserts, it is true that fail they do. This will lead me, I am well aware, to make some very sweeping and some very vague assertions. For the question is an extremely difficult one. Think how little we know about character—think how little we know about art. But, to make a clearance before I begin, I will suggest that we arrange Edwardians and Georgians into two camps; Mr. Wells, Mr. Bennett, and Mr. Galsworthy I will call the Edwardians; Mr. Forster, Mr. Lawrence, Mr. Strachey, Mr. Joyce, and Mr. Eliot I will call the Georgians.[1] And if I speak in the first person, with intolerable egotism, I will ask you to excuse me. I do not want to attribute to the world at large the opinions of one solitary, ill-informed, and misguided individual.

My first assertion is one that I think you will grant—that every one in this room is a judge of character. Indeed it would be impossible to live for a year without disaster unless one practised character-reading and had some skill in the art. Our marriages, our friendships depend on it; our business largely depends on it; every day questions arise which can only be solved by its help. And now I will hazard a second assertion, which is more disputable perhaps, to the effect that on or about December 1910 human character changed.[2]

I am not saying that one went out, as one might into a garden, and there saw that a rose had flowered, or that a hen had laid an egg. The change was not sudden and definite like that. But a change there was, nevertheless; and, since one must be arbitrary, let us date it about the year 1910.... In life one can see the change, if I may use a homely illustration, in the character of one's cook. The Victorian cook lived like a leviathan in the lower depths, formidable, silent, obscure, inscrutable; the Georgian cook is a creature of sunshine and fresh air; in and out of the drawing-room, now to borrow *The Daily Herald*, now to ask advice about a hat. Do you ask for more solemn instances of the power of the human race to change? Read the *Agamemnon*,[3] and see whether, in process of time, your sympathies are not almost entirely with Clytemnestra. Or consider the married life of the Carlyles,[4] and bewail the waste, the futility, for him and for her, of the horrible

---

1 Woolf is here describing two generations of writers. The older generation are those whose major work appeared during the reign of Edward VII (who reigned from 1901 to 1910), including H.G. Wells, Arnold Bennett, and John Galsworthy. The younger generation are those whose work appeared during the reign of George V (who would reign from 1910 to 1936), including E.M. Forster, D.H. Lawrence, Lytton Strachey, James Joyce, and T.S. Eliot.

2 See Introduction, pp. 16-17.

3 First play in the *Oresteia*, a trilogy by Greek tragedian Aeschylus. Clytemnestra is the wife of Agamemnon, king of Argos, whom she kills because he has sacrificed their daughter and has kept the prophetess Cassandra as a concubine. See also *Mrs. Dalloway*, p. 117, n. 1.

4 Thomas (1795-1881) and Jane (1801-66, née Welsh) Carlyle. Thomas Carlyle was a well-known Scottish essayist and historian, and Jane Carlyle was a noted letter-writer (her letters were published posthumously). Their marriage was famously unhappy and reputedly unconsummated.

domestic tradition which made it seemly for a woman of genius to spend her time chasing beetles, scouring saucepans, instead of writing books. All human relations have shifted—those between masters and servants, husbands and wives, parents and children. And when human relations change there is at the same time a change in religion, conduct, politics, and literature. Let us agree to place one of these changes about the year 1910.

I have said that people have to acquire a good deal of skill in character-reading if they are to live a single year of life without disaster. But it is the art of the young. In middle age and in old age the art is practised mostly for its uses, and friendships and other adventures and experiments in the art of reading character are seldom made. But novelists differ from the rest of the world because they do not cease to be interested in character when they have learnt enough about it for practical purposes. They go a step further; they feel that there is something permanently interesting in character in itself. When all the practical business of life has been discharged, there is something about people which continues to seem to them of overwhelming importance, in spite of the fact that it has no bearing whatever upon their happiness, comfort, or income. The study of character becomes to them an absorbing pursuit; to impart character an obsession. And this I find it very difficult to explain: what novelists mean when they talk about character, what the impulse is that urges them so powerfully every now and then to embody their view in writing....

But now I must recall what Mr. Arnold Bennett says. He says that it is only if the characters are real that the novel has any chance of surviving. Otherwise, die it must. But, I ask myself, what is reality? And who are the judges of reality? ...

But now let us examine what Mr. Bennett went on to say—he said that there was no great novelist among the Georgian writers because they cannot create characters who are real, true, and convincing. And there I cannot agree. There are reasons, excuses, possibilities which I think put a different colour upon the case. It seems so to me at least, but I am well aware that this is a matter about which I am likely to be prejudiced, sanguine, and near-sighted. I will put my view before you in the hope that you will make it impartial, judicial, and broad-minded. Why, then, is it so hard for novelists at present to create characters which seem real, not only to Mr. Bennett, but to the world at large? Why, when October comes round,[1] do the publishers always fail to supply us with a masterpiece?

1 I.e., a major book-publishing season.

Surely one reason is that the men and women who began writing novels in 1910 or thereabouts had this great difficulty to face—that there was no English novelist living from whom they could learn their business. Mr. Conrad[1] is a Pole; which sets him apart, and makes him, however admirable, not very helpful. Mr. Hardy[2] has written no novel since 1895. The most prominent and successful novelists in the year 1910 were, I suppose, Mr. Wells, Mr. Bennett, and Mr. Galsworthy. Now it seems to me that to go to these men and ask them to teach you how to write a novel—how to create characters that are real—is precisely like going to a bootmaker and asking him to teach you how to make a watch....

... I asked them—they are my elders and betters—How shall I begin to describe [Mrs. Brown's] character? And they said, "Begin by saying that her father kept a shop in Harrogate. Ascertain the rent. Ascertain the wages of shop assistants in the year 1878. Discover what her mother died of. Describe cancer. Describe calico. Describe——" But I cried, "Stop! Stop!" And I regret to say that I threw that ugly, that clumsy, that incongruous tool out of the window, for I knew that if I began describing the cancer and the calico, my Mrs. Brown, that vision to which I cling though I know no way of imparting it to you, would have been dulled and tarnished and vanished for ever.

That is what I mean by saying that the Edwardian tools are the wrong ones for us to use. They have laid an enormous stress upon the fabric of things. They have given us a house in the hope that we may be able to deduce the human beings who live there. To give them their due, they have made that house much better worth living in. But if you hold that novels are in the first place about people, and only in the second about the houses they live in, that is the wrong way to set about it. Therefore, you see, the Georgian writer had to begin by throwing away the method that was in use at the moment....

... And so the smashing and the crashing began. Thus it is that we hear all round us, in poems and novels and biographies, even in newspaper articles and essays, the sound of breaking and falling, crashing and destruction. It is the prevailing sound of the Georgian age—rather a melancholy one if you think what melodious days there have been in

---

1 Joseph Conrad (1857-1924), born Józef Teodor Konrad Korzeniowski, a Polish novelist who wrote in English, author of *Heart of Darkness* (1899) and *Lord Jim* (1900), among others.

2 Thomas Hardy (1840-1928), English novelist and poet, author of *Far from the Madding Crowd* (1874), *Tess of the d'Urbervilles* (1891), and *Jude the Obscure* (1895), among others.

the past, if you think of Shakespeare and Milton[1] and Keats[2] or even of Jane Austen[3] and Thackeray[4] and Dickens;[5] if you think of the language, the heights to which it can soar when free, and see the same eagle captive, bald, and croaking.

In view of these facts—with these sounds in my ears and these fancies in my brain—I am not going to deny that Mr. Bennett has some reason when he complains that our Georgian writers are unable to make us believe that our characters are real. I am forced to agree that they do not pour out three immortal masterpieces with Victorian regularity every autumn. But instead of being gloomy, I am sanguine. For this state of things is, I think, inevitable whenever from hoar old age or callow youth the convention ceases to be a means of communication between writer and reader, and becomes instead an obstacle and an impediment. At the present moment we are suffering, not from decay, but from having no code of manners which writers and readers accept as a prelude to the more exciting intercourse of friendship. The literary convention of the time is so artificial—you have to talk about the weather and nothing but the weather throughout the entire visit—that, naturally, the feeble are tempted to outrage, and the strong are led to destroy the very foundations and rules of literary society. Signs of this are everywhere apparent. Grammar is violated; syntax disintegrated; as a boy staying with an aunt for the weekend rolls in the geranium bed out of sheer desperation as the solemnities of the sabbath wear on. The more adult writers do not, of course, indulge in such wanton exhibitions of spleen. Their sincerity is desperate, and their courage tremendous; it is only that they do not know which to use, a fork or their fingers. Thus, if you read Mr. Joyce[6] and Mr. Eliot[7] you will be struck by the indecency of the one, and the obscurity of the other. Mr. Joyce's indecency in *Ulysses* seems to me the conscious and calculated indecency of a desperate man who feels that in order to breathe he

---

1 See *Mrs. Dalloway*, p. 185, n. 3.

2 See *Mrs. Dalloway*, p. 113, n. 2.

3 English novelist (1775-1817), author of *Sense and Sensibility* (1811) and *Pride and Prejudice* (1813), among others.

4 William Makepeace Thackeray (1811-63), English novelist, author of *Vanity Fair* (1848), among others.

5 Charles Dickens (1812-70), English novelist, author of *Oliver Twist* (serialized 1837-39), *David Copperfield* (serialized 1849-50), and *Great Expectations* (serialized 1861), among many others.

6 James Joyce (1882-1941), Irish short story writer and novelist, author of *A Portrait of the Artist as a Young Man* (1916) and *Ulysses* (1922), among others.

7 T.S. Eliot (1888-1965), American-born and naturalized British subject, poet, playwright, and critic, author of *The Love Song of J. Alfred Prufrock* (1915) and *The Waste Land* (1922), among others.

must break the windows. At moments, when the window is broken, he is magnificent. But what a waste of energy! And, after all, how dull indecency is, when it is not the overflowing of a super-abundant energy or savagery, but the determined and public-spirited act of a man who needs fresh air! Again, with the obscurity of Mr. Eliot. I think that Mr. Eliot has written some of the loveliest single lines in modern poetry. But how intolerant he is of the old usages and politenesses of society—respect for the weak, consideration for the dull! As I sun myself upon the intense and ravishing beauty of one of his lines, and reflect that I must make a dizzy and dangerous leap to the next, and so on from line to line, like an acrobat flying precariously from bar to bar, I cry out, I confess, for the old decorums, and envy the indolence of my ancestors who, instead of spinning madly through mid-air, dreamt quietly in the shade with a book....

For these reasons, then, we must reconcile ourselves to a season of failures and fragments. We must reflect that where so much strength is spent on finding a way of telling the truth the truth itself is bound to reach us in rather an exhausted and chaotic condition....

... Tolerate the spasmodic, the obscure, the fragmentary, the failure. Your help is invoked in a good cause. For I will make one final and surpassingly rash prediction—we are trembling on the verge of one of the great ages of English literature....

4. From Virginia Woolf, "Modern Fiction," *The Common Reader* (London: Hogarth Press, 1925): 184-95

... Mr. Wells, Mr. Bennett, and Mr. Galsworthy have excited so many hopes and disappointed them so persistently that our gratitude largely takes the form of thanking them for having shown us what they might have done but have not done; what we certainly could not do, but as certainly, perhaps, do not wish to do. No single phrase will sum up the charge or grievance which we have to bring against a mass of work so large in its volume and embodying so many qualities, both admirable and the reverse. If we tried to formulate our meaning in one word we should say that these three writers are materialists. It is because they are concerned not with the spirit but with the body that they have disappointed us, and left us with the feeling that the sooner English fiction turns its back upon them, as politely as may be, and marches, if only into the desert, the better for its soul....

... The writer seems constrained, not by his own free will but by some powerful and unscrupulous tyrant who has him in thrall, to provide a plot, to provide comedy, tragedy, love interest, and an air of probability embalming the whole so impeccable that if all his figures were to come to life they would find themselves dressed down to the last button of their coats in the fashion of the hour. The tyrant is obeyed; the novel is done to a turn. But sometimes, more and more often as time goes by, we suspect a momentary doubt, a spasm of rebellion, as the pages fill themselves in the customary way. Is life like this? Must novels be like this?

Look within and life, it seems, is very far from being "like this." Examine for a moment an ordinary mind on an ordinary day. The mind receives a myriad impressions—trivial, fantastic, evanescent, or engraved with the sharpness of steel. From all sides they come, an incessant shower of innumerable atoms; and as they fall, as they shape themselves into the life of Monday or Tuesday, the accent falls differently from of old; the moment of importance came not here but there; so that, if a writer were a free man and not a slave, if he could write what he chose, not what he must, if he could base his work upon his own feeling and not upon convention, there would be no plot, no comedy, no tragedy, no love interest or catastrophe in the accepted style, and perhaps not a single button sewn on as the Bond Street tailors would have it. Life is not a series of gig lamps[1] symmetrically arranged; life is a luminous halo, a semi-transparent envelope surrounding us from the beginning of consciousness to the end. Is it not the task of the novelist to convey this varying, this unknown and uncircumscribed spirit, whatever aberration or complexity it may display, with as little mixture of the alien and external as possible? We are not pleading merely for courage and sincerity; we are suggesting that the proper stuff of fiction is a little other than custom would have us believe it.

It is, at any rate, in some such fashion as this that we seek to define the quality which distinguishes the work of several young writers, among whom Mr. James Joyce is the most notable, from that of their predecessors. They attempt to come closer to life, and to preserve more sincerely and exactly what interests and moves them, even if to do so they must discard most of the conventions which are commonly observed by the novelist. Let us record the atoms as they fall upon the mind in the order in which they fall, let us trace the pattern, however disconnected and incoherent in appearance, which each sight or incident scores upon the consciousness. Let us not take it for granted that life exists more fully in what is commonly thought big than in what is commonly thought small....

... [T]he problem before the novelist at present, as we suppose it to have been in the past, is to contrive means of being free to set down what he chooses. He has to have the courage to say that what interests him is no longer "this" but "that": out of "that" alone must he con-

---

1 The lamps on either side of a gig, a light two-wheeled one-horse carriage.

struct his work. For the moderns "that," the point of interest, lies very likely in the dark places of psychology. At once, therefore, the accent falls a little differently; the emphasis is upon something hitherto ignored; at once a different outline of form becomes necessary, difficult for us to grasp, incomprehensible to our predecessors....

... "The proper stuff of fiction" does not exist; everything is the proper stuff of fiction, every feeling, every thought; every quality of brain and spirit is drawn upon; no perception comes amiss. And if we can imagine the art of fiction come alive and standing in our midst, she would undoubtedly bid us break her and bully her, as well as honour and love her, for so her youth is renewed and her sovereignty assured.

Appendix C: Political Context

[Readers of *Mrs. Dalloway* at the time of its publication in 1925 would have been aware that a period of enormous political instability was just around the corner for Clarissa Dalloway and her circle. The events of the novel take place on one day in June 1923, as Clarissa looks forward to her party that evening and hopes that the Prime Minister will attend. Readers of the day would know that the Prime Minister at the time was Stanley Baldwin, who had, in June 1923, been in office only one month. Baldwin would shortly call a general election on the issue of tariff reform (see Appendix C4), which he argued would alleviate the economic depression and ongoing unemployment that followed World War I in Britain. However, the general election in December 1923 would cost him the government. Following a hung Parliament and Baldwin's loss of a confidence vote, J. Ramsay MacDonald formed Britain's very first Labour government on 22 January 1924, a government that lasted less than a year. Between June 1923 and May 1937, the British government would change hands five times (see Appendix C5).

Lingering effects of the war and political instability elsewhere in Europe and internationally also contributed to the turmoil in British politics. In his 1915 pamphlet, *War and the Workers: A Plea for Democratic Control* (Appendix C1), MacDonald outlined the ways in which war creates greater hardships for members of the working classes than for the middle and upper classes. The long-term effects of these hardships form the almost unspoken backdrop of *Mrs. Dalloway*, and contributed to the Conservative government's downfall. Other long-term effects of the war surface elsewhere in the novel, perhaps most notably in the figure of Miss Kilman, who lost her position as a teacher because of her German background (though her family had been in England since the eighteenth-century) and her refusal to "pretend that the Germans were all villains" (p. 144). The situation for German-born women in England was even more dire, as a 1915 story from *The Times* indicates (see Appendix C2).

Britain's sense of itself as an imperial power was also waning, a theme that runs throughout *Mrs. Dalloway*. The Amritsar Massacre of 1919, in which troops under the command of Brigadier General Reginald E.H. Dyer fired on a large unarmed crowd of Indian protestors, killing 379, lent fuel to the demand for full Indian independence and helped provoke Gandhi's campaign of mass civil disobedience. As indicated in Sir Valentine Chirol's 1920 article in *The Times* (Appendix C3), British reaction to events in India, and to Gandhi himself, was frequently mixed. Peter Walsh's claim that he has left India because he has fallen in love would, by readers in 1925, have been understood in the context of these events.]

1. From J. Ramsay MacDonald, *War and the Workers: A Plea for Democratic Control* (London: The Union of Democratic Control, 1915)

[James Ramsay MacDonald (1866-1937), Scottish-born British politician and first-ever Labour Prime Minister, was a proponent of evolutionary socialism. The son of a farm servant and a ploughman, MacDonald's social background was markedly different from that of Stanley Baldwin or Richard Dalloway. MacDonald was in a decided minority of his party members in opposing the World War I. His reasons for this were complex. In the short pamphlet from which this excerpt is taken, he outlines only the degree to which war creates greater hardships for the working class.]

In the making of wars the working class has always played a subordinate part; in the paying for them it has had to bear the heaviest burdens. The cost of war is never calculated beforehand. Whilst it is being waged the gains that are to be reaped from it are catalogued and presented with a lavish imagination; when it is over a barrenness in result and an oppressiveness of cost remain as the inheritance of the people....

Let us see what is happening in connection with the present war and so attempt to estimate its cost to labour....

We shall deal mainly with the economic aspect of the question. This is undoubtedly the predominant consideration in the mind of Labour. Not only does it carry with it social and political consequences which the workman fears, but the scarcity of necessities and their increasing cost are, under modern conditions of life, regarded as being of an importance in warfare equalled only by the equipment and conduct of the field forces themselves. It is also from the economic results of a war that there follow the political and industrial agitations which come after the peace and do more than the war itself to change national policy....

The war accounts that are published seem to show that the rich do most of the paying. That is only in appearance, however. The present war had not been going for three months when a tax of 3d. per lb. was put upon tea, yielding for the four months up to the end of the financial year £950,000, ½ d. on a glass of beer (almost altogether a working-class drink) yielding £2,500,000, and an extra income tax (not including super tax) yielding £11,000,000. Leaving out the last, the tax on working-class commodities thus amounts to nearly £20,000,000 per annum, and in order that the workers may hand that sum over to the Exchequer they are robbed of amounts between 10 and 15 per cent. extra, which middlemen add to their profits, so that their special war expenditure amounts already for four months to £4,000,000, and will be over £20,000,000 during the coming year if no new burdens are imposed and the full yield of the new taxes secured.[1]

But that is not all. A very considerable part of the taxation of the rich is passed on to the poor in the shape of reduced wages and increased prices. For instance, while many employers are paying part of the wages of men at the front, not a few of them are charging the cost to the consumer. To this must also be added the enhanced prices of necessities caused partly by scarcity but also by middlemen and others taking advantage of the many opportunities which war affords for the exploitation of the consuming public. During the first four days of the war food prices rose 15 or 16 per cent. and then dropped till the beginning of September when they were 10 per cent. above July levels. Thereafter they rose steadily again until they stood at 19 per cent. higher than July at the beginning of January. Moreover, the articles, like sugar, bread, cheap meat, most used by the poorer sections, are amongst those which bear the heaviest increases, whilst coal prices have gone up nearly everywhere. What was a sovereign[2] for food in July had become only sixteen shillings by the New Year. By increases in cost, one-fifth of the workers' incomes devoted to food has been wiped out by the war.

Even when the worker seems to be specially well done by[,] the benefits he receives are either largely illusory or will have to be borne by his class later on. For instance, the State offers enhanced pensions to soldiers and sailors, their wives, and dependents. This appears to be generous, and the recipients have most certainly a claim to open-handed treatment, but it means that the State is to be crippled in its normal activities, that children will be neglected, houses unbuilt, social reform hampered and postponed, cost of living kept high and stan-

---

1 Prior to 1971, the main denominations of British currency were pounds (£), shillings (s. or /-), and pennies (d.). There were 20 shillings in one pound, 12 pennies in one shilling, and therefore 240 pennies in one pound. It is difficult to establish precise equivalents with regard to purchasing power in 1915, when MacDonald published this pamphlet, and today. However, one indicator suggests that the purchasing power of 3d. in 1915 (the amount by which the price of a pound of tea was raised) is equivalent to £3.59 today using average earnings as the measure. See http://www.measuringworth.com/ppoweruk/.

2 A one-pound coin made of gold.

dards kept low. The price which the neglected and poverty-stricken will have to pay in this respect for the war is that of continued neglect and poverty, and a lowered standard of life all round.

In all this paying, pinching, and suffering there is no equality in sacrifice between the rich and poor. The burden is not only different in degree of weight; it is different in kind. To deprive one of luxuries and superfluities does not belong to the same order of sacrifice as to deprive one of necessaries. A tax on wages is not the same kind of taxation as a tax on incomes. To curtail a family income of £100 a year by an income tax is quite a different thing from reducing an income of £10,000. The coin in which the two victims pay these taxes is struck in different mints. A tax on wages is a tax on life, a tax on incomes[1] is a tax on superfluities.

But we must not confine our attention to taxation, for that is not the principal way in which burdens are heaped upon the poor. War dislocates trade, suddenly withdraws scores of thousands of men from production, blows national capital to smithereens, upsets balances of exchange, and destroys regular markets even when it creates temporary ones; then peace, come when it may, again upsets the economy and industry of the time of war. From this double shock the wage earners are the greatest sufferers—though by no means the only ones—and upon them its result in increased cost of living has the worst effects. When this war is over, prices will rise and the struggle for life will become keener....

Finally, there is the loss of life and the maiming. Here, again, Labour suffers most. The other classes give their share without stint. But when the breadwinner of a working-class family is taken the loss is irreparable. Economic collapse intensifies human grief. A death in a well-to-do family brings tears and breaks hearts, but it does more than that in a poor family. Moreover, the well-to-do have consolations that the poor have not. The sacrifice is only nominally equal, in reality it is very unequal. No pension can make this up. To compensate for it will baffle both the hearts and the heads of men. For generations—long after the inter-class sympathy stirred up by the war has died away—this failure will make itself felt. The death and the maiming of the fathers will be visited upon the children unto the third and fourth generations.[2]

This is true not only as regards the individual workman but also as regards his combinations. The Trade Unions have already spent money accumulated for sickness, for old age benefits, for trade dis-

---

1 I.e., on money received through investment.

2 MacDonald paraphrases God's words to Moses in Exodus 34:7: "... visiting the iniquity of the fathers upon the children, and upon the children's children, unto the third and to the fourth generation."

putes, which will have to be made good later on; they have incurred liabilities for their members who are with the colours[1] which actuarially mount up to many thousands of pounds. These liabilities will take months and years to disclose themselves, but they are there all the same, and will have to be met. In many trades these combinations will emerge weakened from the war, the political effectiveness of Labour will be diminished for the time being, its International solidarity will be broken....

We can sum up:

A lowered vitality, both as regards the individual workman and his Unions, with all that it means to those who have to struggle for daily bread, accompanied by an increased cost of living and of domestic hardship, is the definitely-assured inheritance which wars have given to the working classes....

2. "German Women in London," *The Times* (13 May 1915): 10

INTERNMENT BEING CONSIDERED.
BRITISH WIVES OF ALIENS.
[From a woman correspondent.]

The question of the internment of German women was stated yesterday at Scotland Yard to be under consideration. At the Home Office the authorities said it was a matter for the War Office, and at the War Office it was stated to be a matter for the Home Office.

Meanwhile the German women in London regard the idea with horror. They are asking where will room be found for them—they number many thousands—if the housing problem has proved a difficulty in the case of their interned husbands. Nearly all the single women have been repatriated or have gone with Home Office permits—obtained with great difficulty—to the United States. Many have definitely refused repatriation, having left home through some family quarrel and lived here for many years. When war broke out there was a large number of German women-clerks, typists, commercial travellers, students, and tourists in London, but those with few exceptions have been repatriated. The women who are here now are mainly the British or German wives of German men who have been interned or middle-aged and elderly German women who have lived here so long that they have lost touch with their own country. Their sympathies are, however, German, and they make no attempt to conceal the fact, though German women of the better-classes avoid all allusion to the war when in the company of English people.

1 I.e., in the armed forces.

Work is made absolutely impossible for them with one curious exception—the German cook, whose position has fluctuated since war broke out. In the largest of the servants' agencies it was stated yesterday that German servants had been dismissed almost everywhere and that the German cook was rare in English families. In one of the German women's associations, on the contrary, it was said that though German servants were dismissed at the beginning of the war many applications were afterwards received from Englishwomen, overwhelmed by the servant difficulty, for German cooks, and these women, unless they have been dismissed as a result of the present outcry, are perhaps the only German women in British employment.

There has been a considerable amount of suffering among German women and British women married to Germans since the war. Only 1 per cent. of the German men at large are in employment, and there is much poverty. The German Government through American intermediaries make an allowance, paid through the German Benevolent Society, of 10s. a week and 3s. a week for each child to the wives of interned Germans, while the English Government make a grant, paid through the relieving officer, of 8s. outside the London radius and 10s. inside, and 1s. 6d. for each child to the English wives of interned Germans. Where 6s. or more a week has to be paid for rent and the children require much milk the allowance does not go far. The mental distress of those who have male relatives fighting in Germany and who have been badly frightened by the occurrences of the past couple of days is very great.

Feeling is so strong that anyone with a German name is viewed with suspicion. A distinguished English woman archaeologist, whose family has been resident over 30 years, can obtain work nowhere because she has a German name.[1] The Friends[2] Emergency Committee for the Assistance of Germans, Austrians, and Hungarians in Distress has dealt with over 3,000 cases, trying to find work, generally unavailingly, for German women and men and to relieve necessitous cases. Other societies are also helping, including the Y.W.C.A., the Friends of Foreigners in Distress, and the German Benevolent Society.

---

1 Perhaps a reference to the classicist Louise Ernestine Matthaei, Fellow and Director of Studies at the women's college, Newnham, Cambridge, from 1909, and who served as a possible model for the character of Doris Kilman in *Mrs. Dalloway*. See Introduction, p. 30, n. 1.

2 The Religious Society of Friends, i.e., Quakers.

3. From Sir Valentine Chirol, "India Old and New. I. Mr. Gandhi's Teaching. Hatred of Western Civilization. Saint and Firebrand." *The Times* (23 December 1920): 11

[Valentine Ignatius Chirol (1852-1929) was a British diplomat, journalist, and author. He was appointed to *The Times* in 1891, becoming foreign editor in 1899, a post he held for 12 years. During this time his own publications included *Indian Unrest* (1910) and, later, *India Old and New* (1922). He served on the Royal Commission on the Indian Civil Service, 1912-16.

Chirol identifies India's lightning rod of change as Mohandas Karamchand Gandhi (1869-1948), leader of the independence movement in British-ruled India, and famous proponent of non-violent civil disobedience. Gandhi studied law at University College London, trained as a barrister at the Inner Temple, and was called to the bar in 1891. Following several years in South Africa, he returned to India in 1915 and joined the Indian National Congress (the party most closely affiliated with the Indian Independence Movement), assuming its leadership in 1920, the year in which this article was written.]

The "unchanging East" may still be found in India beneath the fast-changing surface, just as the depths of the ocean are found unstirred by the cyclone that lashes the surface waters into fury. But though it is little more than three years since I was last in India things seemed to have moved during that short period at a more break-neck speed out here than almost anywhere in Europe, though India was far less directly caught up in the whirlwind of the war.

The atmosphere is so surcharged with heat, the horizon obscured by such dense smoke-screens of racial passion, that I can only attempt at first to note down the most prominent features of a situation which a rapid succession of strange events in India and outside India has combined to bring about.

When I left, the famous pronouncement of August 20, 1917,[1] had just opened up to India, as the not unmerited reward of Indian loyalty in the great world-crisis, the prospect for the first time of a real share

1 "On August 20th, 1917, Edwin Montagu [Secretary of State for India] declared in the House of Commons that: 'the policy of His Majesty's Government ... is that of the ... gradual development of self-governing institutions with a view to the progressive realization of responsible government in India as an integral part of the British Empire.' This announcement ... affirmed that a nonwhite portion of the empire could aspire to the same goal of self-government as the white colonies of Canada, Australia, New Zealand, and South Africa had successively achieved" (Danzig 19).

in the governance of the country and of ultimate partnership on equal terms in the commonwealth of British nations.

I return here now on the eve of the first elections for the popular assemblies born of that pronouncement, and I find a large and extremely vocal section of the "politically minded" classes, whose aspirations a whole series of far-reaching reforms embodied in the new Government of India Act were intended to satisfy, banded together to render them abortive. They hearken to a new prophet, and his gospel is as simple as it is massive: "Away with Western civilization! Go back to the ancient ways of the Vedas!"[1]

Nor does the Secretary of State's whilom[2] friend Mr. Gandhi confine himself to generalities. His commandments are precise and particular. He has not only said but written that Western civilization is of its nature Satanic, whereas the civilization of ancient India has no peer, and when it is said that she has not progressed that is her virtue and her anchor and the proof that she is still sound at the core.

He condemns violence as one of the outward and visible expressions of the materialism with which Western civilization is instinct. He therefore deprecates—for the present—any attempt to destroy British rule by open insurgency, though he hints occasionally at what may have to be done ultimately when a *lashkar*[3] of ten million Hindus is ready to leap to the sword. He prefers to rely—for the present—on Indian "soul-force," which, if applied in accordance with his injunctions, will induce the complete paralysis of British rule. It will not even be necessary to drive the British out of India if they will become Indianized, for they can then be tolerated. But if they wish to retain their own culture their place is not in India. The future, anyhow, belongs in the hands of the Indians....

This gospel is not in all respects new, though the form in which it is to be enforced has been invested with the novel and somewhat euphemistic title of "non-cooperation." ...

4. "Prime Minister's Appeal. 'Only Practicable Solution,' Call to Electors." *The Times* (5 December 1923): 12

The following appeal by the Prime Minister[4] to the electors has been issued from 10, Downing-street:—

---

1 Ancient Hindu scriptures.

2 Former.

3 A body or army of Indian soldiers.

4 Stanley Baldwin (1867-1947). For a chronology of Prime Ministers, see Appendix C5.

To-morrow you will be called upon to vote on an issue of the most far-reaching importance to the future welfare of this country and the prosperity of its people.

It is unnecessary for me to draw a picture of the unexampled unemployment from which this country has been suffering during the past four years. You yourselves have seen the suffering which it has created. Indeed, many of you have borne the heaviest weight of the burden with a patience and fortitude which are characteristic of our people.

The cause of the trade depression which has produced this state of unemployment is to be found mainly in the chaos created by the Great War, which has robbed this country of many of its pre-war markets. For the past three years successive Governments have done their utmost, by means of temporary remedies, to lessen the extent of the evil in the hope that European conditions might become sufficiently restored to effect a permanent improvement in our industrial situation. But during the past year events have made it plain that the restoration of Europe has been postponed for many years.

Such was the position with which I was confronted when this winter began. There seemed to be little prospect of regaining the European markets upon which this country largely relied before the war. On the other hand, many foreign countries, owing to the low rate of wages prevailing and the depreciation in their exchanges, were able to export goods to this country at prices with which our industries were totally unable to compete. Thus our industries had to face not only the loss of many of our foreign markets, but also an unfair competition with foreign countries in our own markets. The inevitable consequence was unemployment on a scale hitherto unknown in this country. Over a million of our people are still unemployed; and behind them is growing up a young generation, many of whom, in the absence of an improvement of our industrial conditions, can have little hope for the future, and will be faced with the same hardships as those which now confront us.

There were two alternatives open to me. The first was to continue to deal with the situation by means of palliative measures similar to those which had been adopted in the past. But, knowing as I did that these could not provide a permanent remedy, I decided that this was not an honourable course of action. There remained the other alternative—to appeal to the country without delay in order to secure a mandate for the only solution which appeared to me to go to the root of our troubles. The details of my policy have been laid before the country; but, in brief, the Government propose [*sic*] to protect our industries from the unfair competition of foreign countries, and thus to stimulate home production and enable our industries to give more work and more employment to the numbers of our own people who are out of work.

It is alleged that the Government's proposals will have the effect of increasing prices, and exaggerated statements have been made on this subject to a large extent by opponents who, both in or out of office, have failed to put forward any permanent or constructive scheme for dealing with unemployment and now devote themselves to the easier task of destroying the only practicable scheme which holds the field. I do not admit their arguments. In regard to staple foodstuffs which have been excluded from the scope of the Government's proposals there can be no argument. Wheat, flour, meat (including bacon and ham), butter, cheese, eggs, will be imported into this country precisely as they are to-day.

What we propose to do is to impose duties on imported manufactured goods where the circumstances of the case demand such action. As regards these, I do not believe that our proposals will result in any general increase of price to the consumer, in view of the fact that the growth of home production and the consequent development of normal competition will operate to keep prices at their former level. Moreover, the development of production will lead to a diminution of unemployment, an increase in the number of our wage-earners, greater purchasing capacity, and consequently, a greater demand for our home products.

Our opponents have also urged that the benefits of our proposals will go only to the manufacturer and his workers, and that monopolies will keep prices high so that no benefit reaches the "consumer." But if such practices occur and monopolies arise at home, we shall be able to deal with them. Trusts are no new thing; they exist under free trade; but it is easier to deal with combines in our own country than with trusts created by foreigners abroad.

We do not for a moment accept the exaggerated statements made by our opponents on the subject of prices, but in any case the stimulation of work and the diminution of unemployment are the one issue of paramount importance at the present time, and in proportion as these objects are achieved they will lead to reductions in our rates and taxes. Moreover, I refuse to believe that the people of this country who are fortunate enough to be in employment will allow unfounded apprehensions to stand in the way of the permanent prosperity of their less fortunate fellow-workers and the future welfare of the country. I have sufficient confidence in them to believe that they will regard this problem in its broader aspects and in its relation to the national interests as a whole, and support the Government in its attempt to dispel the heavy cloud of unemployment which, with hardly a ray of hope, has for so long hung over our country.

Pending the full development of our policy the Government, if returned to power, will continue to devote their energies to measures of emergency relief which can help in the direction of giving increased work for the people of this country.

They will also stedfastly [sic] persist in their attempts to promote a settlement of the problems which now beset Europe. They have welcomed the recent indications that this country and her Allies may have the sympathy of the United States of America in their task, and they hope that by means of friendly cooperation with France, Italy, and Belgium Europe may be gradually brought back to peace and prosperity. No other party in the State has shown greater anxiety or determination to preserve the friendship which unites this country to France. In our endeavours to promote a settlement we shall continue to be mindful of the ties of sentiment which unite our two great countries and seek to reconcile them with the interests of the British Empire, which must always remain our primary consideration.

The Government at the same time have proposed as part of their policy to grant substantial assistance to agriculture, the most important of our national industries, by the grant of a subsidy of £1 an acre on all holdings of arable land exceeding one acre, provided that the employer pays a wage to his labourer of not less than 30s. a week. This step should mark the prelude to a period of greater prosperity for all workers on the land.

These are the fundamental issues at stake in the appeal which I have made to the country. The social amelioration of our people is bound up with the problem of unemployment. As I have already announced, I have instituted an inquiry into the possibility of reorganizing our schemes of insurance against ill-health, unemployment, and old age, and of abolishing the discouragement of thrift at present associated with the working of the Old Age Pensions Act.[1] Such reforms as these should prove of great benefit, but no measures of social reform can permanently restore prosperity to this country so long as the disease of unemployment, from which it is suffering, continues unchecked. I have placed before you the remedy which I firmly believe will cure the disease. I ask you to give me your support in order that I may put it to the test.

STANLEY BALDWIN

---

1 This 1908 Act, providing non-contributory pensions for those over the age of 70, was one of many social welfare reforms passed by the Liberal Government between 1906 and 1914.

5. List of British Prime Ministers from 1916 to 1937

7 December 1916–19 October 1922
David Lloyd George, Liberal

23 October 1922–20 May 1923
Andrew Bonar Law, Conservative (resigned due to throat cancer)

23 May 1923–16 January 1924
Stanley Baldwin, Conservative

22 January 1924–4 November 1924
J. Ramsay MacDonald, Labour

4 November 1924–5 June 1929
Stanley Baldwin, Conservative

5 June 1929–24 August 1931
J. Ramsay MacDonald, Labour

24 August 1931–7 June 1935
National Government (i.e., a coalition or multi-party government)

7 June 1935–28 May 1937
Stanley Baldwin, Conservative

Appendix D: Medical Context

[In *Mrs. Dalloway*, Virginia Woolf drew on her own experiences of psychological breakdown in her depiction of World War I veteran and "shell-shock" victim Septimus Warren Smith. And the character of Sir William Bradshaw (the Harley Street physician who prescribes a rest cure for Septimus) is based on one of Woolf's own physicians, Dr. George Savage, a prominent late-nineteenth-century authority on mental illness. As biographer Hermione Lee notes, "Virginia Woolf's clinical history keeps pace with the developing history of English medicine and attitudes to mental illness" (182). These attitudes also formed the backdrop against which so-called shell-shock would be evaluated and treated, and they ranged from seeing mental illness, and "shell-shock," as a form of moral failure (Appendix D1) to more properly psychoanalytic understandings of "shell-shock" as a form of "war neurosis" caused by "processes of dissociation and suppression" (Appendix D2, p. 251; see also Appendix D3). Sadly, Septimus Warren Smith's proposed treatment is based on already old-fashioned and increasingly discredited assumptions about hysteria and war-neurosis (see DeMeester). Similarly, Virginia Woolf never underwent psychoanalysis, though her interest in the work of Sigmund Freud increased in the years following the beginning of World War II (Lee 722-26). They met once, in January 1939.]

1. From George H. Savage, "Moral Insanity," *The Journal of Mental Science* 27.118 (July 1881): 147-55

[Sir George Henry Savage (1842-1941), physician and psychiatrist, was chief medical officer at Bethlem Royal Hospital (a famous institution for the treatment of mental illness) from 1879 to 1888, when he resigned to enter private practice. A co-editor of the *Journal of Mental Science* from 1878 to 1894, and author of the textbook *Insanity and Allied Neuroses* (1884), Savage was long-time physician to the Stephen family and, later, to Virginia and Leonard Woolf.]

The subject of moral insanity has already been considered from several points of view, but I think that when typical cases occur it is well to record them, so that, by a careful examination of published cases, more general information may be obtained concerning this malady. It may seem to the philosopher rather a mistaken way of considering the mind to divide it into intellectual and moral, but we in asylums have constantly to take notice of cases in which the moral side of the patient suffers very much more than the intellectual; and though I should not deem any person capable of being intellectually complete and yet morally defective, I would maintain that the defect on the intellectual side may be so little appreciated, or of so little importance in reference to the individual's relationships with the outer world, that it may be disregarded. In considering the cases at present under notice we shall have to point out that most of them have undoubtedly some defect or excess, if I may use the term, in their intellectual processes. When I say excess I refer to the presence of hallucinations and false perceptions that frequently occur in such cases. In attempting to define moral insanity it is easier to describe what it is not than to come to a comprehensive definition which will include all the cases falling into this group, and no others; and, by way of clearing up the condition, I would say that I look upon the moral relationships, so called, of the individual, as among the highest of his mental possessions, that long after the evolution of the mere organic lower parts, the moral side of man developed; that the recognition of property and of right in property developed with the appreciation of the value of human life, so that the control of one's passions, and of one's desires for possession, and of one's passion for power developed quite late in man, and, as might be expected, the last and highest acquisitions are those which are lost most readily. It is frequently noticed that in cases in which slow progressive nervous change takes place the moral relationships are the first, or among the first, to be affected; and in the same way after an intellectual storm it is no uncommon thing to see the intellect partly restored to its normal equilibrium, but still wanting the highest and most humane of its attributes—high moral control; so in the emotional states of acute mania, of general paralysis, or of chronic insanity we have corresponding defects in this highest intellectual control. From this point we shall have to notice moral insanity, it being in many cases a state or stage of mental disease, and not a fixed or permanent condition itself; so that in very many, if not in all, acute cases of insanity there is a period of moral perversion, just as in nearly all such cases there is a period of mental depression.

... [B]y far the most difficult to handle are those [patients] in whom the intellectual powers seem to be intact, but in whom the social relationships are not fully appreciated.... Probably the most common is to be looked upon as a kind of partial moral dementia. The patients neglect their business, their duties, and their rights, so that they would willingly allow their nearest and formerly dearest relations to suffer in consequence of their laziness; and this they fully appreciate, but fold their hands and do nothing. In some of these cases, technically one may say there is a want of will, a want of power to balance motives. It is not merely a want of memory, a want of perception that if they do not act in the present they will starve in the future, but there seems to be a moral languor that prevents them acting, though they thoroughly appreciate what is said to them. You may tell them that they will go to the Workhouse, and they say, "Oh, yes," or, "We won't come to that, I hope"; but they fold their hands and let happen what may. Cases of this kind, or in this stage, may take to drink, so that we have very complicated cases admitted or readmitted into asylums—patients who, having had an attack of insanity, get well, then break down on their moral side, neglect their business or take to drink, get into bad health and bad social conditions, which produce a fresh attack of mental unsoundness, in which the causes of the outbreak have been very mixed. In some of these cases the moral change is seen in the dislike to family ties, in dislike of wife to husband or of mother to children. One has been surprised that upon sending a patient home to her husband after an attack of insanity she has declined to have any further connection with him, and seemed to have lost all her former inclinations towards him; that in another case a mother, who had been industrious, active, and painstaking towards her children, neglected them, occupied herself in religious observances, or expended a fair amount of energy in looking after other people or their children, leaving her own to starvation and the streets. All these are difficult cases to handle, but they are ones to be recognised; and they are cases that, unfortunately, from my experience, are very unfavourable as far as prognosis goes. In a certain number of cases the moral side of the man seems to be entirely altered through the intellectual; so that a man having delusions [or] hallucinations telling him that he is to be rich, or the Saviour of the world, or is to take twenty wives, may very naturally change his whole habits of life, and become the indolent man, waiting for something to turn up, the prophet that is to convert the world, or the founder of a religious sect. These cases have to be considered from a different standpoint to those we have already noticed. They puzzle one from their general intellectual ability, their chief failing being a want of appreciation that there has been any intellectual loss in themselves. That they have been insane is to them doubtful or untrue. They think that their friends have treated them badly, and naturally feel inclined to act in an unfriendly way towards these relations. Some of these cases cause more anxiety and trouble in asylums than is ordinarily conceived, for they are patients who belie the general belief as to combination. Patients of this kind will not only combine with other patients, but they will organise the others, and in every way endeavour to prevent their doing useful or even necessary work, and are constant obstructives to the discipline as well as to the cure of other patients. The fact has to be recognised that a certain number of patients have moral insanity. As a rule, I should say that moral insanity is associated with intellectual insanity, being either a stage of its onset or a stage of its recovery—a stage of recovery, unfortunately, that may never be completely recovered from; that this moral insanity may be a primary disease, coming on with childhood; that it may be secondary to mental disease; that it may be secondary to physical disease; that it may be simple—*i.e.*, with little or with no intellectual loss—and may be compounded with every variety of intellectual loss; and that when it occurs as the residuum after an attack of insanity, and lasts for twelve months, the prospect of any future improvement is small in the extreme.

2. From W.H.R. Rivers, "Psychiatry and the War," *Science* 49.1268 (18 April 1919): 367-69

[William Halse Rivers Rivers (1864-1922), psychologist and anthropologist, was a university lecturer in psychology at Cambridge University, and, in 1898, a member of the Cambridge anthropological expedition to the Torres Straight. In 1915 he joined Maghull Military Hospital in Lancashire, and in 1916 he was posted to Craiglockhart Hospital for Officers near Edinburgh, where he developed psychiatric techniques to deal with shell-shocked soldiers. His work there has been popularized in Pat Barker's novel trilogy, *Regeneration* (1992), *The Eye in the Door* (1994), and *The Ghost Road* (1996).]

The influence of the war upon psychiatry in Great Britain has been profound and shows itself in many different directions. A most important effect has been to draw psychiatry into closer relations with neurology....

One, and perhaps the most important outcome of this combined activity has been the general recognition of the essential part taken in the production and maintenance of the psycho-neuroses by purely mental factors. In the early stages of the war especial stress was laid on the physical effects of shell explosion, an attitude which found expression in the term shell-shock. As the war has progressed the physical conception of war-neurosis has been gradually replaced by one according to which the vast majority of cases depend on a process of causation in which the factors are essentially mental. The shell explosion or other catastrophe of war, which forms in so many cases the immediate antecedent of the illness, is only the spark which releases deep-seated psychical forces due to the strains of warfare. It has also become clear how large a part is taken in the causation of neurosis by physical factors which only come into action after the soldier has been removed from the scene of warfare.

Not only has war-experience shown the importance of purely mental factors in the production of neurosis, but it has also shown the special potency of certain kinds of mental process, the closely related emotional and instinctive aspects. This knowledge is already having, and will have still more, profound effects upon the science of psychology. This science has hitherto dealt mainly with the intellectual side of mental life and has paid far too little attention to the emotions. Students of certain aspects of mind, and especially those engaged in the study of social psychology, were coming to see how greatly psychologists had over-estimated the intellectual factor. The results of warfare have now compelled psychiatrists to consider from the medical point of view the conflicts between the instinctive tendencies of the individual and the forces of social tradition which workers in other fields have come to recognize as so potent for good and evil in the lives of mankind.

Closely related to this movement is another which has led those dealing with the psycho-neuroses to recognize far more widely than hitherto the importance of mental experience which is not directly accessible to consciousness. Warfare has provided us with numberless examples of the processes of dissociation and suppression by means of which certain bodies of experience become shut off from the general mass making up the normal personality, but yet continue to exist in an active state, producing effects of the most striking kind, both mental and physical.

An interesting by-product of this increased attention to the instinctive, emotional and unconscious aspects of mind has been a great alteration in the attitude of psychiatrists towards the views of the psychoanalytic school. Before the war many psychologists were coming to see the importance of Freud's[1] work to their science, but within the medical profession, the general attitude was one of uncompromising hostility. This state of affairs has been wholly altered by the war. The partisans of Freud have been led by experience of the war-neurosis to see that sex is not the sole factor in the production of psycho-neurosis, but that conflict arising out of the activity of other instincts, and especially that of self-preservation, takes an active if not the leading role. On the other hand, independent students who, partly through lack of opportunity, had not previously committed themselves to either side, have been forced by the facts to see to how great an extent the nature of the psycho-neuroses of warfare support the views of Freud and have made it their business to sift the grain from the chaff

1 Sigmund Freud (1856-1939), the founder of psychoanalysis. Freud's "talking cure" was developed through his work with Josef Breuer, a fellow Austrian physician, and the patient known as Anna O., who suffered from what was then called hysteria (in which symptoms of psychic distress are manifested physically).

and distinguish between the essential and the accidental in his scheme. To such an extent has the reconciliation gone that it has recently been possible for the chief adherent of Freud to read a communication before the leading medical society of London without exciting any trace of acrimony and only such opposition as must be expected when dealing with a subject as new and complex as that under discussion. There are many signs that the end of the war will find psychiatrists and psychologists ready to consider dispassionately the value of Freud's scheme as a basis for the study of the psychoses as well as of the psycho-neuroses of civil life, ready to accept the good and reject the false without the ignorant prejudice and bitter rancor which characterized every discussion of the subject before the war.

Concurrently with the general recognition of the essentially psychical [aspect] of neurosis, there has taken place a great development on the therapeutical side. As a result of the war psycho-therapy has taken its place among the resources of the physician. There is still far from general agreement concerning the value of different forms of psychotherapeutic treatment, but work is steadily going on in testing the value of different methods....

The treatment which has had most success consists of a form of mental analysis which resembles to some extent the psycho-analysis of Freud, but differs from it in making little attempt to go deeply into the unconscious, except in so far as any dissociation present has been the result of recent shocks of warfare. Attention is paid especially to those parts of experience which without any special resistance become accessible to the memory of the patient, and to seek by means of the knowledge so acquired to demonstrate to the patient the essentially psychical nature of his malady. By a process of reeducation he is then led to adjust himself to the conditions created by his illness.

The knowledge already gained, and still more that which will become accessible when those at present fully occupied with the needs of the moment have leisure to record their experience, will be of the utmost importance to the future of psychiatry. Already before the war a movement was on foot to bring about reforms in the treatment of mental disorder, the measures especially favored being the establishment of psychiatric clinics and the removal of curable and slight examples of psychosis from association with more chronic cases. This movement will be greatly assisted by the knowledge and experience gained during the war. Those in the medical profession who are moving towards reform will gain a large body of support from many members of the laity who have come through the war to recognize the gravity of the problem. A large body of exact knowledge will be available to assist those whose business it will be to set the care and treatment of mental disorder on a new footing. Psychiatry will emerge from the war in a state very different from that it occupied in 1914. Above all it will be surrounded by an atmosphere of hope and promise for the future treatment of the greatest of human ills.

3. From Henry Head, "An Address on the Diagnosis of Hysteria," *British Medical Journal* 1 (1922): 827-29

[Henry Head (1861-1940) was a British neurologist who, working with W.H.R. Rivers in 1903, experimented on himself to determine the effects of injury to nerve fibres. In 1926 he published an important two-volume study, *Aphasia and Kindred Disorders of Speech*, based on research conducted with World War I veterans who had suffered gunshot wounds to the head. Like Rivers, he appears as a character in Pat Barker's *Regeneration* (see p. 250). Head was also among the many physicians that Leonard and Virginia Woolf consulted between 1913 and 1915, owing to Leonard's "growing distrust of Savage" (Lee 182). He was one of the two physicians who attended Virginia following her 1913 suicide attempt (Lee 330).]

Our knowledge of the nature and causes of functional nervous disorders has been revolutionized during the last fifteen years, and more recently the prevalence of the war neuroses has aroused a widespread interest in morbid psychology....

[T]here is one series of phenomena where a knowledge of morbid psychology is of profound importance to every medical practitioner; for no branch of medicine is free from the puzzling manifestations of hysteria.... [H]ysteria is mainly associated with abnormal physical conditions. In fact, it might be defined as a morbid mental state, accompanied by physical manifestations and certain forms of aberrant conduct.

These physical signs are as definite and specific as those of any other disease. Hysteria is sometimes said to "imitate" organic affections;[1] but this is a highly misleading statement. The mimicry can only deceive an observer ignorant of the signs of hysteria or content with perfunctory examination.

For the diagnosis of hysteria it is necessary, not only that there should be no demonstrable organic cause for the symptoms, but that the positive signs of hysteria should be present. It is to these positive signs I am anxious to call your attention; but nothing could be duller than a category of the protean conditions which may accompany this disorder. I shall therefore enumerate and describe them solely in order

---

1 "An abnormal bodily state; a disease; a medical complaint or condition" (*OED* online).

to lay bare to you the means by which they can be detected and the state of mind which underlies their appearance.

Freud described hysteria as a "conversion neurosis." This term has been widely adopted, and signifies that the conflict in the patient's mind is solved by some aberrant reaction, which removes him from the situation of doubt and anxiety. If a soldier, unable any longer to face the horrors of the front, became paralysed in both legs, he was automatically relieved from the necessity of facing danger without the obloquy of running away.

Disorders of speech were amongst the commonest hysterical affections due to the strain of war. Sometimes the patient became completely mute, although he wrote voluble accounts of his condition and understood perfectly what was said to him. This is an example of that particular disintegration of some highly developed function so characteristic of hysteria. It is not the physiological mechanics of language that are affected, but the patient is imbued firmly with the idea that he cannot speak ...

The so-called "hysterical stammer," more accurately termed a "stutter," exemplifies another aspect of this disorder....

This illustrates the tendency of hysterical phenomena to consist of a positive disorder of movement, which is so clearly demonstrable in the various forms of tremor. Rhythmic unsteadiness, due to structural disease or want of neural control, is shown by defective power to maintain a certain posture steadily....

Sometimes movement is positively inhibited; the patient says, "I cannot move my leg," and it hangs inert, or is dragged behind him like a log....

When we attempt to express these morbid phenomena in general terms we are struck by their positive nature. There is nothing negative about the manifestations of hysteria; even the anaesthesia is due to refusal to accept impressions, which otherwise run their normal physiological course. Amongst the disorders of motion, the tremor is due to actively repeated movements, rather than to failure of static tone; spasm is the assumption of a definite posture and not the reflex overactivity of some lower function; the so-called hysterical paralysis is the effect of direct inhibition, an active expression of the conviction in the patient's mind—"I cannot move."

Closer analysis of these positive phenomena shows that they depend on three mental factors—proneness to auto-suggestion, a negative attitude to orders from without, and a tendency to the state known as "dissociation." ...

If these are the factors in hysteria, how is this remarkable state of mind induced? It is essentially an irrational answer to a conflict. A young woman, who is a candidate for an examination which she feels is too difficult for her powers, can solve the problem illegitimately by spasm of the right hand. A soldier suffering from fear, knowing he cannot run away, finds a perfect and honourable solution in hysterical paraplegia.

But in many cases the underlying cause is far more subtle. Many of you know the evil effects of not answering promptly a disagreeable letter. Perhaps it remains unopened in your pocket, and all day you feel that some unknown misfortune is about to befall you—you are "off your game," you are certain that you are in for influenza, or at least for a bad cold. All these ills are an expression of the unresolved emotion evoked by that unanswered letter.

This is an example of the evil effects of repression, or an attempt to shirk some unpleasant experience by expelling it from consciousness. But fortunately we can sometimes forget even disagreeable facts without harm. In order that repression may produce evil consequences the idea, charged with emotion, must have been thrust out of consciousness; the patient dislikes it with such intensity that he refuses to face it squarely. The emotion accompanying such an idea may then appear in some substituted form, such as vomiting, headache, or paralysis....

Fear is the most potent reason for repression. All children and animals experience fear; this is suppressed in the adult, who, under normal conditions of civilized life, experiences anxiety only. But deep down lies fear, ready to spring into being when inhibition is removed—as, for example, during sleep. Now in civil life fear of disease is extremely frequent. Some are so subject to this form that they dread each disease in turn as it becomes the fashionable centre of discussion in the popular press. Such fears, dismissed from consciousness without reasonable consideration, are liable to work havoc in the underworld of our minds.

Some relationships are by their very nature liable to be highly charged with emotion. "No man," Bacon[1] said, "can speak to his child but as a father"; and parental fear is the basis of many anxieties. Conversely, however, adoration of a son for his mother, or a daughter for her father, underlies many of the difficulties which may arise subsequently in marriage....

A very important element in the production of a conversion hysteria is a want of capacity to face failure....

I cannot close this discourse without saying a few words about treatment. If possible, the patient should be removed from the usual surroundings and new influences brought to bear. An attempt should be made to switch the dissociated part into the continuity of the

---

1 Francis Bacon (1561-1626), British philosopher, statesman, scientist, and author. The quotation is from Bacon's essay "Of Friendship."

patient's mental life. Every form of persuasion should be exercised to convince the patient that he is able to carry out the action he is convinced to be impossible. Never bully him or accuse him of dishonesty. No one is a greater failure than the medical officer who wishes all hysterics could be shot at dawn. On the other hand, the firm diplomatist with subtle and demonstrable reasons why the patient can stand, walk, or feel, often produces miraculous cures. But it must never be forgotten that in a large number of cases, especially in civil life, removal of hysterical symptoms is only a prelude to the discovery of an anxiety neurosis. The causes for the suppressed emotion must be investigated, or the patient may be left in an even worse condition than that in which you found him.

To the medical man I would say, see that you do your patient no harm by antitherapeutic suggestion; carefully prune your conversation and do not think out your diagnosis aloud.... Be natural, but on guard; you will then be ready to deliver your blow at the moment required. At the same time, remember that your most brilliant conversation is useless with an hysteric; she is interested in herself, not in you.

Nature's moral code, under which we work, is cruel and unrelenting. There is no forgiveness of sins; but, in the medical man, this knowledge should be tempered towards the patient by clinical curiosity and human sympathy. In conclusion, I would say to all who have to deal with these morbid conditions, be as honest in thought as you would be naturally in deed. Act without fear and never lose courage; finally, call nothing common or unclean.

Appendix E: Educational and Social Context

[Access to education, and especially higher education, for women and working people is a recurrent theme in *Mrs. Dalloway*, as it is in so much of Woolf's work. Clarissa Dalloway has no formal education. Miss Kilman has a university degree but (following her dismissal from her teaching position) no opportunity to pursue a profession. Septimus Warren Smith has, prior to the outbreak of war, undertaken a course of self-education "from books borrowed from public libraries" (p. 112), and he has also taken courses from Miss Isabel Pole who "lectur[ed] in the Waterloo Road upon Shakespeare" (p. 113). This is a thinly-veiled reference to Morley College for Working Men and Women, a college at which Woolf herself once lectured (see Introduction, pp. 31-32). Morley College had its origins in the Old Vic Theatre, where, in 1880, Emma Cons opened the Royal Victoria Coffee and Music Hall, intended to provide a temperance alternative to other forms of popular entertainment for working people. The excerpt below (Appendix E1) describes how occasional lectures in the theatre gave rise to Morley College, which was so successful that it moved to premises of its own in 1889. As the "daughter of an educated man," a phrase she employed frequently and especially throughout *Three Guineas*, and a member of the British intelligentsia, Woolf's own attitudes to extension lecturing and working men's colleges were mixed. While she sympathized with the desire of working people for education, she could also be condescending, an attitude that is also apparent in Sir William Anson's speech to a Morley College graduating class, as reported in 1905 (see Appendix E2). While Miss Kilman was, in spite of her *petit bourgeois* background ("My grandfather kept an oil and colour shop in Kensington," p. 150), able to obtain a university degree in History, she was unable to find work in a profession other than teaching. As she exclaims to Elizabeth, "Law, medicine, politics, all professions are open to women of your generation" (p. 150), a development made possible by the post-war Sex Disqualification (Removal) Act of 1919, which opened many of the professions and some positions in the diplomatic and civil services to women (see Appendix E3). It should be noted, however, that the Act did not require universities to admit women to their professional or other programs.]

1. From Cicely Hamilton and Lilian Baylis, *The Old Vic* (London: Jonathan Cape Limited, 1926): 184-87

[The Old Vic was the colloquial name for Royal Victoria Hall, originally named the Cobourg Theatre, which opened in 1818 on the unfashionable south side of the Thames. It was used mainly for melodramas and music hall until it was purchased by Emma Cons (1838-1912), a social reformer, artist (restoring illuminated manuscripts and, in Oxford, stained glass windows), and the first female member of the London County Council. A committed worker for the temperance movement, Cons formed the Coffee Music Hall Company in 1879 to provide wholesome and alcohol-free entertainment, and in 1880 began using the Old Vic as a venue. From these efforts, as described in this excerpt, emerged the Morley College for Working Men and Women.

In 1898 Cons's niece Lilian Baylis (1874-1937) began assisting her aunt at the Old Vic, and became sole manager on Cons's death in 1912. Under her high-minded leadership, the Old Vic became synonymous with Shakespearean production in London. This tradition continued into the 1960s and 1970s, when it served as the first home of Britain's National Theatre.

Baylis's co-author of this history, Cicely Hamilton (1872-1952), was herself an important actor and playwright, as well as a journalist, novelist, and suffragette. Her best-known works were the hit play *Diana of Dobson's* (1908) and the social tract *Marriage as a Trade* (1909).]

For the first few years the Vic's activities were largely non-theatrical. Once a week there was a temperance meeting, plainly labelled as such; and once a week a penny lecture. The men of science who found their way to the theatre and addressed its audience on the movements of the stars or the wonders of the telephone may have been taken aback now and then by the manners of the Vic habitués; playgoers accustomed to exchanging back-chat with red-nosed comedians saw no reason why they should not also exchange back-chat with professors. When one eminent scientist paused in his speech to arrange his mechanical apparatus, the pause was taken for a failure of memory—a dry-up—and a shout from the upper regions bade him 'Go home and learn his lessons.'

All the same the lectures drew an audience and prospered, and were noteworthy for more than their immediate success; they were the small, the unintentional, beginnings of the Morley Memorial College for Working Men and Women. To the general public the Vic is an influence in education because it purveys good art in the shape of drama and music; most of us do not realize that it has also purveyed good science and advanced study. Emma Cons was a born and persistent pioneer; as her coffee taverns broke the ground which was later occupied by Lyons, Lockhart's[1] and a host of others, so her classes in theatre dressing-rooms and paint-rooms preceded the work of Polytechnics. Mr. Booth in his history of the Vic[2] states that, as a result of these dressing-room and paint-room classes, 'a plasterer's labourer gained a scholarship at Cambridge and a rag and paper sorter is now (1916) a Chief Engineer on a P. & O. liner.' When the weekly lectures were placed on the programme there was no thought of Morley College or even of classes; the idea of continuous instruction was suggested by two members of the audience—lads who had attended a science lecture and came round to Miss Cons to ask for further help in their studies. To accede to the request meant thought and trouble; but the thought was given and the trouble taken. A committee was got together to deal with the new and unexpected development; teachers were procured and dressing-rooms converted into class-rooms; and the new educational establishment began its career with four students. The beginning was modest, but the growth was rapid: the four pioneers soon had comrades—so many comrades that more space was demanded and two rooms were knocked into one. The embryo college continued to grow, and before long the process was repeated.

It must be remembered that it was not until 1889 that Morley College took form and shape as a separate entity, with separate premises of its own; until that date, its existence was bound up with that of the Vic—an informal college was run in the actual precincts of a music-hall, and the students who attended it were students of the Old Vic itself! Is there any other theatre in England or elsewhere which, of its own free-will, has combined 'advanced study' with its normal business of music, song and dance? And is there any other college—in England or elsewhere—whose authorities have run a music hall?

2. "Sir W. Anson on Workmen's Colleges," *The Times* (20 September 1905): 8

[Sir William Reynell Anson (1843-1914), lawyer, served as warden of All Souls College, Oxford, and was briefly Vice Chancellor of Oxford University, a post from which he stepped down when he was elected Liberal MP in 1899.]

---

1 Two popular chains of tea shops.

2 John Booth, *A Century of Theatrical Entertainment. 1816-1916. The "Old Vic"* (London: Stead's Publishing House, 1917).

Sir W. Anson, M.P., Parliamentary Secretary to the Board of Education, distributed the certificates to the successful students of Morley College, Waterloo-road, last night. The college is called after the late Mr. Samuel Morley,[1] in recognition of the aid given by him in establishing it. Its object is to bring within the reach of working men and women an education of a general character, with some of the social conditions of college life. This session over 600 students have entered to attend the various classes.

The proceedings took place in the Royal Victoria-hall, which forms part of the same building as the college. The hall was crowded. Mr. E.J. Urwick, president of the college, presided. Among those present were Canon Horsley, Professor Trenton, Miss Cons,[2] Miss Lumsden, Miss Pearson, Mr. F.W. Black, vice-chairman, Miss Eve, Mr. C.R. Buxton, principal, and Miss Sheepshanks,[3] vice-principal.

Sir W. Anson said that on noticing that the Morley College received grants from the Board of Education he had the curiosity to inquire how they were earned. He was supplied with a list of the subjects, and was very much struck by their variety, and especially by the fact that on the science side there were classes in advanced mathematics and botany. It was not obligatory on the students of the college to undergo examination. He could well understand why, in these circumstances, candidates for examination were comparatively few. No one desired to be examined or to examine others. (Laughter.) He had taken part in the examinations in the one capacity and the other. At the time he was frequently examined himself he thought the position of examiner was the proudest and happiest which life could afford. But later on, when it became his duty to examine others, he often wished he could remove to a sphere where they neither examined nor brought up for examination, and where there was some happier way of qualifying for the various functions of life. (Laughter.) Nevertheless, he ventured to submit that examination was a good way of testing their knowledge, of ascertaining whether they really knew what they supposed they knew. One use to which students might

1 Textiles magnate (1809-86), Congregationalist, Liberal MP from 1868 to 1885, and philanthropist. In 1884 he joined the executive committee of the Old Vic, contributed £1000 (one quarter of the total cost) toward the purchase of its lease, and led fundraising efforts for the remainder. (See Booth 63-64.)

2 Emma Cons. See p. 258.

3 Mary Sheepshanks (1872-1960), feminist and educator, in 1897 appointed Vice-Principal of Morley College for Working Men and Women. It was Sheepshanks who, in 1905, invited Virginia Stephen to lecture at Morley College.

profitably put the college was the study of some scientific aspect of the technical work by which they earned their livelihood. A study of that kind would give a fresh stimulus to their everyday labour, the constant pursuit of which day after day might otherwise be dull and wearisome. One the other hand, the members of the college might wisely obtain a complete change of interests by turning their back on the work of everyday life and taking up the study of history, languages, and literature. There was nothing which tended more to increase one's vocabulary of one's own language than the endeavour to translate passages of another tongue into English. The study of literature would bring them not only into contact with the best thoughts of the greatest writers, but would give them lessons in technical workmanship. If they took passages from John Bright's[1] speeches on the Crimean war or from the writings of Burke[2] and Macaulay[3] and lines from Milton or the best poems of Tennyson they would find that to be a great writer meant not only that they must have something to say that was worth communicating, but that they must possess considerable technical skill in the way of saying it. It might be supposed that he was recommending desultory courses of study without any settled or coherent plan for the acquisition of knowledge. He was advocating nothing of the kind. One of the evils of the age was the diffusion of attention, or distraction. They had only to take up any daily paper and look at the headings of its columns to see the variety of the topics to which their attention was invited, and to realize how strong must be their endeavour to keep their minds fixed upon what was really important and essential in life. Therefore he strongly urged them to make up their minds to learn something solid about the writer, the period of history, or the subject which they might take up for study. There was an old saying, which was attributed to Mr. Freeman,[4] that

---

1 John Bright (1811-89), Liberal MP for Manchester and, later, Birmingham, whose 1854 and 1855 Parliamentary speeches opposing the Crimean War were celebrated but ineffectual at stopping the war.

2 Edmund Burke (1729-97), Irish born statesman, political theorist, and philosopher; author of *A Philosophical Inquiry into the Origin of Our Ideas of the Sublime and Beautiful* (1757) and *Reflections on the Revolution in France* (1790), among numerous other books.

3 Thomas Babington Macaulay (1800-59), poet, historian, and statesman. He served on the Supreme Council of India from 1834 to 1838, introducing English education to India through his 1835 Minute on Education, which proposed "to form a class who may be interpreters between us and the millions whom we govern,—a class of persons Indian in blood and colour, but English in tastes, in opinions, in morals and in intellect."

4 This saying is more commonly attributed to T.H. Huxley.

everyone should know something about everything, and everything about something. If they knew a great deal about some one thing they could afford to dissipate their interests about it in different directions. The social side of the institution was of inestimable value; it made it a society of men and women forming a real college. He hoped, therefore, it would always sustain a strong sense of corporate life. He hoped also that the students would come to understand that what this country needed, and needed terribly compared with other nations, was the conviction that knowledge was power, that education was a reality, not the learning unwillingly of a number of unnecessary things, that it meant the acquisition of the habits and the modes of thought which lead to success in life. (Cheers.)

The certificates distributed included those of the University Extension Society, Board of Education, South Kensington Society of Arts, Cambridge University Local Examinations, and Incorporated Phonographic Society.

3. From the Sex Disqualification (Removal) Act (1919)

1919 Chapter 71
An Act to amend the Law with respect to disqualifications on account of sex.
[23 December 1919]

BE IT ENACTED by the King's most Excellent Majesty, by and with the advice and consent of the Lords Spiritual and Temporal, and Commons, in this present Parliament assembled, and by the authority of the same, as follows:

Removal of disqualification on grounds of sex.

1. A person shall not be disqualified by sex or marriage from the exercise of any public function, or from being appointed to or holding any civil or judicial office or post, or from entering or assuming or carrying on any civil profession or vocation, or for admission to any incorporated society (whether incorporated by Royal Charter or otherwise), and a person shall not be exempted by sex or marriage from the liability to serve as a juror:

   Provided that:—

   (a) notwithstanding anything in this section, His Majesty may by Order in Council authorise regulations to be made providing for and prescribing the mode of the admission of women to the civil service of His Majesty, and the conditions on which women admitted to that service may be appointed to or continue to hold posts therein, and giving power to reserve to men any branch of or posts in the civil service in any of His Majesty's possessions overseas, or in any foreign country; and

(b) any judge, chairman of quarter sessions, recorder or other person before whom a case is or may be heard may, in his discretion, on an application made by or on behalf of the parties (including in criminal cases the prosecution and the accused) or any of them, or at his own instance, make an order that the jury shall be composed of men only or of women only as the case may require, or may, on an application made by a woman to be exempted from service on a jury in respect of any case by reason of the nature of the evidence to be given or of the issues to be tried, grant such exemption....

Provision as to women who have qualified for degrees at universities not admitting women to degrees.

2. A woman shall be entitled to be admitted and enrolled as a solicitor after serving under articles for three years only if either she has taken such a university degree as would have so entitled her had she been a man, or if she has been admitted to and passed the final examination and kept, under the conditions required of women by the university, the period of residence necessary for a man to obtain a degree at any university which did not at the time the examination was passed admit women to degrees.

Power to universities to admit women to membership.

3. Nothing in the statutes or charter of any university shall be deemed to preclude the authorities of such university from making such provision as they shall think fit for the admission of women to membership thereof, or to any degree, right, or privilege therein or in connection therewith....

Works Cited and Select Bibliography

[Virginia Woolf was a prolific author. In addition to novels, she published numerous essays, reviews, and short stories; and, since her death, her diaries, letters, and juvenilia have been published. Both her life and her works have generated a great number of biographical studies, critical monographs, critical articles, and editions.

This bibliography makes no attempt to be exhaustive. It includes Woolf's major novels (citations are from the Collected Definitive Edition unless otherwise indicated), other primary works relevant to *Mrs. Dalloway*, a short list of recommended biographies, a list of all secondary material referred to in this edition, and some additional recommended critical material.]

Works by Virginia Woolf

Between the Acts. The Definitive Collected Edition. With an Introduction by Quentin Bell. London: Hogarth Press, 1990. Originally published 1941.

The Complete Shorter Fiction of Virginia Woolf. Edited by Susan Dick. Expanded and revised ed. London: Hogarth Press, 1989.

The Diary of Virginia Woolf. 5 vols. Edited by Anne Olivier Bell, assisted by Andrew McNeillie. New York and London: Harcourt Brace Jovanovich, 1977-84.

"The Hours." The British Museum Manuscript of Mrs. Dalloway. Transcribed and edited by Helen M. Wussow. New York: Pace UP, 1996.

Jacob's Room. The Definitive Collected Edition. With an Introduction by Quentin Bell. London: Hogarth Press, 1990. Originally published 1922.

The Letters of Virginia Woolf. 6 vols. Edited by Nigel Nicolson; assistant editor Joanne Trautmann. New York and London: Harcourt Brace Jovanovich, 1975-80.

"Modern Fiction." *The Common Reader*. London: Hogarth Press, 1925. 184-95.

Moments of Being: A Collection of Autobiographical Writing. 2nd ed. Edited by Jeanne Schulkind. New York: Harcourt/A Harvest Book, 1985.

Mr. Bennett and Mrs. Brown. London: Hogarth Press, 1924. Hogarth Essays Series.

Mrs. Dalloway. London: Hogarth Press, 1925.

Mrs. Dalloway. New York: Harcourt, Brace and Company, 1925.
Mrs. Dalloway. The Definitive Collected Edition. With an Introduction by Angelica Garnett. Edited by G. Patton Wright. London: Hogarth Press, 1990. Originally published 1925.
"Mrs. Dalloway in Bond Street." *The Dial* 75.1 (July 1923): 20-27.
Mrs. Dalloway's Party. A Short Story Sequence. Edited with an Introduction by Stella McNichol. London: Hogarth Press, 1978.
Night and Day. London: Duckworth & Co., 1919.
Nurse Lugton's Golden Thimble. With pictures by Duncan Grant. London: Hogarth Press, 1966.
Orlando: A Biography. London: Hogarth Press, 1928.
"Report on Teaching at Morley College." Appendix B in Quentin Bell, *Virginia Woolf: A Biography*. 202-04.
A Room of One's Own. London: Hogarth Press, 1929.
"The ..." *The Times Literary Supplement*, 17 June 1965: 495.
Three Guineas. London: Hogarth Press, 1938.
To the Lighthouse. The Definitive Collected Edition. With an Introduction by Quentin Bell. London: Hogarth Press, 1990. Originally published 1927.
The Voyage Out. London: Hogarth Press, Uniform Edition, 1929. Originally published by Duckworth & Co., 1915.
The Waves. London: Hogarth Press, 1931.
The Years. London: Hogarth Press, 1937.

Biographies

Bell, Quentin. *Virginia Woolf: A Biography*. 2 vols. London: Hogarth Press, 1972.
DeSalvo, Louise. *Virginia Woolf: The Impact of Childhood Sexual Abuse on Her Life and Work*. Boston: Beacon Press, 1989.
King, James. *Virginia Woolf*. London: Hamish Hamilton, 1994.
Lee, Hermione. *Virginia Woolf*. London: Vintage Books, 1997. Originally published by Chatto & Windus, 1996.
Light, Alison. *Mrs. Woolf and the Servants*. London: Fig Tree, 2007.
Pippett, Aileen. *The Moth and the Star: A Biography of Virginia Woolf*. Toronto: Little, Brown & Co., 1955.
Rose, Phyllis. *Woman of Letters: A Life of Virginia Woolf*. New York: Oxford UP, 1978.
Rosenfeld, Natania. *Outsiders Together: Virginia and Leonard Woolf*. Princeton, NJ: Princeton UP, 2000.
Trombley, Stephen. *'All That Summer She Was Mad': Virginia Woolf and Her Doctors*. London: Junction Books, 1981.

Critical and Historical Works

Abbott, Reginald. "What Miss Kilman's Petticoat Means: Virginia Woolf, Shopping, and Spectacle." *Modern Fiction Studies* 38.1 (Spring 1992): 193-216.

Albee, Edward. *Who's Afraid of Virginia Woolf?: A Play*. New York: Antheneum, 1962.

Banfield, Ann. "Time Passes: Virginia Woolf, Post-Impressionism, and Cambridge Time." *Poetics Today* 24.3 (Fall 2003): 471-516.

Bateman, Anthony. *Cricket, Literature and Culture: Symbolising the Nation, Destabilising Empire*. Farnham, Surrey: Ashgate Publishing, 2009.

Black, Naomi. *Virginia Woolf as Feminist*. Ithaca, NY: Cornell UP, 2004.

Bradshaw, David. Review. [Of Virginia Woolf, *Mrs. Dalloway*, edited by Morris Beja (Shakespeare Head Press Edition). Oxford: Blackwell, 1996 and Virginia Woolf, *The Voyage Out*, edited by C. Ruth Miller and Lawrence Miller (Shakespeare Head Press Edition). Oxford: Blackwell, 1995.] *The Review of English Studies*, New Series, 49.196 (1998): 539-42.

Brown, Bill. "The Secret Life of Things: Virginia Woolf and the Matter of Modernism" in Pamela R. Matthews and David McWhirter, eds., *Aesthetic Subjects*. Minneapolis: U of Minnesota P, 2003. 397-430.

Brown, Susan, Patricia Clements, and Isobel Grundy, eds. Virginia Woolf entry: Overview screen within *Orlando: Women's Writing in the British Isles from the Beginnings to the Present*. Cambridge: Cambridge UP Online, 2006. http://orlando.cambridge.org.login.ezproxy.library.ualberta.ca/.

Browning, Oscar. "The University Extension Movement at Cambridge." *Science* 9.207 (21 January 1887): 61-63.

Bullett, Gerald. "New Fiction." *The Saturday Review* (30 May 1925): 588.

Chirol, Sir Valentine. "India Old and New. I. Mr. Gandhi's Teaching. Hatred of Western Civilization. Saint and Firebrand." *The Times* (23 December 1920): 11.

Clewell, Tammy. "Consolation Refused: Virginia Woolf, The Great War, and Modernist Mourning." *MFS Modern Fiction Studies* 50.1 (2004): 197-223.

Cohen, Scott. "The Empire from the Street: Virginia Woolf, Wembley, and Imperial Monuments." *MFS Modern Fiction Studies* 50.1 (2004): 85-109.

Cramer, Patricia Morgne. "Virginia Woolf and Sexuality" in Susan Sellers, ed., *The Cambridge Companion to Virginia Woolf*. Second Edition. Cambridge UP, 2010. 180-96.

Crawford, John W. "One Day in London the Subject of Mrs. Woolf's New Novel." *The New York Times Book Review* (10 May 1925): 10.
Cuddy-Keane, Melba. *Virginia Woolf, the Intellectual, and the Public Sphere*. Cambridge: Cambridge UP, 2003.
Cunningham, Michael. *The Hours*. New York: Farrar, Straus, Giroux, 1998.
Danzig, Richard. "The Announcement of August 20th, 1917." *The Journal of Asian Studies* 28.1 (November 1968): 19-37.
Daugherty, Beth Rigel. "'A corridor leading from Mrs. Dalloway to a new book': Transforming Stories, Bending Genres," in Kathryn N. Benzel and Ruth Hoberman, eds., *Trespassing Boundaries: Virginia Woolf's Short Fiction*. New York: Palgrave Macmillan, 2004. 101-24.
Davin, Anna. "Introduction," in Co-operative Working Women, *Life as We Have Known It*. Edited by Margaret Llewelyn Davies. With an introductory letter by Virginia Woolf. London: Virago, 1977. Originally published by Hogarth Press, 1931.
DeMeester, Karen. "Trauma and Recovery in Virginia Woolf's *Mrs. Dalloway*." *Modern Fiction Studies* 44.3 (1998): 649-73.
Forster, E.M. "The Novels of Virginia Woolf." *The Criterion* IV.2 (April 1926): 277-86.
Froula, Christine. "*Mrs. Dalloway*'s Postwar Elegy: Women, War, and the Art of Mourning." *Modernism/Modernity* 9.1 (2002): 125-63.
——. "On French and British Freedoms: Early Bloomsbury and the Brothels of Modernism." *Modernism/Modernity* 12.4 (2005a): 553-80.
——. *Virginia Woolf and the Bloomsbury Avant-Garde: War, Civilization, Modernity*. New York: Columbia UP, 2005b.
Gaipa, Mark. "Accessorizing Clarissa: How Virginia Woolf Changes the Clothes and the Character of Her Lady of Fashion." *Modernist Cultures* 4.2 (May 2009): 24-47.
"German Women in London." *The Times* (13 May 1915): 10.
Greg, W.W. "The Rationale of Copy-Text." *Studies in Bibliography* 3 (1950-51): 20-37.
Head, Henry. "An Address on the Diagnosis of Hysteria." *British Medical Journal* 1 (1922): 827-29.
Holmes, J.F. Review of *Mrs. Dalloway*. *The Calendar of Modern Letters* 1 (July 1925): 404-05.
Hughes, Richard. "A Day in London Life." *Saturday Review of Literature* (16 May 1925): 755.
Iannone, Carol. "Woolf, Women, and 'The Hours'." *Commentary* (April 2003): 50-52.
Kelly, Thomas. *A History of Adult Education in Great Britain*. Liverpool: Liverpool UP, 1970.
Kirkpatrick, B.J. *A Bibliography of Virginia Woolf*. Third Edition. Oxford: Clarendon Press, 1980.

Levenback, Karen L. *Virginia Woolf and the Great War*. Syracuse: Syracuse UP, 1999.

MacDonald, J. Ramsay. *War and the Workers: A Plea for Democratic Control*. London: The Union of Democratic Control, 1915.

[McDowall, Arthur Sydney.] "A Novelist's Experiment." *Times Literary Supplement* (21 May 1925): 349.

Miller, J. Hillis. "*Mrs. Dalloway*: Repetition as the Raising of the Dead" in *Fiction and Repetition: Seven English Novels*. Cambridge, MA: Harvard UP, 1982.

Monk, Ray. "This Fictitious Life: Virginia Woolf on Biography and Reality." *Philosophy and Literature* 31 (2007): 1-40.

Muir, Edwin. "Contemporary Writers: Virginia Woolf." *Nation and Athenaeum* (17 April 1926): 70-72.

"New Novels." *The New Statesman* (6 June 1925): 229.

"Prime Minister's Appeal. 'Only Practicable Solution.' Call to Electors." *The Times* (5 December 1923): 12.

Richter, Harvena. "The *Ulysses* Connection: Clarissa Dalloway's Bloomsday." *Studies in the Novel* 21.3 (Fall 1989): 305-19.

Rivers, W.H.R. "Psychiatry and the War." *Science* 49.1268 (18 April 1919): 367-69.

Savage, Geo. H., M.D., "Moral Insanity." *The Journal of Mental Science* 27.118 (July 1881): 147-55.

Schiff, James. "Rewriting Woolf's *Mrs. Dalloway*: Homage, Sexual Identity, and the Single-Day Novel by Cunningham, Lippincott, and Lanchester." *Critique: Studies in Contemporary Fiction* 45.4 (Summer 2004): 363-82.

Shaffer, Brian W. "Civilization in Bloomsbury: Woolf's *Mrs. Dalloway* and Bell's 'Theory of Civilization.'" *Journal of Modern Literature* 19.1 (Summer 1994): 73-87.

Sherry, Vincent. *The Great War and the Language of Modernism*. Oxford: Oxford UP, 2003.

Shields, E.F. "The American Edition of *Mrs. Dalloway*." *Studies in Bibliography* 27 (1974): 157-75.

Silver, Brenda R. *Virginia Woolf Icon*. Chicago and London: U of Chicago P, 1999.

Tate, Trudi. "*Mrs. Dalloway* and the Armenian Question." *Textual Practice* 8.3 (Winter 1994): 467-86.

Thomas, Sue. "Virginia Woolf's Septimus Smith and Contemporary Perceptions of Shell Shock." *English Language Notes (ELN)* 25.2 (December 1987): 49-57.

Vincent, Lady Kitty. "The London Season" in St. John Adcock, ed., *Wonderful London: The World's Greatest City Described by Its Best Writers and Pictured by Its Finest Photographers*. Vol. II. London: The Educational Book Co. [c. 1929]. 430, 435-36.

Walsh, Kelly S. "The Unbearable Openness of Death: Elegies of Rilke and Woolf." *Journal of Modern Literature* 32.4 (Summer 2009): 1-21.

Weinreb, Ben, Christopher Hibbert, Julia Keay, and John Keay. *The London Encyclopaedia*. 3rd ed. London: Macmillan, 2008.

Winter, Jay. "Shell-shock and the Cultural History of the Great War." *Journal of Contemporary History* 35.1 (2000): 7-11.

Wood, Andelys. "Walking the Web in the Lost London of *Mrs. Dalloway*." *Mosaic* 36.2 (June 2003): 19-32.

Wright, Glenn P. "The Raverat Proofs of *Mrs. Dalloway*." *Studies in Bibliography* 39 (1986): 241-61.

Wyatt, Jean M. "*Mrs. Dalloway*: Literary Allusion as Structural Metaphor." *PMLA* 88.3 (May 1973): 440-51.

from the publisher

A name never says it all, but the word "broadview" expresses a good deal of the philosophy behind our company. We are open to a broad range of academic approaches and political viewpoints. We pay attention to the broad impact book publishing and book printing has in the wider world; we began using recycled stock more than a decade ago, and for some years now we have used 100% recycled paper for most titles. As a Canadian-based company we naturally publish a number of titles with a Canadian emphasis, but our publishing program overall is internationally oriented and broad-ranging. Our individual titles often appeal to a broad readership too; many are of interest as much to general readers as to academics and students.

Founded in 1985, Broadview remains a fully independent company owned by its shareholders—not an imprint or subsidiary of a larger multinational.

FSC
www.fsc.org
MIX
Paper from
responsible sources
FSC® C004071